Flood Tide

Book TWO of
The Catalyst

Flood Tide

Book TWO of
The Catalyst

Frank Morin

CONTENTS

1

PLAYING THE PART

A grim, weary army marched through the outskirts of Diodor, the capital of Hallvarr. Soldiers walked with somber faces and downcast eyes. Although ultimately victorious in their recent conflict, they could not celebrate when hundreds of their brothers-in-arms had perished in the fighting.

Worse, today they bore home their fallen leader.

King Leszek's body floated on a glowing cushion of air in the center of the vanguard. He lay with his sword on his chest, pommel under his hands, point at his feet. In his hands he bore yew and stone.

Kevlin rolled his shoulders to relieve some of the tension. He wore a heavy breastplate, borrowed from one of the fallen soldiers. He preferred the mail shirt he'd worn for the past week since the battle at Il'Aicharen, but Harafin had urged him to switch.

He shifted in his saddle and looked forward to where Harafin rode at the head of the column, just behind the honor guard that bore the king's body into the city. The Sentinel wore his customary white robes, and his white beard and hair fluttered in the wind. Harafin's face, which Kevlin could see in profile as the old Sentinel glanced to one side, looked somber. Kevlin could never read Harafin. The old man never did anything without a reason, but that didn't mean he shared those reasons.

The city of Diodor huddled under a chill gray sky that spit occasional drops of rain at the silent multitudes gathered to witness the return of their king. The buildings of the city, draped in black cloth, dripped from heavy rains that had swept through barely an hour ago, giving the impression they were weeping.

Despite the somber mood and grim duty that lay upon the army, Kevlin breathed a silent sigh of relief to see the city. He wasn't much of a woodsman, but in the past couple weeks he'd traipsed around more wilderness than he cared to see ever again. The city held its own dangers, but Kevlin preferred them to the unknowns of the deep forest.

The king's honor guard passed the extensive outer market clustered outside the city wall. As they began to ascend the long central avenue toward the palace, many in the crowds lining both sides of the street bowed or murmured prayers to Serigala. Others held aloft stones and sticks of yew to honor their fallen king.

Kevlin wiped water from his brown hair and straightened in the saddle. He doubted anyone would pay much attention to him, but years of training demanded discipline. A soldier presented his best face when on parade.

As they slowly followed the honor guard, he studied the crowd. The people, almost universally dressed in black, looked like they sincerely mourned the death of their king. He wondered where they found so much yew. He respected each kingdom's burial customs, and had buried comrades from each of the Six Kingdoms.

Nikias stirred in his saddle beside Kevlin. The young man had said little all morning. His moods swings were quick and extreme. Now his previous melancholy bled away as he tugged his form-fitting black leather jerkin straight.

The movement must have drawn someone's attention because a voice called from the crowd, "Nikias! It's Nikias."

Other voices took up the call and soon hundreds chanted the young man's name from both sides of the road.

Nikias grinned and flashed a happy smile. He swung the Bladestaff high over his head in salute. Kevlin, who had learned to watch the long, deadly weapon carefully, ducked aside. Even so, Nikias nearly split his head open with one of the broad, silvered blades that capped both ends of magical weapon.

Nikias shouted, "I have returned." He lifted the Bladestaff higher and the silvered blades burst into blue fire. The crowds cheered their approval. Nikias' grip shifted on the polished shaft that was covered in intricate inlaid silver runes.

Kevlin reined his horse back and shouted, "Careful!"

Nikias, who had already started spinning the Bladestaff, pulled it aside, just missing Kevlin's shoulder. He grinned sheepishly. "Sorry. Forgot you were there."

"You can't afford to do that." Kevlin reined further back, wondering why he bothered. Nikias' attention span was about as long as a hummingbird.

Nikias laughed and spun the Bladestaff around his head and torso in a blur, trailing twin streamers of blue fire.

Colonel Gabral, bearer of the Mace, another of the six great weapons of power, called back over his shoulder, "Control yourself, soldier. You forget our purpose."

Nikias cringed. "Sorry." The flames winked out and he lowered the Bladestaff.

Gabral grunted, but didn't turn again. He looked impressive in his silver-trimmed armor, with his black hair carefully combed and held in place with special creams. Astride his large war horse, he looked imposing, and almost not short.

Kevlin urged his horse up beside Nikias as the crowd settled back to a slightly less somber silence.

Another voice called out of the crowd, "Where's the King's Avenger?"

Nikias grinned and slapped Kevlin on the shoulder. "Here's the man," he shouted loud enough to be heard for several blocks. "Kevlin. The man who avenged the king!"

Nikias grabbed Kevlin's hand and tried to raise it in victory, but Kevlin shook the impetuous youth off. "Stop it."

Too late. As they passed through the city wall and entered the main thoroughfare, the crowd started shouting, "King's Avenger."

Within seconds it became a chant that reverberated from the buildings on both sides. The crowd surged forward and hundreds of hands grasped at Kevlin from all sides.

For a moment, he feared they'd trample him. His horse tried to shy away from the crowd, but they were pressed in too close.

People grabbed Kevlin's hands, touched his leg, or his horse. Many wept, while those too far to reach him saluted and shouted his name.

Nikias laughed again. "They love you, Kevlin." He raised the Bladestaff high and shouted again, "The King's Avenger!"

Colonel Gabral turned around and glared at Kevlin. Of course he'd blame Kevlin for the disturbance. Kevlin couldn't spare the time to glare back. He was too busy trying to fend off the grasping multitude and calm their frenzy. There was enough pent-up emotion in this crowd that their exuberance could easily boil over into a deadly riot.

Then Drystan and Jerrik drove their horses up beside Kevlin, granting a little reprieve. More soldiers pressed in close behind them and helped push the crowd back a few steps further.

"Thanks, brothers" Kevlin said.

Jerrik, who rode on his right side said, "Should we tell them that we killed the other Stalwart?" He pushed one over-zealous spectator back with his leg and growled.

People backed up.

Jerrik was one of the biggest men Kevlin had ever met. His unruly brown hair and long russet beard declared him a citizen of Donarr. They gave him a wild appearance only enhanced by the heavy mail shirt he wore and the huge double-bladed battle-axe strapped to his back.

On Kevlin's left, Drystan said, "It won't matter, brother. A crowd like this can only feed on a single idea at a time."

Where Jerrik's sheer mass intimidated people, Drystan's commanding presence had almost as powerful an effect. The tall, lanky Einarri captain with short blond hair scanned the crowd with piercing blue eyes that radiated nothing but confidence. He used the butt end of his long spear to prod spectators aside a few times, and people quickly learned to give him room.

Kevlin allowed himself a smile. Not yet two weeks as swordbrothers, the two men hadn't always gotten along. He still marveled that they would unite with him through blood, and it encouraged him to hear them calling each other brother.

The crowd continued chanting "King's Avenger", but no longer tried to impede their progress toward the palace.

In front of Kevlin, riding just behind Harafin and Gabral, Ceren glanced back. She met Kevlin's gaze and shook her head, but still smiled as if at a secret joke. She wore her thick auburn hair in an intricate braid.

She wore the same riding outfit she had the night he had first met her. The white blouse looked freshly scrubbed despite their having spent the past four days traveling from the shattered ruins of Il'Aicharen. Over the blouse she wore a dark blue vest. A tan skirt, split for riding, was tucked into long leather boots. She wore no sword. She'd broken hers when she'd killed Wayra.

Then Kevlin nearly killed her when he destroyed the building. Kevlin shuddered at the memory. Only Indira's incredible gift of healing had saved Ceren from that disaster.

Ceren called back, "Unbelievable. Only you could turn a state funeral procession into a circus."

"It's not my fault," Kevlin protested.

Harafin turned. "Did you think not to be noticed? There were hundreds of witnesses. You stood against Dhanjal in full battle rhapsody when the King's own guard could not."

"But that's misleading. I couldn't help it."

Harafin shrugged. "I know that. You know that. In the end, it doesn't matter."

"It does matter," Kevlin muttered. In that final battle Savas, god of War, had bestowed upon him incredible battle prowess while possessing him. Overshadowing the awe of that moment was the sick feeling of revulsion at being held powerless in Savas' will, a puppet that the god had played with.

He'd come closer than anyone else guessed to succumbing forever to Savas' will. If he had, he might have destroyed the entire army.

Indira, who rode beside Ceren, also turned to glance back. She wore her simple green Healer's robe, and her midnight hair hung straight down her back. Kevlin grinned when he met her dark-eyed gaze. He'd managed to win his mail shirt back from her in the last game of Dagger's Folly.

His swordbrothers had lost again. They might be two of the elite warriors of the empire, but they were terrible at cards. As gentle and loving as Indira was with her healing, she was ruthless at cards.

Kevlin hadn't gotten to spend much alone time with her in the past week since the battle at Il'Aicharen. She had been so busy healing, she barely made time for food and the nightly card game that had become a tradition with the company. Kevlin had tried to keep busy as a way to keep his mind off the many unanswered questions he still needed to discuss with Harafin.

Indira smiled and he winked in return. She was turning out to be as fascinating as she was beautiful. Despite his lingering hesitation to allow another woman into his life, he found himself looking forward to the time they spent together.

Nikias nudged him. "Kevlin, you're famous."

"You're exaggerating, like always."

"Am not. You're a hero."

"Sure," Jerrik muttered. "We do half the work, and he gets all the credit." He added in what he probably thought was a whisper, "Just share enough of the glory so I can get a date."

Kevlin laughed. "Done."

He waved to the crowd, and his hand didn't even shake. Over the past couple of days, a strange weakness had left him shaky at unexpected times. He planned to discuss it with Indira, but hadn't found the time yet.

The procession moved forward at its stately walk through the well-ordered streets of the city without further interruption. They climbed a long, gentle hill and finally reached the wide plaza paved with cobblestones that faced the main palace entrance.

No wall surrounded the palace so there was nothing to prevent the throngs from filling the square and the manicured gardens on either side. The palace guard kept the square directly in front of the palace free of onlookers.

The vanguard passed into the open space and halted before the main entrance. The palace reared high overhead, constructed of huge blocks of local brown stone. The huge building failed to instill the same awe that other palaces often projected. Hallvarri buildings were simple and effective. Some people from Tamarr or Freyarr referred to them as unimaginative.

Crown Prince Lievin Dalagan descended wide steps from the deep porch to meet the litter. The honor guard saluted as one and Prince Lievin returned the salute smartly.

The prince was in his early twenties. Despite the grief visible on his face, he stood tall and faced the return of his dead father bravely. He was a handsome man, with thick, black hair, and a famous smile.

Kevlin joined the rest of their party as they dismounted and moved to join the prince and his entourage of nobles cloaked in black.

Prince Lievin greeted Harafin warmly and nodded politely to the rest of their company. They all followed the floating byre of the dead monarch up the stairs to the porch. There, the prince turned back to face the now-silent throng.

He made a subtle gesture to a white-robed Sentinel who stood nearby, and when he spoke, his voice was magnified.

"My people, my friends. Today our hearts are full. We rejoice that our brave soldiers drove the invaders from our lands and proved to the world that we will not cower in the face of even surprise attack."

The crowd cheered as the prince continued. "We have proven that we will stand and face any threat. We will defend our homes, our families, and our nation."

As he spoke, his voice rose in volume, and the crowd responded by shouting louder. Kevlin acknowledged the moving speech, but didn't shout along with the crowd. He had been there. The price they had paid for victory was still far too fresh in his mind.

The prince dropped his voice, forcing the crowd to hush in order to hear. He gestured at the floating figure.

"My father led the charge to defend our homeland. He fell in battle, betrayed by one he thought to be his friend."

As many in the crowd openly wept, Kevlin thought back to that day. He had witnessed Dhanjal's betrayal and murder of the king through the haze of Savas' battle fury. The memory sparked an urge to reach for his sword.

Prince Lievin turned to Harafin who pointed at Kevlin. The prince gestured him forward.

Kevlin moved to stand beside the prince, surprised by the summons. Leave it to Harafin to play games even during the king's funeral.

Prince Lievin declared, "Even in our darkest moment, when evil thought to overwhelm our forces and slaughter our army and lay waste to our beloved land, a hero stood forth to fight for us."

The crowd cheered as Prince Lievin clapped Kevlin on the shoulder. "I present to you the man Kevlin, the man who struck down my father's killer, the man who stood against a Blade Stalwart in full battle rhapsody and defeated him."

"The King's Avenger!"

The crowd roared its approval and began chanting Kevlin's name or "King's Avenger".

As the sound reverberated through the square, Kevlin said, "Your Highness, I didn't do it alone."

Prince Lievin smiled. "But you did it. The people need a hero. Play your part."

Then he announced loudly, "I proclaim Kevlin Truefriend of Hallvarr and name him Lord of the Realm."

The crowd cheered even louder. Before Kevlin could protest the Prince said, "We are forever in your debt."

Prince Lievin bowed to him.

The crowd fell silent as first dozens and then hundreds of people bowed to Kevlin. He scanned the bowing crowd, stunned. The prince had said the crowd needed a hero, and he was giving them one, but what service would he demand in return?

Kevlin still wasn't sure if the battle had been a victory. Dhanjal might be dead, but so was Antigonus. The Shadeleeches had been defeated, but hundreds of people had died.

For five long heartbeats silence reigned before cheering resumed.

Prince Lievin said, "Come, Lord Kevlin." He beckoned the entire company to follow him into the palace behind the floating body of his father.

2

TREMBLING MADNESS

The bulk of the day passed in a blur for Kevlin. Everywhere he went, he was constantly accosted. Men shook his hand or clapped him on the back and congratulated him for his tremendous victory. Women threw their arms around him and kissed him, and many promised to name their next child after him.

Kevlin wasn't prepared for such enthusiasm. He'd lived in Diodor for several months and knew the solid, dependable folk as good natured but reserved. Today they showed none of their normal restraint. He was just happy Indira wasn't around. Some of the women were very enthusiastic.

He finally received a bit of respite that evening as he joined the rest of the company in a private antechamber near the great hall. He got to rest in quiet while they awaited the summons to join the feast honoring their victory and beginning the two-week mourning period for the fallen king.

Kevlin moved to stand beside the hearth where a crackling fire drove back the chill. Drystan stood nearby speaking with Gabral. Both were dressed in their military uniforms. Jerrik lounged in an overstuffed chair with a flagon of something in one huge hand. He waved Kevlin over.

"How are you doing?" the big man asked.

"I'm still alive."

"You don't get it, do you?"

"Get what?"

"These people will give you anything you want. You don't have to let everyone assault you all day." Jerrik grinned. "Although, I wouldn't mind getting assaulted by a few of those ladies who threw themselves at you."

"I'll send them your way next time."

Prince Lievin entered the room with a stunning woman on his arm. The prince looked somber dressed all in black. His companion on the other hand, looked striking in her black silk gown. Tall, shapely, with thick, blond hair and brilliant blue eyes, she drew the attention of everyone in the room like a magnet.

Jerrik surged to his feet beside Kevlin and nearly spilled his drink on himself.

The prince's companion was trailed by a handmaid, a petite, pretty young woman with brown hair. Ceren and Indira trailed the royal party, followed closely by Harafin.

Indira drew Kevlin's eye. Her sable hair shone like silk and highlighted the creamy whiteness of her skin. Tonight she had set aside her customary healer's robe for a royal blue gown. The bodice hugged her torso while the skirt fell in pleated folds all the way to the floor.

Kevlin smiled, thinking back to the kiss they'd shared after the battle. Tonight he'd make sure to get some of her time.

Ceren looked every inch a noblewoman. Her auburn hair was piled on top of her head in a complex arrangement. She wore an emerald green gown that perfectly matched the shade of her eyes, and left her shoulders bare. She looked both vulnerable and alluring at the same time.

She met Kevlin's gaze with a raised eyebrow as if challenging him to make a comment.

He knew better. This woman had proven her courage and cunning on the field of battle. Kevlin had learned to guard his words around her quick tongue and sharp wit.

Prince Lievin said, "My friends, may I present my fiancé, Lady Miren Tylius."

Lady Miren made a little curtsy and they all bowed or curtsied in reply. Then she laughed, a rich sound that seemed to warm the room.

"Enough of such formality." She threw out her arms to include them all. "You are our dear friends."

Then she swept across the room and took Kevlin's hands. He tried to look calm as she kissed him lightly on the cheek. "My dear Lord Kevlin, we cannot thank you enough for avenging Lievin's father."

She smelled like a summer day, and the scent perfectly fit her. Kevlin managed to stammer his thanks, and her smile widened. Then Jerrik nudged him in the ribs.

Kevlin welcomed the distraction. "My Lady, I can't take all the credit. Without my brothers' help, we wouldn't be celebrating a victory today."

If not for the mystical connection he shared with his two swordbrothers, Savas would have owned his soul.

Lady Miren looked from Kevlin to Jerrik with a frown. "How can you two be brothers?"

Jerrik took her hand and bowed over it. "By blood, if not by birth."

Drystan moved to stand beside them and Kevlin said, "My other brother, Drystan Aldacosia."

Lady Miren laughed. "Now I know you're joking." She took Drystan's hand. "I've wanted to meet you for years."

Drystan bowed over her hand, not tongue-tied like Kevlin had been. "Thank you, my lady. But Kevlin isn't jesting. We three are swordbrothers."

"That explains it. I can't wait to hear the story."

"Perhaps during the feast," Prince Lievin said.

While they waited to enter the great hall, Harafin and Prince Lievin discussed the current state of affairs. The Prince shared with them that the emperor himself, along with kings and nobles from the other five kingdoms, had already sent word of their intentions to attend Prince Lievin's coronation in one month's time.

The prince took Lady Miren's hand. "Tonight we'll announce that our wedding will take place that same day."

After everyone congratulated the couple, Colonel Gabral said, "If I may, Your Highness, do you think it wise for so many of the empire's leaders to leave their kingdoms now, at a time of impending war?"

"It's a risk," Prince Lievin admitted. "However, given the lateness of the season, it's unlikely any major assault will be launched before springtime. Still, the empire is already beginning to mobilize."

Harafin said, "I'm glad to hear it." He shook his head ruefully and added, "I would find myself stuck in the wilderness at a time like this."

"I'm glad you were," Prince Lievin replied. "From all accounts, we wouldn't have won without your help."

Harafin stroked his white beard. "The events that transpired in Il'Aicharen will play a pivotal role in the upcoming conflict."

He glanced at Kevlin but his expression was unreadable. Kevlin resisted the urge to look down at his right boot where Oris lay hidden, stitched into the fold of the turned-down upper.

He hadn't connected with the strange essence he had found inside stone since that terrible day. Even now conflicting emotions fought within him as he thought back to that incredible moment. He had never felt anything so wonderful, so *right* in his entire life.

And yet, in the moment he had touched the stone, he'd killed Antigonus, the man he had sworn to save at all costs.

The ShadeLeech Tanathos had turned Antigonus into a Halimaw, and by all accounts, Antigonus was beyond help. Tanathos had very nearly succeeded in his plan to murder the monster that had been Antigonus. His victory would have doomed them all to destruction.

Kevlin had done the right thing, the only thing he could have. He just wished he could feel better about it.

Thoughts of the battle and what he'd done to help win it led to thoughts of the awesome experience of wielding almost limitless power. Under Oris's direction, he'd unleashed a firestorm that broke Wayra's power and shattered the keep.

Suddenly Kevlin craved that experience again. His hands began to shake, and the quiver reverberated up his arms into his chest. The memory of wielding magic seemed to awaken a hunger so intense Kevlin had to bite his lip to keep from growling.

He needed to live that moment again. The need was like a living thing clawing at his innards. Kevlin glanced around. Everyone was focused on Lady Miren as she told a witty tale. No one had noticed his shaking hands.

Kevlin looked to Harafin, but the sight of the old Sentinel only drove the wild hunger to a fever pitch. Harafin had magic. Harafin could give him some, but he didn't. The selfish old fool wouldn't share.

Kevlin felt a crazed urge to launch himself at Harafin and throttle him for being so cruel. Instead, he forced himself to turn away. An open door beckoned and Kevlin staggered away from the group and through the door.

He found himself in a small garden. He made it several steps onto the soft grass before his legs buckled and he fell to his knees. His limbs trembled so badly he couldn't even sit up.

What's happening to me?

Fear sent icy tendrils down his spine, but the driving hunger consumed it.

Then Indira joined him and knelt by his side. "Kevlin, what's the matter?" She tried to help him sit up.

Normally the touch of her hands sent a shiver of warmth through him. Now all he could think of was that she had magic. Her gift of healing had saved hundreds of lives in the past weeks.

"Help me," he begged.

"Of course, Kevlin. Just take off the amulet so I can heal you."

Rage burned through him. How could she be so cruel? He needed magic. Only the amulet could capture her power and give it to him. He couldn't take it off.

Kevlin grabbed Indira's arm and shouted, "Give me magic! Now!"

Indira tried to pull away, her face frightened, but Kevlin tightened his grip. He felt shocked by his actions, but couldn't stop himself.

"Kevlin, stop. You're hurting me."

Kevlin shook her and screamed, "Give it to me!"

Indira cringed away from him, tears glinting in her eyes.

Then giant hands grabbed his wrists and squeezed. The pressure drove his hands open and Indira scrambled away. Kevlin lunged after her, desperate to regain contact, but Jerrik lifted him bodily off the ground and pulled him away.

"Kevlin, stop it," Jerrik growled. "You're acting insane."

Kevlin struggled against Jerrik's unrelenting grasp. Ceren helped Indira to her feet. The two ladies stared at Kevlin in shock.

Jerrik shook Kevlin. "Cut it out, brother."

Kevlin ignored him. He pleaded, "Indira, you're killing me. Just give me a little. Just a little, and I'll be fine."

"What are you talking about?" Ceren asked.

Indira hesitated. "Maybe, maybe I should."

Kevlin nodded. "Yes. Yes. Please."

"I don't think it's a good idea," Ceren said.

"Nay," Jerrik said. He still struggled to hold Kevlin back. "He's not himself."

Drystan arrived. "Is it Savas again?"

Jerrik shrugged. "How am I supposed to know?"

Indira took a single step closer. Kevlin could almost touch her. The need to feel magic made him want to howl.

She said, "I think I can heal him."

"Don't touch him," Harafin commanded, joining them in the small garden.

He stopped beside Indira. "That's the worst thing you could do right now, my dear. It would destroy him."

Indira gasped and retreated. Kevlin howled with frustration as the promised magic moved out of reach. The terrible hunger clawed at him, driving him to redouble his efforts to break free of Jerrik's grasp.

Harafin took a step closer and Kevlin quieted down. Harafin had magic. He could share. Kevlin extended his fingers toward Harafin and whispered, "Please, give me some."

"What's wrong with him?" Ceren asked.

Harafin shushed her with a wave of his hand, not breaking eye contact with Kevlin. "I will share some magic with you if you do one thing for me."

"Anything."

"Take off your boots."

The others looked surprised, but Kevlin didn't care. He'd strip naked if Harafin asked him to. In that moment, he'd murder his own brothers to ease the craving that drove him.

Jerrik eased his hold and Kevlin ripped off his boots and tossed them aside. Harafin pointed a finger at them and a shimmering silver globe appeared around them all.

"What are you doing?" Ceren asked.

"A precaution."

"You're being cryptic again," Drystan said. Harafin shot him a hard look and Drystan raised his hands in surrender. "I know, I know. Trust you."

Gabral, who had been hidden from view behind Ceren, stepped up beside Harafin. "He looks like a rabid animal. We should put him out of his misery."

Harafin pointed at Jerrik and Drystan. "You two stay here. The rest of you, leave us."

Ceren snorted and whispered something to Indira as she led the taller healer from the garden. Gabral frowned and looked like he wanted to protest. A hard look from Harafin convinced him leaving was a better course.

Kevlin crept closer to Harafin and licked his lips. He extended one hand toward the old Sentinel. It shook so badly he could barely hold it up. "You promised."

Harafin held out a hand. A small globe of amber light appeared above his palm and floated across to Kevlin.

Kevlin pounced on it. As soon as it touched him, the amulet resting against his chest grew a shade warmer as it captured the magic and poured it into him.

Kevlin fell back onto the ground and shouted with pure joy as he took the magic and *changed* it the way Oris had taught him, making it his. The power filtered through him, and for a second it washed away the terrible hunger.

Kevlin blew out a happy breath, and only then did his mind come awake, as if out of a terrible dream. What had he done? He'd attacked Indira. The memory seared him to the core.

He rolled to his feet, intent on rushing to her and apologizing, but the hunger returned, stronger than ever.

He glared at Harafin. The Sentinel had more power than he could use, and yet he only shared such a tiny bit. Was Kevlin a dog to receive only scraps?

He held out his hand and demanded, "Give me more."

"No."

Kevlin snarled and launched himself at Harafin, hands outstretched like claws to force the old fool to share.

Jerrik caught him by the shirt and lifted him off the ground. He spun in Jerrik's grasp, but before he could rake the bigger man with his nails, Drystan pinned his arms behind his back.

Harafin said, "Subdue him. I am afraid you will have to be rather firm."

Jerrik grunted as Kevlin kicked him in the ribs. "Sorry brother."

Then he slammed Kevlin onto the ground. Kevlin struck so hard he sank into the soft earth. The impact drove the breath from his lungs and rattled his head. While he lay stunned, Drystan dropped onto his chest and arms, pinning him.

The blow cleared Kevlin's head. The craving for magic still prowled through him, but for the moment it didn't control him.

"I'm all right. Let me up."

Drystan hesitated, but then stood. He and Jerrik remained close by Kevlin's side when he arose.

Kevlin faced Harafin and shame clung like vomit to the back of his throat. "What just happened to me?"

"Have you been feeling shaky lately?"

"Yes."

Harafin nodded. "I should have been watching more closely for the symptoms. I am sorry. I had a lot on my mind."

"What symptoms?" He made it sound like a disease.

"You are suffering from Trembling Madness."

Jerrik moved away from Kevlin. "Is it contagious?"

"No. In fact, Kevlin is the first non-Actinopathic that I know of to experience it."

"What is it?" Kevlin asked, trying to mask a growing fear. Hadn't he just embraced magic? It figured that now it would try to kill him.

"It is the consequence of your experience at the keep of Il'Aicharen."

"You mean, when I . . ."

Harafin held up a hand to forestall him. They hadn't spoken with anyone else about how Kevlin had connected with Oris or his being chosen as its new bearer. Kevlin still could scarcely believe it had happened.

Only the most powerful Sentinels were ever chosen to wield Oris. Harafin had said they would speak more on the matter soon, and had sworn him to secrecy. Only he and Harafin and Sentinel Ah'Shan knew the truth.

Harafin said. "Yes, you handled a considerable amount of magic without the necessary safeguards in place, nor the natural capacity to control it. In such an event, the magic leaves an impression on your mind, a craving, or addiction if you will. The result is the driving hunger that just took control of you tonight. It drives you to acquire magic, and in similar quantities as before."

"That sounds bad," Drystan muttered.

"This has happened occasionally with Sentinels, particularly Accepted, although rarely is the effect as powerful as we witnessed tonight. Only at its most extreme is the phenomenon referred to as Trembling Madness."

"You mean I'm going insane?" Kevlin asked? He'd given so much, tried so hard. Better to have fallen in battle than become a raving lunatic.

"Not exactly. You are sane, but this addiction can be extremely dangerous. It is not dissimilar to the symptoms experienced by users of Aravinda, the Nedikan 'pleasure flower' popular in Freyarr, when they lose access to the drug for any length of time. Should you succumb to this craving and gain access to magic while a slave to it, you would be unable to control it, and could easily unleash terrible destruction."

"That's why you wouldn't give me more magic."

Harafin nodded. "You needed a taste of it to regain control, but now you must drive it away. If you do not, it will only trigger the madness within you."

"How long does it last?" Kevlin asked. Harafin's words terrified him, but he felt a deep reluctance to release the magic. The craving still gnawed at him, but he could still control it.

"With discipline and constant vigilance, you can control it. As your mastery with magic grows, your capacity will increase and the craving will subside and eventually disappear. Now, release the power I gave you."

Kevlin focused the magic into a single drop of power in the center of his chest. He steeled his mind and willed it away. For a second it bucked against his will. The unexpected reaction scared him and he redoubled his efforts to get rid of it.

A column of bright white light shot out of his upraised palm and streaked into the open sky above the garden. It left a burning after-image that remained for several seconds.

Harafin nodded. "Very good." Then he fixed them all with a solemn stare. "Tell no one about this."

Kevlin struggled to focus during the feast. He remembered little of the food beyond the fact that there was a lot of it. The tables groaned under the weight of the feast. Harvest had recently ended and the kingdom was eager to share Serigala's great bounty.

Kevlin wasn't given much time to ponder Harafin's dire pronouncement. As a primary guest of honor, his feast was constantly interrupted by well-wishers.

An entire table was set aside for gifts, and soon it was overflowing. At first, most of them were for Kevlin. In a flash of inspiration, he deflected the request to recount the battle to Jerrik.

The huge Donarri was eager to do so. His heavily embellished account communicated most of the major facts, while leaving out Kevlin's struggle for possession of his soul against Savas.

Thankfully, Jerrik made sure to highlight his and Drystan's contributions. They were both saluted as heroes and for a time, attention shifted from Kevlin to them. Drystan accepted the praise with grace and good humor. Jerrik basked in it, and caught the eyes of several eligible young ladies.

The worst part was that the prince canceled the normal dancing out of respect for the dead king. Kevlin didn't even get to dance with Indira in that gorgeous dress. Worse, he never got a chance to apologize.

He retired late that night to the spacious room appointed to him. As he lay in the darkness, he thought back over everything that had happened in recent weeks.

The battle was over, but he'd have to be a fool to assume his life might return to any semblance of normal. He'd settle for getting some quiet time to spend with Indira.

Surely he could get that much.

3

True Allies

Harafin paused before the door to his bedchamber and turned to face the darkened corridor.

"It is late to be hiding in the darkness, Ah'Shan."

The powerfully built Sentinel moved into the light of the nearby torch, although his face still seemed shadowed by his thick mane of dark hair.

"Harafin, you must end this farce."

"Which farce is that?"

"Don't play games with me. The man Kevlin is a very real danger to everyone around him. Even you must see the folly of leaving him in possession of the stone."

"How did you learn of his condition?"

Ah'Shan snorted. "I'm no fool, Harafin. You think I don't keep wards up? Be grateful that no one else sensed the madness."

"This is no time to make rash decisions," Harafin began.

"Rash?" Ah'Shan cut him off. "Look in the mirror, you old fool. What could be more rash than claiming that untrained, damaged *commoner* is actually chosen to bear our greatest weapon?"

"Oris itself made the choice. I only ratified it."

Ah'Shan stepped closer and pointed a finger at Harafin's chest. "You have the power to un-ratify it. You know the time of trials is upon us. We need a powerful Catalyst to lead us or all will be lost. Do you really think that man can do it?"

"There is much I do not know. Events are moving fast. You are right, we're seeing the beginning of what may prove to be the end of times, and despite hundreds of years of study and preparation, we did not foresee this."

Ah'Shan took a step closer. "Then choose me. You know I'm best qualified for this burden."

Harafin considered the other Sentinel for a moment. "Give me some time."

"We don't have time."

"We do have a little. There are questions I must answer before I change my mind." He placed a hand on Ah'Shan's shoulder. "As impossible as it seems, I made the choice I was convinced was right."

Ah'Shan shook off his hand, but Harafin continued. "If I hadn't lived through those events, I wouldn't have believed I could make such a choice. But I did, and I stand by it until I learn more."

"What more do you need to know? The man is on the verge of madness. With Oris's power in his grasp, he could shatter entire kingdoms."

Harafin said, "I understand the risk. Yet, in addition to the question of the severity of his condition, I need to understand King Leszek's involvement in recent events."

Ah'Shan waved away the point. "He died on the field of battle. Don't trifle with his memory or even you won't survive the wrath of this people."

"He died in battle, and yet I must understand his contract with Dhanjal and what would lead a Blade Stalwart to break his oath once given."

"You play a dangerous game," Ah'Shan warned.

"As do we all." Harafin added softly, "Can you explain why Wayra would turn against us? She nearly facilitated Tanathos' victory. And what was she doing hunting Antigonus even before his call for help came to us?"

"Don't change the subject," Ah'Shan snapped. "Wayra turned from the path I set her on and betrayed us all. Do not try to bring into question my motives."

"I never questioned your motives."

"I am no fool, Harafin. You cannot question Wayra without extending that doubt to me."

"I do not doubt your effectiveness," Harafin said.

"Good. All I know of Wayra is that she met with the king prior to recent events, so she might have been in league with some plot he was tangled in. I did not get a chance to question her."

Harafin studied his old friend for a moment before saying, "Very well. I will see what I can learn from the prince and others here at court."

Ah'Shan turned to go but Harafin called out to him. "I have a favor to ask of you, old friend."

"Name it." He said over his shoulder.

"Keep secret the knowledge that Kevlin was chosen."

"Why?"

"To give us time to act."

Ah'Shan turned to face Harafin. "I will give you the time you ask, but I expect you to act without hesitating." Then he turned and strode into the darkness.

Harafin stared after him. "I never hesitate."

4

A Bit of Help From My Friends

T he next morning, Kevlin avoided the main hall and the constant assaults by the sincere, if annoying, crowds and picked up a simple breakfast from the kitchen. He inquired after Indira and learned she was in the queen's wing.

Kevlin paused in the wide hall that served as a backbone to the northern section of the palace. Seven wings protruded to the north, with the queen's wing in the center. He stood in the wide, arched doorway that led to a plush waiting room filled with padded chairs and couches. A pair of sentries flanked the far double doors that led deeper into that wing.

A comely, middle-aged woman with her brown hair in a bun, sat at a desk near the double doors. She wore the brown and green uniform of a palace servant and smiled warmly at Kevlin when he approached.

Thankfully, she didn't try to kiss or hug him. "What can I do for you, Lord Kevlin?"

It was encouraging to find at least one resident who had returned to their normal controlled self.

When he asked for Indira, the woman grinned. "That woman is a blessing. She treated the queen, who's been so sick ever since hearing of the king's passing."

That would explain why he hadn't seen the queen the day before. So caught up was he with his own problems, he hadn't even thought to ask.

"I'm not surprised. Indira's always eager to help."

"She's ruthless at cards though," the woman added with a grimace.

"Tell me about it," Kevlin chuckled.

He wondered if Indira had any idea how powerful an impact she made wherever she went. Her extreme good looks and unrivaled healing powers won over even hardened veterans. Her cutthroat card dealing seemed out of character, and yet somehow she made it work.

"I'll send for Mistress Indira, but it might be a while." She leaned forward and added in a conspiratorial tone. "She's been teaching the ladies how to play Kings and Beggars."

"I thought that game was frowned on at court."

"Oh, it was."

"I'll wait," Kevlin said. He didn't really have anything to do, so he did not mind.

He wandered over to one of the plush chairs and made himself comfortable. Leave it to Indira to bring a hint of scandal to the respectable court. No doubt she had suggested the game with such innocence the ladies hadn't been able to refuse.

They should have. Indira was going to own them.

Kings and Beggars was a complex card game that usually included thirteen face cards. Twelve represented the kings and queens of each kingdom. The emperor's card trumped them all. Indira possessed a new version that included a card for the keisara. It complicated an already complex game, and Indira had mastered it.

The game was not usually played in the palaces since the objective was to strengthen one's hold over the six kingdoms and eventually usurp power and become emperor. Nobility seemed uncomfortable with the idea of playing with revolution. The card game's popularity had risen after the king of Freyarr had tried to ban it. Since then, the rulers of the six kingdoms hadn't openly criticized it, hoping the fad would pass.

Kevlin barely understood half of the combinations of those royalty cards with the secondary cards representing economy, trade, military, and political intrigue. Different hands allowed for creation of alliances, while others fostered double-crossing and clandestine trading.

The game could take hours. If Indira had convinced the ladies to bet on the game, she'd need more pack mules to cart away her winnings.

While he waited, Kevlin struggled with what to say, how he'd apologize. His hands began to sweat, but at least they didn't shake.

Hopefully she'd arrive in a good mood after crowning herself empress again.

After what seemed an unbearably long wait, the far doors opened. Kevlin surged to his feet, his heart in his throat.

Ceren, not Indira, stepped through the doors. Today she wore her long, auburn hair in a single braid down her back and she wore a simple black linen dress. Even though half the women in the city were wearing similar dresses, Ceren would never appear unremarkable.

"Where's Indira?" Kevlin asked.

Ceren drew him from the waiting room. "She's busy conquering the empire."

"You'd think the ladies would quit."

"You would, but it turns out the ladies of Diodor are very competitive."

Kevlin felt sorry for them.

"Come. We have to talk." She led him down the main hall to a comfortable study lined with books. When she confirmed they were alone she asked, "Do you really think it's safe to be around Indira after what happened yesterday?"

"I'm feeling better. I don't have the shakes right now."

"You're willing to risk Indira's life on the hope that it doesn't return?"

Kevlin said softly, "I just want to apologize."

Ceren placed a hand on his arm. "I know, but Kevlin, how much good would you do if you lost control again and hurt her?"

He dropped onto a couch facing a cold fireplace and ran a hand through his hair. He didn't want to drive Indira away, but he didn't know enough about his condition to feel sure this was the right course.

He wanted to ask Ceren for help, but she confused him. Before the battle at Il'Aicharen, she had actively tried to keep him away from Indira. She hadn't tried to interfere in the past week, but then again she hadn't needed to.

Well, he had proven he wasn't good at relationships. The last woman he'd loved had nearly murdered him. He needed help, and Ceren was the only one he could try turning to.

So he forced himself to ask, "What should I do?"

Ceren settled onto the couch beside him and took his hand. "Give her some time, Kevlin. Things will work out for the best."

"I hope so."

She leaned closer, her emerald eyes sparkling. "What did you learn from Harafin yesterday? What happened to you?"

"He said I have Trembling Madness."

Ceren frowned. "Are you sure?"

"That's what he said. He didn't tell me a lot about it."

Ceren pulled her braid over her shoulder and fiddled with the gold clip holding the end as she stared into the empty fireplace for a moment. "I'll see what I can find out for you."

"Thanks." He doubted Harafin would explain much more, but he needed to know what was happening to him.

Ceren patted his arm one more time and left. As Kevlin turned back down the main hall to search for his swordbrothers, he was grateful that Ceren was there to help.

5

SECURITY QUESTIONS

P rince Lievin summoned the company to the military wing of the palace for a private luncheon. Just as they all settled into seats around a large conference table, the door opened.

Leander strode into the room.

The old Pallian Stalwart looked grim and lines of exhaustion etched in dirt clung to his normally smiling face. His clothing was ragged and debris clung to his normally well-trimmed beard.

Kevlin moved to greet Leander, but Harafin spoke first. "How was your hunt?"

Leander growled and for a second his face reflected the raging fury he'd unleashed at Il'Aicharen when he'd learned that Tanathos was the man who had murdered his family over one hundred years ago.

Kevlin paused two steps away, hand already outstretched in greeting. Leander still looked like he wanted to break things, and Kevlin didn't want to be one of them.

Drystan and Gabral had been the last to see Leander a week ago. They had watched as he threw himself off the eastern flank of the mountain in pursuit of Tanathos. The low clouds that had ringed the mountain had swallowed first Tanathos and then Leander. No one had heard of either of them, despite wide-ranging scouting parties sent to search for them.

With visible effort, Leander shackled his anger. He noted Kevlin's hesitation and managed a smile as he took Kevlin's hand.

"What's for lunch?"

Leander ate ravenously while the rest of the company waited. After downing an entire tankard of cider, he sat back and sighed.

"Thank you for waiting. I haven't eaten much in a week."

Drystan piled more food onto Leander's plate. "Did you find him?"

"No, he escaped."

Gabral frowned and asked, "Then why are you here? I'd think you'd still be hunting him."

Leander speared a chunk of beef with his knife. Kevlin was tempted to protest. He'd already eaten half the platter. At this rate, there wouldn't be enough left for the rest of them. Jerrik liked arm wrestling over food, and Kevlin didn't stand a chance if it came to that.

Leander said, "I intended to hunt him as long as it took. I very nearly had him a couple times, but the animal outfoxed me every time."

He took another drink. "Then yesterday I lost him. His trail completely vanished."

"That's no easy feat," Harafin said, stroking his beard in thought.

Leander shrugged. "The last I sensed of him, he had been racing straight for Diodor."

"He's coming here?" Kevlin asked.

The thought of Tanathos stalking the streets of Diodor triggered a shiver of fear. He wanted to destroy Tanathos almost as much as Leander, but the Shadeleech possessed an overwhelmingly evil presence. Even if they caught him, he would surely cause much destruction before they brought him down.

Gabral frowned. "He can't be. He's a lot of things, but he's no fool. If he comes to Diodor, he'll be destroyed."

Harafin said, "I'll double-check the city's defenses, but you're correct, Colonel. Tanathos would not lightly venture close to the city."

"What if he felt he had good enough reason?" Drystan asked.

Jerrik shook his head. "Even if he thought he could get his hands on Oris again, no one knows who the new bearer is, and he'd never make it back to Il'Aicharen."

"No," Harafin said. "Hathor and the last of the Kestrels are guarding the Heart of the Mountain, and a full company of Sentinels are being dispatched to help with repairs. Tanathos' army is destroyed. He could never win through again."

Drystan said, "But there are still some enemy forces in Hallvarr, isn't that right, Your Highness?"

Prince Lievin nodded. "Commander Tekla is still hunting the one force that razed a town north of Diodor. That force has also vanished."

Harafin frowned. "In those last reports, Tekla refused your order to return to Diodor."

The prince nodded again. "He sent word that he will honor the last command of the king no matter how long it takes."

"Convenient," Harafin said softly with a frown. "I need to speak with that man."

Gabral tapped his fingers on the table. "Perhaps Tanathos is smarter than we give him credit for."

"How so?" Leander asked.

"Think about it. Tanathos disappears while moving toward Diodor." He raised one finger to make the point.

"A strike force of some unknown but undeniable strength also disappears." Another finger raised.

"And in one month, the emperor and most of the senior leadership and nobility of the Six Kingdoms will all be arriving here for the coronation and wedding of Prince Lievin."

He raised his index finger and then pointed the three raised fingers at Drystan. "You say Tanathos might venture close if there's good enough reason."

Drystan nodded. "What better reason than a chance to strike at the emperor and the gathered kings?"

"If he struck with stealth, he might overwhelm the token security forces they would bring to such an event," Leander said slowly with a scowl.

Kevlin hated to think they might be right. Tanathos had proven courageous and audacious in his tactics. He led a strike force across the breadth of the empire undetected. Then he very nearly accomplished the seemingly impossible task of destroying the keep at Il'Aicharen and penetrating to the heart of the mountain to murder the bearer of Oris.

Now the empire's mightiest weapon was tied to a man who could not wield its power.

"If he does, how do we stop him?" Kevlin asked.

Jerrik pointed a chicken leg at Gabral. "You're assuming Tanathos knows they're coming here."

"I think it a safe assumption to make," Harafin said.

"Why?"

Haran scanned the group, holding each eye. "I will be blunt with this company. We know Tanathos conspired with traitors hidden among us to plan his assault."

"Bajaran, Rhea, Dhanjal." Gabral ticked off the names.

"And most likely others," Harafin said. "There are still questions unanswered. Foremost among them is what was the king's connection with Dhanjal?"

Prince Lievin said, "I haven't found the answer to that yet, Master Harafin. I knew nothing of Dhanjal before last week. I had been away for some time on diplomatic assignments for my father. I only returned to Diodor the day before the battle. My father had left word that I was to command here while he was in the field, but no details about what was going on. Everyone who knew went with him."

Harafin said, "Until we know more, we must assume there are traitors hidden within Diodor. Most likely they are already here in the palace."

Gabral patted his perfectly styled hair. "If they're placed well enough, they could pose a serious security threat."

Prince Lievin said, "One man who might know more is my uncle, High Lord Damarist. He is our ambassador on the imperial ruling council."

Harafin nodded. "I am familiar with him. He has been a sitting member on the council for only a few years."

"He'll be arriving with the emperor in a couple of weeks. We can question him then."

"Very well," Harafin said. "For now, I recommend you summon your high command so we can begin to lay plans for the security of the city."

Leander raised a forkful of meat. "I concur. Please pass the butter."

6

A LITTLE TOO CUNNING

The security council met into the afternoon. Kevlin was grateful to finally leave the conference room and stretch his legs after hours of sometimes boring discussions. A servant found him shortly after the meeting with a note from Ceren.

Kevlin found her seated on a wrought-iron bench in a small garden. It was located on the north side of the palace, between two of the seven wings that extended like fingers from the main palace complex. She sat before a gurgling fountain carved to resemble a wolf taking down a deer, a common tribute to Serigala in her form as the Lady Jagen, goddess of the hunt and the moon.

Ceren had set aside her black dress and simple braid. She now wore a white gown with embroidered blue swans scattered across the bodice. Her hair was brushed out and hung in thick waves that cascaded over her shoulders and down her back.

Her red hair and bronze skin made a beautiful contrast with the dress. It amazed him that she could find so many different outfits that fit her so well a single day after arriving at the palace.

He thought back to when they had first met. She had seemed unreachable, a noblewoman, living a life completely foreign to him. Since then, he'd seen her fight, felt the sting of her sharp tongue, and learned to appreciate her quick mind.

Now he had been drawn into those same higher social circles. First his swordbrothers united him to their families through blood, and now

Prince Lievin had proclaimed him a noble of Hallvarr. He'd need to ask Ceren about all that. He had no idea how to act noble.

Ceren waved him over excitedly and he joined her on the little bench.

"What did you find out?"

"Trembling Madness is a rare condition that affects mostly new Accepted sentinels who try to wield more magic than they can handle."

"That's more or less what Harafin told me."

"Did he also tell you it's normally fatal?"

"No. What do you mean, fatal?"

Ceren looked around as if to make sure they were alone, and leaned closer until her head was bare inches from his. She whispered, "It seems this craving for magic can drive people insane, or even kill them."

Kevlin clenched his hands tight. He could feel just a hint of shakiness in them. The craving for magic was there, a dull ache that he'd managed to ignore most of the day. Now, as he thought about it, it roused itself and his hands shook harder. He fought down the urge, and his hands stilled.

Ceren placed one small hand over his and drew his gaze again. "Kevlin, why would Harafin keep this from you?"

"I don't know. We didn't have much time to discuss it."

"That's probably it." She didn't look or sound convinced.

"What are you suggesting?"

Ceren shrugged. "I overheard Harafin say this choosing was unique. Ah'Shan's made it clear he wasn't chosen and he was the only other Sentinel present."

"I don't understand." Kevlin didn't like this turn of the conversation.

"The only idea that makes any possible sense is that somehow Harafin chose a Sentinel as bearer who wasn't at Il'Aicharen."

"I don't think--" Kevlin began.

Ceren cut him off, her face worried. "Think about it, Kevlin. If he did, then he only needs you to stay alive until he can deliver Oris to the next bearer."

Kevlin frowned. He'd sworn to Harafin not to tell anyone the truth about being chosen as bearer, so he couldn't correct her. Besides, what if she's partially right? What if Harafin was planning to choose another bearer soon?

"Kevlin, I can't help you if you don't trust me," Ceren cupped his face in her hands, forcing him to meet her gaze.

She was too clever by half. It was too hard to lie when looking someone in the eye.

"I trust you, Ceren."

"Then tell me."

"I can't. I promised Harafin . . ."

Ceren leaned back, not trying to hide the hurt in her eyes. "Promised to obey him while he withholds information from you."

Kevlin stood and paced away, confused and frustrated. Could Harafin really be using him?

Of course Harafin was using him. That much was certain. What he struggled to believe was that Harafin would spend his life so cheaply. Harafin had made it clear he'd do whatever he felt necessary to protect the empire. He never hesitated, but would he plot Kevlin's death?

Kevlin turned back to Ceren. "I'll ask him about it."

"Be careful." She looked worried.

"I will."

Ceren stood. "I'll see what else I can find for you."

"Thanks. And tell Indira . . ." He trailed off. He couldn't voice the things he wanted to say to Indira. Not to Ceren.

"I'll tell her," Ceren said. Then she smiled. "Oh, I almost forgot. Indira asked me to give you a message."

"Really? Tell me."

Ceren's smile turned mischievous. "I'll have to show you."

She wrapped her arms around his neck. Startled, Kevlin tried to back away but Ceren said, "Don't interrupt."

Then she pulled his head down and kissed him tenderly on the lips."

It was a nice kiss, but Kevlin froze. Indira sent Ceren to kiss him? That was just weird.

But it meant Indira forgave him.

He wrapped his arms around Ceren and kissed her back. If she was going to take a message back to Indira, he'd make it a good one.

She was a good kisser, but he broke the kiss after only a few seconds. It just felt wrong on too many levels.

Ceren had kissed him once before, on the dark night when they had first discovered the enemy fortress, just before she left to seek help. But then while they had chased Tanathos through the heart of Hallvarr, she had done her best to keep Kevlin and Indira apart, to thwart their growing interest.

Now she kissed him like she wanted to kiss him, not like it was a message from another woman.

She held him, preventing him from withdrawing. In that moment, Indira's voice called out from behind them. "Ceren, are you in here . . . oh!"

Kevlin broke away and his heart sank. Indira stood across the clearing, one hand raised to her mouth, her dark eyes wide with surprise.

One question answered, but so many new questions to take its place. So much for reconciling with Indira.

Before he could think how to make things right, Ceren moved across the garden to Indira. "You shouldn't get too close to him, Indira. The shakes are getting worse."

Indira took an involuntary step back, and fear flitted across her face. Kevlin opened his mouth to object, but what could he say? He had grabbed her, hurt her. How could he tell her it was safe to be around him?

Almost as if in response to his thoughts, the hunger for magic stirred in his heart and his body shook with a powerful tremor.

The ladies didn't seem to notice, but it left him cold with fear.

"Don't worry. I'm doing everything I can to help. I delivered your message."

Indira blushed. "But Ceren, I didn't mean for you to. . ."

"I know," Ceren cast a reproachful look at Kevlin. "Things kind of got out of hand."

"Wait a minute," Kevlin protested, taking a step toward them.

Ceren raised a hand to forestall him. "It's all right, Kevlin. I don't blame you. Just keep your distance. You're losing control."

As Ceren led Indira away, Kevlin wanted to chase them, to shout that he wasn't losing control, but that would only prove her point. He stared after them, totally confused.

What by all the gods was Ceren playing at? She'd set him up and he'd fallen right into the trap like a brainless idiot. She claimed to be trying to help, but she'd just neatly driven a wedge between him and Indira and made it look like his fault.

She really was cunning, but not in the good way he'd been thinking. By the Lady! He started to get a headache trying to sort out how to respond.

And to think she'd made him feel guilty for not telling her all of his secrets. Anger replaced confusion and he paced the garden, fists clenched.

Finally he blew out a breath and splashed water on his face to clear his head. He would find Indira and explain things after he talked with Harafin about his condition.

First, he went to look for his brothers. Maybe they could get into a fight. Hitting someone would feel really good.

7

ROGUE FIRE

In the heart of the imperial palace in Tamera, Emperor Zuberi Tegnazian strode into the ruling council formal meeting hall. The emperor was a tall, distinguished-looking man with a handsome face and thick mane of salt-and-pepper hair, who wore his authority as easily as he did his fine robes.

He smiled into the empty hall. He loved how this room smelled. The huge horseshoe-shaped mahogany table around which the council sat added a hint of wood polish to the clean, crisp air. High overhead, a circular stained-glass window that depicted the map of the empire let in a rainbow of light that gave the room a cheery air.

The emperor's aide had served him for most of his thirty-year reign. He knew to wait a moment for Emperor Tegnazian to enjoy the peace of the room that would soon be filled with bustling activity.

The emperor strode toward his throne-like seat at the apex of the table's curve and his aide resumed his running monologue.

"Sentinel Felix will arrive momentarily to discuss security and Sentinel training in your absence. The ambassadors are expected shortly, and all is being finalized for departure of the imperial crown fleet for Diodor with the morning tide tomorrow."

"Very well." Emperor Tegnazian sat in his council chair, his mind working through the hundred details still to be finalized prior to departure.

Crimson fire exploded out of the chair as soon as he settled into it. Flames engulfed him and searing pain screamed from every inch of exposed skin.

As the emperor convulsed in pain, his aide opened his mouth to shout the alarm. A tongue of crimson fire whipped out to envelope him too.

Emperor Tegnazian writhed in the fire, seared by unbelievable agony. Yet he couldn't move, couldn't throw himself from the burning chair.

Through the billowing flames, he saw his personal guards rush into the room. He was denied the ability to scream in agony or grief as waist-thick ropes of fire leaped across the room to envelope them.

The guards fell screaming to the ground. Within the flames they writhed and shrank, as if their flesh was being melted away. Within seconds even their bones dissolved into ash.

The emperor convulsed within the flames and wondered why he still lived. Agony raked his skin and fire poured into his open mouth as he breathed and tried vainly to scream. His innards felt as if they were melting, and yet still he lived.

The outer guard poured into the room and Zuberi wept tears of fire as he watched them fall to the flames. But while the first guards had withered and died, these guards fell to the ground and writhed within the flames like he did.

Emperor Tegnazian tried to form a plea for help, a prayer to the gods, but the pain consumed everything. He could do nothing but stare through the flames and, like an animal, struggle against his invisible bonds even though he knew he could not escape.

Then Ambassador Janezeko of Freyarr entered the room with Urun, the Sentinel from Donarr assigned as the emperor's personal magical bodyguard. Emperor Tegnazian wanted to shout for joy when he saw the heavyset Sentinel.

Urun stopped in the doorway at the sight of the crimson fire filling the council chamber. Ambassador Janezeko charged into the room in a show of courage that surprised and moved the emperor, and then saddened him when he realized the futility of it.

Urun shouted, the words lost to the emperor, drowned out by the thundering rush of flames burning around his head. Ambassador Janezeko skidded to a halt.

He was already too late.

A tendril of fire whipped toward the ambassador, but the Sentinel shouted and threw out a hand.

A spear of white magic flashed across the room to intercept the flames reaching for Janezeko. The ambassador stumbled back toward the door, and Urun backed in that direction, glowing hands raised to ward off the angry flames.

The fire enveloping the fallen soldiers flared, and one of them withered and died. The flames grew stronger, roaring like a dozen lions. A wall of fire shot out to encircle Urun and cut off his retreat.

He shouted again and threw out his hands. Pure white power pulsed out from him in a sphere that drove the flames back.

Zuberi tried to shout his encouragement. Urun would save him.

Then a new tentacle of fire leaped high overhead and, as Urun looked up to track its movement, it drove down through his white sphere of power and speared into his open mouth. Urun convulsed as red fire plunged into his body. His arms and legs shook and his eyes opened wide in a silent scream that died a second later.

The emperor had to watch as Urun shriveled and dissolved under the onslaught of the evil magic.

Within three heartbeats, there was no evidence Urun ever existed. The sight of the Sentinel's horrific death chased Emperor Tegnazian into welcome oblivion.

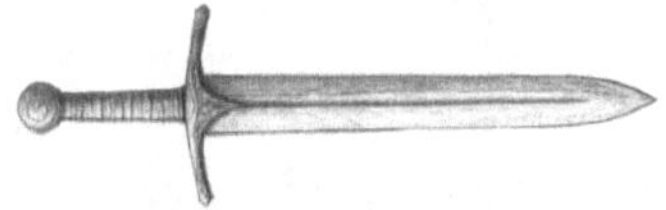

Duke Braden Janezeko, Lord of Parthalan, Freyarri ambassador to the emperor, and sitting member of the Ruling Council, staggered out of the council chamber and fell to his knees. His stomach convulsed, and only with an extreme effort did he keep from vomiting. The image of Urun's grisly death burned so hot in his mind he wondered if it would ever dim.

The sound of rapid footsteps drew his gaze. The captain of the emperor's elite guard arrived, followed closely by the immensely fat Sentinel Felix.

The captain cried, "What's going on here?" He moved toward the open door.

Braden lunged after him and grabbed his arm. "Don't. You'll die." He couldn't bear to watch another person die like Urun did.

"Let me go," the captain snarled. "The emperor's in there."

"You can't help him."

"I can," Felix panted. He adjusted his robes and marched to the door.

"Beware," Braden said, inching toward the door after Felix and the captain.

When the captain saw the emperor writing in the magical flames, he cried out and made to step forward. Felix blocked him with an arm, his gaze locked on the burning room.

"Ambassador Janezeko is right. Stay where you are or you'll only fuel the spell."

"Can you undo this?" the captain asked.

"I mean to try."

Felix stepped into the room, hands raised. Braden nearly pulled him back, but Felix was an Elite Sentinel, in charge of training and security in Harafin's absence. Surely he of all people could deal with this threat.

Crackling flames lashed out at Felix, and Braden took an involuntary step back. Several paces short of the fat Sentinel, the crimson tentacles bounced back off of an invisible shield.

Felix grunted and muttered something to himself. Power crackled through the air like lightning. Hundreds of flashes of blue light rippled across the council chamber and the smell of burning hair drifted to Braden.

Wherever the mini-lightning struck, the fire wavered and retreated. Braden shared a triumphant look with the captain.

Then fire erupted out of the air all around Felix. The heat drove Braden and the captain back through the open door.

In the room, Felix stood within a pillar of billowing flames. Braden could barely see him, couldn't tell if he was burning or not. The memory of Urun being consumed from the inside by the magic nearly caused him to vomit all over the captain.

Felix raised his hands within the flames, but instead of disappearing, the fire burned hotter. Braden shielded his face, and the skin on the back of his hand reddened under the intense heat.

Then the flames winked out and Felix backed to the doorway. He was breathing heavily, but looked unharmed. He placed his hands on either side of the door.

The evil magic grasped toward him again, but a shimmering shield filled the doorway and the flames could not pass.

Felix turned his back on the council chamber and wiped his sweaty face. His robes were singed and the tips of his hair curled under the heat.

He grunted. "Rogue Fire."

"What does that mean?" Braden asked.

Behind Felix, the flames had settled over the emperor and the other guards again. They seemed to pulse in a rhythm far too regular for normal fire. After a moment, Braden realized what it was.

Beside him the captain gasped. "Their heartbeats."

"Aye," Felix said. "Their souls are tied to the flames now."

"The emperor," the captain gasped. "He still lives!"

Felix blocked the man from throwing himself through the glowing doorway. "Yes. I imagine he's in great pain, but he lives."

"I have to save him."

"Then stop being a fool," Felix said sharply. "Go, quickly. Summon the other Sentinels."

"Which ones."

"All of them."

The captain saluted and raced away. Braden tried to compose himself, but before he could ask Felix any more questions, the other ambassadors on the council arrived in a group.

When they learned the situation, they began arguing about what to do. Some suggested they retreat so as to maintain leadership in the empire if Sentinel Felix's shields failed.

Braden said, "Run away then, cowards. Run while those who have the courage to face evil make the important decisions.

There was no more talk about leaving, but of the six ambassadors, there were at least five different ideas about what should be done. The ambassadors from Einarr and Donarr thought alike and usually agreed on most decisions. This proved no different.

They recommended the palace guard be roused and put on high alert to ward against any other attacks. Given recent happenings in Hallvarr, the threat could not be ignored.

The fat ambassador from Meinarr immediately complained about the added cost to the imperial budget. He recommended they pass an emergency motion to raise taxes on all durable goods and foodstuffs to offset expected higher expenditures.

The Hallvarri ambassador said little. He finally commented that this would likely delay the emperor's expected departure. Then wondered if there might be some impact on the expected coronation of his nephew.

The aged Tamarri king, who served also as the host nation's ambassador, managed a weak laugh. "Of course it'll impact the departure, you dolt."

Braden listened to them for a few minutes and then clapped his hands together loudly to draw their attention. "My friends, you are all missing the point here."

"What point is that?" asked the Einarri ambassador, Garitt Talamantez.

He stood straight as a spear despite his fifty years. He kept his steel-gray hair cropped short as if he were still a cavalryman, and he regarded Braden with piercing hazel eyes. The two often argued, but he could sometimes help the man see reason.

"We must consider the fact that even once the other Sentinels arrive and, gods willing, break this evil curse, the emperor will likely be disabled for a period of time. Given the nature of the attack, we may assume it is tied to recent events in Hallvarr as a broader aggressive strategy of pre-emptive strikes aimed at destabilizing our nation in a time of impending conflict."

"Get to the point, you pompous windbag," said the huge Donarri ambassador. Duke Perun Kescog was once one of his nation's greatest warriors. Now middle aged and running to fat, he was still an imposing man.

Braden despised him.

In almost any situation, he and Perun generally took opposing sides. Any chance Braden sometimes had of helping Garitt see reason often died with Perun's obstinate, thick-headed, arguments. The man seemed to think the best way to solve any problem was to hit it enough times with his axe.

Some problems required more subtle solutions, so Braden controlled his frustration. "I could get to the point more quickly if you didn't interrupt, Ambassador."

Duke Kescog snorted. "Braden, you always have to grandstand as if we're in the Great Hall in front of thousands of people. Just say what you have to say, man."

"Very well. I move that we pass a resolution granting interim powers of administration to a successor until such time as the emperor recovers his faculties."

Perun snorted again. "I only need one guess to figure out who you nominate."

Braden spread his hands. "I'll gladly expound upon my qualifications and justifications for the choice unless you have a better candidate in mind."

"It's not a bad idea," High Lord Damarist of Hallvarr said. "We need someone in charge."

Ambassador Talamantez of Einarr shook his head slowly. "Braden, I'm disappointed in you. The emperor's been incapacitated for all of ten minutes and you're already trying to take the throne."

Braden shook his head. "Why turn jealousy into resentment, my old friend?"

"Jealousy?"

"I can't help it that my mind moves faster than most, that I immediately saw the need that none of you yet grasped, and moved to fill it."

Duke Kescog barked a laugh. "That's one way to describe what you do."

A large group of white-robed Sentinels jogged up the hall, interrupting the argument. Felix invited Braden and the other ambassadors to withdraw far enough for the other Sentinels to encircle the doorway with him. He spent a few minutes conversing with them, explaining what he had in mind.

Many of the younger Sentinels murmured in surprise when they heard what had happened, and several of them jockeyed around the doorway for a better view of the cursed flames.

"We are ready," Felix declared at last.

The Sentinels silently shifted positions in what looked at first like random movements. After a moment, Braden realized what they were doing. Each Sentinel placed a glowing hand on the shoulder of another, who in turn placed his hand on yet another. Sometimes several of the younger Sentinels combined, all touching the same older Sentinel. Eventually they formed an unbroken chain with Felix at its head.

The fat Sentinel's impressive girth swelled further, and he began to glow. He threw his hands out wide, palms facing inward. The shimmering shield that had blocked the door swept into the room and expanded around the flames until it formed a glowing half-sphere that encased the cursed fire.

The trapped flames flared ugly red, as if sensing their imminent destruction. Fire blasted in all directions but rebounded from the shield dome. Wherever fire touched the dome, blue light flashed and mini-lightning bolts ripped into the flames and dispersed them.

Felix slowly began to draw his hands closer together. In response, the dome shrank around the flames, driving them inward.

Braden found it hard to breathe as he watched. So much hung on the outcome of this attempt. Beside him, Ambassador Talamantez was grimacing and leaning forward as if he were willing the Sentinels on and yearning to leap into the mystic battle with sword and spear.

The dome continued to contract until it almost touched the outermost soldier who lay within the flames. At that point, the fire flared around the man. His body shriveled and melted under the onslaught, sacrificed to fuel the spell.

The obese Ambassador Severin Gwyre of Meinarr gasped and retched. The stench of his vomit filled the crowded hallway. He croaked, "You must stop. You're killing them."

The captain of the guard said, "No. The emperor is all that matters. Sacrifice every one of us if you must, but save him."

The dome continued to compress. Sentinel Felix's hands began to shake under the strain of holding the spell together. One of the young Sentinels at the end of the linked chain collapsed, his face ashen.

Duke Kescog rushed to the man, dragged him out of the way, and cushioned his head with his own cloak.

"What happened to him?" High Lord Damarist asked.

Duke Kescog said, "They're focusing their strength on Felix. The fellow must have overextended himself."

Another young Sentinel collapsed. This time, Garitt Talamantez drew him from the crowd.

High Lord Damarist asked in a trembling voice. "What happens if they all fall?"

"Silence," Braden snapped. The fool couldn't help himself, but Braden wished he could slap the idiot.

In the room, another soldier withered under the cursed flames and the fire rose up again to assault the shield. After a blinding series of mini-lightning flashes that left Braden blinking fast to restore his vision, the flames subsided around the captured soldiers.

"They're almost there," Garitt breathed.

The Captain shouted, "Stop! Stop, you're killing him."

Sure enough, the emperor now writhed in the flames. He seemed to be shrinking.

He was dying.

Felix brought his arms out wide, and the dome retreated. The emperor continued to writhe in the flames, so Felix snapped his fingers and the dome disappeared.

The emperor sagged in his chair and no longer appeared to be dying under the flames' power. It was as if the flames were sentient and knew the Sentinels were beaten for now.

Tentacles of fire whipped across the room toward the open doorway. Felix raised his hands and a shield appeared in the opening to block the fire. It flared angrily but then subsided again.

Felix turned to face them, his face drenched in sweat. The other Sentinels broke their hold, and many of them sagged against each other.

Felix wiped his face. "This is the most complex enchantment I've seen in over a century."

"Can you break it?" the captain asked softly.

Felix shook his head slowly. "The emperor's life is tied to the spell. It's ingenious, really. If it weren't for that, I could shatter it now. But by linking his life to its continued existence, the curse guarantees I cannot stop it."

"Then he'll die?" the captain asked, his face pale and his shoulders slumped in defeat.

"Not necessarily." Felix blew out a breath. "It is possible one of the High Council knows how to break this spell. Harafin, in particular, has extensive knowledge in this area."

"Send for him at once," Braden said in unison with Perun and Garitt.

Felix nodded. Behind him, the flames flared blindingly. Everyone turned to look. Etched into the stone of the chamber wall was a single sentence.

Abaval will rule the world.

8

A Very Fast Quarry

Kevlin nearly collided with Drystan and Jerrik in an intersection of two halls as he followed the page who had summoned him to meet with the prince.

Jerrik clapped Kevlin on the shoulder and Drystan said, "Summoned to the prince's council?"

Kevlin nodded. "You too?"

"I hope it's something good," Jerrik muttered, rubbing his hands together. "Like the location of those Makrasha. Nothing like a good fight to end the day."

Kevlin shrugged. The page he was following had said only that he needed to report to the prince immediately. They followed him into the military wing of the palace to a book-lined study. Prince Lievin and Harafin were already there, seated in ladder-back chairs around a round table.

Harafin motioned them to a seat. Leander and Gabral entered the room a moment later, followed by Nikias. Leander looked his normal self with freshly trimmed beard and new Stalwart uniform.

They all took seats around the table and waited. A moment later, Ceren and Indira entered the room. Kevlin and the others rose and offered the ladies their chairs. Kevlin watched Indira for any sign of how she felt, but she barely looked at him. She fingered her deck of basic playing cards, an outward sign of worry, but did not start shuffling them.

As soon as the ladies were seated Harafin said, "I have received a Mindlink communication from Tamera."

Kevlin exchanged a puzzled look with Drystan. Sentinels often communicated across vast distances via mind-to-mind connections they called Mindlink. Kevlin knew little about it other than the fact that the farther one reached to make the connection, the effort increased exponentially. To communicate all the way to Tamera was impressive.

Harafin continued. "The emperor is caught in a deadly curse there. His life is in danger."

Gabral leaped to his feet, reaching for the hilt of the Mace that protruded over his shoulder. Nikias followed suit and raised the Bladestaff as if to summon its fire.

Harafin waved him down. "Calm yourselves. You can do no good rushing about, burning things here in Diodor. Felix is leading the effort to contain the curse before it threatens the rest of the palace."

As Gabral sank back into his seat Ceren asked, "Is Tamera really in danger with all the protection surrounding it?"

Harafin said, "Perhaps. The wards guarding Tamera are very powerful, but they were designed to keep an enemy out. It appears an enemy infiltrated the palace and entrapped the emperor in the council chamber."

Kevlin spoke up. "I don't understand. If the emperor survived the initial strike, why can't the Sentinels break the spell? You've said repeatedly that Tamera is home to the greatest number of Sentinels in the world."

"Felix led the effort to do just that, but the emperor's life is linked to the spell and hangs in the balance. From the description of the curse, it rivals one that I have seen only once a long time ago. I managed to diffuse that one, but it was extremely complex."

He swept his gaze around the room. "This information must remain secret. I leave for Tamera at once. I hope to break the curse and save the emperor's life. Hallvarr lost its king. We cannot afford to lose the emperor too."

Gabral said, "I'm going with you. I'm the emperor's champion and must return to his side."

Everyone else around the table chimed in, volunteering in a rush to accompany Harafin and offering their reasons why he should let them come. Kevlin raised his voice with the others. He was not about to let Harafin slip away. He had too many questions that needed answering.

Harafin called for quiet. "I had expected you would feel this way, and you are right. There are many reasons why this company should remain together. We have a work still to accomplish."

Leander raised his voice for the first time. "I will stay here. I must continue the hunt for Tanathos."

Harafin said, "There is more you should hear, my old friend. The curse inscribed a message into the wall of the council chamber. *Abaval will rule the world.*"

"Impossible," Kevlin exclaimed.

Leander's face reddened with anger at the mention of his ancient enemy's secret name. Only in the final moments of the battle of Il'Aicharen when Tanathos had been convinced of victory had he revealed his secret name, the name Leander had been hunting for nearly a century.

Ceren asked, "How is that possible. Tanathos couldn't have reached Tamera already."

"Even if he did, he wouldn't have had time to plan and execute an infiltration of the palace," Gabral added.

"No," Harafin agreed. "Regardless, very few know the import of that name. I am convinced the message was written for us."

"He's summoning us to the palace," Drystan said.

Harafin said to Leander, "I believe you will find your quarry in Tamera."

Prince Lievin spoke for the first time, "Our prayers and best wishes go with you all. There is a large merchant ship in the harbor that just completed minor repairs. It claims to have recently broken the record for passage from Parthalan."

Harafin nodded. "The ship that bore Ah'Shan to Diodor. It will do nicely."

The prince rang a bell to summon a servant and commanded the man to send word to the ship to prepare to receive passengers and to be ready to sail with the next tide.

Harafin said, "Go pack. We leave with the morning tide." As they all rose and moved toward the door, he added a final thought. "When we arrive in Tamera, be on your guard. I suspect we will find much more than one deadly curse arrayed against us there."

9

A Friend's Legacy

Kevlin stood near the bow of the *Ceara* as the large merchant vessel ran south on a beam reach under a strong wind. The *Ceara* was as fine a vessel as any he had sailed on. She was a large, double masted, square-rigged ship.

An ample central hold nestled between the two masts while a quarterdeck began abaft of the mainmast and ran to the stern. She was flying most of her sail, and the crew scurried to the bo'sun's commands. The decks were scrubbed and the equipment orderly.

The feeling of sailing on a well-run ship before a brisk wind filled an empty space inside Kevlin he had not realized existed. He hadn't sailed for years, and stepping aboard the *Ceara* in the pre-dawn chill had triggered a wave of memories that swept through him like a storm surge.

While many of the others had gone belowdecks to escape the biting chill, Kevlin had moved to the bow. Memories long-dimmed by years of neglect flitted behind his eyes. He remembered the years spent growing up on his father's merchant ship with a clarity that startled him. The morning passed quickly and he watched the rising sun with a sense of coming home.

His reverie was broken when one soldier cursed, then bowed toward the statue of Ashera nestled ahead of the foremast at the edge of the forecastle. Kevlin followed the man's gaze and bit back a curse of his own.

The western horizon was thick with ugly red clouds. The weather came from the west so it looked like rain would likely strike later that day. It was the coloring of the clouds that made the sailor swear. Rarely were western clouds colored red before noon. Sailors considered it a bad omen.

Kevlin thought back to the Bloodset that had stained the western horizon shortly before the recent conflict began. This horizon was not nearly so threatening, but he still felt a chill sense of foreboding.

He forced himself to turn away and move belowdecks to join the others. As he passed the statue of Asherah, a fixture on all Meinarri vessels, he couldn't help but bow just a little to her.

He smiled at himself as he descended the ladder. He hadn't offered much service to Asherah since leaving the ocean at age fourteen to seek his fortune. Still, while aboard a ship, the habit was so ingrained from his earliest childhood, he had to pay the Lady at least a little respect. It would be an insult not to, and he couldn't afford to insult any of the gods.

The company crammed into the captain's private dining room for. It was a tight fit, especially with the ladies on board. In addition to Ceren, Indira, and the diminutive archer Adalia, Lady Miren and one of her handmaidens were present. Lady Miren had decided to return to Tamera to comfort her cousin, the keisara, Fideima Tamarr Tegnazian during this difficult time.

Kevlin wished he could have found a way to sit next to Indira. He would have enjoyed the close contact. Instead, he ended up wedged between Jerrik and Lady Miren's handmaiden. He tried not to crowd the young woman too much, but they were pressed so tight in the bench he bumped her whenever he moved.

She looked very uncomfortable, almost sick. She was probably nervous about being forced into such close contact with so many soldiers. He tried to ease her mind as a way to keep from staring at Indira while they waited for the captain to arrive.

"What's your name?"

"Sitara," she said softly.

Kevlin looked more closely at her. Jerrik and even Gabral turned at the sound of her voice. She spoke with such a sweet, clear tone, it was like the song of a bird. Kevlin wanted to hear more.

She was petite, with a round face, delicate features, and straight brown hair that fell to her shoulders. He recognized her as the same pretty young maid who attended Lady Miren the night they arrived in Diodor.

"Well, Sitara, I apologize for jostling you so much."

"It's quite all right, my lord," she said with a little smile, although she refused to lift her eyes from the table.

"Just be happy Nikias isn't here," Kevlin said.

Jerrik laughed. "He'd probably have set the sails on fire by now."

Sitara joined the general laughter, and the sound seemed to float above the others. Lady Miren smiled at her. "It's been lovely having your assistance, Sitara. I'm more than a little tempted to try to convince Fideima to let me keep you."

"You are too kind, my lady."

Captain Sankar squeezed into the room then and ordered them to set to the food. Conversation faded as everyone obeyed with a will. Lunch was surprisingly generous.

Kevlin remembered simple rations aboard his father's ship, but Captain Sankar knew how to treat royalty. The table was filled with an astonishing array of foods, more than most ships' galleys could produce.

While they ate, Ceren asked Harafin if he had any further news of the emperor's condition.

"No, but I am confident Felix will be successful in containing it until we arrive."

As Harafin spoke, Sitara trembled and shrank lower, as if she wished to hide under the table. Kevlin smiled to himself and remembered how awed he'd been when he first met the legendary Sentinel.

Now, after spending the past couple of weeks with him and surviving such an incredible ordeal, Kevlin felt he knew Harafin at least a little. Then Ceren's suspicion about Harafin trickled into his thoughts. He pushed the thought away but knew it would keep returning until Harafin clarified his intentions.

Gabral spoke. "This Felix character sounds weak. Are you sure he's the right man for the job?"

Harafin said, "Don't underestimate Felix. He is one of the few living Sentinels to claim the honor of defeating a Sigrun single-handedly."

"I never heard about that," Ceren said. She leaned forward, her emerald eyes sparkling with interest. "Tell us about it."

When others also called for the story, Harafin nodded. "Very well. During the last great war, when the tide was turning in our favor. One of the Sigrun decided to hunt me down alone to settle a personal score. His name was Zvonko. He was a particularly unpleasant individual, even for a Sigrun."

"He and I had clashed a couple of times and although neither of us won a decisive victory, I had beaten him. He ambushed me in the borderlands and we fought there.

"I defeated him."

Silence settled over the cramped cabin. Those three words spoke volumes. Harafin added, "But that is a tale for a different time. Felix's story follows that event."

"After Zvonko's death, a second Sigrun, a sworn gift-brother of his, decided to finish what Zvonko started."

"What was his name?" Drystan asked.

"I do not know. We had defeated two other Sigrun during that war and he was the newest member of their council. He hunted me, seeking revenge."

Kevlin shuddered to think of one of the Sigrun hunting him. He had only caught a glimpse of their power when they possessed the ShadeLeech Merab in Baldev, but that had been enough. The memory of their declaration that he was marked for death made him suddenly lose his appetite.

Harafin continued. "Before this Sigrun could make an attempt on my life, Felix intercepted him. They fought a mighty duel. When I arrived to help, I found them both lying together, hands around each others' throats."

Lady Miren made a little squeak of fear and covered her mouth with her napkin.

"I apologize if I frightened you. Suffice it to say, the Sigrun lay dead while Felix could barely be called alive. With great effort, I managed to revive him."

Harafin pointed a carrot at Gabral. "That is the legacy of Felix. I trust him with my life."

10

SPINNING THE WHEEL

After the meal, Harafin summoned Kevlin to his cabin, which usually belonged to the first mate. The tiny room was wedged into an awkward corner of the aft section of the ship. It held a single chair, a sea chest, and a bunk.

Harafin sat in the chair, which was bolted to the floor. Leander perched on the sea chest, so Kevlin squeezed between them to the bunk, which lay against the curve of the hull and made for awkward sitting.

Kevlin clasped his hands together in his lap to hide the growing shakiness. He had managed well all morning while lost in his memories. The craving for magic had begun tearing at his self-control during lunch as he sat in such close proximity to Harafin, Leander and Indira.

The prospect of touching magic again soon fueled the fires of the hunger and Kevlin licked his lips even as he fought to remain calm.

"How are you holding up?" Harafin asked.

Kevlin tried to speak, but the thought of more delays suddenly infuriated him and all he managed was a growl. He clutched the edge of the bunk, on the verge of leaping across the tiny room at Harafin. He'd pull magic from the stingy old man by force, if need be.

"Not so good," Leander commented.

"Give me some," Kevlin hissed between clenched teeth. "I need it."

"Show me you are in control, and I will."

Kevlin slammed his head back against the hull, and the pain helped clear his head. He took several deep breaths and forced control over himself. Finally he met Harafin's gaze. "I'm in control. Give me magic before it slips."

"First, a little precaution." Harafin waved one hand and the walls of the tiny cabin began to glow with amber light. Kevlin realized he'd sealed them inside a shield bubble like those he'd used in their first lessons in the forests of Hallvarr.

Kevlin tensed to leap at the wall and absorb magic that way, but Harafin tossed a glowing ball of purple light toward him. Kevlin snatched it out of the air and the amulet hanging around his neck instantly stole the magic and poured it into him.

Kevlin sagged back against the hull, a smile on his lips as he *changed* the magic and made it his. The intense craving flared with desperate hunger, then faded as the magic flowed through him. Feeling almost normal, he sat up and opened his mouth to speak.

The tiny amount of magic he'd absorbed seemed to turn to acid in his veins. Kevlin gasped and fell back as the magic surged up through him like living fire driving toward his brain. Pain exploded through his body and he shouted with panic.

His vision darkened and laughter drowned out his cry. Kevlin wondered if he were laughing or screaming, or just dying.

Then his vision cleared, the pain disappeared like it had never been, and Kevlin gasped with fear.

He no longer lay on the bunk. In fact, the entire cabin was gone, as was the ship.

Kevlin hung suspended high in the air over an empty sea, with nothing but wispy clouds floating far below. A chill wind caressed him, its rushing the only sound.

Kevlin looked around, bewildered, wondering if he was dreaming or if the Trembling Madness had hurled him into insanity.

He started with surprise to find a young man lounging in the air beside him. The youth glowed, as if he'd swallowed a bright star. In his right hand, he held a spinning wheel about as wide across as Kevlin's forearm.

One half of the wheel burned with brilliant, pure white fire. The other half sucked all light into it, so black Kevlin felt like it was trying to suck his eyes right out of his head.

The youth threw his arms out wide and shouted with joy, as if they were the dearest friends, reunited after a long time. He looked so happy, Kevlin couldn't help but smile in return.

He was definitely insane. Then Kevlin knew this being. The name came unbidden to his lips.

"Akillik."

The youthful god of Luck laughed with joy and shouted exuberantly, "Of course! Who did you think it was? Tikir?" He laughed again. "That stuffy old miser never flies."

Kevlin nodded, not sure what to say. Since Akillik and Tikir were opposite halves of Karakol, he hadn't even known the two could appear separately. Then again, how could they show themselves together and still be distinct? But if they were separate, how could they be part of the same god?

Kevlin's head began to hurt.

"It's Kevlin!" Akillik shouted, so loud the nearest cloud shredded as if caught in a sudden gust of wind.

His voice rattled Kevlin to the core, much like Savas' voice had when the god of War had tried to consume Kevlin's soul. It was pleasant but so powerful Kevlin wondered how it didn't shatter his body like it did the distant cloud.

Akillik clapped Kevlin on the shoulder, and his touch exploded through Kevlin's torso like a bolt of lightning. His thoughts scattered and for a moment he knew nothing. He slowly came back to himself as Akillik shouted again as if his previous sentence had never been interrupted, "the man at the cusp of . . . something."

Akillik grinned and brandished his still-spinning wheel. Kevlin stared at it with awe. It was such a constant icon in the Six Kingdoms, he could scarce believe it really existed.

How many times had he spun the Wheel? The thought that calling upon the fickle god's luck actually resulted in a real spin of this magical wheel terrified him. He'd never really believed that using the phrase turned one's fate over to pure chance. He'd always assumed it was just an expression.

Akillik grinned as if he could read Kevlin's thoughts. He probably could.

He leaned closer. "Care to try your luck?"

Kevlin didn't trust himself to speak, so he only shook his head. A thought struck him like a blow to the head.

It's real.

It was all real. Even though Savas had tried to possess his soul, he hadn't expected to see any of the other gods. It just didn't happen. He'd been trying not to think of Savas.

Now seeing Akillik laughing before him while they somehow hung suspended thousands of feet in the air drove home the truth in a way nothing else could have. Kevlin had stepped beyond the realm of faith. He knew now without a doubt that the gods really existed.

He wasn't sure what that meant.

Kevlin couldn't help himself. He laughed with the insanity of it. Akillik joined him and together the two howled their laughter toward the heavens. Kevlin fought down the urge to change his laughter to a scream of fear.

After a moment, Akillik proffered the Wheel again. Kevlin again shook his head, and Akillik shrugged.

"Wise choice."

The youthful god suddenly looked deadly serious, and for the first time during this entire crazy experience, Kevlin felt stark, raving terror.

"You're a man facing lots of choices," Akillik said in a serious tone. "Better make sure you choose wisely."

Then he threw back his head and laughed again. He gave the still-spinning wheel another tug to keep it turning, even though it showed no sign of slowing.

Still chuckling, he added, "Make one wrong choice, and then . . . THEN!" His voice fell, once again serious. "Then you come to me and spin the Wheel and the fate of the world lies in the balance!"

Kevlin wanted to run but couldn't imagine how.

Akillik grinned wide and waved. "See you soon. Say hello to grumpy old Harafin for me."

Then he disappeared.

Kevlin blinked and once more sat on the bunk in the first mate's cabin with Leander and Harafin leaning toward him, faces etched with concern. Daggers of magic drove up through his heart and lungs and rippled up the length of his throat before driving up into his brain.

Kevlin tried to scream, but his throat no longer worked. He couldn't breathe, felt nothing but overwhelming pain. He convulsed back onto the bed as white-hot agony erupted in his brain.

His tongue burned, as if he'd just eaten ten Nedikan inferno beans. His vision darkened, and his ears rang as if a thousand mosquitos were screaming inside of them. His thoughts scattered under the onslaught. It felt like the magic was trying to rip out his mind like it had when it overwhelmed him at the keep under Wayra's onslaught.

How had he escaped it? He couldn't remember.

He tried to fight the wild magic, tried to bend it to his will, but it thundered through his head like a stampede.

Then Leander's will grasped his, like an invisible hand, a rock that grounded him against the wild current. Similar to how his Swordbrothers had loaned him their will to fight free of Savas' domination, Leander's strength helped raise Kevlin out of the flood.

Agony still filled his mind and locked every muscle into a silent scream.

Help me! He hoped Leander could hear his thoughts.

'Protect your mind.' Leander projected an image of a solid shield.

Harafin had taught Kevlin the concept of forming magical shields to protect against rogue Sentinels and Shadeleeches. He hesitated now for two reasons. In his first failed attempt to form a shield, he'd willed it into being inside of his chest. He'd never again make that mistake.

The other problem was that he needed magic to form a magical defense, but it was the magic trying to kill him.

'Defend your mind,' Leander urged, his voice nearly drowned by the roar of magic assaulting Kevlin's thoughts. His strength flowed into Kevlin, blanketing the unruly power and granting a reprieve from the pain. *'This is done by pure will. You must will it so.'*

Guided by the Stalwart, Kevlin formed the image of a fortified castle surrounding his mind, protecting it from the invisible assault. The wild magic crashed against that bulwark and threatened to overwhelm his fledgling defense.

'You must hold fast', Leander spoke into his mind. *'Your will is your defense. Rule your mind.'*

Kevlin reinforced the mental defenses, imagining them as high walls, defended by ranks upon ranks of soldiers.

In response, the assaulting magic took on the image of hordes of Makrasha, storming the walls like they had Il'Aicharen.

Kevlin knew too little about magic, but he knew how to defend a castle. He bent his will to the struggle and rank after rank of swarming Makrasha fell to his mental defenders.

As his control tightened and his defenses held, the Makrasha constructs faded away. Like a spirited stallion submitting to a firm hand, the wild magic calmed, once again pulsing through him like a second bloodstream. It brought strength and peace to his aching body.

Kevlin blew out a shaky breath and opened his eyes. Leander stood over him, one hand pressed to the side of his head. The old man helped him sit up before returning to his seat on the sea chest.

"What happened?" Kevlin asked.

"Something unexpected," Harafin said thoughtfully.

He sat at the very edge of the chair, as if only just resisting the urge to rise to his feet. Even a subtle sign of worry from the powerful old man was a very bad sign. Harafin was never supposed to look flustered.

"Please," Kevlin whispered as he massaged his aching head. "No word games today. Just tell me."

"Very well, but first tell me what happened to you."

"I almost died."

Leander said, "Before that. For a couple of seconds you just seemed . . . gone. Neither of us could reach you. You surprised us."

Kevlin barked a laugh, then winced from a fresh stab of pain in his head. "You were surprised? How do you think I feel?"

"What do you remember?" Harafin asked.

Kevlin hesitated. Part of him wanted to bury the memory of Akillik. They might think him truly insane.

No, anyone else who heard the tale would be convinced he was crazy. Not these two men. They would believe the truth.

What did that say about them?

Kevlin bit back another laugh. He had entered the world these men moved in, a world so far removed from the one he was familiar with, that he wondered if he would ever get his bearings. He had withheld information about Savas' attempt to possess his soul from Harafin for a time, and that mistake had almost cost his brothers their lives. He would not take such a risk again.

So Kevlin took a deep breath and told them about the encounter with Akillik. Neither man spoke until Kevlin finished his tale. He knew they'd ask for every detail, so he tried to include everything the first time around.

He finished by saying, "Then he told me, 'Say hello to grumpy old Harafin for me' and disappeared."

Leander burst out laughing and Kevlin had to laugh along with him. Akillik's humor seemed to have infected him. He should be terrified, but instead he just found it hilarious.

Even Harafin cracked a smile. "That irresponsible young fool. He just simply can't resist."

"You know him, don't you?" Kevlin asked.

Harafin nodded. "Oh yes, I've known Akillik since . . . well, since it was important to know him."

"What does that mean?"

Harafin waved off the question. "We should be asking, why would he manifest himself to you now?"

"Is he trying to possess me, like Savas?"

"No. Akillik doesn't work that way."

"He doesn't work at all," Leander said. He and Kevlin shared another chuckle.

"You're not helping," Harafin said.

"I know," Leander said, still smiling, "But I have a soft place in my heart for fools."

"He's irresponsible, unpredictable, and very dangerous, but Akillik is no fool."

"What does he want?" Kevlin asked.

"I'm not sure. I want you to repeat his exact words again."

Exactly what he'd hoped to avoid. He closed his eyes and repeated again everything Akillik had said. While he spoke, Harafin wrote the words on a parchment Kevlin had not seen him produce, using an odd quill that didn't appear to need to be dipped in an inkwell.

When Kevlin finished, Harafin rolled the parchment and tucked it into his robes. "I will study this and see if I can glean a sense of what game Akillik is playing."

Kevlin said, "I'm just glad that wheel didn't stop spinning while we talked."

"You are wise to fear placing your fate in His hands," Harafin said. "Tell us immediately if He sends you another vision."

"I will."

"Be sure you do. He may manifest himself as a reckless, likable being, but do not be fooled. Akillik is as dangerous in his own way as Savas."

11

SOMETIMES LIFE'S JUST NOT FAIR

Harafin sat back in his chair. "Now, to answer your other question, when you returned from your visit with Akillik, you suffered a mild version of what we call a *Tai Pari*."

"A mild version?"

"Yes. You were lucky I gave you only that tiny bit of magic. Any more, and the *Tai Pari* would have been fatal."

"Explain." Kevlin spoke slowly, with forced calm to hide his rising panic. Bad enough that the Trembling Madness was trying to drive him insane, it was crazy to think the magic that he craved wanted to kill him.

Leander asked, "How is it possible?"

"You must have noticed the state of his channels," Harafin said.

"Of course. He's a mess. But with such a tiny quantity, there should not have been any danger of a *Tai Pari*. Even the newest Accepted could handle that much power safely by pure instinct."

"That was my assumption until now, or I would not have given him any."

"Stop it," Kevlin shouted.

The thought of Harafin refusing to grant more magic set the mindless craving stirring in his heart, but the fear of this unknown danger was quickly escalating into panic. "Stop the lectures and just tell me what's going on. Why is the magic trying to kill me?"

"I'm sorry," Harafin said calmly. "You are rightfully afraid. I will do my best to explain to you what is going on, but you must understand one thing. This is a unique situation, unlike anything we have experienced before. We were discussing it to make sure we understand it so we can explain it to you correctly."

"You gave it a name. How can it have a name if no one's ever had this happen before?"

"*Tai Pari* have occurred, if rarely, in the past," Harafin replied. "But not exactly the way you experienced it. That's what is unique, and what caught us by surprise."

"So what is it? What's a *Tai Pari*, and why does it want to kill me?"

"To understand, you must think back on our first lessons. We discussed how Sentinels use magic."

Kevlin frowned. "We talked about the nature of magic and you claimed it was light, it was tied to the power of the sun, and that somehow it is also spirit."

"Very good. What do you remember about how we wield it?"

Kevlin shrugged. "Sentinels can use their own natural magic or draw upon the latent power all around. They focus it and direct it however they choose."

"Excellent. We did not discuss the mechanics of how Sentinels focus and direct the magic due to lack of time and because your instincts proved very good. However, those mechanics are at the core of the current situation."

"As you mentioned, when Sentinels focus magic, whether it be their own inner power or the latent power around them, they concentrate that power within themselves. In that moment, the power of magic is pulled out of its natural state. Once released by the Sentinel in whatever form they direct, the unspent magic returns to its natural state," Harafin continued.

Kevlin focused on every word, trying to understand, but convinced he was missing most of the meaning. Harafin added, "However, while in its concentrated form, its tendency is to return to that natural state, and it attempts to do so. So the Sentinel must channel and control that magic, keeping it within bounds they set, holding it in that concentrated state to do their bidding."

Kevlin nodded slowly. "That makes sense, but what does that have to do with it trying to kill me?"

"Have patience. I want to make sure you understand this clearly. The first times you wielded magic, you instinctively established adequate controls. However, at the keep, when Wayra's onslaught overwhelmed you, the magic burst those restraints with which you attempted to hold it, like a river bursting its banks."

"Aye, it almost killed me."

He shivered at the memory of the out-of-control magic uprooting his mind and nearly driving him into oblivion. Only at the last moment was he able to breach the final wall in his mind and reach Oris. The powerful presence locked in the stone had changed the magic, calmed it.

That mysterious essence that was Oris had guided him, taught him how to wield the magic. The resulting firestorm he unleashed had destroyed the keep at the same time Ceren killed Wayra. The memory of wielding that torrent of magic, of riding the tidal wave of power, burned so bright in his mind, Kevlin could remember every second in vivid detail.

"That is the key," Harafin said eagerly, enjoying the topic far more than Kevlin thought appropriate. "The magic overwhelmed your mind."

"It was like a flood."

"Exactly. At that moment, you suffered your first *Tai Pari*. In an ancient tongue it means literally a flood tide. It is the phenomenon when magic bursts all controls and overwhelms a Sentinel.

"It does not happen often, but when it does, it generally causes tremendous destruction and often results in the Sentinel's death. Had you not reached Oris when you did, the magic would have killed you and potentially destroyed everyone and everything in the valley."

"I believe that," Kevlin said.

The magnitude of the power had strained his limits to comprehend it. To safely release it, he'd formed a gigantic column of fire that had completely encased the keep and reared hundreds of feet into the air.

He had nearly lost control at one point. The fear of the imminent destruction he would have unleashed upon the valley had given him the courage to accept Oris's direction and regain control.

Kevlin frowned. "I still don't understand how that applies to today."

"When a Sentinel experiences *Tai Pari*, and if they survive, their controls are weakened, increasing the risk of future *Tai Pari*. It's as if the magic senses the weakness and strives to exploit to escape the controls placed around it."

"That's not how it felt," Kevlin protested. "The magic tried to kill me."

"That's where you are a unique case. Your first *Tai Pari* was so severe, your channels were completely destroyed. Magic has free reign to flow throughout your entire being unchecked. The only limitation you place on it is to keep it out of your mind. Since that's where you were overwhelmed the first time, that's the point of weakness where the magic must strike to break free."

"So how do I put controls back in place to keep it from doing this again?"

Harafin and Leander shared one of those mysterious looks Kevlin hated. Did they even recognize how annoying that was?

Harafin said grimly, "We cannot."

"What do you mean?" He couldn't have heard that right.

"May I?" Leander interjected.

Harafin nodded.

"Think of Light, or magic, when it is concentrated to use like a river. The controls placed around it are the banks that keep the water moving in the right direction. The *Tai Pari* is the flood that bursts those banks. Once a river is breached once, it is forever weakened and likely to be breached in the same place again."

"Magic in small quantities is a gently flowing river, easily contained within the banks. In greater quantities, it becomes a swollen torrent that rages against any constraint. Weaknesses are like boulders churning it into rapids and making it that much harder to control."

"You were so completely overrun by the *Tai Pari* at the keep that your controls, the banks placed around the river, have been completely washed away. The magic now flows through you like an unchecked flood every time you attempt to focus or concentrate it."

Kevlin barked a laugh to try to hide his fear. "First you tell me that if I don't wield magic periodically, this Trembling Madness will drive me insane, if not kill me outright. Now you say if I do wield it, the magic will try to kill me. Every time."

"It's not quite as bad as it sounds," Harafin said.

"How is it not as bad as it sounds? And what other surprises have you left out?"

He extended his boot where Oris lay hidden. "Take it back! I don't want it. Give it to someone who knows how to control it. Give it to Ah'Shan."

"I cannot," Harafin said gravely. "You know as well as I that you can only be parted from Oris through death. Do you really want that?"

Kevlin lowered his leg and glowered at the old Sentinel. "You never warned me any of this would happen."

"How could I have known events would turn out the way they did?" Harafin leaned forward and asked softly, "You knew death was possible, even likely for all of us. You accepted those risks as we rode into battle. Do not second guess yourself."

Kevlin couldn't refute Harafin's words, but part of him wished he'd died in battle. Better to die an honorable death than wait to go insane, or possibly hurt the ones he loved when he lost control.

"How to I control it?" Kevlin finally asked.

"We will work on that," Harafin said. "You must hold onto hope. As your capacity and knowledge expand, the threat of the Trembling Madness will diminish."

"But the magic's going to try to kill me every time I try to use it!"

"There is danger in the short term," Harafin acknowledged. "Leander showed you how to shield your mind, and it appears that once you prove your dominance, the magic will subside and allow you to wield it."

"But it's going to do this forever?"

Leander said, "Not necessarily. Sentinels who master themselves and their gift reach a point where they can wield magic without danger. It no longer fights them, but submits completely to their control. If you can reach that point, the threat of another *Tai Pari* will disappear."

"How long will that take?"

Harafin sighed. "To reach complete self-mastery takes Sentinels centuries. That is how we gain the title of masters.

"How many Master Sentinels are there?"

"Twelve."

"Great," Kevlin said sarcastically. "So there's no hope."

"There is always hope," Leander countered with a smile.

Harafin straightened in his chair and said crisply, "Enough of this. We understand the dangers now and know how to deal with them. No road worth walking is without its dangers, and getting depressed over things we cannot change adds no value."

"That's easy for you to say."

"We all face dangers," Harafin replied sternly. "Do not assume yours are the only burdens, or the most grievous to be borne."

"Now," he continued in a friendlier tone, "we will continue your training."

Kevlin wanted to bolt for the door, but he needed training now more than ever. The knowledge Harafin could impart was the only defense against these terrifying threats that seemed to keep multiplying. Just as good intelligence was the best way to defeat a mortal enemy, it seemed just as true in the frightening world of magic.

Then a thought brought him up short. Maybe his future safety was a lost cause? What if Ceren was right? What if Harafin recognized he was doomed and was only trying to keep him alive until they reached Tamera and he could transfer Oris to another Sentinel?

He had to know. "Harafin, why didn't you just Choose Ah'Shan? Life would be simpler for everyone." *Everyone but me.*

"I told you that night after the battle. Oris chose you, not me. I merely ratified the choice, as impossible as it still seems."

"You didn't have to, though, did you?"

Harafin regarded him silently for a moment. "No, I did not."

"Then why?"

"Call it an educated guess."

Kevlin stared. That answer scared him more than anything else Harafin might have said. Harafin never hesitated, never doubted. He, of everyone in the empire, was supposed to know what to do and why.

Harafin continued, "Know this, Kevlin. We are moving into difficult times, times so critical to the future of the world that prophecies were received and recorded hundreds of years ago to help us prepare to meet them."

"You mentioned something about that in Il'Aicharen."

"We have been studying those prophecies, trying to understand them. All to prepare for the bitter conflict about to be unleashed on the world. And we got it wrong."

Leander added, "Looking back at events, there were hints we could have picked up on."

"We should have," Harafin said. "While we battled in the wilderness of Hallvarr, while we chased Tanathos through the heart of the kingdom, I began putting pieces together in ways I had never imagined possible. Events were driving me to seemingly impossible conclusions. When Oris chose you, I had to make a choice too."

"You chose me," Kevlin said softly.

"Yes. More than that, I chose to believe what I had learned instead of clinging to ideas I had honed and polished over two centuries of study. I chose the unknown because it felt right and because I realized that in our arrogance we thought we could predict the future."

Harafin gave a rueful smile. "I have learned in recent weeks that we cannot."

"So what's the use of prophecy?"

"That's a question we've debated for decades," Leander laughed, slapping one knee. "Looks like it's time to start a new round."

Harafin sighed, and it looked like he nearly rolled his eyes. "Not today. Prophecy provides hints, no more, and I trust in their value. There are questions that must be answered, and much still to be revealed, but I believe I made the right choice. If I didn't, then . . ."

He trailed off, and Akillik's words returned to Kevlin. He said, "If we choose wrong, then we're at the mercy of blind chance."

Harafin nodded and scratched his beard, his eyes distant, lost in thought.

Leander said, "It disturbs me more than a little to think Akillik might have been warning us."

"Or making the first move in a mind game," Harafin said. "What better way to ensure his continuance than to misdirect us or confuse us at a critical time?"

"Then what will be his next move?" Leander asked.

Despite having seen Akillik, it still rattled Kevlin to think of the gods as living beings. It unsettled him even more to listen to these old men discussing the gods so familiarly.

Harafin said, "We will discuss this further. For now, back to your training."

"What are we going to do?"

"Drive the magic away."

How could he practice magic without magic?

"Trust me," Harafin said.

The moment of open truthfulness was gone. Harafin was once more being cryptic. Somehow, the shift comforted Kevlin as much as it irritated him.

Kevlin focused the small amount of magic inside of him and willed it to form a small, round shield in front of him. He had used the simple spell several times in the past couple of weeks, and it had saved both his and Ceren's lives.

He lacked much magic, but forming it felt natural after so much practice with this spell. The resulting shield only grew as big around as his outstretched hand. Once all the magic was consumed, Kevlin severed his connection to it. The shield flared and then faded away.

Harafin nodded in approval. "You have mastered the basic shield spell. We will study additional permutations later."

Of course he wouldn't remain on a spellKevlin felt comfortable with.

"Now Kevlin, I want you to connect with Oris like you did at the keep."

Kevlin grinned. He had yearned to re-connect with Oris in the past week, but Harafin had commanded him not to try it alone. Now he eagerly reached for his boot.

"Not that way. At the keep, you connected with it using only your mind. You were not holding it at the time. Try doing that again."

"Is that how the other bearers of Oris used it?" It thrilled Kevlin, and scared him, to include himself in that group that comprised some of the most powerful Sentinels of all time.

Harafin shook his head. "To my knowledge, you are the first to have ever connected with Oris without direct physical contact."

He'd done something those other Sentinels had never done? That bolstered his confidence a little. Maybe they just got comfortable doing it one way and never considered trying something new? He knew so little about what he was doing that he'd never know if he was doing it wrong until after the fact.

Kevlin leaned back against the hull of the ship and thought back to when he had connected with the stone, the one time he had managed to do so. At the time, the magic had been flooding his mind in the *Tai Pari*.

Having a name for the experience did little to minimize the remembered terror. He'd nearly died. It had felt like the magic had driven his mind outside of the confines of his body.

He refused to try that again. He didn't think he could survive it a second time. And yet, in that moment, he had reached out with a thought and somehow touched the stone. Was it that simple?

Kevlin closed his eyes and focused on Oris. He tried to extend his thoughts toward it like he had at the keep, but nothing happened. He envisioned it lying in his boot, and imagined his mind connecting with it.

Nothing. After a couple of minutes of focused effort, Kevlin sat up and shrugged. Harafin and Leander both sat patiently watching him. They looked content to sit there all day.

"I can't do it. Why not?"

Harafin said, "No matter. Each failure helps better define the path leading to success."

With the recent near-*Tai Pari*, it was clear failures concerning magic led to destruction.

"Try holding the stone," Harafin suggested.

"I thought you said not to."

"I had to test a theory."

Kevlin removed his boot. He then whipped his left arm down hard and twisted his wrist. The movement popped a slender stiletto out of its hidden sheath between the layers of his leather wrist guard. He caught the razor-sharp blade and used its fine point to carefully cut the stitches holding Oris in place inside the overhanging top of his boot.

The slender blade, excellent for throwing, proved a good choice. His belt dagger was too big for such fine work. The enchanted silver dagger that hung in a hidden sheath at the base of his neck would have cut the top right off his boot.

If Harafin was going to have him take out Oris very often, he'd have to find a better place to hide the stone. In the meantime, he tried to minimize the damage.

He extracted the little bundle and unwrapped the outer soft leather cloth. His fingers shook with anticipation as he pried open the rune-covered pouch and dumped the stone into his hand.

He was startled anew at how ugly the misshapen rock looked. When Antigonus had handed him the stone for the first time, he'd envisioned many fantastic things Oris could be. At first he hadn't believed the rock was the powerful talisman.

Kevlin flipped the stone in his hand to reveal the interesting side of the rock. He instinctively shifted the stone until his fingers slipped into the grooves along its top edge.

On the front face, a raised emblem that looked to be made out of blue crystal glowed in the bright daylight. It was shaped like a double-edged sword with tongues of flame twisting around its length and extending out toward each of his fingers and his wrist.

The Flaming Sword. He still didn't know what the emblem meant, but both Harafin and Tanathos had been shocked to see it. When Antigonus had given him the stone, it had born the emblem of a six-pointed star. At Kevlin's touch, it had shifted to the flaming sword. Apparently, the emblem was tied to the whole prophecy business.

Kevlin didn't just hope to connect with Oris again. The powerful, strange presence that resided in the heart of the stone had granted him peace and knowledge. He craved the peace and hoped it would share more knowledge. Perhaps it could show him how to deal with the Trembling Madness and *Tai Pari*.

As Kevlin stared at the flaming sword emblem, it drew his gaze deeper. He welcomed the unique sensation of falling into the stone's blue nothingness.

As his mind was drawn into the stone, distant will-o'-the-wisp lights glittered at the edge of his vision and seemed to beckon him on. With a thought, he willed himself forward. He expected to flash past the lights like he had the last time, but gained only slowly on them.

Kevlin willed himself to move faster, impatience driving him forward. A gentle surge washed through his mind, and he welcomed the slow, steady Rhythm of Life. It was a constant in the formless domain of the stone, and finding it again was a good sign. He'd used its universal cadence in the effort to subdue the huge column of fire that had nearly burst from his control at the keep.

Without warning he collided with an invisible wall. The impact jarred his mind. The next pulse of the Rhythm of Life helped him gather his thoughts and he pressed his against the barrier.

He didn't understand. The barrier had blocked his way the first few times he had tried to connect with the stone, but not the last time. On the far side dwelled the powerful essence that was Oris.

Oris, can you hear me? Kevlin threw out the thought and waited, expecting the barrier to fall.

He waited for several long minutes but sensed nothing, felt nothing. In the past, Harafin's voice had called him up from the depths of the stone, a lifeline he had followed back to reality.

This time, Harafin didn't call. Kevlin had never tried to leave Oris on his own and was surprised to find his mind awaken almost instantly when he concentrated on withdrawing.

The two old men sat unmoving, like two statues.

"What did you find?" Leander asked.

Kevlin shook his head. "It's not use. I can't reach it." He voiced the fear he'd carried since the battle. "Did I break it?"

Harafin smiled, and Leander chuckled. "No, my boy, there is nothing you could do to break Oris."

"Then why can't I reach it? I thought it chose me."

"That it did." Harafin looked far more pleased than worried by the setback.

Kevlin frowned. "What are you not telling me?"

"First, let me test my hypothesis."

"I thought you already tested it."

"That was a different one."

"How many are you planning on testing today?"

"This is the last, and the most important."

"So what do we do next?"

Harafin held out a hand. A shimmering butterfly of amber magic formed over it and flitted across the tiny cabin to Kevlin. It settled daintily on his knee. Then it imploded as his amulet captured the magic and poured it into him.

Kevlin took possession of it and re-formed the mental image of the fortified castle around his mind in case it assaulted his control again.

When nothing happened, he grinned. "Hey, I'm okay."

"Very good," Harafin said. "Once you have the Trembling Madness controlled and your mind guarded, it appears it will not rise against you again so soon."

Kevlin breathed a sigh of relief. "We can work with that. If I keep magic with me all the time, I won't have any more problems."

"It's not so easy as that," Leander said.

"Why not?"

"As we explained, concentrated magic like what you feel right now is Light pulled out of its natural state. You can hold it like that for a time, but not indefinitely. Over time, it will flow back to its natural state despite any effort to hold it, like water draining from a sieve."

"That's not fair."

Harafin chuckled. "Much in life is not fair, my boy."

Kevlin glowered at nothing in particular. He'd thought for a moment that he had the answer. They didn't have to crush his hopes so fast.

"Now, try to connect with Oris again," Harafin said.

"Why? I just proved I can't do it?" Harafin's games were getting annoying.

"Just do it. I need to know."

"All right." He did want to connect with Oris, so was happy to try again. Once again gazed into the stone's crystal emblem and allowed his mind to be drawn into its depths.

This time it felt different. He flashed past the will-'o-the-wisp lights like he had at the keep. Without interruption, he connected with the essence, the intelligence that resided in the heart of the stone.

This time he knew better than to probe that connection too closely. The first time he had touched Oris, his mind had been drawn in too deep. He had sensed a vast power, a depth so incomprehensible it had felt like he teetered on the edge of a bottomless chasm. Falling off would have shattered his mind. Some things were too foreign for a mortal to comprehend.

Oris's presence touched his mind. Light and power flooded through him with the force of a waterfall. Had he been standing up, he would have staggered under the force and sheer brilliance of it. Unlike the raging magic that had nearly destroyed him at the keep, the stone's pure magic carried with it a deep and abiding peace.

Kevlin felt immensely powerful, as if he could single-handedly lift the entire ship out of the water. At the same time, a deep calm filled him. The fear that had been nearly choking him vanished, leaving an absolute confidence that he could control this magic without danger.

Kevlin rode the wave of power back to consciousness and met Harafin's gaze. He could feel Oris's light shining in his eyes.

The old men shared a triumphant look.

In his mind, he felt Oris say, "*It is well.*" With the thought came a wave of happiness.

Harafin said, "That is enough for now. Can you let it go?"

Kevlin hesitated. For the first time in days he felt calm and at peace. He didn't want to lose that feeling.

"Don't worry, you will be able to reach it again."

"*Thank you.*" He directed the thought at Oris before slowly withdrawing his mind from it.

The connection broke gently, like the setting of the sun. The stone, which had warmed to the touch slowly cooled.

A fraction of the power that had infused him remained, and it felt right. The fear of having to battle potential *Tai Pari* every time he reached for this place faded, and for a moment he felt confident he could survive these challenges.

He took a deep breath. "Finally. Something went well. Can one of you tell me what just happened?"

"I believe we have unraveled at least a part of the puzzle," Harafin said. "It appears that you can reach Oris only through magic."

"That's not very encouraging. I'm not a Sentinel. Someone will have to give me magic every time."

Harafin said, "It is a start. Now, drive the magic away."

Kevlin reluctantly did so. He opened the nearby porthole window and focused the power into a spear of magic that he threw out the window. It streaked away from the ship, not splashing down until it had neared the distant horizon. It left him feeling empty.

Harafin gave him an encouraging nod. "That is enough for today. Well done."

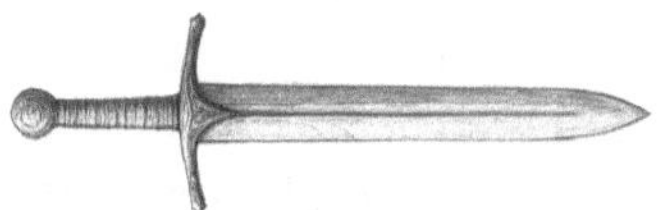

Kevlin knocked on the captain's cabin door. All of the ladies in the company had been assigned the cabin together. Lady Miren's handmaid Sitara opened the door. Behind her, the ladies were seated around a small round table, talking over hands of cards.

Kevlin smiled at Sitara. "I'm glad to see you're looking better."

"Thank you, my lord."

"Just call me Kevlin. The title's so new I keep wanting to look around for this Lord Kevlin who keeps following me."

Sitara smiled and made a little curtsy.

"May I speak with Lady Ceren for a moment?"

"Of course."

Everyone heard the request. Indira had already risen and taken a step toward the door. Now she paused, a look of surprise on her face. Ceren joined Kevlin and they climbed the ladder to the main deck.

Only as he stepped out onto the aft quarterdeck did Kevlin realize his stupidity. Indira had been coming to greet him. He'd blown his chance. He hadn't even acknowledged her, but only asked for Ceren. What must she be thinking?

By the Lady's temper, he was a fool. He turned back toward the ladder, intent on clearing things up immediately, but Ceren caught his arm.

"Kevlin, what's the matter?"

"I'm an idiot."

Ceren laughed, "That's news to you?"

Kevlin managed a smile. He couldn't tell her, not after that kiss in the palace at Diodor.

"What did you want to talk about?" Ceren asked.

Kevlin forced his worries aside. He'd seek out Indira later and explain everything. So he lead Ceren to the stern, far enough from the helmsman that they could enjoy a little privacy.

The ship still ran south at a brisk pace through a light sea. The salty air smelled crisp and clean and the ship rolled with the gentle swell. The sails boomed and the masts creaked. Every sense drank in the feeling of being aboard ship again, and it helped center his mind.

"Have you learned anything new about Trembling Madness?" Kevlin asked.

"Not yet."

"What about *Tai Pari?* Have you ever heard of that?"

Ceren looked at him sharply. "Why do you want to know about that?"

"Just tell me. Have you heard about it?"

"A little. At Il'Aicharen, apparently one old Sentinel suffered a *Tai Pari* trying to defend the villagers." She placed a hand on his arm, scanning his face. "Kevlin, he blew himself up. The explosion weakened the wall. That's why Tanathos managed to breach it where he did."

Kevlin's fear, which had lain dormant since his connection with Oris, spiked to new life. If he lost control, he'd destroy everything and everyone aboard the ship.

He nearly asked her about Akillik. She was from Freyarr and although Akillik had many followers throughout the Six Kingdoms, his most numerous and devout were centered in Freyarr.

Ceren already looked worried, so he decided not to convince her beyond any doubt that he was insane.

"Kevlin, I worry about you."

"Thanks."

"Be very careful."

"I'm glad I have you to help."

12

KEEP YOUR ENEMIES CLOSEST

Sitara perched on the edge of the wide bed in Captain Sankar's cabin and listened to the ladies talk around the nearby table. Both fixtures were bolted to the floor against storms, but thankfully the seas were gentle.

The cabin was comfortable, but very cramped with the five women. Although she would welcome the fresh air if the ladies decided to go topside, she dreaded any time spent out of the safety of the cabin.

Too many enemies surrounded her. The ship was crawling with people, and should any of them discover her identity, they would destroy her.

Her stomach had settled into a hard knot of fear ever since Lady Miren led her aboard the ship. That fear had spiked almost to panic when she had learned Sentinel Harafin was sailing with them. She nearly vomited in the cramped dining room, sitting within striking distance of the terrifying Sentinel. The man Kevlin had saved her life with his distracting conversation.

Lady Ceren entered the cabin and talk turned to the man Kevlin. Sitara listened closely. He seemed genuinely kind. In the palace, she had heard many times about his role in avenging the king's death. Now she was impressed to hear he had played a key role in the recent conflict right from the beginning.

While Healer Indira had taught the ladies several different card games, they had spoken much of events at Il'Aicharen. The knowledge had amazed Sitara and left her more than a little conflicted. She hated to think the ShadeLeech Tanathos had come so close to victory when her love Bajaran had failed. From what Lady Ceren explained, his victory would have doomed the Six Kingdoms.

That bothered her most of all. She was a secret revolutionary, committed to the cause more than ever, and determined to see the fall of the corrupt government. Her motivation was now as much to honor Bajaran's memory and his dream of peace as it was to wreak vengeance on those who killed him.

She struggled with this new knowledge. She was convinced to the deepest corner of her soul that revolution was necessary. She had lived long enough in the imperial capital to witness the terrible injustice of the current system. While the nobles enjoyed spectacular wealth, their own countrymen starved to death or died of curable sicknesses.

The downtrodden and those locked in poverty could never be freed under the current system. Worse, Bajaran had taught her that only by replacing the corrupt heads of the government could peace be finally established with their neighbors to the west.

The reality of the recent conflict left her feeling twinges of doubt for the first time. Tanathos had led an invasion, had plotted to destroy the empire. Were those the actions of a benevolent nation seeking only for peace?

She had touched the Shadeleech's mind and the memory of his profound evil still left her feeling tainted. She supported revolution to establish peace, but he could never have been a partner in peace.

How could the leaders of Grakonia have chosen their envoy so poorly? He must have deceived and betrayed them like he had Bajaran and the others.

Sitara considered the women seated around the table. When she rose to power, these women would stand against her. She hated to think she'd need to destroy them. The more she learned about recent events, the more she found herself applauding their actions. These women and their companions had acted honorably, bravely, and with great self-sacrifice. They had risked all in their efforts to defend the kingdom and preserve the people.

She would have done the same.

Sitara wanted to weep at their blindness. They should be her allies, assisting in the effort to establish real peace. Perhaps she could find a way to introduce true principles to them, to enlighten their minds until they saw the need to throw off limitations of their current lives? They were brave enough to embrace a new order, despite the dangers.

Bajaran had tried to teach her that terrible things would be required to establish freedom. Before now, she hadn't realized the extent of what he was trying to teach her.

While shuffling a thick deck of playing cards with practiced ease, Indira admitted that she and Kevlin were seeing each other. She seemed a good person, a truly humble woman who dedicated her life to help people. At least, she did when not dominating every card game.

Still, Indira posed a dire threat with her powerful gift. The Healer Ithai had shattered Sitara's attempted mind control of the keisara and nearly revealed Sitara's identity. In like manner, Indira could penetrate her illusions. She might not mean to destroy Sitara, but the results would be just as fatal.

Lady Miren said, "I heard Kevlin has been ill."

Ceren assured her he would be fine, but Sitara was a skilled enough liar that she recognized the hint of deceit in the answer. It intrigued her. This might be a nugget of information she could use in beginning to turn these women, who all cared for him.

A knock sounded on the door. Sitara slid off the bed, but the door opened before she could reach it. Harafin poked his head in.

Sitara barely bit back a scream of terror, and it took every ounce of willpower to remain standing so close to him. She dropped her gaze to the floor and shook with tremors of fear.

"I am sorry if I frightened you," Harafin said gently.

Sitara didn't trust herself to speak, couldn't restore her veneer of calm.

Harafin spoke again, "Sorry for interrupting, ladies. I just wanted to invite you all topside for a while. It's a beautiful afternoon."

"Thank you, Master Harafin," Lady Miren said. "I think it's a great idea. We'll join you shortly."

"We should finish the game," Indira protested as she began dealing out a new hand. Cards scattered across the table, all landing exactly in the proper positions.

"And miss this opportunity to escape with our dignity intact for once?" Lady Miren laughed. "We all know you're going to win."

"But I hate quitting early," Indira said.

"I bet it happens to you all the time," Ceren said, tossing her cards to the table. "You never lose."

Indira shrugged, a hint of a smile on her lips. "I have a lot of practice."

Lady Miren rose. "Sometimes I wonder. We've played Kings and Beggars, Dagger's Folly, and Queen's Aplenty and you won everything."

"It's a good thing we weren't betting," Ceren agreed. "She'd own everything we brought with us by now."

Sitara appreciated their banter. It helped ease her fear, but she still sagged against the door after Harafin closed it.

"Sitara, whatever is the matter?" Lady Miren asked.

She turned, her thoughts whirling as she struggled to invent a plausible excuse. Indira was already crossing the room toward her, a look of concern on her face. She reached for Sitara, and one hand glowed with her gift.

Sitara couldn't bear the thought of Indira touching her. She jumped onto the bed to escape.

Indira paused, her expression hurt.

The other ladies all looked shocked by the reaction.

"I'm sorry," Sitara stammered. "It's just . . ." she had to give them a good excuse, or all was lost. "It's just, ever since the keisara was attacked in Tamera, I've been terrified of magic. I can't bear the thought of anyone touching me with it."

Indira said, "I'm sorry for frightening you, but my magic would never harm you. In fact, I think I can help you overcome your fear."

"No," Sitara snapped.

Lady Ceren moved to stand beside Indira. "There's more to this fear of yours, isn't there, Sitara?"

Sitara's mind went blank. Lady Ceren was so clever, so astute. If she started prying, the carefully crafted web of lies that shielded Sitara from discovery would crumble.

Lady Miren saved her. "Oh, leave her be. Can't you see she's terrified? My cousin was traumatized by the attack on her mind. Did you know they haven't found the attacker yet?"

"I did not," Ceren said.

"Think how that would affect you," Lady Miren said. She sat on the edge of the bed and placed a hand on Sitara's shoulder. "Fideima said in her letter she can't bear any gifted person but Ithai to spend more than a few moments in her presence."

Sitara nodded. "Her fear has spread to me, I'm afraid."

"You poor dear," Lady Miren said. "She sent you so far from home before you had a chance to recover from that trauma, only to find yourself far from her side when she needs you most."

Lady Miren's concern seemed so genuine. Sitara had to find a way to turn her into an ally.

"I'm very sorry," Indira said again.

"If there's anything we can do to help, please let us know," Ceren offered.

"Thank you."

Lady Miren clapped her hands together. "Well come on ladies. The game's ruined now. Let's go up on deck and get some fresh air. It'll do us some good."

Adalia, the short archer who had sat quietly in one corner, stood. "Good idea. It be getting stuffy in here."

She was a local of Hallvarr, uneducated yet very skilled with her bow. She'd attached herself to Indira and attended her like a bodyguard.

If Sitara was forced to remove Indira, she'd have to destroy Adalia first.

13

NEVER LET A CRISIS GO TO WASTE

"Sentinel Felix, there's been another attack."

Felix shifted his ponderous weight in the reinforced steel chair he used at his desk and glanced at the messenger. "Who's responding?""Sentinel Nerys."

Felix heaved himself to his feet. "Where is he now?"

"Administrative wing, second floor."

"Have they evacuated the area."

"Yes, sir."

"Good. That will be all."

Felix groaned inwardly as he followed the messenger out into the hall. Operations were being impacted enough. The administrative wing could not be evacuated for long without serious repercussions.

He made his way through the palace complex to the administrative wing and up to the second floor. By the time he arrived, he was sweating and panting. For the hundredth time in the past two days, he was tempted to use magic to help support his bulk, but still rejected the idea.

If he ever gave in to the temptation, he'd never be able to stop himself from doing it all the time. It wouldn't be long before he'd be unable to move on his own without using the crutch of magic. He refused to limit his freedom that way.

Sentinel Nerys met him at the end of an empty hall lined with offices. "Felix, glad you could make it." Nerys was a plain looking man with black hair and brown eyes. He wore the green ribbon of the Kereskedo on his sleeves and at his collar.

"What's the situation?"

"The curse found another hole," Nerys said with a frown. "This time it somehow passed undetected all the way to this hall before we caught it."

"How many casualties?"

"Three were struck down." Nerys nodded toward the end of the hall. "We've quarantined the area but now that it has a hold here . . ."

Felix nodded. "I know. We're losing ground."

He stared in the direction Nerys had indicated, but was too tired to walk any further. Besides, he knew what he would find. The victims would be lying where they had fallen, writhing in constant agony in the cursed flames that fed on their lives but kept them alive.

He wondered how long people could survive the constant agony without going mad. Had the emperor already succumbed?

Within hours of his message to Harafin, the cursed fire had first broken free of the council chamber. They couldn't completely contain it or it would attack the emperor. They wasted precious time before realizing what had happened.

The first time it broke out, the curse had slipped through a drain in the council room floor. It struck down half a dozen people in a lower level before they contained it.

Since then, they had fought a holding battle against it, a battle they were not winning . . .

"It's as if the curse is sentient," Nerys said, echoing Felix's thought.

Felix frowned, "Or perhaps it's being guided, directed by someone in the palace."

"That would be . . . terrible."

"We must consider it. It's clear there are traitors hidden among us." Felix paused, struck by another thought. "I need to think on this. We need to prepare some more proactive countermeasures."

Nerys brightened. "Great idea. In fact, I've been working on something I think will interest you."

Felix maintained a neutral expression. The kereskedo were a new group within the Sentinel ranks, or at least a newly formalized one. Many of their ideas disturbed Felix. The group insisted on pursuing their agenda despite increasing opposition within the broader Sentinel ranks.

When Felix didn't stop him, Nerys continued excitedly. "I've been working on our latest portable shields." He laughed. "They make our early efforts look like child playthings."

"So you wish to donate these new portable shields to workers in the palace?"

Felix was impressed. The kereskedo were brilliant Sentinels and they were pioneering new areas of magical research in ways no one had ever explored. They were many things, but generous with their inventions was not one of them.

He was not surprised when Nerys quickly corrected him. "Not exactly. You see, the earlier models were effective, if crude. They sold surprisingly well. But once people see the benefits of the new model, I believe many of our existing customers will want them."

"How does that help us?"

Nerys clapped him on the shoulder, "Don't you see? What are they going to do with all those old shields? I mean, they're still potent for months unless triggered."

When Felix didn't speak, Nerys said, "We can take them back, maybe even give returning customers a partial credit toward purchase of a new model. Then we can sell those older models at a steep discount to workers here in the palace who couldn't afford them at full price."

Felix stared. "You want to turn this emergency into a marketing campaign?"

Nerys' smiled faded. "Well, if you say it that way, it sounds cold-hearted and reprehensible. I'm just trying to help."

"Help who?" Felix felt tainted just discussing the idea.

The kereskedo sold their inventions, artifacts imbued with enough Sentinel power to perform specific tasks for short periods. The recently-invented portable shield cloaks were but one example. It seemed a uniquely evil thing to take the glorious gifts that Sentinels worked decades to perfect and distill them down to nothing more than merchandise sold to the highest bidder.

Worse, the nobility showed an insatiable appetite for the inventions along with a disgusting disregard for custom. The Kedos had been actively marketing their wares for less than a year, and their inventions were already becoming signs of status. The prices the upper-class were willing to pay for these trinkets were staggering.

Nerys said. "Look, we've never had a replacement product like this. So far everything's been brand new. We haven't had time to improve upon existing models. I think this is the answer to the dilemma. It'll help everyone."

Felix said, "I cannot condone it. You're trying to capitalize on fear for your own profit."

"I am not."

Felix cut him off. "If you want to donate those . . . items to critical personnel, I would applaud the gesture. However, I will not allow you to take advantage of people the way you suggest."

Nerys retreated a step, his face now angry. "You just don't have the vision, Felix. You never had."

He turned and stormed off.

Felix dismissed Nerys from his mind and turned his thoughts to more important things.

14

QUESTIONS OF FATE

The storm that had threatened earlier blew off to the north and the afternoon turned warm and sunny. Everyone crowded the *Ceara's* decks to enjoy the weather. Kevlin was pleased to see no one looked seasick. Hopefully the good weather held.

He avoided the ladies gathered in the stern. They were listening to the helmsman explain about steering the ship. The young man was clearly motivated to keep the attention of five attractive women. It looked like he would gladly talk the day away if they let him. Kevlin longed to speak with Indira, but he wanted to catch her alone.

Harafin and Leander were lost in a deep discussion, and Kevlin didn't want another headache, so he avoided them. He hadn't seen Sentinel Ah'Shan all day and was grateful for it.

He and Ah'Shan had disliked each other from the start. Their dislike had culminated in a fistfight outside of the keep of Il'Aicharen. Kevlin had beaten Ah'Shan, but the Sentinel knew about his protective amulet now. Kevlin doubted the man would prove as easy to defeat again. He wasn't the leader of the Kestrels for nothing.

Jerrik and Gabral were competing in imaginary battles, describing their forces and how they would attack or counter-attack. Their discussion broke down into shouted insults every minute or two as they accused each other of cheating.

Kevlin found Drystan standing alone near the bow. The lanky Einarri warrior moved easily with the gentle roll of the ship and stared out at the glistening sea.

He greeted Kevlin warmly. "I haven't sailed before. This is amazing."

"Seriously?" Kevlin couldn't imagine not knowing the sea.

Drystan shrugged. "Horses and boats don't really get along."

Kevlin nodded. His father had hated taking on horses or worse, cattle. The mess and stench lingered for weeks after the animals were unloaded.

He realized he knew little about Drystan beyond his legendary reputation and incredible fighting skills. Drystan had united Kevlin to his family by blood. Kevlin knew nothing about them other than a few scraps of information he had picked up, and some calculated tidbits passed to him from Ceren.

"Tell me about your family," Kevlin said.

Drystan was happy to oblige. He spoke of the endless Einarri plains, of the waving sea of tall grass they traversed upon their matchless stallions. Kevlin was startled to learn Drystan was married and that his eldest sone had only just been born before Drystan had been ordered to Tamera.

"What are their names?" Kevlin asked.

"My wife is Keelin," Drystan said with a smile, his voice thick with emotion.

At one point in his life, Kevlin had planned to marry. Unfortunately the woman he loved turned out to be a murderous traitor. She had nearly killed him, and he'd spent years running from those memories and the enemies still bent on his destruction.

He glanced toward the stern of the ship but couldn't see Indira. He wanted to make things right with her, wanted to kiss her again, but the thought of marriage made him nervous.

Worse, he had no idea what Indira might be thinking. Did she already expect things of him?

Was he already failing?

"My son's name is Rhys," Drystan added.

"I hope you get to see them again soon."

"Me too. Keelin's father is Ambassador Talamantez. He sits on the ruling council." Drystan grimaced. "He has a crazy idea to make me a ruler in his place."

"Miserable," Kevlin agreed.

Drystan didn't pick up on the sarcasm. "I'd hate it. I just want to ride the plains with my family and my tribe."

He spoke with great pride of the Chandana, the powerful tribe his father led as herdmaster. "Our bloodlines run pure and deep."

Drystan talked about the responsibilities of being son of the herdmaster and, when he was home, battle master of the tribe. Despite the long peace with Grakonia, the Einarri had been fighting constant skirmishes with the Nedikans along their southern border for decades.

Drystan spoke of the constant vigilance required to guard against the Nedikan raiders who slipped north across the border looking for horses to steal and women and children to kidnap and sell as slaves.

As he listened to his Swordbrother, Kevlin was deeply impressed by Drystan's love and dedication to his family and tribe. Kevlin had jumped ship at fourteen and hadn't spoken with his family or even sent them word in years.

They ate dinner on deck to enjoy the late afternoon sun. After the meal, Harafin again summoned Kevlin to his borrowed cabin. As soon as Kevlin seated himself on the small bunk, his hands began to shake and his mouth went dry. He'd felt fine all day, but the craving returned with a desperate intensity.

He struggled for a few seconds to bring it under control. It was not as hard as last time. He clung to the hope that he was getting the hang of this.

Harafin encased the room in its glowing amber bubble shield and then tossed Kevlin a ball of crimson magic. Kevlin cringed at the sight of it.

"Lesson number one tonight," Harafin said. "There is importance to the color you choose to associate with your magic. It is true that the ShadeLeeches prefer blood-red magic. However, you cannot allow yourself to fear red magic above other colors."

Kevlin still shivered as he changed the magic captured by the amulet and made it his.

"Now, connect with Oris," Harafin said.

Kevlin reached for his boot until Harafin shook his head. This lesson included the mind trick of touching the stone without using his hands. So he closed his eyes and focused. A finger of thought touched Oris, and it sucked his mind into its deep blue depths.

He felt its vast presence, which rose with him back to consciousness. It felt like a tiny spark in the back of his mind that maintained their connection.

Renewed strength and comforting peace washed through him with Oris's presence. He breathed deep and savored the feeling of complete wellness.

"Very good," Harafin said. "I want to work a little more on your shields."

Kevlin grinned. Usually Harafin's lessons left him feeling stupid and hopelessly lost. He looked forward to showing Harafin what he could do with shields.

"You have improved greatly with fashioning external shields," Harafin added. "Tonight we will build upon what Leander taught you regarding inner shielding."

Kevlin sighed. Harafin never made things easy.

"As you learned, these are psychic shields, not physical constructs."

"How does that work? Are they real, or just all in my head?

"They are very real, and critically important, especially for you."

He reviewed what Leander had demonstrated in building psychic shields to protect the mind. With the experience of fighting down the *Tai Pari*, the explanation made sense. Hopefully he could pick up other new principles without having to nearly die to understand them.

Magic wasn't Kevlin's strength. He'd only touched it for the first time mere weeks prior. He was no Sentinel, and it still made no sense that he carried Oris, the empire's greatest defense.

Harafin stepped across the room and placed a hand on Kevlin's head. His voice spoke into Kevlin's mind. *'Come, I will help you build them again.'*

Guided by the old Sentinel, Kevlin again formed the image of a fortified castle around his thoughts. The psychic shields rose and solidified, and Kevlin embellished the castle with a grand, central keep and several graceful towers.

"Ha! How's that?" he asked with pride.

Harafin returned to his chair. "Let's see."

An invisible hammer-strike of focused power struck Kevlin's mental towers and shattered them. Kevlin winced from the resulting mental jab.

Knowing he'd never really have a chance against Harafin didn't squash a flash of irritation that he'd failed. He'd had to practice many times before forming decent physical shields. When they had failed, he'd felt similar mental stabs of pain.

He had once constructed a huge, bowl-shaped shield to protect Ceren and himself from the first attack by Wayra and her Kestrels. The constant pounding of their magic against his shields had felt like a dozen midgets had climbed into his head and pounded his brain with hammers.

Kevlin re-formed the shield, raised the towers, and reinforced his inner fortress. "Try again."

Harafin struck again. This time the shields wobbled, one mental tower crumbled, but the rest of the fortress held. Even as Kevlin smiled in victory, Harafin struck a second time. The shields imploded and Kevlin winced. One of the midgets was back.

"How did I beat you?" Harafin asked.

"You're too strong."

"Was my first blow too strong?"

Kevlin thought about it. He'd served as an officer for a time in one mercenary company, overseeing a siege company in Donarr. He hadn't worked on the siege engines himself, but had learned a great deal from the engineers who did.

One of the key principles of their work was that a single stone rarely knocked down a wall. Their challenge was to strike the same place over and over again. The repeated barrage would weaken and then topple the wall.

It was the same principle, but there had to be more or Harafin wouldn't have pointed it out. After a moment, he realized the answer and raised his shields again.

"One more time."

This time, Harafin's first blow was more focused, and nearly shattered the shield. Kevlin winced at the pain but held on. Before Harafin could strike again, Kevlin shifted the shield.

Where a city wall was fixed, his mental shields didn't have to be. Harafin might intend to strike the same place twice, but Kevlin didn't have to play by the same rules.

As expected, the second blow struck in the same place as the first, right between Kevlin's eyes. Kevlin's shield rocked again, but held.

Harafin smiled. "Well done. I had hoped your training would provide insights non-military Sentinels often overlook. Keep your shields strong, and yet flexible. It is a foundational principle you will need as we learn other lessons and master new skills."

"Teach me another." If he had to learn this, he'd rather get it over with as fast as possible.

"Ponder what you have learned. The best knowledge is knowledge gained through personal insight."

He should have known. Harafin would give him bits and pieces, but never make it easy. Still, he was proud of tonight's progress.

"Whenever you touch magic," Harafin added. "First and foremost, you must shield your mind. Not only to protect from the Trembling Madness and the *Tai Pari*, but from other gifted minds."

Kevlin shuddered as a memory surfaced. For a moment, he was again a little boy aboard his father's ship, a little boy being tortured by magic wielded by a Sentinel.

If only he'd known then what he knew now.

Harafin added, "The mind is the ultimate battlefield. If you can breach another's shields, you can destroy them from within."

Some principles were eternal. Only after breaching a city wall could an invading force destroy the defenders.

Then he frowned. "If you destroy someone's mind, you don't have to defeat them physically. So why didn't you do that at that hidden fort, or when we faced Tanathos and the other ShadeLeeches? You fought them with fire and lightning and tangible magic."

"If there had been more time, I would have attacked their minds, but they were well shielded and the effort would have taken too long. One must choose their battles and know the risks."

"What risks?"

"Think about it. If I had paused to scan their mental defenses or sought to breach the walls around their mind, I would have been vulnerable to their direct attack. I could not both break their psychic shields and defeat their physical attacks that the same time."

Kevlin had once turned the tide against a strike force of Raghneidur and their Canavars when they had gotten distracted. He'd have to remember this principle also transferred from his previous life as a mercenary into his new, magical world.

"The battle of the mind is often the most dangerous and the most effective," Harafin continued. "Guard yourself well, for in Tamera our enemy will strike from the shadows where they will have the luxury of time to prepare attacks against the mind."

"You really think we'll be fighting in the palace?"

"I believe it best to be prepared. Soon, I will teach you the battle of the mind."

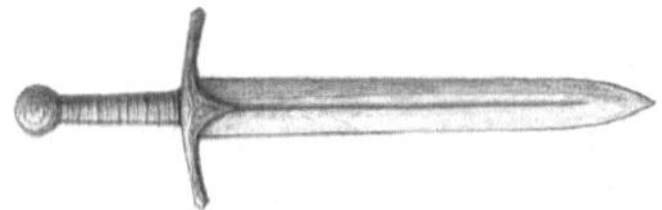

After Kevlin disappeared up the companionway ladder to the upper deck, Ah'Shan knocked on Harafin's door and stepped inside.

The powerfully built Sentinel said, "I wish to sit in on your sessions with this ungifted bearer of Oris."

"That may be a bit premature. So far we are only covering the basics."

"How is that even possible?" Ah'Shan snapped. "The man has no gift. Why do you insist on playing with his life, and with the fate of the empire?"

Harafin considered Ah'Shan. He had known the man for almost two centuries. Ah'Shan was a tremendously gifted Sentinel, and one who Harafin had long suspected would rise to become bearer of Oris after Antigonus. Recent events were giving him a glimpse into Ah'Shan's character he had never known, glimpses that suggested why Oris had not chosen him.

"Patience, my old friend. My reasons will become clear with time."

Ah'Shan snorted. "Have you discussed the prophecy yet?"

"That which has been required thus far."

"So you've explained to this helpless fool that after he suffers long enough from this power you've thrust upon him, you expect him to die to save the empire?"

"That's one interpretation, but we've proven that we understand the prophecy less than we thought we did."

"Always the optimist, even when logic dictates otherwise. Of all the sections of prophecy, this one is most clear. *Drown thyself in the fires of the world's creation and deliver up the lives of the chosen sacrifices. The Flaming Sword will be quenched in the rebirth of order, and lives offered up will give new life to balance.*"

"I will ask you not to speak with him about this."

Ah'Shan barked a laugh. "So you fear I may be right."

"I fear only that we jump to conclusions."

He refused to allow Ah'Shan to see that he did, in fact worry about that section of the prophecy. The Catalyst would be called upon to make many hard choices. Other great men had been forced to seal their works with their blood. If Kevlin was required to do the same, would he be willing to do so? Worrying about it now would only instill doubts before Kevlin could handle them. So much still remained to be taught.

If fate did require the ultimate sacrifice, Harafin would pay whatever price to ensure the continued existence of the world. He would not hesitate. Stakes were too high, and the fate of the world hung in the balance. So much rested on the man Kevlin.

It scared him more than he would ever admit.

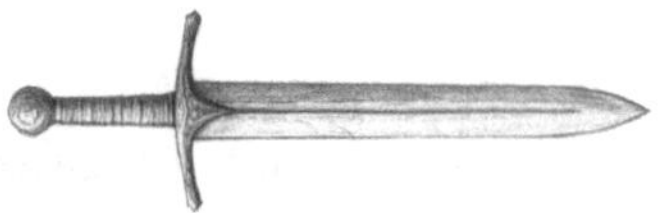

Kevlin slipped away from Harafin's door and escaped up the ladder only seconds before Ah'Shan stormed out of the room. Their words rang through his mind like a death knell.

Why hadn't Harafin told him?

What else wasn't he telling him?

He moved to the bow of the ship and settled into a sheltered spot near the rail. He'd returned to Harafin's cabin to ask one final question when he'd overheard the Sentinels' voices.

He hadn't planned to eavesdrop, but felt uncomfortable interrupting Ah'Shan, so he'd stood close to the door, one hand raised to knock. He'd been surprised neither of the men had sensed him there.

Maybe they had.

Did they want him to know that he was little more than a sacrificial offering?

Harafin said they couldn't interpret the prophecy. From what he'd revealed, their understanding of other passages had proven incorrect. Still, the passage seemed pretty clear.

Kevlin sat there for a long time, pondering what he'd learned and trying to make up his mind what to do about it. He liked none of the options he considered.

In the end all he could decide was to learn all he could from Harafin and use that knowledge to seek a way out. He hadn't asked for any of this, and he wouldn't allow Harafin or anyone to set him up to die just because some dead guy who spoke in riddles ordained it so.

15

BROTHERLY KINDNESS

The next three days passed uneventfully. Kevlin met with Harafin each morning, but the sessions were short. The time was spent practicing concepts Harafin had already taught. In each session, Kevlin searched for hints that Harafin knew he had overheard the discussion with Ah'Shan, but detected nothing.

The regular immersion in magic helped keep the Trembling Madness at bay, but the *Tai Pari* proved a more difficult challenge. On the morning of the third day of the voyage, the magic fought his control with a ferocity that left him gasping and trembling.

The rogue magic swarmed his fortified defenses just as the Makrasha had stormed the keep at Il'Aicharen. Kevlin tried to reinforce his shields, but Harafin had to step in to prevent his mind from becoming overwhelmed again.

"You must practice," Harafin said. "I won't always be around to save you." He looked worried, and that terrified Kevlin. Was Ah'Shan right? Was all this some twisted sort of torture that ended in blood sacrifice?

Kevlin spent much of the day seated at the bow, eyes closed, practicing his shielding. The others soon learned to leave him alone, even though he wouldn't tell them what he was doing. By the next afternoon, he discovered some valuable insights.

The first big breakthrough came with the realization that the walls around his mind didn't have to be round. He discussed the benefits and liabilities of different types of fortifications with his swordbrothers and then with Gabral. Gabral commanded an exhaustive knowledge on the subject and, after an initial moment of cautious hesitation, spoke eagerly about it.

Kevlin practiced with various mental structures, raising mental fortifications in seconds. He eagerly waited to test them out against Harafin, but the next morning, Harafin looked exhausted and suggested Kevlin practice with Leander.

"What's wrong?"

"I'm just tired. I spent several hours yesterday in Mindlink conversations with Felix, helping him develop new ways to hold the curse at bay."

"It's really that bad?"

"This is the most complex curse I've ever heard of. I believe we will have only one chance to defeat it."

Kevlin sought out Leander, but the Stalwart refused to summon his Sentinel powers. He had renounced them when he took the vows to become a Stalwart. During the battle at Il'Aicharen, the shock of learning Tanathos' secret name had driven him to draw upon those long-unused powers, but he would not do so again.

"I cannot risk it," Leander said. "Those powers are too closely tied to destruction. If I unleashed them upon you . . ." He paused, looking grim. "I don't know if I could stop until you were destroyed."

Kevlin decided shields could wait.

Leander smiled the old, jovial smile Kevlin knew. "Don't worry, lad. I've had a few days now to regain my composure. Chasing Tanathos proved taxing spiritually as well as physically. For a time, I opened the door to the uncontrolled fury that consumed me after the murder of my family."

"I'm glad you feel better." Kevlin had caught a glimpse of Leander's fury and never wanted the Stalwart angry with him. "So am I. Uncontrolled anger is a force of chaos, and too often it results in destruction far beyond what may be intended."

It was good to see Leander's indomitable good humor returning and that he was back in control.

Kevlin tried to speak privately with Indira, but couldn't get her alone. He saw her on deck and during meals, but Ceren and Lady Miren always hovered nearby. Lady Miren had a quick wit and a ready laugh, and she helped keep the company's spirits high, but every time Kevlin tried to draw Indira aside, Lady Miren would insist on joining them.

"I have to protect the virtue of every lady in my company," she insisted. Then she laughed at Kevlin's shocked expression.

Indira made it clear she wanted to speak with him too. She said, "Let's play a hand of Sailor's Grief. If I win, we get some alone time at the bow."

Lady Miren just laughed.

Kevlin appreciated her concern for the ladies, but her insistence on chaperoning them was becoming irritating.

Adalia, who shadowed Indira at all times, tried to help. "Let 'em alone, m'lady. If'n Kevlin tried nothing on Indira, I'd shoot him in parts wot would calm him down real fast."

Kevlin retreated at that point. He'd get time with Indira once they docked. He turned to his brothers, and they were happy to help him pass the time.

He sparred with both Drystan and Jerrik and spent hours getting beat up by them. He poured his frustration into the matches, and his swordbrothers beat it all out of him.

For half a second, Kevlin longed for the battle prowess Savas had bestowed upon him while trying to possess his soul. He'd stood against both Jerrik and Drystan, had fought like a god.

Better to get beat up.

He had fought like a puppet of a god, moved by Savas' invisible strings. Had he accepted Savas' control, would he have retained any shred of self?

"We have to try something different," Jerrik said as he helped Kevlin rise from getting knocked flat.

Drystan nodded from where he sat against the wall of the quarterdeck, sharpening the head of his spear. "You're right. Kevlin's got to adapt his style."

Kevlin wiped sweat out of his face. He fought with the Taiseluz style, which already provided tremendous flexibility. What he needed was to be faster, or stronger.

These men were masters of their fighting styles as much as Harafin was a master of magic. He needed to learn what they could teach.

"What do you suggest?"

Drystan rose smoothly to his feet. He put down his spear and drew one of his long-knives. "I'm glad you asked."

Kevlin soon wished he hadn't.

That night at dinner, he could barely sit upright. Every muscle ached with fresh bruises, and he nearly fell asleep in his dinner plate.

Ceren grinned across the table at him. "Kevlin, you look terrible. What happened?"

Jerrik grinned. "Kevlin enjoyed a little brotherly kindness today."

"If that's kindness, I'd hate to see you argue," Lady Miren said.

Kevlin ate without talking much and had just decided that he could fall asleep leaning against the bulkhead and no one would ever notice when Harafin spoke.

"Tomorrow morning we will arrive in Tamera."

"We made good time," Lady Miren said.

Captain Sankar, who was joining them in the cramped dining room said, "Aye. We might just beat the record."

Kevlin roused himself. This ship recently broke the record for fastest time from Parthalan. He had his suspicions that Sentinel Ah'Shan had tampered with the winds during that trip, which should disqualify it. He couldn't allow them to unfairly claim a second record without verifying it.

"Has anyone . . . helped us along?" Kevlin asked.

Harafin said, "I have not."

"There," Captain Sankar said quickly. "All well and good and above board."

Kevlin was too tired to argue further.

Harafin said, "You all know the import of our mission. However, I want to impress upon you that even after we break this curse, the danger will be far from over."

"Is there another curse?" Lady Miren asked.

"No, but I am convinced this curse, despite how great a threat it poses directly, is but the first strike. This is the opening move designed to draw this company to Tamera."

"How can you say that?" Gabral asked. "The emperor's life is in danger. Are you so arrogant that you think yourself more important than he is?"

"I do not."

Kevlin reached for a glass of water to try to clear his mind. He wished he had room to splash it on his face but Sitara, who again sat pressed against him, would surely not appreciate that. He needed to think. He wanted to argue with Gabral. How could the short colonel decry arrogance in others?

Harafin continued, outwardly unperturbed. "It is not arrogance that makes me think there is more at stake here, but logic. If the emperor's life was really the target, why is he not dead?"

While Gabral frowned over that, Leander spoke. "Perhaps it is the ultimate goal of the curse. Whoever created it knew that to kill the emperor immediately would remove any obstacle to Felix or another Sentinel immediately destroying it. From the reports you've been receiving, it is causing great disruption in the palace despite the best efforts to contain it."

"Perhaps," Harafin said, "but that is a short-term gain. They have to know we'll break it eventually."

Leander repeated, "Perhaps. Unless there is a timeframe embedded in the curse in which the emperor's life will be forfeit anyway. Can the enemy really ignore such a prize as the emperor's life?"

"That depends on what they're trying to accomplish. However, your point is valid. Yet another reason to reach Tamera with all speed."

Harafin regarded the rest of them. "Be on your guard tomorrow. There are many questions to be answered before I would consider Tamera a safe haven."

16

THE THIRD LEVEL OF BREAD PUDDING

They reached Tamera with the rising sun. Kevlin came up on deck when the lookout shouted the sighting. The morning air was chill and a thin fog clung to the calm sea.

He always preferred to stand in the bow to greet a new port, but this time the ladies beat him to it. They stood in a close knot, chatting excitedly about the city.

Indira, her cheeks flushed with the cold and with excitement, grinned at him. "I can't wait to get home. I've missed it."

"I always liked returning home the best," he agreed as he drank in the sight of her. He drew closer, but Lady Miren took his arm.

"Lord Kevlin, have you been to Tamera before?" She wore her long blond hair loose and it cascaded down her back in waves of gold.

"A few times. I passed through the outer reaches of the city occasionally, and as a boy we docked here at least once a year."

"Excellent. You can be our local guide."

"Hardly that, my lady. I've seen only a fraction of it, and never the inner city. We always docked in the common port so I've never even seen the formal port where we're headed."

Lady Miren shrugged. "Then we'll explore it together."

Her enthusiasm was contagious. "I have a better idea. Let's have Indira show us around."

Indira grinned. "I've got a few things I definitely want to show you, Kevlin." She met his gaze boldly, and a shiver of heat raced through him.

Lady Miren linked her other arm with Indira. "I think this is going to be a visit to remember."

Adalia, who gripped the rail next to Indira said softly, "Just as long as we set our feet on dry land."

The others began arriving. Drystan and Jerrik described the basic layout of the city, including the spokes, the four major thoroughfares that radiated out from the palace and down through the city.

When Lady Miren asked about their favorite places in the city to visit, Jerrik laughed. "You won't be wanting to visit any of those places, my lady. Not your crowd."

Gabral proved to have an extensive knowledge of the city and recommended several attractions for the ladies. He told them about the high-class shopping along the Golden Road, and strongly recommended they explore the sunken gardens.

Ceren pointed, exclaiming, "Look, there it is."

Tamera filled a wide plain that rose up to a plateau that towered over the sea. This early in the day, most of the city still lay cloaked in shadow. Atop the plateau, the greatest wonder of the imperial capital shone like a beacon.

Known simply as the Great Dome, the tallest structure in the capital seemed to burn like a miniature sun in the early morning light. It greeted the day, first to taste the morning's rays, and last to relinquish its gleam to the twilight.

Kevlin remembered seeing the glittering dome from his father's ship miles out into the Tamerlane Sea when the rest of the capital had already slipped below the distant horizon. He'd never entered the dome, and the thought of finally getting to do so thrilled him more than he'd admit.

As the *Ceara* approached the northern port, the sun climbed high enough to illuminate more of the city, but their vantage limited their view. The outer city wall ran along the edge of the sea, up to the steep flanks of the plateau that housed the central palace complex. Few buildings in the poorer districts rose high enough to glimpse behind the wall. The closer to the plateau, the grander the buildings.

They reached the formal port with the morning tide and the sailors brought the large ship smoothly into the sheltered bay. A harbor tug was already waiting for them, and they docked at the central deep-water dock with hardly a pause.

Harafin had orchestrated their arrival with consummate skill. If he ever left the ruling council, he could make a fortune as a merchant.

An escort of threescore imperial cavalry awaited their arrival at the foot of the quay. Harafin summoned the party together and said, "Your baggage will be transported for you. We leave for the palace at once." Even before Drystan could ask, Harafin added, "And yes, the horses too."

Drystan glanced at the hold where the animals were stabled.

Kevlin clapped him on the back, "They'll take good care of the horses."

"I know," Drystan said, glancing at the riderless horses awaiting them. "It's just, I haven't ridden Jasindar for days. I should be the one to release him from the ship."

Kevlin didn't blame Drystan for looking forlorn. Jasindar was a magnificent animal, a purebred Einarri stallion, one of the finest of the Chandana herd. Kevlin wasn't sure he had ever seen the stallion's equal.

If he ever got to ride such a horse, other mounts would never seem adequate. The Einarri connection to their horses ran even deeper than that, however. Kevlin decided to learn more about it. He was now united by blood to the Chandana. He needed to understand them.

"How about we take a ride tomorrow? You can teach me about our tribe."

Jerrik joined the conversation. "Horses don't like me much."

Kevlin hadn't heard the big man join them. For such a giant, he could move quietly.

Drystan grinned. "That's because you're too fat."

Jerrik flexed. "Muscle weighs more than fat, little brother."

"The bigger they are . . ." Drystan started.

"The harder they clobber you," Jerrik finished.

Drystan laughed and his eyes glinted in the early morning light. "We're going to have to test that theory real soon."

"Absolutely," Jerrik grinned.

A wide gangplank was lowered over the side and Harafin descended while the sailors were still securing it. He led the group to the waiting procession. The ladies were assisted into a plush, open carriage, and the rest of the company mounted waiting horses.

They moved out immediately. The normally busy docks were clear and open. They passed rows of large merchant ships waiting to unload or take on new cargo. Sailors lined the decks to watch them pass. Farther out in the port, several broad-beamed military vessels swung gently in the current against their anchor chains.

The group passed through the outer wall via a gate that could easily accommodate four wagons abreast. Inside the city proper, they turned right onto the Golden Road, the northernmost of the four spokes, and kicked the horses into a gentle canter.

Even here where the city elite came to shop and show off their finery, the road remained open. There were no soldiers holding the lane open, but people remained on the sides of the cobbled street watching, although many pretended not to.

Kevlin, who rode just behind the open carriage, watched Indira more than he did the opulent shops lining the street. He didn't have the money to shop in this section of the city, and even if he had, he doubted they would let him in. Lady Miren and Ceren oohed and ahhed over various shops, and at one point, Lady Miren called out to ask if they could stop for a moment.

They did not. So the ladies eagerly planned their return. Indira didn't seem distracted by the wealth on display. She cast several glances back at Kevlin, and spent the trip conversing with Lady Miren's handmaid, Sitara, who looked uncomfortable sitting so close to Indira.

Adalia stared at the rich shops with wide-eyed amazement. The tiny archer from Baldev had thought Diodor a marvelous place of unbelievable riches. It couldn't compare with the opulence of the Golden Road.

They passed an open-fronted shop filled with weapons and armor and an entire rack of intricately carved bows. Adalia nearly fell out of the carriage trying to keep the shop in view for as long as possible.

They slowed through a series of steep switchbacks that zig-zagged up the slope to the gate in the inner-city wall. A dozen spearmen in the emperor's colors stood at attention as they passed. The gate was a fifty-foot tunnel boring through the massive inner wall, with a second gate guarding the far end. They exited the tunnel into brilliant sunlight and their first unobstructed view of the palace compound.

Kevlin gaped. The palace complex of the inner city eclipsed anything he'd ever seen. It didn't inspire awe, but rammed it down one's throat.

Immense. That one word captured the essence of the view. The central palace was still a mile distant, beyond the palaces, towers, and massive buildings that made up the city-within-the-city that was the palace complex of Tamera. The Great Dome towered high above everything, its sphere seeming to glow with inner fire. None of the other buildings in the inner-city complex stood even half as tall.

"By Jagen, this place be huge," Adalia said in the carriage.

Kevlin tore his eyes off the Great Dome to glance at the tiny archer. She looked around with eyes so big they seemed about to burst from her head. The other ladies tried to hide their amazement but were not entirely successful.

Kevlin followed Adalia's gaze to their right to a beautifully manicured park. Thick green lawns with wide-spaced shade trees and hedges shaped into fanciful creatures ran all the way to the edge of the cliff. The Tamerlane Sea extended to the far horizon beyond.

Gabral, who rode in front of the carriage, saluted to the left. They were approaching the Tamarr palace. The long, imposing structure flanked the road for a full quarter mile. However it seemed a bit inconsistent.

It was fashioned out of heavy gray stone, and yet it was surrounded by a polished cedar porch that led to dozens of wide openings that looked like they had been punched through the walls as an afterthought. The openings were flanked by fluted columns, ornate carvings, and marble statues, almost as if to prove they belonged.

Leander urged his horse up to ride beside Kevlin. "Hurts the eyes, doesn't it?"

"Sort of."

He chuckled. "It's in transition."

"What do you mean?"

"This was originally built as a fortress. You can still see it. But over the past twenty years, they've been remodeling, trying to compete with Freyarr for the most ornate, pompous structure."

The only part of the palace that still looked grim and solemn was the central section. Wide granite steps led up to heavy iron doors flanked by two statues of Salawin with the Sword of Justice raised as if to strike down anyone who dared enter.

"The high courts," Leander explained. "No place for mercy in that hall."

The park on their right gave way to a long, unbroken wall of polished, white granite, lined with dozens of statues of the emperors who had ruled over the past two centuries. Kevlin gave them only a brief glance, before gazing again at the central palace.

They rode into the main courtyard that spanned a quarter mile. Kevlin, like most of the company, nearly hurt his neck trying to look in every direction at once. The central palace loomed above them to the right, capped by the towering bulk of the dome. Its famous white marble walls seemed insufficient to hold up the incredible structure.

The road emptied into a circular boulevard that enclosed a beautiful garden with cobbled paths. Flower beds encircled the garden, bursting with a riot of colors. The garden in turn encircled a deep hole in the ground at least a hundred yards across. It plunged out of sight into the earth, but out of its center rose a tall fountain on a stone pedestal. Water cascaded high into the air before falling in a circular waterfall down into the depths of the gaping hole.

Three other main avenues emptied into this central boulevard. Flanking those other roads and encircling the central courtyard opposite the main bulk of the central palace stood the palaces of each of the Six Kingdoms.

They each stood equidistant from the central palace, tiny by comparison, as if kneeling at the feet of their ruler. Other than their size, they shared no common traits. Kevlin couldn't process the details, but each palace had been designed to represent its kingdom and to stand apart from the others.

In front of each of the six palaces, facing the central courtyard, stood statues of each nation's god. They reared thirty feet into the air and shone in the morning light. Kevlin refused to look at the statue of Savas that flanked the golden road opposite the statue of Salawin.

The company trotted around the central boulevard and up to the main stairs that led into the central palace complex directly under the Great Dome. Hundreds of people could ascend those stairs together and not feel crowded.

A crowd of well-dressed men and women waited to greet them. A very elderly man struggled to maintain order but was ignored by the others.

"That's Damodar, the Chief Steward of the palace," Leander said, nodding toward the old man. "The loud-mouthed, self-important officials are the ambassadors."

The ambassadors surged forward to greet Harafin. Behind them, a terribly fat Sentinel who was already sweating despite the chill morning, greeted Harafin with a loud shout.

Harafin raised a hand in greeting. "Ho, Felix."

He barely paused to acknowledge the ambassadors and other nobility arrayed to greet them before plowing through their ranks toward the main entrance. He called out loudly, "Assemble everyone immediately. I will do nothing until we have freed the emperor."

The Chief Steward frowned and glanced toward the stable hands who were taking the horses. Many of the young men were watching Harafin and talking excitedly among themselves.

As Kevlin passed through the immense main entrance with the others, he wondered at it. Clearly there was an ongoing effort to suppress information about the curse. Those efforts rarely worked as planned, and often back-fired.

His thoughts trailed off as he stepped into the palace. He had been impressed by the Great Dome from the outside. Nothing could have prepared him for the unbroken view all the way up to the peak of the dome so far overhead it seemed impossible the structure could have been crafted by human hands.

The open space dwarfed any other building Kevlin had ever imagined. Ten thousand people could fit in the open hall under the dome. Seven levels of balconies and railed walkways ringed the walls of the dome, but only stretched halfway up the structure. Hundreds of people moved about their various tasks high above the floor.

Five stories above him, an ornately carved carriage with no wheels floated off the end of an open balcony and crossed the immense empty space in a graceful arc. A dozen people sat in the carriage, and several of them waved at the staring spectators below.

Beside Kevlin, Jerrik muttered, "I hate coming here."

"How could you hate this?" Kevlin finally managed to close his mouth that had fallen open in wonder.

Jerrik frowned at nothing in particular and said softly, "Makes me feel . . . small."

Chuckling, Kevlin hurried to follow the others who were crossing the wide marble expanse of the floor. Harafin headed toward a magnificent grand staircase that arced up in twin arms to the second level.

Only when he nearly stepped in what looked like a huge puddle of water did Kevlin really look at the floor.

"Sherah's Teeth," he whispered as he glanced around and tried to take in the full scope of what he saw.

It looked like they were walking through actual waves. He nearly stumbled as his mind expected him to step onto a wave crest instead of landing on solid, flat marble. Beyond the waters, Harafin was striding through a range of tall mountains. Kevlin blinked a few times, but the illusion of depth did not dissipate.

"Don't try to see it here," Drystan said, nodding toward the stairs. "Look from up there."

"Where are we going?" Kevlin asked.

Gabral, who was trying to not look impressed, pointed at the yawning opening of a vast hallway that started on the next level. "That hall leads back to the imperial palace where the ruling council chamber is located."

"I thought we were in the imperial palace."

Gabral snorted. "Not hardly. There's lots of palaces here. The entire inner city is called the Greater Palace Complex. Each kingdom has their own palace outside. Right now we're standing in the Great Dome, which is the centerpiece of the Tamera Palace proper, but the complex is so big it's broken down into smaller sections."

He waved toward a huge opening in the north wall of the Great Dome on the main level, thick with people. "The Northern Kingdoms Admin Palace lies over there. You saw it from outside, the long wing that faces the northern edge of the central boulevard." He nodded toward the south. "Same thing over there, just for the southern kingdoms."

Ceren, who had moved closer to them as they walked said, "I read about all this, but I can hardly believe it."

At the top of the grand stair, Kevlin and the others paused to look back over the wide expanse of marble floor they had just traversed.

The sight took Kevlin's breath away. Stretched across the entire expanse of the dome floor was a detailed map of the empire. All Six Kingdoms were portrayed in spectacular detail. The waves he'd thought he was wading through were part of the Tamerlane Sea, which was the one landmark given less space than it deserved.

More than the breathtaking detail of the mosaic, it was the three-dimensional effect somehow embedded into the artwork that amazed him most. Kevlin stared for several seconds, trying to penetrate the illusion, but from this distance it looked even more realistic than when they had been walking through it.

Indira stepped to the rail beside him. "I could stand here all day looking at this."

Kevlin took her hand, but now that he finally got the chance to speak with her, his words failed him. He wanted nothing more than to look into those big, dark eyes.

Ceren slipped up beside Indira. "Come on, or we'll be left behind."

The rest of the party was already marching down the long hall. When the three of them jogged to catch up, Ceren somehow ended up between Kevlin and Indira. When they rejoined the party, the two ladies rejoined Adalia, leaving Kevlin at the rear of the troupe with his brothers.

They walked through a hall wide enough for thirty people abreast. It reared at least two stories tall and ran straight west for a hundred yards.

Gabral said, "We're about to enter the area reserved for staffers who work for the various imperial departments not directly affiliated with any of the Six Kingdoms. It's known as the Imperial Palace."

"So this is where the emperor lives?" Kevlin asked. He was having trouble absorbing so much information on such a huge scale. That, coupled with getting separated from Indira again was making him cranky.

"Wrong again." Gabral actually smiled. "The Emperor's Palace lies north of the Imperial Palace. The Great Hall is south of here, with other support buildings I've never visited surrounding them. I've lived here for three years. It takes a while to sort it all out."

Kevlin stopped trying to digest all the wonders and just focused on following Harafin. Until today, he'd considered himself widely traveled, but he now felt like a country fool.

The halls were thick with people, many of whom watched the company with guarded interest and occasional glares. Most of the attention was directed at Harafin and the ambassadors, who strode down the center of the hall without slowing. Their heavy escort ensured people got out of the way.

Of course, most of the stares were then transferred to the women who walked in the center of the group. More than one person started bowing to Lady Miren, while others stared after her, frowning.

Kevlin asked Drystan, "Why are they doing that?"

"She looks a lot like the keisara."

Made sense. The keisara was the emperor's wife, and she definitely would require respect. They ascended several more staircases and then turned down a wide corridor flanked by two Sentinels. The hall stood empty and a sense of foreboding hung in the air.

They were drawing close to the curse. A few minutes later, they stopped in a wide atrium facing a set of ornately carved double doors.

"Are you sure you want to approach from this side?" Felix asked Harafin.

He nodded. "Get everyone down here. There's more room to work."

"Master Harafin, I'm so glad you're here."

Keisara Fideima Tamar Tegnazian swept into the atrium from a side corridor, surrounded by half a dozen Sentinels and two dozen guards. Everyone bowed or curtsied.

Kevlin stared when he rose from his bow. Lady Miren did share a striking resemblance to the keisara, but failed to project the same aura of magnificence. The keisara took Harafin's hand in greeting, then turned to greet her cousin.

Sentinels began to arrive, along with many Stalwarts dressed in the various colors of their orders. Soon the atrium filled to overflowing with more than fifty gifted men and women.

Harafin raised his hands for attention. "Thank you for coming and offering your strength. Assemble yourselves, and we will begin." He turned to face the double doors and declared, "The curse dies now."

The Stalwarts and Sentinels shifted, forming long chains as each person grasped the shoulders of the person in front of them. The chains of each order of Stalwarts remained distinct, as did several different groupings of Sentinels. The lines snaked around each other before ending with the senior Sentinels and Stalwarts who stood arrayed behind Harafin.

Harafin turned to the keisara. "Your Majesty, I recommend you withdraw."

Keisara Fideima shook her head, standing tall and looking regal. "I will not leave, Master Harafin. I will witness the salvation of my husband. This curse has caused us so much pain and I will not flee." When he tried to protest, she added, "If I'm not safe here among all of you, there is no place in the palace I would call safe."

Harafin inclined his head in a small bow. "Very well. No matter what you see, you must not enter the council chamber until I authorize it."

He swept his gaze over the ambassadors, who stood gathered in a group to one side. "That goes for all of you."

They all eagerly agreed. Harafin pointed to two Sentinels who stood apart from the long chains of men and women. "Shield them."

A shimmering silvery shield formed around the keisara and the small group of ladies with her. Another formed over the ambassadors.

The keisara clasped hands with Lady Miren, who leaned close and whispered words of comfort. Ceren stood on the queen's other side and Indira hovered nearby. Adalia clenched her hands as if fighting the urge to string her bow.

Kevlin felt it too. Tension and anticipation hung thick in the air, mingled with fear. His hands itched to hold a weapon even though he knew it would do no good against the mystic forces they faced here.

As a hushed anticipation settled over the group, Drystan whispered to Kevlin, "Maybe we should've been standing closer to the ladies."

Jerrik chuckled, a deep rumbling that drew many disapproving glares. "Coward."

Harafin spoke softly. "Begin."

Scores of hands began to glow as Sentinels and Stalwarts alike bowed their heads in concentration. The air became charged like during a thunderstorm, and a breeze picked up.

Leander, Ah'Shan, and ten other men and women who stood at the heads of the various chains of living power, raised their hands in unison. They did not touch Harafin, but lifted outstretched hands in his direction. Ropes of pure white light leapt from each of them, meeting at a single point in the center of Harafin's back.

Harafin, who faced the closed double doors, squared his shoulders but showed no other outward sign of the influx of power. So much raw power flowed through the room that Kevlin could feel it, like whispers across his skin.

Only then did he realize the danger.

The Trembling Madness roared to life and shattered his mental restraints. Kevlin swayed and would have fallen if Jerrik had not caught him.

"Kevlin, stand your ground," Jerrik growled.

Kevlin barely heard the words. He clasped his head with both hands and squeezed, as if the pressure could help him maintain his sanity. He swayed as he fought to resist the overpowering urge to leap upon the nearest Sentinel and take the man's magic.

They wouldn't miss a little. Just a little, that's all he needed. They were so cruel to deny him. He deserved it just as much as Harafin did. No, he deserved it more. Harafin could get his own.

Kevlin took a step forward, toward Harafin. His face contorted into a mask of hatred and his fingers curled into claws. He would take the magic, all the magic. He deserved it.

Drystan caught his shoulder. "Kevlin, stop. Harafin's about to open the doors."

"Leave off," Kevlin growled. "I need it."

"Uh oh," Jerrik groaned. "Bad timing, Kevlin."

Kevlin took another step, unable to stop himself. Part of him still resisted, but that part was fighting a losing battle inside the broken remnants of his mental fortress.

Another voice was clamoring so loud, those whispered doubts were hard to focus on. Why not take it? He deserved it. He needed it.

His hands started to shake and a crazed laugh bubbled in his throat. Ceren turned at the sound and her eyes widened at the sight of him. Indira also turned, and she looked terrified. Protected in their shield, they couldn't help or flee.

Jerrik and Drystan grabbed Kevlin's arms and restrained him. He struggled against them and opened his mouth to scream at them to let him go.

A gauntleted fist smashed him in the face and snapped his head back so hard he pulled a muscle in his neck.

Kevlin's legs buckled, and he sagged between his brothers. His vision blurred, and the pain smashed through the raging madness like a splash of icy water. He drove the invading magic out of his mind and reinforced his broken shields. When the unruly power crashed against his defenses again, this time he held.

Kevlin coughed, and a cloth was shoved over his mouth to silence him. He could barely breathe, and struggled to free himself.

Gabral's voice hissed into his ear. "Stand down, mercenary, or I'll kill you right now."

Kevlin didn't doubt Gabral's sincerity. The short colonel had disliked him from the start and seemed eager to find an excuse to kill him. He would have several times if Harafin hadn't intervened.

Kevlin had thought they were over that. Apparently not. He was disappointed his brothers didn't intervene.

Jerrik and Drystan held him up until he could stand on his own. Gabral stood close in front of him, glowering and watching him closely, as if looking for an excuse to hit him again.

Kevlin whispered, "I'm all right. Let me go."

His brothers slowly relaxed their grip and Drystan said, "That was quick thinking, Colonel."

Gabral smiled. "Happy to help." Then he turned his back on them. The Mace, which he now held in his hand, began to burn with blue fire that rolled up and over him, encasing him in its protective power.

Kevlin hated to admit Gabral had done the right thing. He would have lost control otherwise. The Trembling Magic had subsided, but he maintained his shielding in case it rose to challenge his sanity again.

The entire incident had taken only a few seconds, and no one outside of the small group seemed to have noticed. Then again, all the Sentinels and Stalwarts packed in around them were concentrating so hard, they wouldn't notice if the building started to collapse.

The wide double doors burst open so hard that Kevlin was surprised they didn't spring from their hinges. Harafin stood alone in the opening, hands spread wide, with blue lightning arcing between them. His body glowed with pure white light and he radiated an aura of absolute power.

Kevlin reinforced his already strong defenses against the Trembling Madness. It tested his mental barrier, but subsided when he maintained control.

Beyond the double doors lay the ruling council chamber. At the far end stood the long, half-moon curve of the gigantic council table. The room glowed with angry red light that pulsed slowly.

The glow emanated from the head of the room where the figure of a man showed dimly through a pillar of crimson fire. Another column of fire burned several feet to the left, although the bulk of the table concealed whatever lay within it.

As soon as the double doors opened, the condensed flames surged high, burning all the way up to the ceiling. Tendrils of flame whipped across the room toward Harafin.

The old Sentinel threw his hands out and shouted a word Kevlin could not understand, but that rippled through him like a cyclone of sound.

A curtain of blue-white light exploded into the room, burning so bright it blinded Kevlin. The crack of thunder pealed so loud Kevlin cried out, clutching at his ears. A second shockwave of sound struck with stunning force and tumbled him to the floor. His brothers landed on top of him, and Jerrik's elbow drove into Kevlin's ribs, driven by his immense weight.

Kevlin clenched his eyes shut and kept his hands clapped over his ears, but it was a futile effort. It reminded him of the night he first met Antigonus, a few short weeks ago. It felt like years. Antigonus had summoned a bolt of lightning against Rhea, and Kevlin had again stood far too close.

If only Antigonus had managed to kill Rhea with that bolt, things might have turned out so different.

Hands pulled Kevlin to his feet and he forced his eyes open. People stood nearby, but he only saw them as shadowy figures surrounded by gray. He blinked several times, and his vision slowly returned.

Silence enveloped him, and his head felt thick, like it was packed with wool. It took a moment to recognize Jerrik standing beside him. The huge Donarri warrior tried speaking, but Kevlin couldn't make out the words. It sounded like Jerrik was talking underwater.

Jerrik frowned and twisted Kevlin around. Drystan stood behind him with Indira. She looked concerned and had one hand half-extended toward Kevlin.

He wanted to step forward and take that hand, wanted to feel the warmth of her touch. But as soon as he saw her, the wild craving for magic stirred. The longing to touch her was overshadowed by a new urge to grab her and force her to give him magic.

Kevlin reached for her, but she must have noted the change in his face because she retreated. Drystan intercepted Kevlin and cocked back an arm to show he'd share some of Gabral's tonic against insanity if Kevlin didn't stand down.

Kevlin closed his eyes and fought to control himself. He hated losing control, but the thought of hurting Indira drove him to redouble the height and strength of his mental walls. It took a few seconds, but he surrounded his thoughts with impenetrable wards, and the madness subsided.

He could see better now. Sounds started to register, but dimly. Indira was already gone. His brothers stood nearby, casually flanking him. A knot of Sentinels clustered around the double doors to the council chamber, so Kevlin couldn't see inside the room.

Felix pushed out through the crowd and started speaking and gesturing wildly. The gathered Sentinels reluctantly disbanded.

The room was scarcely recognizable. The polished marble floor had buckled in four places, its entire expanse cracked and charred. The walls were blackened and pockmarked with craters as if they'd been attacked with siege weapons. The huge stained-glass window in the ceiling was simply gone, and the immense, crescent-shaped table lay in smoldering piles of ash.

There was no sign of the cursed crimson fire.

Harafin stood beside the emperor's throne-like chair while half a dozen Stalwarts and green-robed Healers lifted the emperor onto a stretcher and began hustling him from the room. The keisara, who was openly crying, hugged Harafin and kissed him on the cheek before rushing after the emperor's stretcher.

Lady Miren embraced Harafin, then followed. Harafin waved to Ceren, who stood nearby. Kevlin couldn't hear what he said, but she gave a brief curtsy and ran after Lady Miren.

Sentinels who walked past Kevlin all shared a look of profound awe that fit well his lingering deafness.

Drystan handed Kevlin a small piece of parchment. It read, *'Don't let anyone know you're still not well. They might try to heal you.'*

Kevlin sighed. He needed to speak with Harafin. The Trembling Madness seemed to be far worse here in the palace. At the same time, he felt deeply frustrated that the others could be healed while he stumbled around like a cripple.

Colonel Gabral walked past and didn't bother hiding his smile. He said something, but Kevlin heard only a muted whisper.

Within moments, the hall was crowded with workers, soldiers, and bureaucrats. It was as if they had been hidden behind an invisible dam that had broken now that the curse was gone. Kevlin stood on the fringes of the flood and watched people hurry by, while the noise of their passing sounded like distant echoes. He felt alone and completely useless.

Jerrik and Drystan appeared a few minutes later and signaled him to follow. They led him down a dozen different halls and descended more flights of stairs than Kevlin remembered climbing on the way in.

After walking at least two miles through the palace compound, Kevlin felt hopelessly lost. He knew they had left the Imperial Palace behind because he saw fewer people dressed in the green and gold of the emperor's staff and now saw mostly soldiers in the uniform of the imperial guard.

Eventually they stopped at a plain white wooden door that looked exactly like hundreds of other doors lining the last three halls they had followed. The simple, utilitarian hall made it clear they were far from important sections of the palace.

Drystan consulted a circular wooden chip about the size of a silver crown and nodded. He handed Kevlin the chip. The symbol 3-BP-18-44 was etched into the top of it.

"What's this?" Kevlin's voice still sounded to him like he was speaking with cotton stuffing his cheeks.

Jerrik leaned close and shouted into his ear. "It means, sub-level three, section bread pudding, hall eighteen, room forty-four." His voice sounded like a whisper.

Kevlin frowned. "Bread pudding?"

Drystan shouted in his other ear, "He means Bracken Parthalan." At Kevlin's blank stare, Drystan shrugged. "I'll explain when you can hear."

Jerrik shouted, "Bread Pudding is easier to remember."

"You're confusing him," Drystan said, then pushed open the door to reveal a small but comfortable room with a sturdy bed, small table with washbasin, and wardrobe. Kevlin's pack lay on the bed.

Jerrik shouted, "Your quarters. Welcome home." Then he passed Kevlin a bit of parchment with two other sets of codes on it. "Our rooms."

Drystan shouted, "We have to report to our ambassadors. We'll track you down later."

The two left in different directions. Kevlin chose the course of wisdom, lay down on his bed, and fell asleep.

17

SNAKES AND WORMHOLES

Kevlin awoke to a knock on the door and smiled. It felt great to hear again.

A young woman in the palace uniform of green and gold stood in the hall. Her brown eyes and curly brown hair bounced when she curtsied, but gave him no hint as to her nationality. Her skin was fair, so probably not Freyarr. Beyond that, Kevlin couldn't tell.

"Lord Kevlin?"

"Kevlin is fine. I just woke up. Using titles so soon makes me a little nauseous."

The young woman cracked a smile.

"What's your name?"

"Marjani, my lord. I'm here to summon you to the emperor's council."

Kevlin stepped into the hall and shut the door. He should probably change into something nice before being presented before the emperor. Unfortunately his spare clothes weren't much better, and they'd emerge from his pack even more wrinkled than what he'd been sleeping in.

"Marjani, can I ask you something?"

"Anything, my lord."

"Where in the name of the seven gods am I?"

"Why, Lord Kevlin, you're in the palace."

Kevlin laughed, and Marjani smiled. As she led him down the hall, she asked, "Are you new to the palace, Sir Kevlin?"

"I am. Which palace are we in right now?"

"The Underground Palace."

"I haven't heard of that one."

"There are quite a few. It can take a while."

Kevlin looked around but it didn't look like they were underground. The halls were plainer than the fancy main halls, but didn't need torches to light the way, and the air didn't smell musty or dank.

"How is it possible?"

While they walked, Marjani explained that the entire greater palace compound was built upon several sub-levels carved down into the heart of the plateau.

"The entire palace compound? But it's huge."

"It is. The inner city stretches exactly one and a half miles north to south, and almost twice that east to west."

She explained that the sub-levels were used for guest housing, barracks, storage, and a multitude of other supporting functions. It was an entire city unto itself. A grid-work of sunken gardens situated throughout the inner city provided fresh air and light. That light was reflected throughout the complex through a series of mirrors.

At night the fountains placed in the center of every sunken garden glowed with enough light to maintain the sub-levels in perpetual twilight. Every fountain glowed a different color, and Marjani highly recommended Kevlin explore some of them. They were among the city's famous attractions.

"So how do I find my way back to my room later?" Kevlin asked.

Marjani showed him brass plaques mounted at each hall intersection with codes similar to the one he carried. She showed him how to read the codes. Each of the Six Kingdoms was responsible for the upkeep and maintenance of sections of the sub-levels closest to their individual palaces. The key was to know which sub-level he needed, and which section. Every section was named after a city in the kingdom sponsoring that part of the Underground Palace. He was assigned Bracken-Parthalan. Bracken was the name of an outer suburb of the great trading city of Parthalan in Freyarr.

"So," Marjani concluded. "Once you know the system, it's fairly simple. Head toward the Freyarri-controlled under-city, find your sub-level and section, and then use the brass plaques on the walls to find your hall and room."

"If you find me wandering the halls, please show me the way home."

"I work in the first sub-level, but I'm a floater so I get around a lot. I'll keep my eye out for you."

Kevlin grimaced. "Where I come from, floaters are . . . something different."

"Meinarr?"

"Yes."

"Bodies found floating in the sea. I hear that a lot."

Marjani showed him how to locate the stairs to higher levels, and eventually led him to one of the sunken gardens. She said this one glowed emerald green at night, so he could use that as a landmark when he tried to find his way back.

They climbed the staircase carved into the circular outer wall of the garden. Apparently every garden had similar stairs. This garden was plush, but only a fraction of the size of the central garden situated in front of the Great Dome. Wildflowers carpeted the lowest level and surrounded an entire orchard of apple trees heavy with ripe fruit.

"The harvesters should be picking those any day now," Marjani said. "There will be fresh fruit in the dining halls next week."

They surfaced finally and wound their way along cobbled paths through the upper section of the garden. Marjani said, "I took you this way so you can get a sense of the layout. It's possible to travel between any of the buildings in the greater palace complex without going outside if you have the security clearance."

The central boulevard passed not far from where they stood. To the east, the Freyarr palace seemed to glow in the midday sun. Unlike the Tamarr palace, the Freyarr palace was open and airy. High, arced entrances lined the walls, and several small domes capped various sections of the roof.

Marjani noted his gaze. "The Freyarr Palace is one of the wonders of the inner city. The original palace was torn down thirty years ago for the new one." As she led him toward the Great Dome's main entrance, she added, "The Fire Stalwarts run a gambling house in honor of Akillik. It's worth going in just to see the wealth on display."

Kevlin glanced back at the palace before they were swallowed up by the Great Dome's vast expanse. He thought back to the disturbing interview he'd had with the god of Luck. He wouldn't willingly draw closer to Akillik than he had to.

After a long, confusing walk, Marjani led Kevlin to a council chamber situated in the Emperor's Palace. Kevlin found most of the company already gathered, and he suddenly wished he'd found a way to find a change of clothes.

Drystan and Jerrik wore parade uniforms of their respective nations. Gabral wore his silver-trimmed imperial guard uniform and a wine-colored cape with his house emblem on one side and the emperor's seal on the other. He'd managed to cut his hair already, and every heavily-oiled lock was situated perfectly. At least Harafin and Leander looked unchanged.

Kevlin felt deeply self-conscious as a servant ushered him into the small conference room. Emperor Tegnazian sat in an overstuffed chair situated next to a crackling fire. Two Healers attended him. Three Sentinels and two dozen guards had been stationed in the hall approaching this room. He'd been ordered to surrender his sword and belt dagger outside.

Security was tight, but they hadn't noticed the stilettos concealed in his wrist guards or the enchanted dagger hidden at the base of his neck. He didn't correct the oversight.

Kevlin bowed deeply when the emperor looked his way. He was suddenly nervous at the prospect of meeting this great man. Emperor Tegnazian, born on the very day the last great war ended, had reigned for the past three decades during a time of unprecedented peace.

Widespread belief held that as long as Emperor Zuberi Tegnazian ruled, there would be no war with their enemies to the west. Kevlin wondered how the man would handle the likelihood of renewed hostilities.

The emperor spoke in a rich, resonant voice. "Lord Kevlin, welcome."

"Thank you, Your Majesty." Kevlin was impressed the emperor knew him.

The emperor beckoned him closer and even extended a hand for Kevlin to take. Kevlin dropped to one knee and bowed again.

"Lord Kevlin, the King's Avenger," Emperor Tegnazian said warmly. He looked tired and the curse had left his hair bleached white, but his voice remained strong. "We all owe you a debt of gratitude for what you did in Hallvarr."

Kevlin stammered his thanks. He had been surprised by the adulation in Diodor, but could understand it at a certain level. He hadn't expected much recognition outside of Hallvarr, nor did he want it. It only reminded him how skewed everyone's understanding of events there had become. There had been no heroics involved in his fight with Dhanjal. He felt like he was lying to everyone.

The emperor waved them all to seats and dismissed his attendants with orders not to disturb the meeting. "Where are the two brave ladies from your company that I heard so much about?"

Harafin said, "Lady Ceren offered to act as liaison with your wife. She should arrive shortly from their first meeting."

The emperor smiled. "Excellent choice. From all accounts, that young woman is very cunning."

The word was a good choice. Ceren had indeed been given the title of Cunning by Antigonus, a reference to the prophecy of the Catalyst Antigonus was trying to force to fulfillment. He'd been wrong about many things, but although the prophetic title of Cunning didn't belong to Ceren, she had proved herself resourceful and brave.

"My ward, Indira, asked to be excused," Leander said. "She was needed urgently in the hospital."

"Very well. I'll get right to the point. Harafin, I've thanked you once already, my friend, but I want to thank you here with your company. I owe you my life. Again."

Harafin nodded graciously.

The emperor continued. "You will not have time to rest, I'm afraid. This attack has shaken the city and weakened morale. With war looming, we must be strong."

Gabral interjected. "Certainly news of your recovery will help."

"Perhaps. However, word of the curse was aggressively suppressed. So word of my recovery cannot be widely communicated without highlighting the secrecy, which would just reinforce suspicions among the populace that their leaders lie to them. My wife's brilliant announcement of a ball to celebrate the engagement of her cousin to Crown Prince Lievin will probably do more to help. People will see us healthy, enjoying ourselves, and willing to celebrate despite grim tidings. In the meantime, I summoned you to hear your candid assessment of the situation, and to prepare for our response."

"Should I summon the rest of your security council?" Gabral offered.

"Not yet."

Leander spoke. "Who knew the name Abaval?"

"Almost no one."

Leander added, "Can you provide a list? That will be our best focus for investigation."

The emperor nodded. "Myself, Field Marshall Ankur, Sentinel Felix, the ambassadors."

Leander's eager expression faded to a grimace.

Harafin said, "Then it was not such a closely guarded secret after all."

"Perhaps not," the emperor conceded.

Harafin rose and paced to the fire. "What concerns me the most is the curse was cast by a Shadeleech. There is no doubt. And yet, the palace defenses should have prevented such a creature from penetrating into the inner palace. The shields are keyed to recognize sthenic energy and trigger an alarm."

"What if they dropped all connection to their power?" Leander asked.

"It might be possible," Harafin admitted after a moment's thought. "But they would have to sever all connection to their power, to their enslaved Makrasha, and even to their shielding, leaving them completely helpless. I don't believe they would do it, nor am I convinced a single Shadeleech could then cast such a curse without taking another life."

"Have there been any unsolved murders recently?" Gabral asked.

"We'll have to inquire of the palace guard," the emperor said.

Harafin shook his head. "Even if a Shadeleech penetrated the defenses by rendering himself completely helpless, murdering someone with his powers would certainly trigger the palace defenses."

"Are you certain?" Leander asked. "They are a series of layered shields surrounding the palace. Do they extend even to the inner halls?"

Leander's comment triggered a thought, something Kevlin had been wrestling with during his solo practice sessions with his mental shields. He filed the information away for later consideration.

Harafin crossed the room to an ornately carved column in the far corner. "I will double-check." He placed one hand on a carved knot shaped like a clenched fist.

"Could Tanathos really have done it?" Kevlin asked.

"It's remotely possible he traveled this far in the time he had," Leander said. "If he bent his entire will to it and sacrificed several of his slaves. However, I doubt he could have penetrated to the inner palace without assistance, even if he did strip himself of all power."

Kevlin doubted Tanathos would allow himself to be left helpless. He shivered to think of Shadeleeches wandering the halls of the palace.

Drystan said, "If he did make it in time, and even if he somehow slipped into the palace, he couldn't have brought his strike force in with him."

Gabral shook his head. "No. There's no way."

Jerrik spoke for the first time. "Then where are they?"

The emperor said, "That presents an opportunity. I'll order the palace guard to send scouting parties into the surrounding countryside. Perhaps they'll uncover evidence of these marauders."

Harafin cursed in the corner and his hand flared with bright white light. He remained that way, for half a minute before turning. "Interesting."

Kevlin was getting used to his often-understated expressions. Harafin found the prospect of enemy armies hidden in Hallvarr interesting, and the thought of facing multiple Halimaw only 'difficult'.

"What have you found?" the emperor asked.

"I discovered a wormhole in our defenses."

Harafin seated himself with a satisfied smile. "It was quite ingenious, like a snake. It twisted through some of the weaker portions of the shield, deflecting the regular shields around itself until it became all but invisible. I nearly missed it, but it leads right to the inner palace."

"So Tanathos did breach the shields," Kevlin said.

"No. No Shadeleech could have done this. Only someone with a detailed knowledge of our shielding technique could have. They also needed access to the matrix of defensive spells built into the very walls of the palace. Only then could they have breached our defenses undetected."

His voice became grim. "Only an Elite or Master Sentinel could have done it."

Drystan tapped a small table in front of his chair. "That should narrow down the list of suspects quite a bit."

"Unless Bajaran did it before he left," Leander said.

"Could he have done that?" the emperor asked.

Harafin considered the question for a moment. "He had access. That begs the question, is this somehow part of the original plot we thwarted recently in Hallvarr, or something set in motion in response to events there?"

"I'm getting a headache," Jerrik said, tugging on his unruly beard. "Just tell me who to kill."

Leander chuckled. "To speak to Harafin's question, we must first determine what the attackers hoped to accomplish."

The emperor looked surprised. "Isn't it obvious? Their intention was to cripple the government in one brilliant, daring stroke."

"I am not convinced that was the reason," Harafin said.

The emperor looked a little disappointed. "Then why else attack me?"

Gabral said, "If they wanted you dead, they had plenty of time to do it. They didn't kill you, so what were they after?"

Gabral managed to keep a straight face while he presented the same argument to the emperor that Harafin had made on the *Ceara*. Kevlin wanted to borrow Jerrik's gauntlet and punch Gabral in the mouth.

Harafin didn't seem to mind. "Exactly. I don't think the attackers forgot to key the curse to take your life. They proved far too clever, and this attack shows a level of planning rarely seen outside of the highest levels of the enemy circles."

"Perhaps they meant to cause a panic," Leander said. "From what I've heard, a few more days of that curse and they would have succeeded."

"I don't know what these hidden assassins hoped to achieve," Emperor Tegnazian said in a loud voice. He rose and surveyed the small company. "But I'm certain of one thing. This hidden enemy, be they a lone assassin or a conspiracy a hundred strong, must be rooted out."

He swept an arm across the room to include them all. "My security forces have been compromised. I summoned you here today because of all the forces at my disposal, this company alone I trust above all others."

He declared in a ringing voice, "You are hereby commissioned to discover the identities of these traitors before they strike again."

He seated himself and said to Jerrik, "Then my good man, by all means, kill them all."

18

CIRCLES OF POWER

Ceren sat on a small, plush sofa in the keisara's private sitting room at the very top of the Keisara's Tower. This was a room where only Fideima's inner circle of friends were ever invited. She could barely contain her excitement.

The spacious room took up the entire upper floor and was comfortably furnished without being ostentatious. Ceren approved of all of the keisara's choices for furniture, placement, fabrics, and coloring. Of course, it was nothing but the platform upon which to enjoy the breathtaking views.

The tower room boasted eight huge windows that provided unbroken vistas in every direction. The Keisara's Tower was one of the two identical towers placed at either end of the central keep of the Emperor's Palace, which sat near the western edge of the plateau.

Ceren could look down at the cliffs that plummeted several hundred more feet to the Tamerlane Sea, which stretched to the western horizon. Ships far out in the sea looked like tiny toys.

The Great Dome glistened in the midday sunlight to the southeast and blocked her view of the southern half of the city. Other windows offered spectacular vistas of the myriad towers and keeps and domes of the inner city complex. Beyond the Northern Kingdoms Admin Palace, she glimpsed the Tamarr and Freyarr palaces, the thick inner city wall, and the vast expanse of the northern half of Tamera.

She could have stood at the windows and absorbed those views for hours. Instead, she sat demurely on the sofa facing Keisara Fideima and

Lady Miren, who shared another sofa. Sitara stood at attention to one side. Another of the keisara's handmaidens, named Omolara, who could have passed for a younger sister of Lady Miren, stood on the other.

Ceren was glad Sitara was present. Otherwise, so much gorgeous blond hair in one place would have made her far too self-conscious. She was so thrilled she wanted to squeal like a little girl. This opportunity dwarfed everything she'd ever dreamed. She composed her mind and her face and reminded herself to breathe.

"Lady Ceren," Keisara Fideima said, "I'm so glad you were available to attend me today."

Ceren wanted to shout, *Are you kidding? I'd have sacrificed my cousin to get an audience with you!* But she only said, "It's my pleasure, Your Majesty."

The keisara motioned toward trays of sweetbreads and chilled fruit wine on the table and invited Ceren to help herself. She did so, and only through a lifetime of training in her father's palace did she manage to act calm and not spill it all over herself.

Keisara Fideima chatted with Lady Miren, but watched Ceren. She realized this was the first test, a simple way for the keisara to judge her character and fortitude.

After they all sampled some of the food, the keisara said, "It's my understanding that you traveled with Master Harafin recently and witnessed some of the tragic events in Hallvarr."

"Yes, Your Majesty."

"Tell me, do you believe Master Harafin will succeed in rooting out the traitors hidden here in the palace?"

Ceren smiled. "I have no doubt. Master Harafin does not hesitate. When he sees a threat, he destroys it." As she spoke, she jabbed her arm out in an imaginary sword thrust.

Lady Miren jumped and then giggled at herself. The keisara looked startled but masked her emotions too well for Ceren to read more.

Ceren wanted to slap herself for making a scene. "I'm sorry for startling you. I'm afraid I'm still a little jumpy from battle."

Keisara Fideima raised a single eyebrow in surprise. "You actually . . . participated in battle, Lady Ceren?"

"I did," Ceren said, thrilled to have cracked the keisara's façade. "In fact, I rode with the assault force that broke the siege at Il'Aicharen."

"Oh my," Lady Miren exclaimed. "Did you . . . kill anyone?"

Ceren dropped her gaze to her hands. "Yes."

She raised her eyes to see them both staring at her as if seeing her for the first time. "I killed Makrasha."

She shivered at the memory of the huge, foul beasts and their flat, green eyes and deadly hengaruk. Then she remembered the one Makrasha, maw gaping wide as it tried to bite her head off.

Kevlin had killed it, had savaged it in a terrible fury. Neither of them had known that Indira was protecting her at the time. He had thought the beast was killing her.

She forced the memories away. The ladies were watching her closely. She took another drink of her chilled wine. "Again, I apologize. Some of the memories are unsettling."

Keisara Fideima asked, "How did the battle end? Accounts are scattered and incomplete."

Ceren knew what she was asking. Where was Oris, and who was the new bearer? Knowledge was power, and this was the most closely guarded secret Ceren had ever known. She was deeply frustrated that she hadn't cracked it yet herself, but she wasn't about to reveal that failure to the keisara.

"I'm sorry, my own memories are a little vague. After I killed the rogue Sentinel Wayra, the burning tower collapsed on me and I lost track of some time."

"You killed Wayra?" the keisara exclaimed.

"Yes, your majesty." Time to tie it all together. "But I succeeded primarily because Master Harafin stood against Wayra, against the full might of the keep's activated defenses. He battled with power no other Sentinel could have matched. Her distraction proved fatal."

She leaned forward. "Master Harafin will find these traitors and he will destroy them."

"And you'll help him," Lady Miren said with a little clap of her hands. She lifted her glass. "You are the bravest woman I've ever met. Gods bless you."

Keisara Fideima lifted her glass as well. Ceren bowed her head to accept their praise, a little smile on her lips.

Things were working out better than she could have hoped.

19

Performance Anxiety

S itara pushed open the plain wooden door and slipped into the simple guest room. Identical to hundreds of similar rooms in this rarely used section of the underground palace, it provided a secure meeting place.

She had already swept the room with her mind and confirmed Remiel alone waited inside. When he caught sight of her, he jumped to his feet from the small bed where he'd been lounging. He grinned and crossed the room in two steps to wrap his arms around her.

He smelled clean and fresh and was wearing a hint of cologne. His strong arms held her with unusual gentleness. As usual, his thick, dark hair was perfectly styled and he still looked like a sixteen year-old. If she didn't hate him so much, she'd admit he was very handsome.

"I've missed you, Angel."

Of course he missed her. When she'd agreed to this pig's terms of service, she'd forced him to agree to take no other women to his bed until she was finished with him. Her long absence must have tested his will.

She felt no pity for him.

When he tried to kiss her lips, she pushed him away. "You'll get your payment when I finish my report."

He retreated and leaned against the wall near the bed, but his eyes stayed glued to her. For once he actually tried to keep his gaze focused on her face instead of mentally undressing her while they talked.

"So how did the trip go?" he asked. "Tell me about Diodor."

"Tell your master I made contact and expect delivery." The code phrase was all she dared share with him.

Masego was her master too, but that didn't mean she had to treat Remiel like an equal.

"You're here," Remiel said, his usual cocky smile on his face. "So I figured you were successful."

"Then why require I come to tell you what you're clever enough to figure out alone?"

They both knew why. By insisting on a meeting, he could claim another payment. She hated remaining trapped in this agreement, but Masego hadn't offered to amend it for her. She doubted he ever would, doubted he ever spared her discomfort a single thought.

Remiel advanced and took her hands. His smile faded and he gazed into her eyes with unusual intensity. "Can't I miss my best girl?"

"Don't mock me," she snapped.

Sitara moved to the bed and perched on the edge. Her brief freedom from Tamera had been fraught with danger, but she'd loved escaping Remiel's touch. Only by returning could she complete her mission to succeed in the revolution. Only then could she truly honor Bajaran's memory, but she hated the price she was forced to pay.

When she reached for the ties to her bodice, Remiel surprised her. He took her hand and drew it back from the laces.

"Don't bother, Angel."

She wasn't sure what disgusting plan he had in mind for her and barely checked her rage. For the thousandth time, she was tempted to unleash her powers upon him, torture his body, and take the essence of his soul to feed her strength.

When the time was right, she would do just that.

Remiel retreated to the door, but his smile looked forced and his eyes a little sad.

"Angel, I..." He sighed, one hand on the doorknob. "Listen, if anyone asks, just tell them you had a good time."

Then he left.

Sitara stared after him, hardly believing he would leave without taking advantage of her again. He'd always enjoyed that part of their secret meetings the most.

She snorted when she considered his last words. As if she spoke about him with anyone. She had no close friends. She couldn't trust anyone, not even these men who she had turned to for help after Bajaran's death.

There was no end to Remiel's bloated ego. Even when he couldn't perform, he still worried about his reputation.

Sitara exited the lower levels before he changed his mind. She drove him from her thoughts. Her next interview would be far more dangerous and important.

20

A CHANCE TO SPIN THE WHEEL

Kevlin stood in a corner of the now-crowded council chamber. Sentinel Felix, along with the ambassadors who made up the ruling council, sat around a table that had been brought in for the meeting.

Maps and charts and dozens of other documents that seemed to serve no purpose lay scattered across the table. Kevlin watched in growing amusement as a steady stream of aides delivered the unused documents only to replace them with yet more documents a few moments later.

It was nice to have something to distract him, even something so small. The discussions at the table were more than a little disturbing.

When everyone first arrived, the emperor announced that the company including Gabral, Kevlin, and his swordbrothers were to be added to his personal guard. With so many of the guard killed or disabled by the curse, it made sense. The ambassadors seemed pleased, particularly the Einarri ambassador, Garitt Talamantez, Drystan's uncle.

Then discussions turned to improving security without triggering riots in the streets. Kevlin learned that the inner city gates had not been closed in decades, and there was evidence that major repairs would be needed before the gates could be made operational.

The emperor insisted that a full legion of imperial guard patrol from the inner wall down through the upper city to the outer wall. The original city of Tamera once fit inside that outer wall. Now only upper-class mansions fit there, separated from the rest of the populace by the ancient wall.

Suggestions were made to increase the token police force that currently guarded the outer city wall. That sparked arguments about how many forces, which kingdoms would provide them, and who would pay the bills.

The immensely fat ambassador from Meinarr, the bald Duke Gwyre, immediately proposed increasing various taxes to pay for the expected rise in expenditures. That sparked additional arguments about budgets and percentages that soon left Kevlin's head spinning.

It soon became apparent that some of the ambassadors argued only to guarantee they didn't agree with certain other men around the table. Other times, they suggested proposals that were clearly absurd only to then offer a compromise that seemed to provide unfair benefits for their kingdom. It didn't look like they would accomplish much of use today.

Leander leaned against the wall next to Kevlin and whispered, "They'll be at this all day."

"At least," Kevlin agreed with a wry smile.

"Come with me," Leander said.

Kevlin followed him to the door and slipped out. No one challenged them or called them back in. Leander paused a dozen steps down the hall and Kevlin asked, "Shouldn't we stay in there?"

Leander chuckled, "Perhaps, but you heard the emperor. Our assignment is to ferret out traitors. Your post as his guard is just a cover. I think it's time to begin the hunt."

"What do you have in mind?"

Leander started walking and Kevlin fell into step beside him. He recovered his weapons at the security checkpoint and followed Leander back to the main hallways. He even recognized some of the landmarks this time.

Only then did Leander say, "The emperor let slip that Bajaran's quarters haven't been searched yet."

"How is that possible?"

Leander shrugged. "It's a big place. Details are easy to overlook, but I think it's a good place to start."

He eagerly followed Leander back to the Great Dome and out the main gate. They took the central boulevard around to the south. As they walked, Kevlin studied the palaces of the various kingdoms.

Just south of the airy Freyarr Palace loomed the blocky Meinarr Palace. The granite walls were fairly plain, with little ornamentation. The building sported fewer entrances than the other palaces, but they were heavily used.

Leander said, "The major mercantile trading house is located in the Meinarr palace. Takes up the entire second floor." He chuckled. "Don't let the somber look fool you. More money changes hands in that palace in an hour than in all the other palaces combined in a week."

South of the Meinarr Palace, across the wide avenue of the Iron Spoke, stood the Donarr Palace. Kevlin wasn't surprised to find it was really a fully functional castle, complete with outer wall, guard towers and portcullis. Looking at it, he could imagine himself back in Donarr during his mercenary campaigns. Those were some of his happiest days, right up until Chayah betrayed and tried to murder him.

South of the Donarr Palace stood the simple rectangle of the Hallvarr Palace. Its clean, straight lines and tasteful ornamentation seemed out of place amidst the opulence of much of the rest of the inner city. Although Leander assured him all the palaces were allocated the same amount of space, this one appeared somehow smaller than the others.

An open dome sat at the close end of the roof and seemed to be heavily used. Leander explained it was an observatory run by the Pemburu Stalwarts and frequented by university students.

South of the Hallvarr Palace, across the avenue of the Port Spoke, Kevlin expected to find the Einarr Palace. Instead, he found an open expanse of gardens, mature trees, and small fountains surrounding half a dozen widely scattered low buildings. In the center of the space stood a giant tent that reared three stories high and looked far more permanent than any tent should.

Leander noted his gaze. "The Einarri don't like big, blocky structures. They house a lot of their administrative functions belowground, although most of their staff manage to work in the buildings you see there."

"Their palace is a tent?"

"Only the ambassador's offices." Leander pointed beyond the palace. "They've turned the entire southern edge of the plateau into a cavalry training ground. Most of the time when I need to find an Einarri official, I go there to look."

Kevlin filed away that piece of information for the next time he needed to find Drystan. He followed Leander to the far southern edge of the central palace compound where a tall tower made of white granite stood flanked by a wide, low building fashioned of gray stone.

"The Sentinel Tower," Leander said.

Kevlin studied it as they approached. It was very wide and simple, unadorned. When they reached the open main floor, they passed many white-robed Sentinels. Singly or in quietly chatting pairs, they moved about their business with a more sedate pace than most of the people Kevlin had seen scurrying about the main palace. A wide stair of white marble ascended along the outer wall to their right, and an identical stair descended to their left.

"Most of the classrooms are on the lower floors," Leander said. "While the offices and living quarters of the senior Sentinels are above. The bulk of them live and work in the next building, which also houses the university.

Leander led the way through the tower into the university building, through a wide central hall. After almost one hundred and fifty paces, he turned down a side hallway, descended one level and turned yet again. They entered a simple hall of whitewashed stone.

Kevlin looked for the brass plaques that marked hall addresses, but saw nothing similar here. "How do you know where you're going?"

"Non-actinopathic folk can't see the signs. It's a way to ensure only Sentinels or their guests access these areas."

After three more turns, Leander finally stopped near the end of a hall, in front of a simple white wooden door. It looked exactly like every other door they'd passed on this level.

"Not big on individuality here, are they?" Kevlin asked.

"The palace is too big for that. This way, it keeps costs down." Leander smiled. "At least that's what the bureaucrats say."

The old Stalwart glanced around to ensure they were alone in the hall, then snapped his fingers. His enchanted war hammer popped into his hand and he grinned as he hefted it.

He smashed the door off its hinges.

Kevlin caught a glimpse of the room. A large, canopied bed, several book cases, and a trunk at the foot of the bed. Then the entire room exploded into flames that engulfed it and roared into the hall.

The heat blistered his skin and carried a sickly smell, like burning oil. Kevlin retreated from the fire.

"What did you do?"

Leander stood in the door and ignored the flames pouring out of the room and washing over him. As a Stalwart, he was immune to magical harm.

Magic. The sight of so much of it triggered the Trembling Madness. It crashed through his mind before he could form his mental shields, shattering his self-control. He lunged past Leander and into the room. The amulet grew hot against his chest as it sucked in the magic of the fire that engulfed him.

Kevlin laughed aloud and spun in circles, arms thrown wide, in an effort to capture as much magic as he could. As it poured into him, he changed it and gloried in its power.

What had he been waiting for? Why hadn't he forced someone to give him this much magic sooner? The memory of the torrential flood of magic he'd controlled while at the keep of Il'Aicharen returned and he ran around the room, trying to scoop up flames with his hands.

"Kevlin, stop," Leander shouted from the doorway, but his words were drowned by the roaring of the fire. Kevlin ignored him and whirled faster. He had to take as much as he could before Leander interfered.

Leander rushed into the room and began pawing around the burning furniture, looking for something. Kevlin kept an eye on him. If the old fool tried to take the magic for himself, Kevlin would throw him out of the room. He could make his own. This was Kevlin's.

Magic roared through Kevlin's limbs, filling him with power, although it was still but a pittance compared to what he'd controlled in Il'Aicharen. Kevlin threw back his head and laughed through the flames.

Then the captured magic bucked against his control. It reared inside of him in a single, convulsive thrust of pure power driving toward his brain. His defenses were already breached by the Trembling Madness, so the unruly magic poured into his mind like a savage horde of Makrasha.

Kevlin collapsed to the floor, clutching at his head and screaming from the agony tearing through his skull. The insane craving for magic burned away, but his mental fortress was already breached.

Magic tore at his mind, attempting to shatter it so it could burst free of his control. He writhed on the floor, his thoughts scattered, unable to rebuild his shields. The flames of the room coated his mouth with the taste of charred grease, and pain pulsed through his head like a thousand drums. His fingernails scraped against the smooth stone of the floor as he tried to hold onto reality.

Then the pain vanished and silence dropped over him like a shroud.

Kevlin blinked and sat up. Everything around him seemed frozen in time. Leander, not two feet away, hung in mid-air, caught in the act of dropping to his knees beside Kevlin. The flames were stuck in mid-flicker. The air smelled crisp and carried a hint of clover.

He looked to his left and scrambled backward in surprise. Akillik lay on a tongue of fire, using it like a hammock. The youthful god laughed when he saw Kevlin, a rolling exclamation of pure joy.

"Good to see you again, Kevlin." He lay on His head back and used His spinning wheel as a pillow. It didn't slow, but He didn't seem to notice. "Lucky amulet you have there."

Kevlin clutched his shirt where the amulet lay hidden, and a sudden fear blossomed in his chest. Would Akillik really target the amulet? He couldn't imagine anything more disastrous.

Akillik laughed again and lifted his wheel for Kevlin to see. It began to slow.

"No!" Kevlin shouted. "Keep your luck." He forced his eyes closed, forced the image of the wheel away.

His body trembled with the effort of not looking. He gritted his teeth against the overpowering urge to look. If he allowed Akillik to play His game, if the Wheel came up against him, he'd die in a heartbeat.

"Spoilsport," Akillik said. Then He laughed again. His voice spoke close beside Kevlin's ear, a whisper that crawled into his mind and shook him with its power.

"Next time we meet, the test will not be so simple."

Pain ignited again in Kevlin's mind as time resumed. He welcomed the deadly struggle against the unruly magic. If he lost this, he'd only die.

The struggle against Savas had made it all too clear that stumbling into a god's power would cost his very soul.

Kevlin laughed against the terror that made him want to curl up on the floor and surrender. He threw all the insanity, all the fear, all the pain he possessed into the laughter as the *Tai Pari* threatened to crush his mind.

He sounded like Akillik.

Then Leander arrived, his mind a bulwark of strength. He poured peace across Kevlin's thoughts, like a wave of reinforcements driving the invaders from Kevlin's mind. The respite gave Kevlin the seconds he needed to rear high the mental shields he'd practiced on the ship.

In seconds, he stood atop his fortified mental battlements and screamed defiance against the torrent of uncontrolled magic. Let it come, and he would dominate it this time.

Very good, Leander's mindvoice said. *You've made excellent progress. I saw him again. Akillik.*

We'll talk about it later. I need to try to salvage . . . something.

Kevlin groaned as he opened his eyes and sat up. Magical flames burned all around them, obscuring everything in the room. He coughed, and then coughed again.

"Hurry," Leander said through a cough of his own. He ran to the wall where a bookcase burned, but when he reached for the books, he yelped and backed away.

"What is it?" Kevlin called through another cough.

"We have to get out of here. Real fire's taking over. And real smoke."

The two supported each other as they staggered toward the door, but Leander fell to one knee, coughing so hard it was a wonder he didn't spit out a lung and a few other organs.

Kevlin lacked the strength to lift him. There didn't seem to be any air left in the room. He noticed for the first time the intense heat. It beat against him, sucking his strength. He sank to the floor next to Leander.

Kevlin started to crawl. His fingers scraped the smooth stone as he dragged himself toward the promised salvation of the doorway. His other hand clutched Leander's collar, dragging the still-coughing Stalwart along.

The flames intensified and the skin of his face cracked under the heat. He couldn't breathe, couldn't see. He closed his eyes and kept pulling, but the truth dawned on him with terrifying brutality.

They weren't going to make it.

A shadowy figure appeared in the doorway. Through a gap in the smoke, Kevlin recognized the white robes of a Sentinel. More gathered in the hall behind. He pulled Leander another agonizing inch forward, clinging to hope while trying to hold his breath. The Sentinels could put out the fire.

The flames surged into a firestorm far more intense than it had been before. Furniture vaporized and the very walls started to melt.

Kevlin covered his face with an arm, but he felt his shirt smoldering. The heat could not be survived for long. He collapsed to the ground beside Leander, his burning lungs trying to draw another breath. The air singed his throat and sucked every bit of moisture from his mouth. It tasted like a charnel house, the foul stench gagging him.

Beside him, Leander mumbled something, but Kevlin couldn't hear over the roaring of the flames. The hairs of Leander's beard were curling, blackening under the heat.

Then the fire winked out.

Kevlin sprawled on the floor, but the stones were searing hot instead of refreshing as he had hoped. So he staggered to his feet and helped Leander rise.

Sentinel Felix stood in the doorway, arms still raised. He laughed when he saw Leander. "Only your Faith could withstand Rogue Fire, my friend."

Then he frowned. "Kevlin? What are you doing in there?"

"Trying not to burn to death," Kevlin croaked.

Felix stepped into the room. "How did you survive that firestorm? You're no Stalwart."

"No, he's not," Leander said. "He's not nearly disciplined enough." He clapped Felix on the shoulder. "Thank you. Another few seconds and you would have had to scrape what was left of us off the floor."

"I'm not joking," Felix said. Behind him, several other Sentinels crowded into the doorway, listening.

Kevlin was still too shaken by the recent *Tai Pari*, the Trembling Madness, and the vision of Akillik. He couldn't think of a plausible explanation, but didn't plan to reveal the secret of the amulet.

He glanced at Leander, who looked equally stumped.

"Let me through so I can explain."

Indira pushed through the crowd and her voice caressed Kevlin's ears, bringing the first real relief. She wore her green Healer robe and it was spotted with blood. She looked tired.

Kevlin moved to her side as the tiny archer Adalia joined Indira and took her arm. "Careful. Ye kin hardly walk, Indira."

Felix made a little bow. "Healer Indira, you're always welcome. How can you explain this?"

Indira faced Felix, her chin high, her hair brushed back from her face.

Leander spoke before she could. "This is a matter that should be discussed in confidence."

Felix waved the other Sentinels away. They grumbled as they drifted off, but none of them openly protested.

Leander said, "Indira has recently discovered a previously unexplored aspect of her gift."

Indira nodded. "I can shield others with my power, even when not actively healing them." She glanced at Kevlin. "Although standing in that fire guaranteed you needed my help."

"I'm very impressed," Felix said. "After you've had a chance to rest, I'd love to hear how this works."

He headed for the door but paused. "Leander, I want to know what was going on in here. Soon."

After he left, Kevlin took Indira's hands.

She asked, "Are you all right? What were you thinking?"

"I'm fine, but you lied? For me?" Her integrity was a major reason anyone still played cards with her. If word got out that she'd lied, no one would believe her fantastic skill with cards was completely honest.

A little color rose in her cheeks. "Well, you weren't helping. You looked like your thoughts had all melted. Besides, it wasn't exactly a lie. I mean, I didn't actually tell him I shielded you. I just sort of . . . implied it."

Kevlin laughed, and Leander joined him. "You're the queen of justification."

"Well, you're very welcome," Indira snapped. She turned and marched off.

Adalia shook her head. "Ye coulda handled that better." Then she trotted after Indira.

Leander clapped him on the shoulder. "Are you going to chase her?"

"Should I?"

"Don't ask me. I've lived a century longer than you, my boy, and I still can't understand women."

That didn't help.

Kevlin started to run.

21

TEACHING TIME WITH MASEGO

Sitara hurried down the wide central stair of the Sentinel Tower into the lower levels. She glanced back occasionally to see if anyone might be following. None of the Sentinels who passed her even seemed to notice her. She thanked the anonymity of the palace livery she'd borrowed before making the trek across the palace complex.

She knew she was being foolish to worry. If anyone had suspected her, they would have detained her already. Still, she had taken an awful risk lingering by the door to Bajaran's room after the crowd began to disperse.

Thank the gods Indira hadn't noticed her. The healer's abrupt exit had caught her by surprise, and had Indira been paying better attention, she might have spotted Sitara rushing away around the next corner.

Indira terrified her. Now that she knew Indira's secret, she was doubly glad she hadn't allowed Indira to touch her on the ship. She'd have to exercise extra caution around the healer. The woman's sweet façade was as effective as Sitara's own voice in convincing people to underestimate her.

Sitara reached the third sub-level and breathed a sigh of relief. Actually, things were going very well. She'd learned some very intriguing things from the Lady Ceren in the Keisara's Tower today. Even better, she'd escaped Remiel's touch for another day.

No doubt he'd find an excuse to meet with her again soon and make up for the lapse. The world would never know the depth of the sacrifice she made to bring to pass Bajaran's dream of a new world. It didn't matter. She'd make any sacrifice to honor the memory of the greatest man she'd ever known.

To fulfill her plan, she needed more help. She thought of the man Kevlin. Even protected by Indira's shield of Faith, he'd showed great courage to enter the inferno of Bajaran's room. She had caught a glimpse of the melted walls and heaps of ash that had been the furniture. Nothing remained, no trace evidence that might lead anyone to her.

This man Kevlin was a true hero. He might be one she could recruit to her cause. He was beloved by the people, and she felt he was a man one could trust. He'd be perfect.

Sitara buried those dangerous thoughts as she sought out the heavily shielded classroom where she met with her teacher. If he learned what she planned--.

An unexpected blow to her mind dropped her to the floor mid-stride. She bit back a scream, clamping down on her lip so hard that blood began to flow.

A thought drove into her mind like a hammer, *You useless, undisciplined wretch. Have you forgotten everything I taught you during your little vacation?*

No, master.

Masego's voice cut at her mind like a razor. *I told you to come with your shields up, and mind focused. Do you think I have time to waste?*

There were too many Sentinels. She couldn't even allow herself to feel terrified that he might have caught a glimpse of her plans.

I don't accept excuses. Another mental blow rattled her, and sparked her anger. She had risked so much, done so much for him.

His Mindvoice laugh mocked her thoughts.

Mock this. Sitara formed her newly designed shields and locked them into place around her mind, faster than ever before, and drove his thoughts away.

A heavy blow slammed into a single segment of her shield, just as she expected it to. She instantly rotated the shield and braced herself. A second mental strike slammed into the same place as the first. Her shield held, but a shockwave still rippled through it into her mind. She again shifted her shields to a new configuration.

After Tanathos had broken into her mind, she'd spent the rest of the journey to Diodor practicing her shields. She'd used every available moment in that city to continue her practice. Her duties to Lady Miren had not consumed as much time as her work for the keisara had, and she'd put the time to good use. Her shields were now a complex, multi-layered fortress of protection.

The base of her neck tingled with the telltale sign of a Mindlink connection. Sitara bared her teeth at the empty wall in victory. Then she made a tiny opening and accepted the connection.

Masego drove his thoughts through the opening in an attempt to breach her defenses. She was ready for him and severed the connection with a single, brutal slash across his thoughts. It was hard enough to have caused him pain.

A moment later, the tickle returned and she cautiously opened another connection.

Much better. The thought from Masego held no hint of mockery. *Finally, you're learning something.*

Not from you, she thought to herself. To him, she projected the reply, *Thank you, master.*

Report on your mission.

Success. She allowed a little pride. *I made contact with the Shadeleech. Your instructions were delivered.*

Good. He will prove useful.

Master, he nearly destroyed me, but seemed to recognize your name.

As I expected.

How could Tanathos know her master? She shuddered at the memory of the Shadeleech's cesspool of a mind. Even the memory of his evil thoughts tainted her. Masego was ruthless and cruel, but Tanathos was pure evil. *How can you ally with such an evil creature?*

Don't confuse using him with an alliance, Masego responded. *Would you prefer Harafin to chase us or him when we steal the stone?*

Sitara leaned against the wall, hugging herself against the chill fear that returned any time she considered Harafin. She'd nearly lost her composure several times on the ship. To think she'd eaten in the same room with the legendary Sentinel and still lived.

What else have you learned? Masego asked. *Where is Oris? Who is its new Bearer? Did they come to Tamera with Harafin?*

I cannot answer any of those questions, Sitara stammered.

Masego didn't respond for three long heartbeats and her fear grew. He finally spoke, his Mindvoice icy cold. *You test my patience. How could you spend so much time with his company and not learn this?*

What do you expect me to do? Sitara asked. *I didn't dare try to influence anyone or even touch my gift on that ship with Sentinels in arm's reach all the time. I'm no use to you dead.*

Your ignorance is beginning to tire me.

I'm only ignorant because you haven't taught me, Sitara shot back. She braced herself for a punishing blow. Her master didn't like to be challenged.

I teach when you prove you're worthy, Masego said. *You have proven nothing.*

Even Lady Ceren doesn't seem to know who the new Bearer is, Sitara said. *The keisara asked her, but she dodged the question.*

She was hiding the truth.

I don't think so. The only people who might know are one of the soldiers who fought beside Harafin at the last.

Names?

The man Gabral.

No. It would be unwise to challenge him.

There were others. Drystan and Jerrik, and the man Kevlin.

She hated having to offer the man Kevlin to her master. He had shown kindness to her and probably saved her life on the ship. She had plans for him, but couldn't lie to Masego now.

He was the Steward and much in Harafin's council. One of those three are most likely to know the secret.

I will arrange to question one of these men, Masego said, his voice no longer angry. *Lady Ceren might still prove useful.*

If she knows, she will not speak of it.

That is no matter. Your lesson begins now. I will teach you to mine the thoughts of another for information you seek. You can sometimes steal their darkest secrets while they remain unaware.

Sitara listened eagerly as Masego began to teach. If only she'd known this earlier, she could have taken what she needed.

Then she thought back to the time Masego had possessed her, body and soul. It had been necessary to deflect Sentinel Omolara's suspicions, but had left her feeling utterly violated. She'd sworn never to submit to such a violation again.

She needed this new skill, despite how it would violate others. She hated to think what she did for the revolution paralleled his evil works even a little. It wasn't really the same thing. She didn't intend to possess anyone. She would only skim information. She wouldn't harm them unless she found no alternative.

A mental blow snapped her mind back to the lesson. Masego snarled, *If you wander again, I'll leave you crippled on the floor.*

I'm sorry, master. I'm still tired from the journey.

Deal with that on your own time. One final point. Do not attempt this on a gifted mind, even an unshielded one. They will sense your presence.

I'll be careful, Sitara promised.

So many secrets.

22

ROGUE FIRE

Kevlin stood at a long window in Harafin's quarters in the Sentinel Tower and stared at the panoramic view of the city. Of course Harafin's apartment took up the entire top floor of the tower.

Kevlin could have stared at the city for an hour. The view helped ease his frustration. He'd chased Indira, but she'd told him to leave her alone. Hopefully with a little time, she'd forgive him. He needed to find a way to make it up to her. Maybe Adalia would tell him what restaurants Indira liked.

From Harafin's window, he could study the city flowing down the gentle slope below the plateau of the inner city and filling the eastern plain. He could easily trace the four spokes that split the city into distinct quarters and extended all the way to the distant horizon. At the outermost edge of the city, the imperial highway wrapped around the plain, connecting the city with the Six Kingdoms.

The door opened and Harafin entered, followed by Ah'Shan. Kevlin and Leander had been escorted up to the tower room only moments before. Leander had expected the summons, so they had just waited for it near the main entrance to the Sentinel Tower.

Leander beckoned Kevlin to join him on a pair of wooden chairs in the sitting room. Their clothes were still singed and reeking of smoke.

Harafin regarded the pair of them. "That was rash."

"Necessary," Leander countered.

Ah'Shan dropped into an overstuffed chair. "You should have waited for a Sentinel to go with you. We might have been able to salvage something."

Leander said, "That's unlikely. Even if you or Harafin had joined us, you might not have recognized rogue fire soon enough to prevent the destruction of any evidence."

"Perhaps," Harafin said. "We shall never know."

Ah'Shan growled, "Bajaran was thorough. I wonder what he was trying to hide."

"That's assuming Bajaran set that trap before he left," Leander said. "It's just as likely that someone else didn't want to be connected with him."

Harafin said, "We have too many questions already. Let's not add to the list."

Leander began to reply, but Harafin leaped to his feet, waving him to silence. He strode across the room to a carved column that looked identical to the one in the emperor's council chamber they recently left. He placed a hand on the same carved fist, and closed his eyes.

After a moment, he dropped his hand and slowly turned. "I felt a minor quiver in the shielding around the palace."

"Tanathos?" Kevlin asked, standing, eager to chase down the Shadeleech.

"I do not know. By the time I connected with the shield matrix, they were gone."

"Where were they?" Leander asked.

"I cannot tell," Harafin said with a frown. "The contact was very weak. I will have to fine-tune the shield parameters to provide better directional location for the next contact."

"If he hasn't already turned and run," Kevlin said. Some of what Harafin was talking about made no sense, but Tanathos had proven he was good at running.

Harafin did not look bothered. "I do not believe he will run yet. I still think the curse was designed primarily to draw us here. Now that we've arrived, I expect the enemy is already preparing their next strike."

Kevlin hated giving the enemy the first move.

"We should strike first then," Leander said.

Harafin chuckled. "I'd love to. Point me to the enemy and I will gladly destroy them."

Ah'Shan leaned forward in his chair. "Is it possible to extend the shield matrix?"

"Of course," Leander agreed. "Only the palace complex is shielded. Extend the shields around the city."

Harafin shook his head. "The shields were never designed to extend so far. It may be possible to do what you suggest, but the power required to maintain such a spell for any length of time would be staggering."

"It's worth it," Leander said.

"I cannot agree. With so many Sentinels residing here, managing the levels of latent magic is already a challenge. It's a struggle to maintain sufficient for daily usage and also fuel the existing shield matrix and the multitude of other fixed enchantments. The balance is extremely fine. Establishing a long-term, full-city shield matrix would drain all the latent magic from the area."

"The Sentinels can deal with it," Leander said.

Ah'Shan scowled. "That's easy for you to say. Your gift wouldn't be affected. We'd be the ones weakened."

"Ah'Shan is right," Harafin said. "If the enemy's next attack is more powerful, which is likely, we would have insufficient latent magic for our Sentinels to go into battle."

Leander paced to the window, head bowed in thought. He turned, his voice solemn. "Activate the palace defenses."

That surprised Kevlin. Harafin had spoken of Rhisart, the then-Gerent of Il'Aicharen who had activated the keep's defenses there. With that power, he had fought off the entire attacking horde for days. Upon his death, Wayra had gained control of those powerful defenses and nearly destroyed them all when she turned against them.

It made sense that Tamera might be imbued with similar defenses. Hopefully there were better controls in place to make sure that power never fell into the wrong hands.

"No," Harafin said. "I cannot."

"Do it," Leander urged. "That would grant you more than enough power to blanket the entire city with a shield strong enough to pinpoint the enemy. We could destroy them before nightfall." His hand clenched at his side, as if anticipating calling his mighty hammer.

Harafin shook his head. "I understand your eagerness, my friend, but the defenses were never designed for such a purpose. Activating the defenses drains vast stores of magic. It would likely take years to fully reset them."

"We need that power now," Leander insisted. "There's time to replenish the store."

"We are moving into a time of war. What if we had a real emergency?"

"This is an emergency," Leander snapped. "Someone cast rogue fire inside the palace, Harafin. Rogue fire!"

Kevlin hoped Leander could keep his anger under control. If his family had been murdered and he knew the murderer was hidden close by, he'd use any option available to hunt them down. He feared what might happen if Harafin said no again.

So he interjected. "What is rogue fire?"

Leander paced to the window and stood looking out, his expression grim.

Harafin watched him for a moment before speaking. "Rogue fire is the hallmark spell of Kyllikki, one of the twin rulers of the Sigrun council."

"It's an extremely dangerous spell," Ah'Shan added. "One that all Sentinels are forbidden to use."

"More than that, Kyllikki jealously guards its use even among the other Sigrun," Harafin said.

Sigrun, Kevlin thought. *Forbidden spells*. He'd asked the question to ease tensions, not make himself more afraid. Could one of the Sigrun have infiltrated the city?

As bad as Tanathos was, he didn't want to stand within a thousand miles of a Sigrun.

"What does it do?" he dared ask.

"It destroys," Ah'Shan said simply.

Harafin added, "The great irony in rogue fire is that it started as a practical joke."

"A joke?" That raging inferno in Bajaran's room hadn't been a joke. Kyllikki had one twisted sense of humor.

"When they were young, before they rose up against our nation and overthrew it, Kyllikki and his twin brother Nyyrikki loved practical jokes and excelled in inventing ways to torment the other students."

Kevlin had to remind himself that Harafin was over a quarter of a millennia old. Every time the old man spoke of the Sigrun and times before the formation of the Tamerlane Empire, it surprised Kevlin. Harafin had lived through so much history. He knew things the history books had forgotten.

So much of it had been so bad. It was a wonder Harafin hadn't moved to an abandoned island somewhere for a little peace.

Harafin continued. "Rogue fire is as powerful as it is simple. Kyllikki invented it to burn another student's research notes. Any of the common spells used to extinguish fire only make it stronger. The poor student who was its first victim torched an entire room and barely escaped with his life."

"I have no doubt Kyllikki was himself surprised by how very powerful it proved to be. He extinguished it himself before it could do more damage, and before any of the teachers realized what was happening."

Harafin's voice turned grim. "He never showed such restraint again. He used rogue fire in several of his earliest attacks against the Sentinel High Council."

For a moment, Harafin looked his age as a great sadness weighed him down. He whispered, "Such a simple spell."

Ah'Shan said, "The more power directed against rogue fire to quell it, the faster it grows."

"It was uniquely effective against some of the most powerful Sentinels of the day," Harafin said. "Their very strength was their downfall. They didn't have time to realize their mistake before they were consumed."

"And now someone used it in Bajaran's quarters," Leander said. "Can't you see, we need to stop this now?"

"It manifested also when the curse first struck," Felix declared as he pushed open the outer door. He leaned against the doorframe, panting. Kevlin was surprised he hadn't heard Felix's wheezing breath long before the fat Sentinel arrived.

"I didn't know that," Harafin said.

Felix staggered across the room and dropped onto a sofa that groaned under the load. He wiped his sweaty face and managed a weak smile. "Sorry I'm late. And yes, when I first tried to contain the curse, it struck with rogue fire." He shook his head. "Nearly had me for a minute, there. That's why I knew how to deal with it today. I've had it on my mind."

"All reasons why you should activate the defenses," Leander reiterated.

Harafin hesitated. "I still feel that step inappropriate." He held up a hand to forestall Leander. "I have a feeling, a premonition, that we will need those defenses, and soon. However, I believe I can improve on the current situation."

Harafin rubbed his hands together, a look of anticipation on his face. "I will extend the shield matrix down the spokes, like feelers, if you will, to trigger a warning if a Shadeleech crosses."

Ah'Shan barked a hard laugh. "Brilliant. No one travels far without crossing one of the spokes sooner or later."

"How difficult is it to make that change to the matrix?" Leander asked. "It has stood unchanged for over a century."

Harafin considered the question. "It won't be easy. However, I assisted with laying the foundation for the original matrix so I understand what must be done."

"I'll share my strength with you," Leander said.

"That's not necessary. I can manage."

"Allow me to help anyway. It will ease my heart to know I helped put the plan in place."

"In that case, by all means."

Leander visibly relaxed. "Very well. We have a plan. I'll organize patrols of Stalwarts throughout the city."

"That's an excellent idea," Felix said. "We should add Sentinels to the regular city guard patrols. If there's a Shadeleech hidden in the city, they'll need Sentinels to bring him down."

"Unless we find him first," Leander said with a wolfish grin.

23

PALLIAN STALWARTS

When Kevlin and Leander exited Sentinel Tower, Leander said, "Since you're not scheduled for guard duty until tomorrow, I'll give you a tour of our citadel."

"Lead on." Kevlin had never been inside a Pallian citadel and was eager to see it. Besides, after talking about rogue fire and Sigrun, he preferred staying in Leander's company as long as possible.

They crossed the central palace courtyard, rounded the corner of the Donarr Castle, and followed the Iron Spoke toward the inner city wall. The citadel sat on the south side of the road behind a screen of mature oak trees.

It looked like a cross between a castle and a church, and was flanked by a high wall of ancient stone. They passed through the huge, ironbound main doors into a vaulted room. It was illuminated by tall, stained-glass windows situated between heavy support columns, rearing almost all the way to the ceiling.

Leander pointed out several Stalwarts to their left, who attended walk-in patients daily. To the right, more Stalwarts were seated around heavy tables piled with books.

Within seconds, word spread of Leander's arrival, and Stalwarts dropped what they were doing and rushed to greet him. Leander seemed to shed years, and beamed like a father returning to beloved children. Students offered to bring him food, hot cloths for his face, and clean clothes. They seemed ready to burst with excitement.

Leander politely refused every offer and said, "If studies are so boring today that you feel driven to find excuses to leave them, then come to the practice field."

The students cheered and rushed out a large rear door. Several older Stalwarts, who had lingered at the rear of the crowd, took advantage of the lull to greet Leander more calmly.

"Styra Leander," one of them said, "I'm happy for your safe return, but I did have plans for those students today."

Leander clapped the man on the shoulder. "I know. You can have them tomorrow. Today, we hold assembly."

That startled the man, but he only said, "I'll summon the brethren." He led the other teachers out a small door on the south side of the room.

Leander headed after the students, with Kevlin in tow.

"What is that they were all calling you?" Kevlin asked.

"Styra is an honorific referring to my title. As leader of the Pallian order, I am the Styrskena, or guide."

"Sorry, I didn't know to call you that."

Leander chuckled. "No, my boy. It's used only in the citadel, or among the Pallians. Anywhere else, it's not appropriate."

"But it's what you are, isn't it."

"I am a Hammer Stalwart. That is enough most days."

Leander led him through a set of wooden doors to a wide hallway that ran a surprising distance. Kevlin realized they must have passed through the wall behind the main building. He had assumed the church-fort was the heart of the citadel, but it turned out to be only the figurehead.

The citadel complex proved extensive, with four long granite buildings enclosed by the high wall, all facing a central field of close-cropped, dense grass.

When they emerged into the noon sunlight, fourscore Stalwarts stood in orderly ranks facing them. The Stalwarts raised their war hammers in unison and shouted, "Styra Leander, welcome home!"

Leander raised both hands in blessing. "Thank you, my friends. May your hammers be swift and your hearts wise."

"Now," he added with a wide smile. "Show me what you have learned in my absence."

The Stalwarts split into pairs for sparring. They fought with skill to match their enthusiasm. More than one ended up injured in their mock battles. The partners of the injured dropped their hammers and lay glowing hands of healing onto their injured companions.

An extremely stocky fellow with a shaved head joined Kevlin and Leander. He was a little shorter than average but his shoulders strained the limits of his jacket, and his thighs were as thick around as Kevlin's waist. He greeted Leander heartily, and his blue eyes twinkled with suppressed laughter.

Leander clasped hands warmly with the powerful Stalwart. "Kevlin, this is Leda Basak, my second-in-command and Ledskena of the citadel. He runs things while I'm away."

Kevlin clasped hands with Basak. Power radiated through the man's grip. Kevlin was glad they were meeting as friends. He had no doubt Basak could throw him over the wall if he wanted to.

"Pleasure to meet you," Basak said with a deep but surprisingly gentle voice.

Leander said, "Basak, why don't you spar with Kevlin? He's getting a little rusty."

"Gladly." Basak snapped his fingers, and a war hammer popped into his hand.

"I'm not that rusty," Kevlin protested out of habit, but he welcomed the chance to spar with the man.

"I watched you spar with your brothers," Leander said. "You need it."

"I thought your hammer was the only one that did that reappearing trick," Kevlin said.

"I cheated a little."

Kevlin drew his sword and faced off with Basak, eager to test the man's skills, but a little nervous too. He'd seen Leander fight. The old Stalwart was unmatched in battle. Even Jerrik and Drystan combined had fallen behind in the fighting.

When Leander had learned the true name of Tanathos and realized he was the ancient enemy who had murdered his family, his rage had been terrifying. He'd single-handedly destroyed a force of attacking Makrasha. He'd struck them down with such ferocity that the monsters had fought each other to escape his deadly hammer.

They began slowly to warm up and feel out each other's skills. Kevlin was eager to test the new forms he'd been practicing with his swordbrothers. After the first moment, Basak attacked with more intensity. Kevlin grinned and his body tingled with energy as his focus centered on the battle. Within seconds, he and Basak were dueling without reservation.

Basak wielded the heavy hammer easily, and his blows carried tremendous power. Kevlin moved fast, flowing around the stocky fellow, focusing on deflecting the blows just wide enough to slip around them.

His world contracted as it always did when he fought with the sword until nothing existed but him and his opponent. Their weapons rang again and again as they shifted across the width of the field, each seeking an opening to touch the other. Kevlin's muscles burned with the thrill of battle and the familiar ache from the shock of absorbing Basak's hammer on his blade. The air smelled of dust and crushed grass.

Then Kevlin moved just a bit too slow. His feet slipped out of position, and he caught the full weight of a hammer strike on his sword. The blow slammed his sword back against his chest, and he felt a hot flash of pain as his own blade bit into his shoulder.

He stumbled and dropped the weapon. His wrist throbbed from being twisted back so hard.

Basak dropped his hammer and it disappeared. "Sorry, Kevlin. I thought you'd catch that one."

"So did I."

"May I?" Basak extended his hands.

"Of course."

Only when the amulet captured Basak's healing power and poured it into Kevlin did he realize his mistake. He stumbled away from Basak's hand, but it was already too late.

"What's the matter?" Basak asked.

Kevlin ignored him. Cold fear shivered down his spine as he *changed* the magic and desperately began forming his psychic shields. A rising sense of euphoria swept through him with the small amount of magic. It was quickly replaced by the desperate craving for more, and he had to fight to keep from leaping at Basak to beat more out of him.

Maybe if he fell and pretended to be hurt, Basak might try to heal him again? Kevlin dropped to his knees, but bit his lip to swallow the words bubbling in his throat that would beg for power. For a second he wavered, uncertain why he was resisting. Why was it a bad thing to have magic? He deserved it after all.

No, that wasn't right. He needed control. Kevlin panted as he fought to center his thoughts and remember who he was. His mental image of himself standing atop his fortified defenses began to waver, and laughter rippled up his throat.

For a moment he hung there, teetering on the brink, barely holding at bay the urge to give in to the craving. Kevlin growled as he re-formed his wavering defenses and held to the image as a bulwark against the Trembling Madness.

Slowly the madness subsided, and Kevlin's knotted muscles began to relax. Only then did he realize he'd clenched his fists so hard, his nails had torn through the skin.

Leander stood next to Basak, watching him. Other Stalwarts had approached, curious.

Kevlin said, "Sorry about that. It's just . . ."

He couldn't finish. The magic rebelled against him and slammed into his mental shields. The shock rattled him and he lost his balance, falling to one knee. Without his recent training, his shields never would have survived the assault. They wavered, but held, and he reinforced the shields, summoning a mental army to man the walls and repel the assaulting hordes.

The unruly magic drove against his mental defenses again and again. Each time, Kevlin's shields weakened just a little, until he barely held on. He expected Leander to step in and support him, but no help came and he couldn't spare energy to call for help.

You will obey me, he shouted in his mind at the boiling magic, and he led a counterattack to sweep the walls of his mind clear. That final wave broke and retreated.

The magic then settled into a calm trickle of power flowing through him like a second bloodstream. Where it had been tearing at his innards in its wild attempts to break free of his control, now it healed and soothed.

Kevlin reinforced his shields further and directed the magic against his injured shoulder and wrist. He lacked the knowledge to actively heal it, but the little power available to him bonded to those injured areas and the pain eased.

Kevlin blew out a breath and then climbed to his feet. He felt exhausted, as if he'd really fought a desperate battle. More Stalwarts had gathered, and Leander stood close beside him. The old man offered a steadying hand.

"Are you all right?" Leander asked.

"I think so."

"Very good." Leander added to the assembled Stalwarts, "My friends, what you witnessed here is a delicate matter, one that has my personal attention. I ask you all to keep it in confidence and trust me to deal with it."

Every Stalwart agreed, and many looked relieved. Basak said, "Kevlin, I'm sorry. I didn't mean to hurt you."

"It's all right. It's not your fault."

"Can I heal you?" Basak asked.

The pain had lessened, but not disappeared. His wrist ached, and he found a deep cut in his shoulder when he inspected it.

"I should have been wearing my armor," he said with a grimace.

He didn't want to remove the amulet, didn't want anyone else to know about it, but he also didn't want to keep bleeding. Then he had a thought. When Oris had taught him how to change the magic captured by the amulet and make it his, it had shown him something else.

"Just a minute." He closed his eyes, took a chance, and reached out with a thought to touch Oris. He was pretty sure Harafin wouldn't approve, but he was the bearer after all, wasn't he?

He connected with the stone, and its power rose through him like the rising tide. It filled him with peace and confidence.

Kevlin threw out the thought, *How do I let him heal me?*

An idea flashed into Kevlin's mind, and in a second he understood. *Thank you.*

The stone's presence withdrew. Kevlin opened his eyes and grinned. "Got it."

Leander frowned. "I think we need to talk. Soon."

"How about over lunch?" Kevlin realized he was famished.

With a tiny trickle of magic, he extended feelers of thought to the amulet and, using the knowledge just imparted from Oris, he disabled its power.

"You can heal me now."

Basak hesitated for a second before laying hands on Kevlin. Healing magic flowed through Kevlin, drove away exhaustion, and knit his wounds.

He'd never controlled magic while at the same time getting healed by another's power. How did the two powers not collide? How did Basak not sense his power? Kevlin watched Basak, but the stocky Stalwart made no outward sign that he recognized the power in Kevlin.

Basak completed his ministration a moment later. "You're sound."

"Physically at least," Kevlin said with a wry grin.

"Call the Assembly," Leander said.

"At once, my Styra." Basak headed for a small door at the base of a squat tower, and a moment later a brass bell tolled three times.

"How did you do that?" Leander asked.

"It's kind of complicated."

"We'll talk about it later, then. Are you protected now?"

Kevlin reached out with a trickle of magic and re-engaged the amulet's powers. "Yes."

"Come." Leander led the way into one of the other long buildings. The Stalwarts who were still milling about the practice yard all fell in behind.

Only then did Kevlin realize the danger of what he had done. If he had released all the magic while the amulet was disabled, he might never have been able to enable it again. Why had Oris shown him how to do it?

They descended two levels below the citadel and entered a cavernous room. Void of any furnishings, it was sheathed with wood paneling painted pearly white. Leander climbed three steps onto a platform that ran the length of one side of the room, and motioned Kevlin to follow. Basak joined them a moment later.

He clapped Kevlin on the shoulder. "That was an excellent match."

"It would've been better if I'd won."

Basak smiled. "Never going to happen."

That guaranteed he'd have to try again.

While they talked, Stalwarts filed into the room. They all dressed in simple, unbleached woolen clothing, although the styles varied. They ranged in age from youths to ancients who could barely walk. A low murmur of many whispered conversations echoed through the huge room as they awaited Leander.

When more than a hundred people filled the room, Leander held up his hand. Silence fell over the crowd. "It is good to be home."

Everyone beamed in response, every face expressing love for their leader. Kevlin was moved by the depth of their devotion to the old man.

"Dire times are upon us," Leander continued. "Times in which we will be called upon to exercise the tenets of our faith. As some of you may have already heard, we suspect a Shadeleech is lurking in the greater Tamera region."

Most of the Stalwarts looked surprised, and excited murmurs rippled through the crowd.

"We suspect it may be Tanathos, the same Shadeleech we battled recently in Hallvarr." Leander paused and his face turned hard. "The same man who murdered my family a century ago."

Silence gripped the crowd, and tears glistened in many eyes. The soft creaking of hands adjusting grips on hammers sounded loud in the silence.

"Today the hunt begins," Leander declared.

A hundred hammers rose in unison and the crowd shouted their willingness to follow.

"The time has come to take hammer to hand," he cried over the tumult, answered by another cheer.

"You must be the shield against the darkness and the hammer of justice."

Every Stalwart responded in unison, "We will."

Leander raised both hands in blessing and chanted solemnly, "May the Light grant forgiveness to those who repent." As he spoke, his hands began to glow softly with a pure, white light.

"We offer all the opportunity to choose," the crowd answered together. They raised their left arms, palms forward, hands glowing.

"May we bring mercy to those in need."

"We pledge our gift," the chant rose in strength, and with it the intensity of the light. It reflected off their faces and the walls and filled the room with pure white brilliance.

"May we bring justice to those who deserve it," Leander chanted.

"We pledge our hammers," they cried. The light grew around them until the room shone like noonday.

"May we be ever loyal to the Creator and the Light."

"We pledge our lives!" The shout reverberated through the hall and seemed to be reflected and amplified by the light.

Leander snapped his fingers and his war hammer appeared in his right hand. Hammers were raised throughout the room in unison. Kevlin alone stood as an outside witness to the amazing spectacle.

As one, every Stalwart chanted in a great swelling chorus.

"Light."

"Mercy."

"Justice."

With every word, the light swelled until Kevlin had to shield his eyes from it. Echoes reverberated through the chamber and through Kevlin's soul. The light flooded through him, rippling across his skin with tangible strength. It swept him away, lifting him with the strength of faith and determination of these people.

As he embraced the moment, he followed a sudden prompting and placed a hand on Leander's shoulder. In that instant, Leander's hammer burst into brilliant blue fire, and magic poured into Kevlin.

The amulet captured it, and he *changed* it. Then he reached out with his mind and connected with the essence of Oris. It rose to occupy a tiny corner of his mind, and power surged through him with the first pulse of the rhythm of life.

A vast strength filled him, so intense it nearly lifted him from his feet. It filled his soul with peace, and colored his vision with a light blue haze.

Every Stalwart glowed, surrounded by the light of their powers. Kevlin stared in wonder at the pulsing living power within each Stalwart.

They were glorious.

So lost was he in the vision that he hardly noticed as he drew his own sword and held it high. The echoes from the chant were dying down, and the light of their extended hands dimmed as they lowered them. The movement of his sword drew every eye as he raised it high.

With his mind floating in Oris's power, he released a flow of energy into his sword and whispered a single word.

"Fire."

Blue flames pulsed into existence along the blade of his sword in a mirror image of the fire still burning around Leander's hammer.

Kevlin spoke into the silence, words that came unbidden to his mind. "The time of the choosing is at hand. The inner vessel must be purged or none will withstand the coming conflict."

Leander shouted, "Time to cleanse the inner vessel!"

The gathered Stalwarts raised their hammers again and shouted, "Cleanse the inner vessel."

It is well. The thought drifted through Kevlin's mind softly, and yet so powerful that it nearly drove him to his knees.

He dropped his sword arm and the flames winked out. Oris faded from his mind. Leander released his hammer and it vanished. The assembled Stalwarts lowered their hammers and the spell that had wrapped them all faded to memory.

The focused unity of the room dissolved, and Stalwarts chatted among themselves. Kevlin caught snatches of conversation. Many discussed their desire to help Leander bring his family's murderer to justice. Others cast curious looks at Kevlin and discussed his surprise participation in the assembly.

Apparently it was highly unusual for someone not of their order to attend, let alone speak. Many times, he heard the phrase, "Cleanse the inner vessel."

Although he had said it first and it had felt so right at the time, he wondered now what it meant. He doubted it was a call for everyone to volunteer for extra duties in the kitchens.

"That was unexpected," Leander said with a smile.

"I'm sorry. I don't know what got into me."

"It's all right, my friend," Leander said. "Unexpected, yes, but the more I think on it, the more I realize it was necessary."

As the gathered Stalwarts drifted from the assembly hall. Leander added, "I've been pondering this very point for days. I'm convinced you were right."

He stared across the room and his voice grew deadly serious. "A time of cleansing is indeed upon us."

24

THE PRIVILEGED FEW

Kevlin stepped into the immense open space under the Great Dome and paused again to stare. After leaving the citadel, he'd wandered the inner city, exploring while mulling over the mission to track down the hidden enemy.

The problem was, they didn't know who the enemy was. The palace complex was so vast, the lack of direction left him feeling uneasy and irritable. Worse, Leander had made him drive away all his magic before he left the citadel.

Now he stepped out of the flow of foot traffic and paused beside a thirty-foot mural. The beautiful painting depicted the cliffs of Tamera from the sea, with the Great Dome shining high above everything else. He wasn't sure why the artist felt they could enhance the awe-inspiring view from the inside of the Great Dome with a painting of a view from miles away.

Kevlin scanned the railed walkways and balconies that ringed the lower half of the dome. He'd have to figure out how to get up there. The view would be magnificent. If he dropped a watermelon from such a height, he could probably cover half the room with fruit. Maybe he could convince Drystan to try it.

Above the highest level of balconies, a series of wide, stained-glass windows ringed the dome. Colored light streamed in through the western windows. Higher still, the dome reared in unbroken glory to a circular window set in the very top. It looked tiny, but probably spanned twenty paces. The vertical ribs that formed the skeleton of the dome were cleverly incorporated into gigantic murals painted across the inside of the dome.

Kevlin stared until his neck started to hurt. He was surprised no entrepreneurial official had brought out a dozen couches for rent to make the viewing easier. Then again, bureaucrats and imagination didn't usually go together.

The murals varied so much in style and content that for the first time he wished he knew something about painting. Two murals alone, set across from each other on the north and south ends of the dome, consumed a tenth of all of the painted space. They both depicted pivotal battle scenes from the empire's history.

The one on the north showed in spectacular detail the five day battle that drove the Sigrun and their armies out of the far western borderlands in the early days of the empire. It detailed the shattering of those lands, complete with exploding mountains and gaping fissures.

The southern mural depicted the decisive battle in the last great war when the Grakonian armies were overrun, led by the Six. It included a giant image of Antigonus wielding Oris, with ribbons of blue fire connecting him to the Six.

Flanking the massive battle murals were paintings done in soft colors and vague images, a style popular in the last century. Kevlin found little value in the murals even though they most likely contained some sort of symbolic meaning. He was too much of a realist.

Why paint a fuzzy woman? If she was as good looking as the artist suggested, who wouldn't want to see more detail? If she was ugly, well he could understand it then. He wondered if the entire style had arisen because one influential artist hadn't wanted to offend his wife.

The rest of the dome was covered with dozens of different scenes in as many styles, including various bearers of the Six. There were paintings of the gods, although they featured far less than Kevlin would have expected.

When his neck cramped from looking up so long, he scanned the other awed dome-gazers like himself. Then he turned his gaze to the sea of humanity flowing past.

How could they ferret out the traitors? It was unlikely that Tanathos was hidden in the inner city. Harafin would find him. If Tanathos had indeed penetrated the shield matrix, he'd try again. The key was identifying the traitors who helped him.

Kevlin had no idea where to start. The palace was a city unto itself. The entire greater palace complex was the heart of the city and the seat of power and commerce. Many thousands of people came there every day, plus the untold numbers who lived in the vast complex.

Just standing in the dome, he could never identify everyone walking past. The many uniformed guards declared a strong military presence, including soldiers dressed in the uniforms of every kingdom. Others wore the green and gold of the palace guard. Scores of others palace servants and staffers hurried by, dressed in similar colors. He even saw a few dressed in the crimson and white of the emperor's personal guard.

A thousand conversations filled the huge open space with a constant low buzz. Kevlin caught words spoken in every dialect of the empire. Somehow the air remained fresh despite the sea of humanity passing through on their innumerable errands.

Nobility frequented the space far more often than Kevlin had expected. The walked with heads high, decked out in all their finery and trailed by aides and guards.

Crowds of merchants moved among them, dressed richly and wearing flat-brimmed hats in their guild colors. Hundreds of other people not so easily identifiable crowded past, dressed in wildly different garb, drawn to the capital for purposes as diverse as they appeared. Any one of them could be a secret enemy, waiting for an opportunity to strike from their positions of anonymity.

As he pondered the problem, Kevlin rejoined the flowing crowds that crossed the wide expanse of the dome's floor like living rivers. He paused beside a large stone map that rose on a pedestal standing in the illusory Tamerlane Sea covering the floor, at the spot that should be the island of Il'Marinen, the Sentinel capital.

The map detailed the entire inner-city complex. Inlaid glass depicted various palaces in different colors, making it easier to see how everything was organized.

He studied it for several minutes, memorizing as much of the city layout as possible. A bronze plaque next to the map explained the dome's history. The massive structure was one of the first aboveground buildings raised after the underground complex was completed. It took only five years to construct, due to focused efforts by dozens of Sentinels who assisted with the work.

Even though it had been raised in large part through magic, it still stood as an engineering marvel. The wonderful floor mural with the three-dimensional effect had been added for the empire's centennial celebration. Surprisingly, the painting of the floor used no magic.

It had been completed in eighteen months by the master painter, Tahleiy. Even more surprising, Tahleiy was a Nedikan captive who spent ten years of indentured servitude working in the dome. He not only oversaw painting of the floor, but also painted many of the ceiling murals.

The painting of the ceiling had been an ongoing effort since the dome was first built, and the last one had been completed only the night before the empire's two hundred year celebration.

Generations of artists had worked on the structure. The vast scope of the work left Kevlin feeling small.

Several green-and-gold clad officials answered visitors' questions from a nearby booth. The vast array of imperial departments and kingdom-specific agencies amazed Kevlin. He expected to see the various military departments, as well as commerce and agriculture. Other departments included waste management, palace administration, and infrastructure. But he'd never considered there might be a department for the Collection and Removal of Excrement from the city, known as CARE.

The sheer volume of information made Kevlin impatient to move on. He rarely thought this hard for this long. If he kept it up, he'd risk suffering a brain cramp.

He plotted a course to the department of Imperial Resourcing, where he could pick up his new uniform. He'd join the crowds following the larger-than-scale imperial highway network on the floor map. The ocean waves might be fake, but why risk stumbling when he could walk on smooth roads?

"Kevlin!"

Surprised, he turned to find Marjani, the young woman who had led him to the council room earlier.

"Hello, Marjani."

She curtsied with a smile. "My Lord Kevlin, you're not an easy man to find."

"You're lucky you found me. I was just getting ready to get lost again."

"Please find yourself by the fourth afternoon bell," she said. "Ambassador Damarist has asked that you report to the Hallvarr Palace."

"That's not for a couple hours."

"I wasn't sure how long it would take to find you." She cocked her head to one side. "I'd be happy to give you a tour, unless your heart is set on getting lost."

"I'd love a tour. I can get lost any time."

Marjani led him back outside. Now that the sun had passed its zenith and begun slipping toward the western horizon behind the Great Dome, some of the inner palace already lay under a blanket of shadow. The water in the cascading fountain of the central garden glowed with brilliant white light, each droplet like a tiny flame.

He was tempted to ask Marjani if she knew how to find Indira. Strolling through that twilight garden together might just be enough to smooth over his many blunders.

"When do the fountains start glowing?" he asked instead.

Marjani pointed out two other fountains set in front of distant palaces that hadn't started glowing yet. "Each fountain is lit when they fall into shadow."

"Makes sense." He'd have to explore the different lights and ask Adalia what Indira's favorite color was. He wasn't sure what the patron color for card hustlers was.

Marjani led him through the central garden, close to the fountain so he could watch the water tumbling deep into the earth to the pool at the bottom. As he considered how much power it would take to light the water like that, he felt the madness stirring to life.

"Lord Kevlin, it's this way," Marjani said as he started moving toward the stairs to the bottom.

"I told you not to call me that," Kevlin snapped.

"I'm sorry." She curtsied, her expression hurt. He realized what he'd done, and forced control.

"No, I'm the one who's sorry." He ran a hand through his hair and grimaced. "Sometimes . . . I do stupid things."

"You don't have to apologize to me, Kevlin."

"Yes, I do. You've shown kindness to me. I don't care who you are or who you think I am, I can't repay you with cruelty."

"Apology accepted." She gave him a real smile, and the sparkle returned to her eyes.

Why hadn't it been this easy to apologize to Indira?

They crossed the garden and followed the Silver Spoke between the Tamarr and Freyarr palaces. The afternoon sun was warm, but a cool sea breeze added a chill to the air. People packed the main thoroughfare and hurried to complete their business before the sun set.

Marjani led Kevlin onto a side street, along the city side of several of the palaces and past countless support structures. They paused at an open-sided restaurant where Kevlin purchased sweetbreads and chilled juice concoctions from Freyarr for them.

As they continued their tour of the inner city and wound their way toward the inner city wall, Marjani pointed out a grand, three-story building ringed by a wide, covered porch. A crowd of richly dressed nobles packed the porch and thronged the open door. A grinning pair of Sentinels with wide, green stripes marking their sleeves and collars made a token effort to urge restraint on the crowd.

A gilded sign hung above the porch read, "Kereskedo Custom Talismans."

"What's a Kereskedo?" Kevlin asked.

"They're the fastest growing business in the palace. Everyone wants their merchandise." Her voice took on a wistful tone as she stared at the crowd jostling to get into the shop. "They only market to nobility. I've never been allowed inside."

"What's got that crowd so worked up?"

Marjani shrugged. "They probably announced a new product release. Each is more amazing than the last, and they've become status symbols in the upper classes. There are only a limited supply of each product, so demand is huge."

It warmed his heart to see the normally puffed-up nobility acting like lesser people when shopping.

"The Kedos refuse to sell to servants," Marjani explained. "They insist the actual user of the products be present."

"Who are the Kedos anyway?"

Marjani pointed toward the two Sentinels flanking the doorway. "They are."

"Sentinels?"

"That's what makes it so wonderful."

Kevlin had assumed the Kedos sold perfumes or some other rare, useless item only nobility would want. He'd never heard of Sentinels acting as merchants. The very thought made him shudder. Whatever they sold, there would be no way honest, non-actinopathic merchants could compete fairly.

"What do they sell?"

"Magically-imbued items," Marjani gushed.

"Like what?"

"All sorts of things!"

She explained that the group of Sentinels explored ways to imbue common items with a specific magical property. Their first commercial product had been a small lamp that emitted a powerful light. It could illuminate a room with bright, even light for up to ten hours. Unfortunately it worked only once, so nobles only brought them out for important events. One more way to impress each other with how much they spent.

The Kedos had tried a few more household items, but the single-use limitation proved an insurmountable barrier. Then they made the decision that changed everything by turning their focus to personal defense. They produced a vest that could emit a blast of air strong enough to topple anyone within half a dozen paces. It was marketed as a defense against muggers or assassins.

The product had become an instant sensation.

"Every noble house insisted on purchasing one," Marjani said. "The Kedos scrambled to fill the orders, but they kept rolling in despite an obscene climb in prices." She glanced back at the shop as they moved farther down the street. "Since then, they've produced many more products, each more amazing than the last, and each more expensive."

Kevlin considered the information as they toured more of the inner city. They even climbed the high inner-city wall and enjoyed spectacular views of the upper city. Rich mansions were built into the gentle slope between the plateau of the inner city and the wide plain of greater Tamera.

After another hour exploring the inner city, Marjani led him back toward the Hallvarr Palace. They once more passed the Kereskedo shop, which now stood all but deserted.

"They must have sold out of the new product already," Marjani commented.

Kevlin grinned. "For once, having a title might be useful. Let's go take a look."

Marjani eagerly agreed, and Kevlin led the way inside. A huge room took up the entire first floor of the building. It was richly appointed in dark woods and shining brass fixtures. Crystal cases were placed strategically around the room displaying the Kedo wares.

A Sentinel with the green Kereskedo ribbons on sleeves and collar approached. He was a plain-looking man with an average build. His robes were made of fine silk, and several opulent rings flashed on his fingers.

His smile faded as Kevlin's rather charred and dirty clothing registered. "I am sorry," he said brusquely, "but servants are not allowed in this establishment."

"My lord Kevlin," Marjani said with unusual gravity. "Do you wish to file a formal complaint against this insolent merchant?"

The Sentinel, who had already begun to turn from them, spun back around, his eyes wide. He made a tiny bow. "Lord Kevlin, the King's Avenger?"

Kevlin decided to play the part, even though he still hated to think of Sentinels competing as merchants. Having grown up in a struggling merchant family, the thought of Sentinels stealing business angered him.

Besides, this self-important man was breaking a tradition older than the empire. Sentinels were to serve and protect against the Grakonians, and share their knowledge with the Six Kingdoms. In return, their needs were all provided for.

He assumed an indignant expression. "Who did you think I was?" He moved toward the exit.

The Sentinel scooted around Kevlin and wrung his hands together. "Please, my lord. Don't be so hasty. You'll have to forgive me, but we've had an exceptionally busy day. Now that I know you, you're exactly what I should have expected."

Kevlin decided to let the comment slide. "I had been interested in considering your products, but it sounds like you're sold out."

"Only our most recent model," the Sentinel corrected. "Allow me to introduce myself. I am Sentinel Nerys, head of the Kereskedo and owner of this establishment." He waved his arm to take in the display cases. "Since this is your first time here, please let me introduce our products to you."

Kevlin hesitated before nodding. As the man directed them to the nearest display cabinet, Kevlin shared an amused look with Marjani.

Sentinel Nerys gave them a detailed tour of the shop, explaining each of the items. Kevlin struggled to conceal his growing amazement. From the first air-blast vest, the Kedos had enhanced their products dramatically. Richly appointed vests, petticoats and jackets were the most popular items, and Nerys insisted they accepted custom orders. Nobility could drop off a favorite article and the Kedos would imbue it with the purchased enchantment.

Enchantments varied widely. They viewed brightly glowing hats, then gloves containing focused energy allowing the wearer to punch through locked doors. They fingered silk shirts pitched as better protection than full plate armor.

One entire rack featured ornately carved wooden staves and rods that could shoot everything from blasts of fire to ropes that would tie up targets on their own. Each item was designed so that a specific action would trigger the one-time enchantment, like buttons or cords. Others, like the staves, had a section that could be twisted or pressed.

Marjani pointed at a simple wooden box sitting on a corner shelf. "What does that do?"

"Nothing, yet, my girl," Nerys said. "It's an experimental model for multi-projectile distribution. Only one of its kind. Not yet available for sale."

He directed them to a large glass case in the center of the room. It contained personal magical shields, the most popular items. In addition to manual triggers like the other enchantments, these also included an automatic trigger if the article of clothing imbued with the power was cut or struck very hard.

"We call it the Ever-Vigilant Bodyguard," Nerys declared. "It will protect against even the unseen assassins."

The wonder of it drove away Kevlin's earlier dislike of the merchant. The man was right, no one else in the world could offer such products. Kevlin was still not sure if it was right to market such things, but he began to share the enthusiasm of the store's other clients.

Marjani, her eyes glowing with excitement said, "This must be extremely popular."

"Oh, yes, young lady. Rumors of secret assassins and distant conflict have driven up sales fifty percent."

He then pointed to a full-length leather jacket cut in a popular style. "And this, my Lord Kevlin, is our latest model, the item that sparked the run on the store earlier today." He added with great pride, "We sold out in less than four hours, and already have a waiting list of over one hundred orders."

"What is it?" Marjani asked excitedly.

"We call it the Personal Army."

Nerys explained that the jacket contained an eight-hour shield enchantment that would trigger automatically at need. He then pointed to sets of four buttons lining both cuffs. Each button triggered additional enchantments, customizable by the buyer, from magical ropes to blasts of fire, to rapid-fire arrows.

Kevlin touched the garment, awed by the potential. This could change the world. If their assault force in Hallvarr had been equipped with these jackets, they could have overrun the Grakonian forces while suffering only a fraction of their losses.

He gripped Sentinel Nerys' hand. "Amazing!"

Nerys grinned. "Thank you, my Lord Kevlin. Your endorsement means a great deal."

"You could revolutionize how we approach warfare," Kevlin said.

Nerys grinned. "Imagine, my lord, you could go into battle with power to rival the Shadeleeches, or even the Six. You would stand apart from all other men."

Kevlin frowned. "Why not outfit an entire army with these?"

Nerys laughed. "You jest, my lord."

"No, I'm completely serious."

"You don't understand. Common soldiers could never afford a jacket like this."

"Well, if you could sell so many, I'm sure you could lower the prices and still make a wonderful profit."

"That's not the point," Nerys said, his tone offended. "These wares are intended for the privileged few, the nobility, those worthy of additional protection."

"The worthy few?" Kevlin repeated slowly, each word tasting like rotten meat.

"Of course," Nerys said, not noticing his reaction. "If anyone could access the powers of Sentinels, it would lessen the wonder of it. Our powers would become . . . common."

"It doesn't matter that you could save lives?" Kevlin asked.

Sentinel Nerys shrugged. "If we did all that, there would be no need for the vaunted Kestrels or the other Sentinels to protect everyone, would there?"

"I suppose not," Kevlin said. "Thank you for explaining things so clearly."

He headed for the door, with Sentinel Nerys following in his wake. At first the Sentinel merchant asked which item he wished to order, then pleaded for an order. As Kevlin was about to reach the door, he begged for an endorsement in exchange for a free gift.

Kelvin paused in the doorway. "Why do you want my endorsement so badly?"

"You're the King's Avenger," Nerys exclaimed. "The most famous man in the empire at the moment. Think of the prestige your endorsement would mean."

Kevlin resisted the urge to grab the man and shake him by the collar. "Not today."

As he led Marjani down the steps, Nerys called after him, "I look forward to speaking with you again. Feel free to visit any time, or stop by our two new locations in the upper city and the central marketplace."

The man might be a Sentinel, but he'd embraced all that Kevlin hated about the merchant class. He sullied all Sentinels by association. The wonder of what the Kedos had accomplished only heightened his frustration.

Marjani trotted to keep up with him, her brown curls bouncing with every step. "That was amazing. Thank you so much."

Kevlin reined in his anger and tried to focus on the wonder of the inventions. "I'm glad you enjoyed it."

"Wouldn't it be great to own one of those?"

Kevlin shrugged. "I doubt we'll ever see them again."

25

THE JOYS OF POLITICS

T he Hallvarr Palace was situated just south of the Donarr castle, flanking the Iron Spoke. As Kevlin and Marjani approached the huge rectangular stone structure, Kevlin glanced up at the spherical observatory visible on the roof. "I'd like to see that up close."

"Later, perhaps."

Kevlin turned to find Harafin approaching.

The old Sentinel said, "I hope you don't mind, but I will join you in your visit to the ambassador."

"Be my guest."

"Apparently the good ambassador's schedule is extremely booked. I received word he could not see me for several days."

"That's strange," Kevlin said. "He summoned me, but I have no idea what he wants to talk about. You'd think he'd have given you this time."

Harafin thanked Marjani for finding Kevlin, pressed a coin into her hand, and dismissed her.

She gave Kevlin a deep curtsy. "I had a great time. I hope you did too."

"Very much, thanks." With all the strife and intrigue he'd been dealing with, it was nice to spend time with a genuinely nice person.

Harafin led the way into the Hallvarr Palace and up to the third floor. He swept through a set of wide double doors and waved aside an attendant who rose to greet him.

"I will see the ambassador now." Harafin pushed open the thick, mahogany door on the far side of the room.

Kevlin followed Harafin into a large study lined with bookshelves. A fireplace with a small fire and a wide mantel took up most of the wall to the left. Several comfortable chairs sat facing the fireplace. Three padded wooden chairs faced a long but simple wooden desk across the room. A window behind the desk looked south toward the Einarri palace park.

Ambassador Damarist stood beside his desk in a heated conversation with a young, dark-haired staffer. The ambassador was a tall man whose rich clothing hung a little loose on his gaunt frame. His brown hair was a bit disheveled, and his eyes a little wild.

When the door opened he shouted, "I told you I'm not to be disturbed."

When he recognized Harafin, he cringed back in surprise. "Oh, Master Harafin. I'm deeply sorry." He waved away the young man, who looked to be about sixteen. The youth slipped out of the room and closed the door behind him.

"Hello, Borehl," Harafin said in a friendly tone. "I hope you don't mind, but Kevlin graciously offered to share his allotted time with me. There are a few things we need to discuss."

The ambassador skirted Harafin and took Kevlin's hand in both of his. "Ah, my Lord Kevlin. So good of you to come." His long-fingered hands were thin, and trembled against Kevlin's.

He motioned them to take seats and retreated around his desk to his overstuffed leather chair. He pulled a silk handkerchief from a pocket and dabbed at his face.

"I have a few questions about recent events in Hallvarr," Harafin said. "Particularly concerning the death of your brother, the king, and his connection with the Blade Stalwart, Dhanjal."

Ambassador Damarist sighed. "My poor brother. What a tragedy. That's why I summoned you today, Sir Kevlin, to thank you for avenging him."

"I'm glad I was able to help."

"You have our condolences," Harafin said. "What can you tell me about the king's relationship with Dhanjal?"

"I'm afraid I've been away from Diodor far too long." The ambassador picked at a rolled parchment on his desk.

"Prince Lievin said you were in regular contact with King Leszek. Surely he would tell you should he choose to contract with a Blade Stalwart."

Ambassador Damarist looked up finally. "These questions, Master Harafin, lead to dangerous territory. Are you sure you wish to tread there?"

"I believe events in Hallvarr are tied to the attack on the emperor. Tell me what you know."

"I doubt you'll find the answers you seek." He paused, his expression grave. "I must ask you to hold what I tell you here in the strictest confidence."

"I will hear what you have to say before I make any promises, but know that I will not treat your words lightly."

"My brother suffered from a rare malady of the mind," the ambassador said. "In recent years it manifested itself through increasing paranoia."

Harafin frowned. "I have heard of no such sickness."

Ambassador Damarist managed a weak smile. "Then it appears our efforts to conceal his condition were successful."

"Why did you not tell me? We could have helped."

"I don't think so. Sentinel Hathor was in my brother's counsel, and his healing attempts proved unsuccessful. The best he managed was to slow the progression of the sickness."

"Hathor did not speak of this to me," Harafin said.

"My brother made him swear on penalty of death that he would not. You see, he was convinced unknown enemies were plotting to kill him. That's why he had so many forces armed and ready to march. How else could he have rushed off to battle with so little preparation?"

Harafin sat back in his chair, his face unreadable. "Tell me about the Blade Stalwart."

Ambassador Damarist shrugged. "I learned that Dhanjal was available, and I referred him to my brother. I had hoped the services of such a mighty warrior would ease my brother's mind."

"So you hired Dhanjal?" Kevlin asked.

"No. I informed my brother that he was available."

"How did you find out about Dhanjal?" Harafin asked.

"Through Ambassador Janezeko, of course."

Harafin looked surprised. "Ambassador Janezeko?"

"Yes. He helped set up the contract transfer."

"What was he doing with a Blade Stalwart?"

"I have no idea. I'm afraid you'll have to ask him."

Kevlin wasn't surprised the interview was providing nothing but a referral to someone else. The higher one reached in the chain of command, the more adept they became at passing the latrine shovel to someone else.

Could the king really have been going insane? That shifted his memories of the recent conflict, casting shadows where before things had seemed clear.

Harafin said, "I find it more than a little disturbing that neither you nor Braden informed the council of your involvement with this Blade Stalwart."

"You must understand my position," Ambassador Damaris said. "I do not defy the emperor's wishes lightly, but had I informed him, he would have wanted to know why my brother felt it necessary to contract with Dhanjal. That might have led to exposing my brother's condition."

"That would have been for the best. Thousands of lives might have been saved."

"I've thought of that," the ambassador snapped. He ran a hand through his already-disheveled hair. "But how could I have known Dhanjal would betray my country? No Blade Stalwart has ever reneged on a contract. At the time, the benefits outweighed the risks."

"I can understand your position," Harafin said. "But that does not excuse you for taking the wrong course."

"Don't pretend to be so morally superior, Harafin. If word spread that my brother was mad, he'd have been de-throned."

"His son is more than capable."

"That's not the point. It would have led to chaos. Doubts about Lievin's capacity would have been raised. It would have put the kingdom at risk."

"Perhaps."

"I have to watch out for my kingdom. The council certainly wouldn't help."

"We would have offered aid."

Ambassador Damarist snorted. "You might have wanted to, but don't pretend to think the council would have acted. We did nothing to help Donarr, even when it was on the verge of annihilation."

The two began arguing about council policies and decisions. Kevlin listened to the exchange with growing amazement. He hadn't realized the ruling council was so fractured.

He had lived the conflict in Donarr and knew how close the Raghneidur had come to destroying the kingdom with the help of the traitorous General Stigandr. Kevlin had been one of the general's legion commanders, and had nearly died when he discovered the plot. He'd helped alert the kingdom, which had saved it from destruction, but he'd lost his career and the woman he had loved.

Of course, trying to murder him had been an effective way to indicate she wanted to end that relationship.

He'd heard from Drystan about the ongoing Nedikan incursions into Einarr, but hadn't realized they also raided Freyarr. As a mercenary, he'd been involved in many of the minor conflicts scattered throughout the empire over the past ten years, but he'd still believed the Six Kingdoms enjoyed overall peace.

The half century since the last great war was touted as a time of perpetual peace. That claim was looking more and more tattered. Politicians always tried to paint situations in the most favorable light for themselves, so he felt more disappointed than surprised.

With open warfare looming with an expected Grakonia invasion next year, the empire was teetering on the brink of difficult times.

"Enough," Harafin said finally. "Now is not the time to second-guess every decision the council has made. You know my position and counsel has always been to help."

"I know, but I cannot ignore the fact that your counsel is regularly ignored. I did what I did out of patriotism to my kingdom, which will always trump loyalty to the empire."

Harafin stood, his expression grave. "Be careful who you say that to, Borehl. You're not in your kingdom."

"Are you threatening me?" Ambassador Damarist also rose to his feet.

Harafin shook his head. "Just a warning. Difficult times lay ahead and loyalties will be tested to the limits."

"I know where my loyalties lie, and don't tell me about difficult times. My brother was murdered on the field of battle."

"I'm afraid what your country experienced is just the beginning."

"Then don't be surprised when I place our needs above anything else."

They took their leave, and as they descended the stairs from the palace to the central courtyard, Harafin said, "That was unexpected."

Harafin's understatements drove Kevlin more than a little crazy sometimes.

"What do you think?" Harafin asked.

"I'm not really sure. I can't tell if he's lying about King Leszek or not. I didn't spend enough time with the king."

"I will most assuredly speak with Ambassador Janezeko."

"Did we learn anything useful in there?" Kevlin asked.

"Perhaps." Harafin led the way toward the Sentinel Tower. "But here in the inner city, truth can be a fickle thing. Let us hope we can find it before time runs out."

26

DEATH OF A MUFFIN

In Harafin's quarters at the top of the Sentinel Tower, they ate a late lunch with Leander. An entire table of food had been prepared for them, so Kevlin dug in with a will and stuffed himself.

As they ate, the two old men asked him to recount his last visitation from Akillik.

"He's such a meddler," Harafin scowled when Kevlin finished. "No doubt, He'd love nothing more than to damage that amulet of yours, or cause it to be stolen."

"Do you think He will?" Kevlin asked, gripping it under his shirt. What would he do if he lost the amulet?

"Don't play His games," Leander said. "Don't give Him the chance to try."

"You mean He won't just decide to do it?"

"Not unless he feels driven to intervene," said Harafin. "His greatest power stems from His Wheel, so He plays His own game with it all the time. People know Him as the god of Luck. He would risk much by breaking His own rules and making a decision without basing it on chance."

"He's trying to goad you into playing the game for Him," added Leander. "And preparing worst-case scenarios for you when you do play."

"What if the Wheel spins in my favor?"

"That's the risk He takes," Harafin said. "But if you fall into His trap and play His game, eventually it will spin against you."

"That would be very bad," Leander said solemnly.

"How do I get Him to leave me alone?" Kevlin asked. He'd been stalked by Savas in Hallvarr. The god of War had attempted to possess his soul. Only by a razor's edge, and the mystic connection with his swordbrothers had he broken free. He wished the gods would just leave him alone.

"It is no simple thing to thwart a god," Harafin said. "Focus on the task at hand. Hopefully Akillik will find something else to amuse himself."

"That almost scares me more," Leander said. "At least right now we know what he's focused on."

"Exercise caution," Harafin urged Kevlin. "Now, it is time to continue your training."

Kevlin felt a rush of exhilaration with the anticipation of getting magic. He scooted to the edge of his chair, hands gripping his legs to suppress the urge to grab Harafin to make the transfer easier.

He'd tasted magic earlier today, so managed to restrain the urge. When Harafin tossed a small, glowing ball of magic at him, he caught it with forced calm.

As soon as the magic poured into him from the amulet, he raised reinforced battlements around his mind. As expected, the magic bucked against his control and hordes of imaginary Makrasha assaulted his defenses.

Kevlin grabbed his head and clenched his eyes shut as he marshaled his defensive forces and threw his will into defending his mind. Whispers of thoughts floated up from the assaulting force.

Why restrain the power when so much could be done with it?

Why hadn't he thought of that before? Harafin said he needed more magic to blanket the city with the shield matrix and locate Tanathos. Kevlin had all the magic he needed.

He could summon power from Oris, more power than any Sentinel. At the keep, he had defeated Wayra, melted the keep to the ground. Not even Harafin could do that.

Kevlin's resolve weakened and the ravening hordes gained a foothold on the walls of his mind. The thought of again wielding so much power, of saving the city like he had saved Il'Aicharen, appealed to the part of him that liked being hailed a hero.

Sweat beaded his brow as he struggled to decide. He could do so much good. All he had to do was dare to wield that power again.

Then the image of the keep collapsing into a pile of burning rubble rose in his mind. Ceren had nearly died when he destroyed the tower. How many would die if he chose to surrender to these temptations now?

It would be worth it, the thought came. *Sacrifice is necessary to achieve a greater good.*

Everything crystallized with that thought. Kevlin rallied his will and drove the insidious temptations away. How many innocents might he destroy if he embraced the temptation to hunt Tanathos at any cost?

He could never live with such destruction on his hands.

With his will fixed and immovable, the unruly magic settled, one more beaten into submission. He hoped it tired of fighting him before his will broke.

"Are you all right?" Harafin asked.

"Of course I'm not all right," Kevlin snapped. "Why do we keep pretending otherwise? Have you considered what'll happen if I slip?"

"Don't," Harafin commanded.

The destruction at Il'Aicharen had been contained because he'd had a focused target. Here in the heavily populated city, there'd be no limit to the destruction he could cause.

Harafin must have a plan to deal with that eventuality. The old Sentinel always thought ahead, and he never hesitated.

His last word was probably as much a warning as it was encouragement. Kevlin doubted he'd survive if Harafin had to step in during another *Tai Pari*.

Of course, if the prophecy Ah'Shan had mentioned was real, Harafin might already be planning to sacrifice Kevlin. He wondered how far he could get if he made a break for the door and just kept running.

"I think you need to take Oris and find its real bearer."

"Think of what you're saying," Leander said.

"I am."

If Oris chose another, Kevlin's life would be forfeit. He didn't want to die, but he was starting to see there might not be any good way out. Better to end things on his own terms, and not as a blood sacrifice or a mass murderer.

"You know I cannot take it," Harafin said. "You were chosen. The situation is difficult, and part of me wishes it were otherwise, but you are chosen and we must face that fact."

"How can you be so certain?" Kevlin wished he shared Harafin's faith.

"How can you not be? You know it chose you."

"Tell me what convinced you I was the right choice." It had felt right at the time, but now Kevlin doubted the accuracy of his memory. More and more, the situation seemed a terrible farce.

Harafin leaned back in his chair. "As I mentioned on the *Ceara*, the idea that you might be the prophesied catalyst came as a shock. I have studied for two centuries the clues and signs concerning these days. Against all odds, they began to manifest through you. I will admit it was not easy to consider that we might have mis-read the prophecy."

"What clues?"

"We should continue your lesson."

"I need to know," Kevlin pleaded. "I'm not a Sentinel, and if I continue down this road, at best I might die without taking a lot of innocent people with me. I need to know why you're so sure, because people I care about are at risk because of me."

"He has a point," Leander said.

"Very well." Harafin paced to the window. "Several things you said echoed passages of the prophecy too closely to be ignored."

"Like what?"

"For example, on the way to the hidden fort you said 'I was born upon the waters of the sea, was forged into a man in the heat of battle, and I've shed blood in every kingdom of the empire'."

"How can you remember that?" Kevlin only remembered because of the strange mood that had settled over him that day.

"Those words echoed one of Antigonus' favorite passages of the catalyst prophecy, the passage he was trying to fulfill by embarking on the journey where you met him."

If only Antigonus had thought that one out longer.

"The prophecy states, *O Sea, rejoice! Thou shalt lift the Catalyst in thy waves. An offering of blood shall be received by the lands of thy companions, and all shall lay claim to thee. Battle shall be thy headmaster and form thee in his unyielding crucible.*"

"That's a little thin," Kevlin said.

"Actually, it's surprisingly close," Leander interjected. "You just have to read past all the flowery language."

"It was close enough that I made the connection," Harafin said. "You made other comments on our journey that echoed other passages, but I'll review only the strongest clue."

"Tell me," Kevlin urged.

"Your swordbrothers."

"Why them?" It was unusual to form a triple swordbrother bond, but now unknown.

"You remember my concern when I saw you used Bajaran's cursed dagger in the swordbrother ceremony?"

"Aye." It was a miracle they hadn't died. That blade, which Kevlin wore in the hidden sheath at the base of his neck, could kill in seconds. It had weakened even Antigonus, leaving him defenseless against Tanathos. Bajaran had died in the forests of Hallvarr, but his blade had found its mark.

Yet, when Kevlin had used that blade in the swordbrother ceremony, it hadn't destroyed them. He had felt something from Oris, and a strange tingling, but nothing more.

Harafin said, "The prophecy speaks of you, of the Three."

"That's the whole Strength and Cunning thing, right?"

"Exactly. The section in question reads as follows: *Look for the Catalyst at the time of the Choices, for a Choice shall deliver unto thee the blood of Strength, and another the blood of Cunning. Through the miracle of life over death shalt the union be created: the One with Strength and with Cunning. Three shall be One, and without the Three, the One shall fall.*

"How could you possibly read anything useful in that gibberish?"

Harafin smiled. "Practice."

"So, how does this relate to Jerrik and Drystan?"

"Not only is such a triple oath of swordbrothers unusual, but there is the reference to blood."

That part was easy. They had to cut their hands to mingle their bloodlines.

"The fact that your blade did not kill you is the 'miracle of life over death'. Did you never wonder how you gained the ability to draw upon their strength and cunning?"

"How did you know about that?" They hadn't discussed it in detail, but Kevlin had managed to share thoughts with his brothers a couple of times. Their strength and discipline had helped him defy Savas.

"I spoke with Jerrik about it."

"He didn't mention that."

"I asked him not to."

"Why?" What other secrets was Harafin holding from him? Who else in the company was he counseling with about Kevlin and not telling?

He'd asked Kevlin to keep secret the fact that he was Oris's new bearer. It shouldn't surprise him that the old man would do the same with others. It just seemed such a waste. Why not get things out in the open?

"I have my reasons. Suffice it to say that the connection you enjoy with your brothers is unique among non-actinopathic. It provides strong evidence that you are, in fact, the Catalyst we sought."

"Why can't prophecies be more specific? Wouldn't it have been simpler if it just said, Kevlin and his swordbrothers are the Three?"

"I've sometimes wished the same thing," Leander admitted.

"They can be cryptic, and require study, ideally by one who also holds the gift of prophecy," Harafin said. "But think about it. If the enemy, who wishes to see the prophecy fail, knew your name, how long would you be safe?"

Harafin had a point. Then again the Sigrun, speaking through the mouth of the possessed Shadeleech, Merab, had told Kevlin he was marked. They did know his name.

What if they had found him before Harafin did? That was a chain of thoughts that would lead to hiding in a closet.

"It proves frustrating at times, but it is a necessary complication," Harafin added. "Now, back to your training."

Kevlin wanted to explore the prophecy business more. It might provide some clues how to escape the mess he was locked in. Unfortunately, it looked like prophecies were only useful after events had already happened.

"Today we begin working with the elements," Harafin said.

That sounded like a great way to wreak havoc on an unprecedented scale. It sounded perfect for when they caught up with Tanathos.

They started by conjuring fire. First they lit the logs in the fireplace, then formed it in the air above their hands. Kevlin enjoyed a close affinity with fire. It danced and flickered to his command, each tiny flame dancing in time with the rhythm of life.

These tiny flames paled against the memory of when he'd controlled the towering pillar of fire that brought down the keep and the traitor Wayra. That moment was seared permanently into his mind.

Maybe it was time to live it again?

At the sudden urge, he formed a six-foot pillar of fire in the room that scorched the stone floor. The insatiable hunger of the fire resonated with the desire pounding through him to unleash it upon any who stood in his way.

"Kevlin, control," Leander snapped.

Only then did Kevlin realize what he was doing and snuffed it out. He had to be more careful. The Trembling Madness was so insidious, it was turning him into his own worst enemy.

"It's all right," Kevlin assured the old men. "I'm in control."

"Good," said Harafin, openly calm. "I think it best we leave fire for now and move on to air."

The concept of air as a substance with weight that could be handled seemed strange at first. Then again, winds were strong enough to drive great ships across the sea, and he'd spent the first fourteen years of his life aboard his father's ship learning to harness the power of air.

Handling air without a sail proved much harder than working with fire, or rather it required a more subtle approach. Fire leapt to life at his command and obeyed his will without question, like a well-trained dog. Trying to manipulate air was more like guiding a spirited stallion.

Under Harafin's patient instruction, he managed to form it into a solid wall, or solidify it under objects and lift them off the floor. It required intense concentration that left him as exhausted as a sparring match.

After he lifted a chair to the ceiling and gently lowered it again, Leander said, "When we first entered the Great Dome, you noticed the floating carriage, yes?"

"Aye. That was amazing."

"It uses the same principle."

"Then why isn't it used more often? Why not just fly wagons between cities? Why not fly people?" The idea could revolutionize travel.

"The carriage you saw is unique, the only one of its kind," Leander explained. "It's a gimmick to impress visitors."

"Why not make more?"

Leander said, "You just lifted a chair, and you're exhausted. How long do you think you could fly a wagon?"

"I'm new at this," Kevlin protested. "Experienced Sentinels could do it a lot easier."

"To some degree, that is correct," Harafin said. "But the cost in effort outweighs the gain. Horses deliver wagons safely and with adequate speed without draining the nation's Sentinels."

There had to be a way to apply the principle. Kevlin decided he'd return to the idea once he understood more about magic. If it didn't kill him first.

After a brief rest they moved on to water. He was relieved to find it almost as easy as working with fire. Harafin taught him how to change its temperature, cooling it by bleeding its heat into the surrounding air, and then reversing the process. They practiced filling glasses, creating sheets of water, or scattering it into a heavy fog, which was then thinned to mist before dissipating it throughout the room.

"You cannot just make things vanish," Harafin explained. "You can destroy something if you wish, but cannot just unmake it. Everything has mass, and although that mass can be redistributed, it cannot just cease to exist."

Kevlin frowned. "I've seen you destroy things. You do it all the time."

"I will demonstrate." Harafin pointed at a leftover dinner roll. It floated into the air, then disappeared with a flash.

"You just destroyed it," Kevlin said. A thin wisp of smoke marked the spot where the roll had floated only seconds ago.

"No. I did not unmake the roll. I merely broke it down to its smallest component parts and released them back into the room. There is a difference. I never said it had to take very long. Now, you try."

Harafin instructed him to form a barrier of air around the sacrificial muffin. He chose a whisperberry muffin. He hated the bitter aftertaste, and its fate seemed appropriate. The idea was that the shield would contain the particles when he shattered the muffin. Then he'd vaporize what remained with fire.

The reality didn't go so well. When Kevlin tried to shatter the doomed pastry, he lost control of the shield and spewed tiny fragments around the room. He grimaced as he wiped whisperberry juice off his face. That muffin had gotten its ultimate revenge.

Harafin cleaned up the mess with a wave of his hand.

Leander just laughed. "Not bad. Better than my first attempt."

"Everyone does better than you did," Harafin agreed. "You failed to damage the apple in any way."

"Well, I did bruise it against the teacher's head," Leander laughed.

Harafin explained. "The apple knocked out the instructor. None of that class of first year Accepted had any idea how to react."

"Trying to explain to the healer what had happened was a low point in my actinopathic career," Leander said.

Kevlin had never imagined these powerful old man as incompetent Sentinels in training. He resumed the exercise a little more relaxed, and managed to successfully obliterate a piece of white cake after only a few more attempts.

Harafin decided they would wait until they left the capital before attempting to practice altering the weather or calling lighting from the sky.

"Good idea," Kevlin agreed.

Harafin rubbed his hands together, "Now, I will teach you Mindlink."

27

GUARD DUTY

Kevlin marched through the halls of the Emperor's Palace at the rear of the emperor's retinue. The new breastplate chafed against his shoulders under his crimson-and-white surcoat emblazoned with the seal of the emperor's personal guard.

He'd spent a restless night after leaving the Sentinel Tower, and his dreams were plagued by faceless assassins. The Mindlink training had proved more difficult than he'd expected. The concepts were complex and he never would have succeeded had Harafin not recommended he appeal to Oris. The stone had illuminated his understanding, and he'd finally grasped the concepts.

Now he struggled to focus, his thoughts straying back to the lesson. It didn't help that he hated guard duty. Guarding the emperor was even more boring than guarding low-life merchant smugglers.

At least they were walking now. His eyes had glazed during the mind-numbing hours the emperor sat listening to petitions. Now he and most of the ambassadors were heading for the council chamber to review heightened security measures. Ambassador Damarist had excused himself, while the aged King Tamar who served as his nation's ambassador, withdrew to rest.

The remainder of the company proceeded quickly through the halls of the Imperial Palace. Everyone made way for the emperor, and the guards stationed regularly along the halls ensured the way remained clear. Even as they walked, the ambassadors began arguing about the costs of the adopted measures, and how to pay them.

Beside Kevlin marched the captain of the emperor's personal guard. Named Belenus, the man bore a striking resemblance to Terach, the man Antigonus had chosen as Strength, who had died defending Antigonus from Dhanjal. His build was the same, although Belenus' black, close-cropped hair bore streaks of gray and his eyes were brown instead of blue. Like many of the elite Tamarri soldiers, Belenus bore a Pala strapped to his back. The long-handled, single-edged sword was their signature weapon.

He thought back to the memory of Terach kneeling on the floor, impaled by Dhanjal's scimitar. Again he saw the light of life fade from the brave soldier's eyes, again watched as Terach's blood burned from photophor powder.

Terach's death still disturbed him. Kevlin and Ceren had been forced to leave Antigonus behind, and barely escaped with their lives. So many deaths had resulted from that failure.

At least Dhanjal's had been one of them.

Belenus did not speak much as they followed the obese Meinarri ambassador, Duke Gwyre, who had fallen behind the rest of the company. The huge ambassador sweated profusely and panted as he tried to hurry along.

The emperor and the other ambassadors were so caught up in their discussion, they didn't notice. Kevlin wondered if the fat man would collapse. What would they do? Would Captain Belenus insist they carry him?

It'd take a dozen men. Kevlin silently urged the fat man to keep his feet.

Captain Belenus had made it clear that he didn't welcome Kevlin and his brothers' temporary assignment to the emperor's guard. "I don't care who you are," the captain had said during their briefing. "Better men than you have trained for years to qualify for this post."

"Trot a few of those better men over here," Jerrik had growled, "and we'll see if they're ready."

Drystan had intervened before the argument turned into a brawl. "We're here on the emperor's orders, Captain. We'll follow your lead, and you can even pretend we're your regular guard. But we have a mission to do and expect you to stay out of our way."

"Endanger the emperor, and I'll remove your head."

Drystan had only smiled, his eyes sparkling with eagerness for battle.

"If you lot did your job right the first time, we wouldn't have to come clean up your mess," Jerrik added.

That had nearly started a fight, but Captain Belenus showed discipline, if not grace.

Colonel Gabral, the final member of their five-man team, had stood a little apart from the rest of the group. He finally spoke. "Enough. You're acting like children. Do your job Captain, and let us do ours."

Now Kevlin strode beside Captain Belenus in an uneasy silence at the rear of the group. Belenus had lost a lot of good men to that curse. Kevlin understood too well the anger a good leader felt when men under his command died.

Drystan and Jerrik, assigned as point guards, led the group into a large atrium at the junction of four halls. The path circled a small garden, complete with an oval-shaped pool and a spraying fountain. A pair of apple trees hunched under a heavy load of ripe fruit, and three white ducks splashed in the water. High above, at the peak of the vaulted ceiling, a circular window let in a brilliant shaft of bright golden light.

As the group reached the small garden, Drystan raised a hand to signal a halt.

"Why are we stopping?" the emperor asked.

Drystan pointed to the hall ahead. Beyond the small garden, eight soldiers dressed in the colors of the emperor's guard marched into the room in a double file.

"Are we expecting an escort?" Drystan asked.

"No," Captain Belenus said from where he and Kevlin still lingered at the rear of the party with the obese Ambassador Gwyre.

Echoing footsteps announced more soldiers, who marched out of the halls to either side. Still more approached from behind. Every group was identical, with eight soldiers in double file, marching in step.

As the four groups converged on the emperor's party, Jerrik called out, "Stand down, soldiers, and clear the way."

The soldiers continued their advance. They made no threatening moves, but they didn't have to. This situation was all wrong.

The main party bunched together near the pond, with Gabral in front. If only Ambassador Gwyre had caught up. He'd stopped as soon as everyone else did, and remained a good ten paces apart from the others.

Kevlin was tempted to kick his ample behind. Did the fat between his ears not register that they were in danger?

Jerrik shifted left, while Drystan took the right flank. Kevlin turned to watch the men approaching from behind. Four of them bore wide shields, which was uncommon in the palace.

The emperor called out, "Who is your commander?"

A grizzled-looking fellow with steel-gray hair saluted from the first company. "I command, Your Imperial Majesty. We are here to provide additional protection. There is unrest in the palace."

"There," Ambassador Janezeko from Freyarr said with a smile, as if he had just won an argument. "No need for your overly developed sense of caution today."

As the groups converged on the emperor's party, Captain Belenus shouted, "Ware. These are not my men!"

Pandemonium shattered the tranquil atrium.

Soldiers charged from every direction, and the air filled with the wicked hiss of swords ripped from sheaths. Four soldiers from the right-hand column raised crossbows and fired on the emperor's party.

Drystan leaped in the way, his spinning spear deflecting three of the bolts wide. The fourth slammed into his shoulder, punched through his light chain armor, and sank deep into his shoulder.

On the left flank the soldiers had advanced closer, and they charged Jerrik from mere feet away. He bellowed his own battle cry, threw his arms out wide, and leaped into the double column. He slammed into the charging rank like an angry bull and plowed right over the first four soldiers.

Most of the company fell in a heap with Jerrik in the center. Fists and daggers flashed from all sides as the fight degenerated into a wild brawl.

Kevlin drew his own sword and moved to face the shield-bearing soldiers charging their rear.

Captain Belenus shouted, "Hold them off!"

Instead of flanking him like he should have, Belenus left Kevlin to stand alone while he moved to intercept three soldiers who had slipped past Jerrik's wild brawl.

Kevlin bit back a curse. Facing disciplined shield-men alone without a shield of his own, left him at an extreme disadvantage. If he didn't slow their charge, they'd run right over him and fall upon the emperor's party.

So Kevlin charged to meet them.

Battle lust swept through him and he shouted his defiance and fear. Finally, someone to hit.

He focused all his pent-up frustration into a lunge at the left-most of the leading pair of soldiers, and slashed his sword just above the top of the man's shield. The soldier responded too slowly, and Kevlin's blade slashed his eyes. The man screamed and staggered.

Kevlin kicked at the bottom edge of the shield of the man's partner, which the man had shifted to strike at Kevlin's unprotected side.

Kevlin connected first. His foot drove the bottom edge of the shield into the man's kneecap and snapped the knee back with an audible pop. The soldier lurched to the side, and Kevlin slammed the hilt of his sword into the man's helmeted head. The soldier dropped like a stone.

Kevlin retreated a step and glanced around to see how the rest of the company was faring.

Not so good.

Unable to wield his long spear single-handedly, Drystan had thrown it at one of the crossbowmen. The man lay dead with the spear driven through his throat.

As Kevlin turned to look, other soldiers threw a net over Drystan. He struggled to throw it off, but the men leaped on him with clubs and drove him to the ground with heavy blows to his torso.

Jerrik was still brawling with half a dozen men, and blood flowed freely from the group. Kevlin couldn't tell how much of it was his brother's, but he cringed to see it.

Gabral had moved forward to intercept the company charging through the small garden. He had drawn the Mace, which started to burn with blue fire, and he hefted it and beckoned the soldiers on.

Instead of closing with him, three of them threw small pouches that struck his armored torso and exploded into clouds of white powder.

Gabral cursed and swiped at his eyes. He swung the Mace in wild arcs, but the powder temporarily blinded him and the soldiers skirted around him and charged toward the emperor's main party.

Captain Belenus had engaged three soldiers who had slipped around Jerrik. He dropped two of them with lightning strikes of his Pala, but the final soldier withstood him for critical seconds. Four knife-wielding soldiers charged past the entangled Drystan and leaped at the fat Ambassador Gwyre, who had finally tried to join the rest of the group.

Kevlin needed to stop the six soldiers facing him. No one would come to his aid. If he failed, more ambassadors would die today.

Suddenly a boring guard duty sounded wonderful.

"Come on!" He raised his sword, preparing to charge.

A soldier without a shield stepped out of the file. He carried a coiled whip. It flicked out with amazing speed and curled around Kevlin's ankles. The soldier yanked before Kevlin could sever the whip.

Kevlin stumbled, but regained his balance. Then the lead soldier lunged and shield-bashed him in the face, knocking him off his feet.

Two soldiers ran past him toward the emperor's party. Half-blind from pain and blood that ran into one eye, he slashed wildly at them. His sword bit into one of their legs and the man screamed.

Then the others leaped on Kevlin with clubs and began beating him. His breastplate absorbed most of the blows, but he caught one heavy strike to the side of the head, and his vision blurred.

He twisted under the weight of his attackers, but lacked purchase to fight them off. His thoughts became fuzzy, but he wondered why they didn't just kill him. Instead, many hands grabbed him and began dragging him away.

As he struggled, he caught sight of the rest of the battle. Two soldiers had leaped upon Ambassador Gwyre and plunged their daggers repeatedly into his fat torso. Blood spurted wide and he screamed and beat futilely against them.

Even as the obese ambassador fell, Captain Belenus charged in with a dazzling double slash that decapitated one attacker. Two others appeared, and he dropped them in their tracks. The last attacker shouted in victory and withdrew his bloody dagger from the ambassador's chest.

Then he shuddered and slowly toppled to the side. Behind him, Ambassador Janezeko stood clutching his own bloody dagger.

Beyond Janezeko, four other attackers had reached the emperor's party. The trim Ambassador Talamantez from Einarr and the hulking Ambassador Kescog from Donarr pushed the emperor behind them.

Kevlin twisted harder to watch, unable to tear his eyes away, even though he wanted to vomit. These men would be slaughtered before his eyes, men he was responsible to protect. He and his brothers had failed, and the entire company was about to be overrun.

He forgot these two were raised as warriors, not diplomats.

Ambassador Talamantez twisted past one sword, chopped the attacker's hand, and stripped the sword out of the man's numbed fingers. He clobbered the surprised attacker with the hilt, then slashed the throat of a second attacker.

Beside him, Duke Kescog blocked a heavy blow with one meaty forearm. The sword bit deep and blood gushed down his arm, but he ignored the wound and punched the man in the face. The blow drove the man into the ground where he lay motionless.

Ambassador Kescog scooped up his sword and stood side by side with Ambassador Talamantez. He shouted and beckoned several attackers on, but they hesitated.

In that second, Gabral raised the Mace high and its brilliant blue flame rolled down over him. A wave of fire exploded out of the mighty weapon and incinerated everything within ten feet of him in a blinding flash of deadly fire. Four soldiers caught in the blast died with their flesh boiled right off their bones, leaving them little more than smoking piles of charred meat.

With a final swipe to clear his eyes, Gabral pointed the Mace at one soldier who had circled the group and now leaped at the emperor, sword raised. The long top spike of the Mace fired off and slammed into the attacker's back, driving him to the ground at the emperor's feet.

Gabral charged several attackers, cursing loudly. He ignored their feeble attempts to strike him, and smashed them to the ground with heavy blows of his enchanted weapon.

At the same time, Jerrik surged to his feet in the middle of the brawling fight he'd been entangled in, shedding opponents like water. Roaring like a berserker, he picked up one attacker and threw the man across the room into the gang of men trying to drag Drystan away.

The hapless fellow crashed into the group and they all fell in a heap. Drystan untangled himself from the net and staggered to his feet. Although bruised and battered, he drew one of his long-knives from the sheath on his back. As his attackers regained their footing, he attacked.

Drystan moved through their ranks like a cyclone, the silvered steel of his long-knife flashing in the golden morning light. Men tried to intercept him, or tried to escape. None were successful. He shouted no battle cry, made no threats or curses.

He just killed them all.

With the tide of battle turned, the remaining soldiers broke and fled. The four men dragging Kevlin dropped him and ran.

Kevlin untied his ankles, scooped up his sword, and gave chase. He staggered like a drunkard for the first few steps, but battle fury boiled away his pain. He sprinted after the fleeing attackers, hungry for the chance to beat them to death.

Behind him, Emperor Tegnazian shouted, "Colonel Gabral, take some of them for questioning."

Kevlin grimaced. Hopefully Gabral would capture a few. He didn't intend to leave alive any of the ones he chased.

The men fled like deer down the hall and around a sharp corner. Kevlin charged after them, shouting curses. He rounded the corner and skidded to a halt. All four of them hung suspended in a shimmering wall of blue light, like flies trapped in honey-coated paper.

Beside the wall stood the fat Sentinel Felix. "What's all this, then?"

28

MIND TRAP

Sentinel Felix healed Ambassadors Kescog and Talamantez while Kevlin and the others stood guard. Ambassador Gwyre had died before Felix arrived, and the pitiful wreck lay in a pool of his own blood.

Emperor Tegnazian paced near the duck pond in a towering fury. He stopped occasionally to look at the fallen ambassador and the dead attackers strewn around the room. Then he would scan the captured attackers huddling in a small group guarded by Colonel Gabral. Several times he grimaced and clenched his fists, as if restraining an impulse to personally beat the captured men.

Sentinel Felix used Mindlink to notify others of the assault, and reinforcements soon came pouring in. Kevlin and his brothers fanned out to face the newcomers, swords drawn, and ordered them back until Captain Belenus could vouch for them.

Many of the soldiers glared at the distrust, but Kevlin didn't care. The attackers had used stolen uniforms, and they had nearly succeeded.

Leander arrived with a score of Hammer Stalwarts. They pushed through the emperor's guard without slowing, and ringed the emperor's company with hammers at the ready. Captain Belenus joined his men scowling at being displaced, but he swallowed his protest and ordered his men into a second ring of defense. A couple of the Stalwarts moved to attend to Drystan and Jerrik's wounds. Kevlin had only suffered minor injuries by comparison, and the lingering battle fury helped him keep the pain at bay.

The emperor, followed by the ambassadors, stalked over to the prisoners, ten in all. He pointed at their leader, and Gabral collared the man and pushed him to his knees before the emperor. He looked thoroughly beaten. He'd apparently tried to resist capture, and Gabral had shattered his shoulder. His arm hung useless, and blood dripped from his fingers.

"By whose orders did you do this?" Emperor Tegnazian demanded.

The man coughed, then winced and spat blood on the floor. "Orders came from M. . ."

He screamed, clutched his head, and pitched sideways to the floor.

Sentinel Felix rushed over, but Leander beat him to the fallen man and placed glowing hands on the side of his head.

"He's dead."

Felix placed a hand on the man's chest and closed his eyes in concentration. After a moment, he nodded. "Mind trap."

"Say that again," Emperor Tegnazian ordered.

Felix dusted off his hands. "A mind trap killed this man. I've seen it used by Shadeleeches in the past. If a servant tries to speak something forbidden, usually the name of their master, the spell snaps their mind."

Ambassador Janezeko said, "You're saying this man was hired by a Shadeleech?"

"Or someone who employs the same techniques."

One prisoner who sat nearby said, "We didn't know, honest. We were just hired to . . ." He also screamed and collapsed.

Felix, moving with surprising speed, grabbed the fallen man. For several seconds, he leaned over the man before dropping him with a curse.

"Too slow." He turned to the rest of the prisoners, who were all staring at their fallen companions in stark terror. "Say nothing, for your lives."

Felix moved to one of the soldiers, grabbing him by the collar when he cringed away. "Sit still, man. I'm not the one you should fear."

He concentrated over the seated man, who sat rigid, barely breathing. After a moment, Felix grunted.

"It is as I feared. Your Majesty, I need Ah'Shan to conduct a thorough exploration and break the trap. He's the most skilled in the technique.

I did learn a little. Their captain may have known more, but this man knew none of the specifics. They arrived just yesterday from Hallvarr."

He added with a smile, "And I know where they were barracked right here in the palace."

"Very good," Emperor Tegnazian said. "Captain, send a detachment of your men to these traitors' barracks. Search them, and take into custody anyone else you encounter there."

Captain Belenus saluted and turned to issue orders.

Leander said, "I'll send along a pair of Stalwarts. If these men are working for a Shadeleech or rogue Sentinel, you may need them."

Emperor Tegnazian's eye fell on the dead Ambassador Gwyre, now covered by a soldier's cloak, and he sighed. "Make arrangements for Severin's funeral."

After turning away, he added, "Summon Sentinel Ah'Shan to interrogate the prisoners in the dungeon, and send for Harafin."

29

POLITE COMPANY

Kevlin stood against the wall in the same small council chamber where he had first met the emperor. His battle fury had faded, and he ached with every movement. He should have insisted on a healing after all.

The ambassadors, still wearing their blood-stained clothing, sat around the table, a subdued group. Several other guards and Stalwarts ringed the room, and more were stationed outside. Now that the fighting was over, the excess in caution seemed laughable.

At least with the extra protection, Drystan and Jerrik had been excused to recover from their wounds. Even though Felix had healed the worst of their injuries, they needed rest to fully recover. Kevlin suspected they were going to need all their strength soon.

Emperor Tegnazian paced between the table and an overstuffed chair near the fireplace. He held his hands clasped behind his back, his expression locked into a scowl. His clothing was stained with the blood of the attacker Gabral had killed at his feet.

A white-robed Sentinel entered the room. He looked to be middle aged, with the bronze skin and blonde hair common to Freyarr.

He performed a perfect, formal bow. "Your Imperial Majesty, I am Sentinel Durgesh, reporting for duty as a member of your personal guard."

"You're late," Ambassador Kescog growled.

Sentinel Durgesh nodded respectfully to the hulking ambassador. "I heard of the recent, unfortunate events and I apologize for my tardiness. I was meeting with my master, Ah'Shan to discuss most effective strategies to counter any unexpected aggression."

Kevlin recognized the signature black ribbon sewed to the cuffs and collar of the Sentinel's robes, marking the man a Kestrel. The Kestrels were a militant order, founded by Ah'Shan half a century ago and led by him still. They trained heavily in the battle arts with the stated goal of preparing to fight in the vanguard of the next battle with the Grakonians.

Kevlin didn't trust them. Wayra had been a Kestrel, and she had turned on them at the battle of Il'Aicharen and nearly guaranteed Tanathos' victory.

Leander, who sat in one of the comfortable chairs closer to the fireplace said, "You may not have noticed, but it's time for practice, my boy, not theory."

"Again, I apologize," the Sentinel said. He had a smooth, cultured voice and seemed outwardly unruffled by the cool welcome. "Now that I'm in attendance, I can assure your safety in the event of another attack."

Emperor Tegnazian strode to the table and slammed his fist onto the wood. "There can be no next attack!" He ran his angry gaze around the room. "This is our home. We cannot assume the enemy is free to attack at will. They. Are. Not." He stood tall, with fists clenched at his side. "I rule here, not these nameless traitors. I will have order, I will have peace."

The door again opened and Harafin stepped into the room. Emperor Tegnazian rounded on him. "Finally! What are you doing about this, Master Harafin?"

If he was surprised by the angry greeting, Harafin didn't show it. He merely nodded in greeting. "I'm deeply saddened to hear of the loss of Ambassador Gwyre, and I'm relieved that the rest of you are safe."

Emperor Tegnazian regained control with a visible effort. "Thank you, Harafin. It has proven to be a trying day. I'm glad you're here."

Harafin moved to an empty seat at the table. "What do we know about the men who attacked you?"

Ambassador Talamantez from Einarr spoke. "Sentinel Ah'Shan is interrogating them now."

A breathless soldier slipped into the room and snapped a smart salute. At the emperor's nod, he reported, "Sire, we have initial reports of the search of the attackers' quarters."

"That was very efficient," the huge Ambassador Kescog from Donarr said.

The soldier reported that the raid on the barracks found them empty. However, a locked trunk was broken open to reveal a dozen of the signature cloaks of the Wolves, the elite Chandravernan guard of Hallvarr.

As ambassadors began arguing about the significance of the find, the emperor ordered silence until the soldier finished. He said they tracked down the ship the men had arrived on. It was a diplomatic courier from Diodor, but had burned to the waterline less than an hour ago in the formal port. There were no survivors. The city guard were combing the dockside taverns looking for any crew who might have been on shore leave.

The soldier withdrew and Emperor Tegnazian drove one fist into his other open palm. "We are blocked at every turn."

Ambassador Damarist of Hallvarr chose that moment to arrive. As soon as he stepped inside, Emperor Tegnazian pointed an accusing finger at him. "You. Where have you been?"

"I'm so sorry," Ambassador Damarist stammered. The man looked even thinner than Kevlin remembered, and he shook under the emperor's angry glare. "I came as soon as I could."

Emperor Tegnazian said in a steely voice, "Perhaps you can explain why the men who just tried to assassinate me came from Diodor on a government courier ship and had in their possession cloaks identifying them as Chandravernan Wolves?"

Ambassador Damarist paled and opened his mouth as if to protest, but no words came out.

Ambassador Janezeko from Freyarr spoke into the silence. "It's interesting that you just happened to excuse yourself long enough to be absent when we were attacked by your countrymen."

"I protest," Ambassador Damarist squeaked finally. "I know nothing of this. Braden, how dare you accuse me of colluding with these attackers?"

"You have to admit, there's a lot of evidence pointing toward Hallvarr," Ambassador Talamantez said. His face was expressionless, showing nothing of what he might be thinking.

"No," Ambassador Damarist protested again. He turned back to the emperor. "You know where my loyalties lie."

Kevlin had been trying to reconcile his memories of Diodor and its population with these new accusations. The people there seemed deeply loyal to their king and kingdom.

Then again, so much had occurred in Hallvarr recently, could more secret traitors remain hidden among the population there, perhaps even in the palace? Ambassador Damarist said the king had been suffering a form of madness.

Was revolution part of that madness?

The Ambassador's question brought to mind his recent declaration to Harafin that his loyalty to his kingdom would always trump his loyalty to the empire. Was he really saying what he seemed to be saying now?

Kevlin rubbed his temples to ease a growing headache. He didn't have the brain power for intrigue. As much as his skull still ached from the beating he took during the battle, he preferred that kind of pain to these mental games. At least then he had a chance to fight back.

Harafin made no comment. Apparently he planned to let the ambassador's remark go unchallenged.

Emperor Tegnazian said, "Borehl, there's too much evidence here for me to ignore."

Ambassador Damarist shook his head slowly. "Someone is setting me up, and you're allowing them to do it." He raised his hands slowly until his closed fists met in front of his chest. "Why not bind me now and take me to the dungeon?"

Ambassador Janezeko made a silent clapping motion with his hands. "Excellent show, but the melodrama is a little over-done."

"Enough, Braden," the emperor snapped. "This is no laughing matter. Borehl, how do you suggest these suspicions be put to rest?"

The ambassador thought for a moment. "I will send for Commander Tekla. He knows all of the Wolves personally. He can identify these attackers as imposters."

"And if they prove to be Wolves in truth?" the emperor asked.

"Then I swear we'll find out who ordered the attack. I did not, and I personally guarantee we will execute whoever did."

The emperor nodded. "Send for Tekla."

Harafin interjected. "Ah'Shan is interrogating the prisoners. Perhaps he will learn more."

The emperor seated himself at the head of the table. "Now tell me, how can we safeguard the city when we cannot even safeguard the palace? Word has already spread throughout the city of the attack."

The huge Ambassador Kescog said, "I have already ordered the regular city watch doubled in case of unrest."

"That's not going to help," Ambassador Janezeko said.

"No, it won't," the emperor agreed. "Not for long. We need a victory. I want these traitors rooted out."

Leander rose and paced toward Harafin. "We're overlooking something here." At the emperor's nod, he continued, "We can no longer afford to ignore the fact that at least one Actinopathic person is likely involved in these recent attacks. We suspected a Shadeleech, but there must be a Sentinel working with him. We should focus our energies on ferreting out that traitorous Sentinel."

"Here, here," Ambassador Janezeko said heartily. "I agree completely."

Sentinel Durgesh said, "I must protest. Your personal vendetta against the Shadeleech Tanathos is well known, and is clouding your judgment. This divisive talk only makes matters worse." He smiled coldly at Leander. "I recommend you be excused, and perhaps restrained before you hurt yourself."

Kevlin felt tempted to strike down the snake right there. In any other situation, such an open insult would have been grounds for a challenge. By the looks of the assembled ambassador's faces, even here in this council where arguing seemed to be a well-developed art, the man's bluntness was unusual.

"Go ahead, restrain me," Leander appeared outwardly calm, but his fist clenched slowly once at his side.

Sentinel Durgesh returned Leander's stare, but made no further move.

"I stand by what I said," Leander added. "I recommend we start by casting Truth on you, Durgesh. Your failure to report for duty just happened to leave the emperor vulnerable."

"You dare question me?" The Kestrel's superior cool façade cracked.

"Contact on the shield matrix," Harafin cried, slapping his hand onto the table. "I just felt a tremor on the Iron Spoke, above the central marketplace. A Shadeleech just crossed the road."

Leander lunged for the door, followed closely by Sentinel Felix. Kevlin wanted to rush after them, but his duty prevented him from leaving.

"May the gods grant they find him this time," the emperor declared.

Kevlin urged the old Stalwart on. This was the proof they needed. Tanathos really was here in the city.

The day of reckoning for Tanathos had come. The Shadeleech was a terrifying enemy, but Kevlin longed for the chance to face him. He would avenge Antigonus and the hundreds of others killed at Il'Aicharen.

If Leander found Tanathos on the streets of the city, gods help anyone caught in the middle.

30

A Healer's Touch

Indira stepped into the sprawling hospital ward situated at the edge of the central marketplace of Tamera. The cavernous chamber bustled with activity, with scores of injured and sick people being treated by Healers and Stalwarts of several different orders.

Indira wove through the crowded aisles, past cots with patients tended by nurses while they waited for their turn to be healed. The diminutive archer Adalia followed close behind.

Indira smiled. This was her domain. Here she could do so much good. The suffering of the sick and injured tore at her heart and she thanked the creator daily for blessing her with such a powerful gift of healing.

"There be a lot of sick folk here," Adalia commented a little uneasily. "There be no plague here, be there?"

"No. Tamera is a big city. There are always sick and injured."

She sighted a group of Pallian Stalwarts near the back of the huge room and moved in their direction. She had developed a deep love for most of the Pallians. "With so many orders of Stalwarts residing in the city, and with the Healers' College located here, we all take turns providing free access to healing services."

"All this be free?" Adalia scanned the huge room again, eyes wide with the wonder of it.

Indira smiled and twisted her long midnight hair into a simple braid in preparation for getting to work. "It's one of the benefits of living near so many Stalwarts."

Adalia nodded. "I never seen a Stalwart or a Healer till I was twelve."

The Pallian Stalwarts greeted Indira warmly, particularly Edana, a broad-faced woman with many laugh lines. She was Indira's regular partner in the popular Sickle and Wheel card game they held weekly.

Edana gave her a hug. "I'm so glad you're back! We've been on a terrible losing streak since you left."

"I'm sure we'll set it to right," Indira said.

"Are you kidding?" Edana laughed. "We're positioned for a huge win! They're giving me a ten-to-one rating for tonight's game. With you as a ringer, we can recover triple what I've lost."

Indira loved the game, but she didn't play for the money like Edana did. She always felt a little bad taking coins from Stalwarts, although she did enjoy raking the professional gamblers.

"What about the patients?" Indira asked.

Right now, she just wanted to heal. Embracing her gift centered her mind and brought peace, which she had enjoyed less and less in recent days. She still felt irritated with Kevlin, and longed to think of nothing but helping others.

"We're a little short on the rotation today, with Styra Leander sending so many into the streets to hunt that Shadeleech," Edana admitted.

"Shush." A blocky Stalwart standing nearby glanced around to make sure none of the patients overheard. Indira didn't know his name. "No one's supposed to know about that."

Indira hoped Leander would be careful. He was such a good man, and her heart ached to think of the loss of his family. During their recent adventures in Hallvarr, she'd finally come to understand how he could justify striking down men like Tanathos. She wished people didn't have to fight. It caused too much suffering.

"Looks like more patients than normal," Indira said, scanning the rows of patients again.

"There sure are," Edana said. "People are restless."

"What do you expect?" the blocky fellow said. "Battles in Hallvarr, rumors of the emperor being sick, and now some kind of assassination attempt. It's got folks jittery."

Edana nodded. "And with the ball tonight, free ale is being distributed to the commoners. They're already getting drunk and starting to fight, and it's barely noon."

"Well, let's get to work." Indira wished people didn't get hurt so much, but she was happy to immerse herself in her work.

Adalia hovered nearby as Indira moved to the first patient, a pretty young woman with terrible bruises on her face. Her lips were split and her eyes almost swollen shut. She sat patiently despite obvious pain.

Indira gently touched the woman's tangled brown hair as she embraced her healing gift. It filled her immediately, shining through her soul like bright sunlight that filled her with warmth and peace. She focused on the injured woman and began the soft chant that helped her direct that power into her patients.

The strength of her gift vibrated through her like living music that rose in counterpoint to her chant and intensified as it connected her to the woman. Her healing sight focused on the woman's injuries, and their extent shocked Indira.

The young woman bore a patchwork of bruises across most of her body, and in some places newer bruises were piled on top of old ones still unhealed. Indira's hands shook with sorrow as she felt the woman's terrible pain.

Indira directed her gift to flow through the woman's mind to grant her peace. Then she attacked each bruise, draining away the hurt and restoring the damaged flesh.

Nearly fifteen minutes later, she opened her eyes and removed her hands from the young woman's head. A wave of weariness set her legs trembling, and she dropped onto the cot beside the woman. In some ways, healing consumed as much energy as pitched battle.

The young woman stared at her with eyes filled with wonder. "You're an angel come to life."

"Nothing so grand as that," Indira said.

Adalia crouched nearby, frowning. "What took ye so long with this one, Indira? Getting rusty?"

Indira took the young woman's hand. "What happened to you? You've been beaten many times."

The young woman looked down, and her hair slid across her face. "It's nothing."

"But it is," Indira insisted. "Who did this to you?" She gently pushed the young woman's hair out of her face. The girl was crying softly.

Adalia leaned forward. "Tell us and we can help."

"My boyfriend thought I was seeing another man. He got angry."

Adalia snorted. "That's a lot of elk droppings. Indira said ye've been beat lots a times."

"He's a suspicious type," she whispered.

"Coward," Adalia snarled. "I wish I knew where to find him."

The young woman pointed a shaky finger. "He's right over there. This time, some men caught him beating me and they beat him in turn."

Halfway across the room a big, heavily-muscled man with short, black hair was just rising from a cot. A Pemburu Stalwart had been attending him. He noticed the young woman pointing at him and shouldered past the Stalwart, moving in their direction.

"You're gonna need more healing than that, girl!" he shouted.

The man's audacity amazed Indira. It angered her too. She rarely allowed herself to feel anger, for it interfered with her healing.

Not today. As the trembling young woman tried to flee, Indira pushed her back down. "Don't move."

She stepped into the man's path. "You will not harm this girl."

Nearby, the stocky Stalwart reached for his hammer, but Edana held him back and whispered something to him.

The burly boyfriend closed on Indira without slowing. He shouted, "Get outta my way." When Indira didn't move, he tried to drive his shoulder into her.

The fool.

He collided with her shield of Faith and rebounded as if he'd run into a brick wall. He tripped and crashed onto a cot, which buckled under the sudden weight.

Adalia moved to Indira's side, arrow already knocked. "Nice move, that. Now it's my turn."

As the man surged to his feet, Adalia said, "I'll give ye three seconds ta git outta here afore I shoot ye."

He barked a laugh. "I'm gonna take that bow outta your hands, little lady, and spank you with it."

Adalia fired. The arrow punched through the man's hand and drove into his thigh, pinning his hand to his leg.

He screamed and staggered, his expression shocked. Adalia knocked another arrow in single, fluid motion. Silence descended on the rest of the hospital as all eyes turned to watch the spectacle.

"Two seconds left," Adalia said coldly.

"You can't do this!"

"One second." She drew the string back.

He bolted, crying out for help, moving awkwardly with his hand pinned to his leg.

"Too slow." Adalia fired again. The twang of the bow sounded loud in the silent room. The arrow drove deep into the man's meaty backside.

He screamed and collapsed in a heap. He held up his free hand and begged for mercy, for help, and finally for the city guard.

A Fire Stalwart moved toward the man and shouted at Adalia. "Enough. You made your point."

Adalia shouted back. "If'n I hear bout you laying a finger on this woman again, my next bolt's gonna hurt ye a lot more than them little pricks I just gave ye."

She reached for another arrow, but the man shouted, "I won't touch her, I promise."

Adalia spat on the floor and turned her back on the fellow as the Fire Stalwart moved to help him. "Coward."

Indira hugged Adalia. "That was well done."

Adalia raised an eyebrow. "Not gonna cry that he got hurt?"

"Not this time."

The young woman was staring from the tiny archer to her huge boyfriend. Adalia said, "Find yerself a different man. That one's no good."

"I will." She hugged Adalia and strode from the room with a grin on her face.

The nearby Pallian Stalwarts congratulated Adalia. One of them commented to Indira, "I'm surprised you stepped in front of that guy. You don't usually take sides."

"In Hallvarr I learned a few things. I saw the face of evil and learned it has to be confronted sometimes."

"I heard you learned more than that," Edana said. "Tell us how you shield others when you're not healing them."

Indira blushed. She didn't like all the attention, but she was eager to share the wondrous ability she'd discovered with Kevlin's help. Thinking of him brought to mind the few times she'd kissed him.

Part of her wished they'd had more time to explore their relationship, but part of her was happy she had a little distance. Kevlin affected her deeply, and the intensity of her feelings scared her. She was glad Ceren was around to help him figure out the terrible Trembling Madness.

"How about a demonstration?" Indira asked. When they all agreed, she asked Adalia, "Will you help me?"

Adalia shrugged. "Sure. Whatever ye need, Indira."

Indira said to the stocky Stalwart, "Hit her with your hammer."

"Remind me to ask what ye want first next time," Adalia muttered as the Stalwart advanced.

Indira embraced her gift again. It soared into her heart, filling her with glorious joy. As the Stalwart raised his hammer to strike, Indira extended her gift to wrap Adalia in its protective embrace.

She couldn't reach Adalia.

In Hallvarr, she'd managed for the first time to extend her shield of Faith beyond herself. She'd saved Ceren's life. Now her Faith wavered and didn't flow out to cover Adalia.

The Stalwart's hammer swung in a deadly arc.

"Stop!" she shouted.

He tried to check his swing, but had already committed to the blow. The hammer slammed into Adalia's side and, with an audible crack of breaking ribs, knocked her from her feet.

Indira rushed to the fallen archer, who moaned with pain, barely conscious. She laid hands on her tiny friend, and this time her gift flowed out without hesitation. Indira poured everything she had into the healing. With desperate speed, she drained away Adalia's pain, knit the bones, and restored the battered flesh.

After several minutes, she removed her hands and sank to the floor, exhausted.

Edana helped Adalia sit up, and Indira clutched the tiny woman's hands. "I'm so very sorry."

"Have a care next time," Adalia said, tone sharp. "I kin get paid to get hit, you know."

Indira sighed with relief. At least Adalia's indomitable spirit hadn't been damaged.

Edana asked, "What happened?"

"I don't know," Indira said with a frown. "I couldn't do it."

31

THE LIGHT OF A TRUE CAUSE

Sitara answered a soft knock on the door of the keisara's private sitting room. A page passed a folded note to her. She expected it to be addressed to her mistress, or to Lady Ceren. They were the only two in the room, chatting over afternoon tea.

It was addressed to her. Sitara opened it, but the paper was blank. That could only mean Masego.

He risked much to contact her in the light of day. Sentinel Omolara had left the room only moments ago on an errand for the keisara. If she'd lingered and noticed the note . . . Sitara shivered.

The ladies remained engrossed in their conversation, so Sitara risked embracing her Actinopathic gift. It came slowly, trickling into her soul as if the conduit had nearly closed.

She tried harder, yearning to feel it return to the glorious light of its pure power. It came, but pooled just under her skin as if blocked from penetrating further.

She hated to think that the Sentinels were somehow blocking her access. They didn't know she was a secret revolutionary. How could they do this to her? It was one more example of the tyranny ruling the empire, one more motivation to restore order to the world.

She focused a sliver of power on the note, shielding it from view of the ladies. As expected, light flashed across the paper and revealed a short line of text.

Seek out Remiel during the ball for instructions. We strike tonight.

Then the paper burst into flame. Sitara forced herself to hold it in her open palm for the two seconds it took to vaporize into smoke. She clenched her burned hand and imagined it held concealed her now-racing heart.

Tonight they would take the man Kevlin.

She had tried to direct her master toward one of the other soldiers, but he'd fixated on Kevlin. Sitara hated to lose him as a potential ally, but perhaps she could find a way to help him escape her master? If she could, he'd be primed and ready to help her destroy Masego.

Sitara crossed the room to stand behind her mistress. The pure light of her gift seeped away through her mental fingers. Sitara savored the last vestiges of that power. The day would soon come when she could embrace that power for as long as she wished, without fear of discovery.

After a slow breath to steady herself against what was to come, she opened her soul to the power of darkness. In stark contrast to the reluctance of her Actinopathic gift, this power crawled eagerly into her soul, staining her with its filth. She resisted the urge to gag and to scrub at her arms. No amount of soap would help.

With the darkness clinging to her innards, she focused its power and prepared for the next delicate step. Using the technique her master recently taught her, she turned toward Lady Ceren, who was explaining to the keisara about regulating merchant guilds in her home city of Agoreaun.

Sitara extended a finger of thought and probed Lady Ceren's mind. The woman was not gifted, but she possessed a formidable will that provided natural shielding. Sitara could break through, but the trauma would alert Ceren of the danger.

She eventually found a weakness and her thoughts slithered deeper. She hated having to suck truth away like a criminal, but it had to be done. Such sacrifice was necessary for the greater good, even from one who had only ever shown her kindness.

Soon, Sitara would own Lady Ceren's secrets.

32

HAVING A BALL

Kevlin stepped through the yawning main entrance to the Great Dome with hundreds of other party-goers flowing into the building like a river of living color. Once inside, he slipped out of the main current and found a place near the outer wall where he could watch without being trampled.

Tens of thousands of people, dressed in their best finery, filled the immense space and packed all seven levels of open walkways clinging to the dome's lower walls. Still more people poured in from every entrance. A thousand different perfumes filled the air with a potpourri of scents that mingled together into a unique aroma.

The windows just above the highest level of open walkways that normally let in the daylight now shone silver with their own inner brilliance. The light cast a soft glow over the dome, creating a gentle twilight.

The air vibrated with the low roar of thousands of conversations, while musical troupes from each of the Six Kingdoms struggled to be heard. The musicians were situated on the floor map on top of each capital city. Nearby dance floors were marked off in the Tamerlane Sea. Couples whirled together in some, while large groups stepped to the complex patterns of the most popular dances of the day in others.

Kevlin grimaced. On a good day he barely managed to keep from tripping his dance partner. The last time he attempted to participate in one of the intricate group dances, he had started a brawl. Today, surrounded by the upper tier of society, he wanted nothing to do with the dancing.

At least he didn't look entirely out of place. He'd discovered a pile of new clothing in his room along with a note from Marjani. The young woman was a marvel. Tonight he wore a pearl-gray cotton shirt under a charcoal vest and the finest pair of deep green trousers he'd ever owned. He felt comfortable, but remained unremarkable and anonymous in the crowd.

The nobility and wealthy merchants didn't share his restraint. The ball was an excuse to empty their jewelry vaults, and they seemed intent on out-sparkling each other. Men and women both wore jewels of every color imaginable. Some of the men wore military uniforms, but they were the minority. The others sported the most recent fashions from every corner of the empire.

Frilled shirts under bright doublets and waistcoats seemed most popular. Their owners often wore smug expressions as they mingled with those wearing somber colors and floppy, plumed hats popular a month ago. The variety of color and style overwhelmed Kevlin's ability to absorb it all.

Despite their best efforts, the men were at most a backdrop against which the women shone. Spectacular gowns that fell to the floor in pleated folds seemed most popular with women from sensible Hallvarr. Tamarri ladies sported wide hoop skirts that consumed vast amounts of space and challenged their dance partners to draw near enough to clasp hands.

Many of the Freyarri ladies with their bronzed skin wore silks that clung to their torsos and caressed their legs as they moved. The merchant women of Meinarr adopted styles from the nations they most traded with.

Hairstyles varied more than Kevlin had ever seen. From long, flowing tresses dripping with jewels, to complex patterns piled high over their heads, the variety seemed endless.

Kevlin eventually spotted tables piled high with a mouth-watering array of delicacies. They were scattered around the hall along the edges of the imperial highways marked in the floor map, and offered foods from each kingdom. He picked up a drink and a meat pie and tried to make himself useful.

He didn't want to insult any of the chefs, so tried to sample a bit of everything. He had to pace himself to avoid getting too stuffed, and was grateful the party was supposed to last all night.

A raised platform had been erected between the twin arcs of the grand staircase for the emperor and the keisara. The ambassadors and other high nobility mingled there above the crowd. Kevlin caught sight of Harafin and Leander, but enjoyed the anonymity of the lower crowd.

The entire night was orchestrated to highlight the emperor's presence. Seeing him well and enjoying the entertainment would do much to quell rumors of sickness or assassination attempts. There were sufficient imperial guards in view to maintain the peace, and Kevlin knew there were many more hidden among the crowd.

As Kevlin scanned the room, he caught sight of Jerrik descending the grand stair with a beautiful brunette on his arm. The giant Donarri soldier dressed conservatively in his best uniform and towered above the crowd. Kevlin moved to intercept him.

When Jerrik caught sight of him, he boomed out a loud hello that chased off several partygoers and cleared a space for them to talk. Jerrik's companion said something to him that Kevlin couldn't hear, and slipped away through the crowd.

"Who's your friend?" Kevlin asked his huge blood brother.

"A distant cousin." Jerrik watched the woman go. "Too bad she's engaged to a friend of mine."

Drystan stepped out of the crowd with a tall, willowy woman whose light brown hair hung in a simple braid down her back. She looked young, an image reinforced by her peach-colored dress that left her slender arms bare. A sleeping baby hung in a pack on her back.

Drystan slipped an arm around the woman's narrow waist. "Brothers, I'm thrilled to introduce you to my wife, Keelin."

Jerrik laughed and wrapped her in a hug, engulfing her in his meaty arms. When he stepped back, she grinned and her blue eyes sparkled with mirth.

"It's a pleasure to meet you, Jerrik."

"Ukko's Beard, Drystan finally did something right marrying you."

She laughed and laid a hand on his arm. "We're going to get along well."

Kevlin took her hands and bowed over them. "So pleased to meet you."

"So you're the Kevlin my husband now calls brother?"

"I surely am, and indebted to him and Jerrik for welcoming me into the families."

She hugged him and said into his ear, "Then I too welcome you, Kevlin, my new brother."

She smelled of sunshine and wild grasses, and her warm words set him at ease. He had worried what his brothers' extended families would think when they found out about the Swordbrother oath.

"I can't wait to hear the tale," Keelin said.

"There's much to tell," Jerrik said.

"Later," Drystan said. He slipped his arm around Keelin's waist again and looked like he never planned on removing it. He gazed at her with open devotion.

Kevlin wondered at his brother's ability to leave his young bride. She was tall for a woman but looked vulnerable beside the powerful warriors.

"How long have you been in the capital?" Kevlin asked.

"I just arrived today. I didn't want to miss the ball."

"Good timing," Jerrik said.

"It's been a busy day," Kevlin agreed.

Keelin ran a hand over Drystan's injured shoulder. "I heard about the fight." She touched Drystan's cheek and said in a teasing voice, "You survived pitched battle in Hallvarr, and you fall to a bunch of ruffians on your first day back in the capital. You're getting slow, dear one."

Drystan laughed and hugged her close.

Jerrik said, "The emperor was lucky we were there. His regulars would've been swarmed under."

Keelin frowned. "You didn't say anything about the emperor."

Drystan looked around to make sure no one was listening, despite the fact that they could barely hear each other. "We're not supposed to talk about it, love."

She cocked her head to one side and raised an eyebrow.

Drystan chuckled. "Well, not much."

Kevlin said, "We got lucky. The ambush was very well planned."

"Doubly lucky, I say," Jerrik said. "They should've killed you both. Fools tried dragging you away instead."

"Why would they do that?" Keelin asked.

Drystan shrugged. "The Sentinels are going to interrogate them after they break some kind of mind trap. We don't know why they tried to kill the emperor."

She shook her head. "Something doesn't add up, dear one. If they only wanted to kill the emperor, they would've killed you to get to him."

"Are you disappointed I survived?"

"Never, love, but their actions don't make sense."

"I have no idea," Drystan said. "They made a mistake, and paid the price." He took her hands in his and turned her toward the nearby troupe playing a traditional Einarri song. "I don't plan to spend my evening talking about them. I plan to spend it with you."

Together they slipped through the crowd and merged seamlessly into the group of dancers moving to the intricate steps of the song. Drystan and Keelin moved together so perfectly that Kevlin smiled as he watched them dance.

Drystan always fought as if he moved to a dance he alone heard. Now he moved to the music with his wife as if they understood its demands better than anyone. They flowed around each other with a grace unmatched by any other couple.

"Sir Kevlin, I hope you're enjoying yourself tonight."

Kevlin turned and found Marjani standing beside him. She wore a simple but elegant green and gold dress, and her curly hair was held back with a large comb.

"I am, thank you."

Jerrik asked, "Who's your friend, Kevlin?"

"This is Marjani. Marjani, this is my brother, Jerrik."

Marjani craned her neck up to look at Jerrik. "How is it possible? My lord Jerrik, you're Donarri or I'm blind. Kevlin's from Meinarr."

Jerrik grinned and took her hand. "We're brothers by blood, but not by birth."

"Well, you've got a quick tongue for a big man. If there's anything I can do for you, just ask."

Jerrik pointed toward the Donarr band. "They're playing my favorite song. Join me."

Marjani laughed. "That's a drinking song."

"Aye. My favorite."

Marjani curtsied. "I *am* assigned to make sure guests have a good time."

"Then come. Show me a good time."

They moved off through the crowd and Kevlin chuckled to watch them go. Jerrik was always on the lookout for a girl to chase, but Kevlin had expected him to pursue eligible noble ladies.

Kevlin forgot all about his huge brother when he caught sight of Indira and Ceren descending the grand stair. The sight of them snuffed out any thoughts but getting to Indira's side.

He plowed through the crowd to intercept her, and drank in the sight of her. Everything else faded to gray around him. The constant roaring of the crowd dimmed to a whisper as she consumed his senses.

Indira wore a long white and black satin gown that left her graceful neck and shoulders bare. She had piled her midnight hair atop her head in a complex style similar to the one Ceren wore. Around her neck she wore a simple silver chain. Her creamy skin glowed in the soft light.

As Kevlin moved to intercept her, Ceren stepped between them. Ceren again wore a gown in emerald green that matched her eyes and complemented her smooth, olive skin.

"Kevlin, I don't think it's wise for you to get too close to Indira."

Kevlin nodded a polite greeting to Ceren without taking his eyes off Indira. He reached for Indira and she took his hand with a dazzling smile that filled him with soaring joy. They moved closer together, and Kevlin yearned to kiss her full lips.

"Indira," Ceren said in an exasperated voice. "We talked about this."

Indira shrugged. "I'm sorry, Ceren. I just don't feel it's dangerous here."

Kevlin slipped an arm around Indira's waist and breathed deep to capture a hint of her gentle perfume. Standing so close to her again, he couldn't believe he'd allowed anything to distance them.

"I've been working with Harafin," Kevlin assured Ceren. "Everything's under control."

"It's a risk you don't have to take," Ceren protested.

Kevlin led Indira toward the center of the floor. "Actually, we do."

They crossed the vast hall without speaking. Kevlin exulted in the simple pleasure of walking with her. He saw no one else, barely noticed where they were walking. Only when they stepped onto the dance floor as the Meinarr troupe began one of the few dances Kevlin actually felt confident with did he pay attention.

As they stepped to the stately, intimate dance among the other couples, Kevlin said, "I've missed you."

"Me too." Indira glanced to either side as if to make sure no one could hear them. Then she asked, "How . . . how have you been?"

Memories of the ambush, desperate struggle, and death of the Meinarr Ambassador flashed into his mind. He saw again Akillik and his burning Wheel, and felt the remembered terror of the *Tai Pari*.

"Doesn't matter." He forced it all away. "Right now I'm better than ever." He touched her cheek. "How about you?"

She startled him by leaning her head against his shoulder, her expression worried. His heart nearly burst with the thrill of feeling her in is arms, but he couldn't imagine what might be bothering her.

She whispered so softly he barely heard. "I tried protecting Adalia today. It didn't work."

"Is she all right? What happened?"

He was such a fool. He'd been so focused on the enemy concealed within the palace, he'd overlooked the more vulnerable targets.

Indira slid one hand down his cheek, setting his skin on fire with her touch. "We're fine. It's nothing like that. I was just trying to demonstrate how I protect others, how you taught me."

She blushed, and he didn't even bother resisting the urge to kiss her lightly on the lips. She didn't pull away.

"Tell me about it," he urged.

She did. As they danced close together and ignored the rest of the world, she poured out her concerns. She'd failed to protect Adalia. Worse, she'd caused the tiny archer pain. Even worse, she feared she might not be able to protect anyone again should the need arise.

Kevlin listened until her words trailed off. "I don't think you should worry about it so much. I know you. You'll work it out."

"You think so?"

"You're stronger than you think, Indira. You saved my life, and the lives of more people than I can count. You saved Ceren at the tower. So you had a bad day? Don't let it get you down."

She smiled. "Thank you."

"Besides," he added. "Maybe I'll finally get to save you for once."

She laughed, and he kissed her again. She kissed him back, and the feeling of her lips pressed to his set his heart singing.

In that moment, all was right with the world.

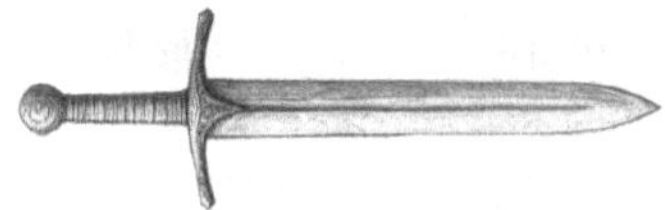

Ceren stood at the edge of the dance floor and watched Kevlin and Indira. She maintained a calm façade that revealed none of her conflicting emotions.

She loved Indira like a sister, but she'd worked too hard to arrange things here at the capital. She couldn't allow Indira and Kevlin to destroy everything before she could reap the fruits of her work. Some things were too important for any distractions to interrupt. The stakes were far too high to fail.

Ceren made up her mind and moved purposefully away through the crowd. It was time to act.

33

AN HONEST PAIN

R emiel again waited for Sitara in their normal trysting spot. He jumped to his feet when she arrived, but hesitated to embrace her. She didn't encourage him.

He grinned. "Tonight, Angel. We're taking the man Kevlin tonight."

"How?"

"Don't worry about that. You've got a different part to play."

Sitara drew closer and embraced her gift. It came without its recent hesitation, but still barely penetrated her skin. Its peace comforted her in the face of what was surely to come.

Connected with her gift, she felt his excitement like a nearby flame. Whatever had hindered him during their last meeting no longer interfered with his emotions.

"Tell me," she said, steeling herself against her coming duty.

"Masego himself will dig the information out of the man," Remiel said, taking her hands with trembling fingers. "Under cover of the party, we'll take the bearer. They'll be complacent, thinking the secret is sure."

"And the stone?" Sitara asked. Capturing Oris had been Bajaran's bold declaration of revolution. Had he succeeded, so much would have been different.

"We'll take it and flee tonight," Remiel said. He squeezed her hands. "It's really happening, Angel."

He sounded excited, played the part perfectly, but her actinopathic senses caught an undercurrent of fear. It shouldn't surprise her that all servants of Masego felt fear around him.

"How are we getting out?" she asked.

"That's where you come in," Remiel said, growing more serious. "You are to meet the Shadeleech Tanathos and bring him into the palace."

"What?" Sitara trembled with fear and sat on the edge of the bed.

He still held her hands and surely felt her fingers trembling. "It's all right, Angel. The plan's set. I'll give you all the details. All you have to do is act out your part."

That was easy for him to say. He'd never met the terrifying Shadeleech. Even with her body safe hundreds of miles away from Tanathos, he had nearly destroyed her when she touched his cesspit mind via Mindlink. That contact still haunted her dreams.

Remiel settled beside her on the edge of the bed and drew her to him. He held her with surprisingly gentle arms and stroked her hair.

"It's all right, Angel. You can do it."

This unexpected tender moment unnerved her. Remiel had never done anything like this before. In the past, he had always delivered his message, then demanded she submit to him and allow him to claim his payment.

"I'll be fine," she lied, pulling away from his embrace.

"Are you sure?" He studied her face, another unusual choice. Usually he focused his lecherous gaze on other parts of her.

"I'll do my duty," she promised, her mind turning from Tanathos to Kevlin.

She'd try to shield him from Masego's cruelty if possible. All he had to do was surrender the name of the new bearer. Masego would focus on that greater prize, and perhaps she could save Kevlin's life.

It might prove the perfect moment to turn him. If she could win that man, she'd gain access to his formidable allies. With careful planning, she could raise the forces she would need to destroy Masego just as he overthrew the current government.

Remiel pulled her to him again and stroked her hair, his face leaning on her head. "Tell me about your family."

Sitara recoiled. Did he think to gain extra leverage over her? If so, he'd chosen the wrong questions. She hadn't spoken with her family in years and wanted nothing to do with that life.

"Tell me about yours," she retorted.

He actually did. "I grew up right here in Tamera. My father died when I was young, and my mother spent most of her time caring for my sickly little sister."

Remiel took her hands in his and talked about struggling to provide for his family, to find work in an often cruel city. His story resonated strongly with her. These were the very injustices she sought to overthrow, the changes that motivated her to carry on with Bajaran's work.

She touched his mind with her power and was surprised yet again to find no mental shields blocking her access to his thoughts. Using the technique Masego had recently taught her, she skimmed his thoughts, drawing images from recent days.

He was ashamed.

The truth stunned her. She barely felt when he gently drew her back into his arms and held her while continuing his tale. She barely heard his words as images flashed through her mind.

Remiel was ashamed of what he had done to her, what he forced her to do. He hated himself, but couldn't think of a way out of the bargain. More than anything, he feared Masego.

She blocked the flow of images. She couldn't handle that much truth. It contradicted too much of the simple hatred she felt for this man.

Remiel stood. "I don't usually speak of these things, Angel, but I wanted you to know. You're different and I hope one day . . ." His voice trailed off and his face reddened.

She didn't want to ask, but the words came unbidden to her lips. "You hope what?"

"It doesn't matter," he said quickly and turned toward the door. He paused in the center of the room. "I'm sorry we don't have more time, Angel. I've got things to set up for tonight."

He placed a folded parchment on the dresser. "Your instructions are all in here. I'll see you later."

Sitara scarce believed he'd left her again without claiming his payment. The thoughts she'd gleaned from his mind rattled her to the core. She hated to think he might not be Masego's evil lackey. Her new confusion clouded her hatred, and that made her angry.

Good. Anger would be her best defense against Tanathos.

34

ONE DROP OF CHAOS

As the final notes of the dance hung in the air, Kevlin leaned forward to kiss Indira again. She closed her eyes and tipped her chin up to meet him.

As their lips touched, the amulet poured a trickle of magic into his chest.

Kevlin released Indira and stumbled away as he *changed* the magic to gain ownership of it. Had Indira slipped and touched him with her power? Had someone else done it?

Indira opened her eyes. The confusion on her face made it clear she had no idea what was going on. She hadn't done it.

The distraction proved disastrous. The magic revolted against his control and drove into his still-unprotected mind like a burning dagger. Kevlin clutched his head and staggered into another couple.

The man pushed him roughly away and Kevlin dropped to one knee. His vision faded to black. The magic roared like invading hoards as it tore down the mental barriers he struggled to raise against it. He smelled burning hair and tasted blood.

It was such a small amount of magic, but it tore at his shields with terrible force. Panic flickered at the edge of his thoughts. He wasn't sure he could stop it this time.

Then everything stopped and silence as deep as a tomb settled over him. Kevlin looked around, even though he didn't want to see. Everyone appeared frozen in time around him. Indira hung with one foot extended and one hand reaching toward him, her face locked in an expression of concern.

A flash of light drew Kevlin's gaze up toward the gigantic murals painted on the upper half of the dome. A brilliant silver light raced across the dome, like a living snake. It flashed between widely spaced images, pausing at each one for a single heartbeat.

Gods. Kevlin hadn't noticed these subtle images of the gods concealed amidst the broader murals, but the light outlined each one before moving one. The images continued to glow softly after the light left them, and they seemed to pulse as if about to move.

"Sherah's Teeth," Kevlin muttered fearfully.

"They're not that special, really."

The rope-like light ended its mad dash across the dome at the image of Akillik. It flared like a sunburst, and the youthful-looking god emerged from the mural, laughing as if he'd just heard the funniest joke ever. Tonight, as if in honor of the grand event, Akillik wore a glittering waistcoat that looked like pure gold.

"What?"

"Her teeth. They're really not that special. Why do you always talk about them?" Akillik drifted down toward Kevlin. "If you're going to talk about Asherah, there's a couple other features that deserve a lot more attention, you know."

How could he possibly respond to that?

Akillik laughed again. "No, maybe not. She might destroy you." He glanced up at the softly glowing image of Asherah in another mural. "Want to find out?"

"No!" Akillik was more than Kevlin wanted. He couldn't handle two gods.

"You're right," Akillik shrugged. "She'd just ruin the fun." He laughed louder than ever, threw out his arms and shouted, "And there's so much fun to be had tonight!"

Kevlin noticed for the first time that the Wheel spun so fast it blurred in the young god's hand. The blurring intensified until it looked like many wheels spun simultaneously in the same space. The sight gave Kevlin a headache, but he couldn't look away.

"Yes, my good man," Akillik whispered, leaning close. "So many people taking chances tonight. So many spinning the Wheel, grasping for Luck to win a fair lady's heart, to dance, to plot the death of an enemy. So many giving their souls into my care, entrusting me with their fate!"

He snapped the Wheel toward Kevlin and the blurring vanished. The Wheel began to slow, and Akillik's expression became intent. "What about you, Kevlin? Ready to try your luck?"

Kevlin shook his head, his mouth suddenly too dry to speak. He'd often spun the Wheel in the past, but never really understood the true scope of what he did. Now that he saw it, he didn't want to ever again willingly trust his fate to this crazy god.

"What do you have to lose?" Akillik whispered as he hovered just above Kevlin's head. The Wheel slowed until it barely moved.

The Black side, so dark it sucked the light out of the air around it, was spinning up.

Akillik whistled. "Might not be a good time, really." Then he laughed again, this time a hard, unfriendly laugh.

Kevlin found his voice. "I don't want your luck. Just leave me alone."

Akillik rose a few feet and gestured around at the dome. "Think about it, man. If the Wheel spins for you, you'll be the greatest hero ever to walk the earth."

He descended again and extended the Wheel toward Kevlin. "If it spins against you, you could destroy everything." Akillik grinned. "Either way, no one will ever forget your name. Well, no one that lives, anyway."

Anger helped center his mind. Akillik claimed to be different, but just like Savas, he wanted only to destroy, to control Kevlin's life.

"I will not!" Kevlin shouted. He snatched a goblet from the hands of a nearby lady and threw it at Akillik. It disappeared in a flash of golden light before reaching the god.

Akillik floated higher, but his whisper floated back down. "You can't hold out forever, Kevlin. The longer you do, the greater the consequence."

His eyes blazed with power, and he looked far older and far more dangerous than ever before. "In the end, I always win."

Then he disappeared.

Pain crashed in on Kevlin's senses. He grabbed his head as magic tore through his mind, ripping at his thoughts and pushing the limits of his control.

A new thought floated to the surface of the turbulent battlefield of his mind. *Why struggle? It could all be over. All I have to do is give in.*

Sweat drenched Kevlin's shirt and dripped from his face. His muscles quivered as if he'd been fighting for hours, and pain pounded through him. All he had to do was let go, release the magic.

Indira dropped to her knees beside him. He couldn't focus on her, but he felt her presence, smelled the gentle fragrance she wore.

If he surrendered, what would happen to her?

Kevlin groaned with the effort and marshaled his scattered thoughts for a counterattack. He formed the image of himself standing atop his broken battlements, sword held high, ringed with blue fire.

He leaped off the wall, driving into the attacking horde.

You will obey me, by the gods.

Akillik's mocking laugh rang through his mind, and he cursed himself for the choice of words. But he didn't allow fear of Akillik to distract him. With every ounce of will he could muster, Kevlin led the charge against the magic.

He sought the peace of discipline and strength he'd felt while linked to his brothers in battle. The rogue magic beat against him, but he fought back with growing intensity.

He tasted dirt, and the sounds of steel rending flesh sounded in his ears as memories of real battles flickered through his mind. Kevlin rocked forward, groaning, barely suppressing the urge to shout aloud his battle cry.

The tide shifted in his favor and the magic retreated. He raised the reinforced battlements around his mind and populated them with invisible forces. As his control improved, the rebellious power subsided and submitted to his control. It flowed through his limbs, healing and refreshing his body where seconds earlier it had torn at his flesh to escape.

Kevlin blew out a breath and sat straight. Indira hovered close beside him, one hand extended toward him, but not quite touching. A few other people were looking on in concern.

Let them think he was drunk. If only life were that simple.

Kevlin wanted nothing more than to lie down, but he still knelt on the dance floor. The band was just beginning the first chords of another song, so he had to move.

"Are you all right?" Indira asked, finally touching his shoulder.

"I'm alive."

She helped him up and they moved off the dance floor. Kevlin suddenly felt ravenous, so they moved to one of the food tables and he piled a plate high and started wolfing it down.

"I don't often encourage binge eating after an injury," Indira said. "Slow down and tell me what happened."

"I'm not sure. Someone touched me with magic."

"Who?"

"I don't know." He shrugged and popped a sugar-coated pastry into his mouth.

"Why?"

"Who would even know to try?"

Indira looked around at the sea of humanity on every side, frowning.

Kevlin took her hand. "I have to find Harafin. He needs to know about this."

"I'll come with you."

Kevlin slipped a hand around her waist and leaned on her as they moved slowly across the floor. She frowned as they walked and Kevlin asked, "What's wrong?"

"I saw you fall," she said softly, her grip tightening around his waist. "I wanted to help you, but I didn't dare. For the first time in my life, I didn't know what to do."

"You did the right thing."

"But I didn't," she said with surprising heat. "Kevlin, the right thing is always to help and to heal, but I can't do that with you."

Her intensity surprised him. "Indira, sometimes the best way to help is to let someone deal with a problem alone."

"That doesn't make sense."

A dark-haired youth dressed in the green and gold of the palace staffers interrupted. He looked strangely familiar, but Kevlin couldn't place where he might have seen him before.

"Sir Kevlin, Master Harafin wishes to see you at once."

Kevlin smiled ruefully. "How did he know?"

The young man pointed toward the wide corridor leading toward the Southern Kingdoms Admin Palace. "He is waiting for you in one of the sunken gardens."

Kevlin sighed. If Harafin wanted privacy, he must have somehow felt the almost-*Tai-Pari*. What would he do?

The servant gave Kevlin directions, but then blocked Indira from joining Kevlin. "Pardon, Lady, I was told Sir Kevlin needed to come alone."

"It's all right," Kevlin told her and kissed her cheek. "I'll find you later."

"Be careful."

He glanced back twice, and she remained there, watching him. He hated leaving her right when things had been going so well. Hopefully Harafin would be quick, because he planned to enjoy this party.

The crowds thinned rapidly as he moved away from the Great Dome. He found a side corridor and descended to the second sub-level as instructed. He munched on the remnants of the food on the plate he still carried, and in a few minutes arrived at the sunken garden.

It was a simple one, with half a dozen pear trees already harvested for the season, and several benches scattered around the clearing and near the doors. The cascading fountain glowed with an amber light.

Since this level of the garden stood empty, Kevlin moved toward the stairs leading down to the lowest level. Harafin was taking the privacy a little far this time. It wasn't a good sign.

Fifty feet from the stairs, he stopped and spit out the food he'd been chewing. Eight men dressed in black clothing and armor erupted out of the shadows of the stairs in a silent charge.

Kevlin was not wearing his sword.

35

A Bit Of Fun

Kevlin pawed his belt, then cursed the fool who had banned long weapons from the ball. He could only do one thing. Run.

Two more black-clad men stepped into the doorway behind him.

Not good. The men advancing from the stairs spread out and the ones not brandishing heavy clubs produced a pair of nets.

That was just not fair.

Kevlin drew his belt dagger. It was a pathetic show of defiance, but he didn't have anything better. He tried to bolster his confidence by reminding himself he'd been in worse situations. That sparked an idea. The only worse situations he could think of were being nearly consumed by magic.

He had a little magic.

Connor threw his dinner plate at the advancing men, who lurked almost within striking range of those nets. As the food tumbled through the air, he focused on the piece of white cake he'd been saving for last. He wrapped it in a sphere of air and held it suspended in front of the lead attacker's face.

The man laughed. "You gonna fight us with a pastry?"

"Watch carefully," Kevlin said with forced confidence. "That piece of cake is going to save your life."

At the same time, he focused on the invisible connection with his swordbrothers. This time he felt it, vibrant and strong.

Brothers, he called to them. *Help. I'm under attack*! And he pushed to them the location.

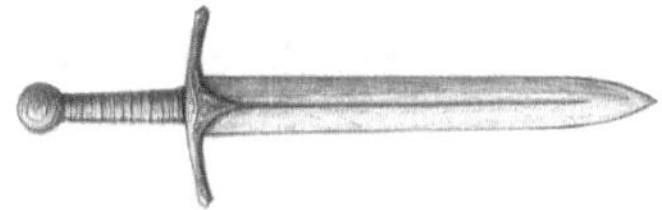

Jerrik cursed and spun away from a voluptuous blonde with coppery skin who wore a stunning red silk gown that caressed her as she moved. The beautiful young woman kept talking, as if she didn't notice him leaving.

She probably hadn't. She was the youngest daughter of a minor Freyarri noble house, known for her good looks, not her brains. Plus, she'd been drinking a lot.

Jerrik threw his drink at a young nobleman with a wide-brimmed floppy hat who didn't move out of the way in time. The idiot caught the cup in the face and toppled to the floor.

Jerrik charged right over him, shouting, "Ukko's Beard, get out of my way!"

His voice carried over the constant din of the ball, and people scattered out of his path. He didn't slow for the few too stupid or too drunk to move in time, but just bowled them over.

He pushed them harder than strictly necessary. Jerrik loved a good fight better than anyone, but Kevlin's timing was terrible. That girl had been getting very friendly.

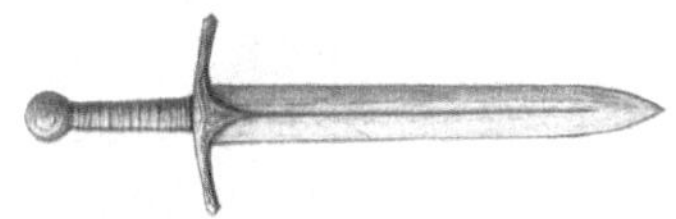

Drystan raced from the dance floor and wove through the crowd with his customary grace. Despite the press, he barely slowed, and people spun to watch him race for the wide southern exit where he met up with Jerrik.

Few noticed the willowy young woman with a sleeping baby strapped to her back who shadowed his steps and kept pace with him the entire way.

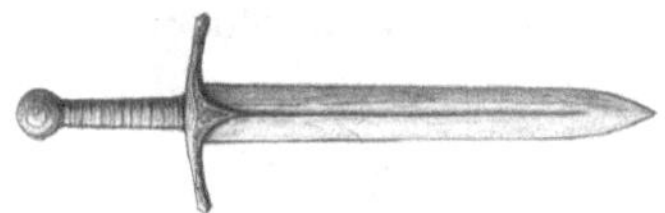

The lead attacker barked a laugh and said to Kevlin, "You're proving a lot more entertaining than most. All right, laddie, tell me how this little piece of cake is going to save my life."

Kevlin used the recently-learned technique and exploded the cake inside its containing sphere of air. It shattered in a brilliant flash of cream and fire. Three seconds later, it was reduced to a greasy smear.

Kevlin released the sphere of air and a cloud of black smoke wafted over the attackers, who cringed away. He spoke into the silence. "First one to take a step forward gets his head blown up just like that cake."

They all stepped back.

Several exchanged nervous glances and one, a thin fellow with a scraggly beard said, "No one said nothing about him using magic."

The leader clapped the fellow on the shoulder. "Risk is part of the business." He shoved the man forward.

The unlucky fellow stumbled several steps and shrieked like a little girl.

Kevlin cursed. He didn't have enough magic left to kill the clumsy fool. So he poked him in the eye with an invisible finger of power.

The man howled and rolled around, clutching at his head. That helped a little, but Kevlin needed something more. He didn't have enough magic left now to even blow up another piece of cake.

The leader grunted. "Nice trick. Take him, lads."

The black-clad soldiers advanced again, forming a loose circle around Kevlin, clubs raised.

Time to change tactics. He preferred steel over magic anyway.

Two net-wielding men stepped into range and hefted the net to throw. Kevlin brought his right arm down hard to release the stiletto hidden in his wrist-guard.

He was glad he had decided to keep it on, worn under the loose sleeve of his new shirt. The tiny blade sprang out and he caught it with a practiced motion.

Kevlin threw it just as the men committed to throwing the net. The stiletto caught the right-most of the pair in the eye and sank to the hilt. The man screamed and fell into the net, tangling it.

The second pair weren't deterred, but threw their net, forcing Kevlin to dive out of the way. He rolled and drew Bajaran's cursed silver dagger from its hidden sheath at the base of his neck.

He came to his feet closer to the outer door. One of the men stationed there meet him with a heavy blow of his club.

Kevlin tried to dodge, but the club smashed his left shoulder. Something cracked and pain exploded all the way down Kevlin's arm. His belt dagger fell from numb fingers.

He stumbled and slashed wildly with the silver dagger, scoring a light cut on the man's arm.

It was enough.

The fellow screamed and dropped his club. He staggered back against his companion and screamed again, a high-pitched wail of agony. It reminded Kevlin of the sound he'd heard a sailor make when attacked by a shark.

That kind of scream a man doesn't forget. The other attackers paused, staring at their companion.

The doomed soldier collapsed, clutching at his wounded arm as his fingers blackened and began to smoke as if being charred from the inside. Tendrils of blackness crawled up his neck, just under the skin.

He screamed again as the fingers of blackness reached his face. He convulsed, then lay still, his dead eyes fixed on the ceiling high above. His companions recoiled from the sight.

Kevlin gritted his teeth against the pain pounding through him like a high sea and focused the tiny bit of magic still remaining to him on the silver dagger.

"Fire."

A ripple of blue flame appeared around the dagger, coursing the length of the blade. A single tongue of fire slipped off the point and dropped to the floor where it burned for a second before being joined by another, and then another.

Kevlin hefted the burning blade, drawing every eye. Battle fury swept through him, helping to drive back the pain. He planted his feet, beckoned with his dagger, and snarled, "Who wants to die next?"

The leader spat. "Those were good men you killed, laddie." He hefted his club. "I'm gonna break your arms and legs for that."

Kevlin had never met a more determined group of mercenaries. Most soldiers for hire would cut their losses and run. It wasn't fair.

A distant echoing laughter sounded in his ears.

Curse you and your Wheel, Kevlin shouted the thought. *May you get stuck in the mud of Asherah's displeasure!*

Kevlin shifted toward the wall in hopes of getting his back to it, but the mercenaries cut him off. He turned a steady circle to keep them in view.

The men hovered just out of reach while two of their number prepared the net again. He tensed to launch a desperate charge before they could snare him.

Jerrik charged into the room, bellowing his battle cry, "Kamen Seig!"

Without slowing, he caught up one of the heavy benches situated near the door and heaved it. It blasted two mercenaries into the next world.

The leader shouted at his net-wielding men, "Throw already." To the others, he gestured at Jerrik. "Kill that one."

Drystan joined the fray. He sprinted into the room, wielding nothing but a pair of short daggers.

One soldier intercepted him, club raised to strike.

Drystan spun around the man in his trademark move and whipped his tiny blades across the man's throat as he passed. The mercenary clutched as his neck as his life blood spurted between his fingers.

Drystan had already closed on the next man and, with a flying leap, slammed both knees into the center of the man's chest. He drove the fellow to the ground and struck him in the temple with the pommel of one blade.

The sight of his brothers invigorated Kevlin. He charged the men with the net. They threw it.

Maybe that wasn't such a good idea.

Kevlin dove forward and tried to roll under it. The impact on his wounded shoulder drove a shocking wave of pain through him and he ended up in a heap at the feet of the mercenaries.

One of them kicked Kevlin in the head. The blow rattled him and he lost his grip on the silver dagger. The flames winked out.

The other mercenary scooped up the blade. Kevlin struggled to bring his vision into focus as the man leaned over him with the weapon.

"Too bad I can't kill you," the man said. "But I'm going to keep this little knife as a gift."

Kevlin kicked him in the knee.

When the man lurched forward, Kevlin grabbed his wrist and drove the silver dagger back into his stomach. The blade cut through his boiled leather armor like butter and sank deep into his stomach.

The mercenary screamed and collapsed. Kevlin pulled out the blade and turned toward the man's companion. That one, in true mercenary spirit, turned and ran.

Keelin arrived in the doorway first.

The mercenary bore down on her with a shout and raised his club to smash her and her baby out of the way.

Drystan and Jerrik were fully engaged with the other mercenaries and didn't see the danger. Time seemed to slow as Kevlin helplessly watched the mercenary bear down on Keelin.

Instead of fleeing, Keelin reached under the strap of her baby's pack and extracted a two-foot leather cord capped with a metal ball. As the mercenary closed on her, she danced aside and flicked the strange weapon at him.

The metal ball smashed into his forehead. His head snapped back while his feet kept moving, flipping him over backward. He landed on his head and didn't move.

Keelin stepped over him and moved to Kevlin.

As she settled daintily to the ground beside him, Kevlin stammered, "How did you . . . ?"

"Oh, dear," Keelin said with a warm smile. "If that impressed you, I'm afraid you're in for rather a shock when you see me back home."

"You're not like most new mothers."

"I'll take that as a compliment. Now, tell me what hurts."

The tide of battle turned against the mercenaries. Jerrik picked up the leader and threw him into two of his other men and then wrapped the three of them in their own net. Drystan took another mercenary's club away from him, clobbered him on the head, and broke the legs of the last two mercenaries as they tried to flee.

"Now that you've finished, why don't one of you tell me what's going on?" Harafin stood in the doorway, with Leander close behind.

"They started it," Kevlin said.

Jerrik clapped his huge hands together, threw his head back and roared, "And by the gods, we finished it!"

Harafin gestured with one hand, and glowing prisons formed around all of the still-breathing mercenaries. He stepped into the garden and asked, "Why did they do this?"

Kevlin shrugged and then groaned from a new wave of pain from his injured shoulder. Keelin helped him stand. "I don't know anything about them. I was looking for you."

"You think they planned this?" Jerrik asked.

"Clearly," Harafin said. "They meant to take Kevlin."

Leander moved to Kevlin's side and began examining his shoulder. "Again, the question is why."

Harafin said, "That is exactly what we are going to find out."

36

THE FACE OF EVIL

Sitara, dressed in an elegant midnight-blue silk gown and matching cloak, stepped through the brightly lit outer gate of the Port Spoke of the inner city wall. She blended in with the dozens of other party-goers passing in both directions around her and no one paid her any heed.

She descended the wide boulevard into the upper city for a quarter mile before slipping into a darkened alley near a richly furnished stable. As she stepped into the shadows, she opened herself to the power of the night. Darkness eagerly crawled into her and clung to her innards, filling her with power and revulsion in equal measure.

Sitara focused a bit of that power into her eyes, and the dim world previously concealed by the cloak of night clarified. Usually she would have preferred a torch or any natural, clean light. Her tainted power penetrated the darkness farther, but tinted things a slight shade of crimson, as if everything she looked at was on the verge of bleeding.

She took a deep breath and forced calm over herself. She double-checked her mental shields, then strode down the alley with more confidence than she felt.

As she neared the far end of the building, a man-sized, hooded shape separated itself from the other shadows and moved to intercept her. Sitara's heart quickened in fear, despite her efforts to maintain calm.

She braced herself against an expected attack, but felt no more than a whisper of contact. Instantly she altered the angles of her shield.

Instead of attacking, the dark figure brushed back his hood to reveal dark hair and eyes covered in roiling blackness that shamed the other shadows.

Tanathos made a short, mocking bow. "Greetings, sister of the true blood."

Sitara shuddered at the oddly intimate greeting. She still struggled with the fact that her master agreed to ally even superficially with this creature. His presence radiated pure evil, and a primal instinct deep inside her soul urged her to attack and not relent until one of them lay dead.

His death will serve a purpose, she reminded herself.

Masego's plan had better work. If only she could watch as Harafin destroyed this arrogant, disgusting creature. That his death would help shield their escape with the prize motivated her to keep her peace.

"We don't have much time," she said. "You know what must be done. Do it."

Tanathos' lip curled back in a silent snarl and he stepped closer. She forced herself not to shrink back from his presence, but clenched the fabric of her gown tight in one fist. It helped relieve a little of the tension that threatened to snap her resolve.

"You fear me, girl. A hint of wisdom in one so young."

His condescension reminded her of Masego, and anger burned away some of the fear. She leaned just a hair closer to him. "Don't try my patience or my Master will need to find another pet Shadeleech to do his bidding."

Tanathos raised a hand and it burst into red fire.

"Put that out, fool," Sitara hissed.

Her throat felt drier than ash and she struggled to keep her breathing normal. Pushing him was insane, but allowing him to believe she feared him would be suicidal. She tensed behind her mental shields and prepared a counterstrike should he try to hit her.

Tanathos dropped his fist and the crimson flames snuffed out. He took a step back, a twisted smile on his lips. "Your spirit is strong. It will feed me well."

"I'm going to wait in the street," Sitara said. "Be quick. Tell yourself you're tough as many times as you need to believe it. When you're done, purge your powers and join me. We don't have much time."

She forced herself to turn her back on him and walk slowly toward the street. At every step, she expected a brutal attack and wanted to scream from the tension that knotted her insides. It seemed to take forever to reach the corner at the front of the building.

There she sank onto a metal bench and clasped her shaking hands in her lap. She breathed deep and wiped her suddenly sweating brow.

All too soon Tanathos joined her. He now wore a wide-brimmed hat that cast a deep shadow over his eyes. He dressed in black trousers and shirt with a crimson vest, covered in a dark cloak. Not exactly high fashion, but not so unusual as to draw the guards' attention.

Sitara rose from her seat. "You're purged?"

He gave her a quick, jerky nod.

"Good. Stay close or I won't be able to shield you from the Sentinels posted at the gate."

Tanathos moved close beside her and slipped an arm around her waist. She had to bite down hard on her lip to keep from squealing and fleeing his touch.

"You're too close."

Tanathos chuckled. "You fear my touch?"

"Don't flatter yourself. I might be recognized, and if we look like a couple, it could draw unnecessary questions."

Tanathos removed his hand and withdrew a single step. Sitara quickened her pace. The sooner she accomplished this mission, the better.

They climbed the slope of the upper city and passed through the open outer gates into the long tunnel that bore through the enormous inner-city wall. The air was surprisingly chill, and the passage echoed loudly with the many footsteps on the hard stone road.

Sitara purged the clinging filth of her dark power, despite the stark terror she felt standing so close to the Shadeleech. If she waited any longer, that dark power would trigger the guardian wards placed at the entrances. Despite that danger, she couldn't have left herself powerless had she not known Tanathos had purged his Sthenic magic too.

A squad of soldiers was stationed at the far end of the tunnel, along with a pair of Fire Stalwarts and a pair of Kestrels. The group inspected everyone entering the inner city.

No long weapons were allowed, so the guards collected and catalogued every sword, long-knife, and even staves. They handed the owners a receipt to allow them to collect the weapons on their way out.

Tanathos dragged Sitara to a stop. "How do we pass?"

"We wait."

"For what?"

"You'll see." It might be petty, but she savored the little bit of power her knowledge granted her over him.

He was very much at her mercy right now. If only she dared the wrath of her master enough to reveal him to the Sentinels.

"Don't play games with me," Tanathos snarled.

Sitara leaned against the tunnel wall and watched people pass by. She glanced at Tanathos. "The game is not mine. We both dance to my master's tune."

"He is not my master."

"You're here at his bidding, protected by his will and pleasure, are you not?"

Tanathos said nothing, and leaned against the wall beside her. "How long do we wait?"

The sound of many footsteps marching in cadence drew Sitara's gaze to the outer gate. "The wait is over."

Approaching at a steady march came a large party surrounded by the shimmering silver haze of a Sentinel shield. Within the shield, half a dozen guards flanked an enclosed palanquin carried by eight burly men.

As the last pair of guards marched past, Sitara gestured to Tanathos and jogged after the entourage. The rear quarter of the shield flickered and disappeared. The last two guards parted without looking back at Sitara.

She slipped between them and moved forward until she walked just behind the litter-bearers, with Tanathos on her heels. As soon as they passed, the rear guard closed ranks behind them and the shield flowed back down over the entire party.

Tanathos focused on the palanquin in front of them, his expression neutral. Despite her loathing of him, his outward calm impressed her. Could she walk so calmly into the heart of a Shadeleech fortress, completely cut off from her powers?

Hopefully he thought she'd help plan everything. In fact, she barely concealed her own amazement. Everything was falling into place exactly as Remiel had predicted.

How could Masego arrange this? How could the Sentinel shielding this party be in league with him? She wished she knew their name or could at least see their face. She longed to know other secret revolutionaries. The very fact that she walked within a few feet of one encouraged her.

Was the noble involved, or ignorant of the deception being played out right behind them? If Masego could arrange so much so quickly, with help from those placed so high, what else might he be capable of?

That worried her. She needed more information to plan her coup. Let Masego orchestrate the downfall of the current, corrupt regime, but she couldn't let him consolidate power. She needed to build her own forces.

The company passed through the inner gate and paused at the command of the gate company captain.

"What's all this, then?" the captain asked.

One of the Sentinels on duty moved to stand beside the captain. "Lower your shield and be inspected."

Sitara bit her lip. This was not part of the plan. If they lowered the shield, the Sentinels would surely sense Tanathos. Even purged of his powers, he was so steeped in Sthenic energy that some residue would surely trigger the guardian spells.

The front of the shield flickered briefly and a richly dressed servant stepped through to face the captain. The shield solidified behind him. He held out a sealed parchment to the captain.

"We are authorized to pass, Captain. High Lady Damarist is worried about assassins who might be out and about tonight and received permission to maintain an active shield to and from the Great Dome."

"I assure you, we are safe here," the captain started.

"Be that as it may, Captain. The High Lady made her decision and her party was vetted before leaving her mansion." He extended the parchment again. "Let us pass."

The captain broke the seal and read the parchment. He frowned but stepped aside and waved them through.

Sitara fell into step with the others, but her mind raced. High Lady Damarist? Could the ambassador's wife really be knowingly helping Masego? Could his influence extend so far?

After the group passed the Sentinel Tower, the rear of the shield flickered and disappeared. The rear guard parted again, and Sitara drew Tanathos out of the protecting circle.

She struggled to open the channel to her own Actinopathic gift. It came after a terrifying pause, a weak shadow of its normal strength. The revolution could not come too soon.

The Sentinels had managed to nearly block her completely from her gift. That, more than any other fact, confirmed the need to throw down their rule.

Sitara wrapped an invisible shield around the two of them and led Tanathos southwest, behind the Sentinel Tower, toward the dark, outer edge of the plateau. As they passed the white tower, Tanathos growled low in his throat.

Sitara reached out with a whisper of thought and probed his unprotected mind.

He snarled and grabbed her cloak. "Keep your thoughts out of my head or I'll rip your throat out right here."

Sitara forced herself to stare into the roiling blackness covering his eyes under his wide-brimmed hat. "To kill you, all I need to do is drop my shield. Are you prepared to die?"

Tanathos released her, and she saw the first flicker of real fear on his face. The sight bolstered her confidence. Even Tanathos could feel fear. He could die just like any other man.

Silently they circumvented a long, low cedar hedge and approached a squat stone building set apart in an open courtyard. Inside, it held only a set of simple stone stairs descending into darkness.

"The catacombs," Sitara said, and led him down.

37

BEGIN THE HUNT

Kevlin stood in a long, low-ceilinged room deep in the dungeons under the central palace. He and his Swordbrothers waited while Harafin examined the captured mercenaries. Leander had stabilized the worst of the injured.

Harafin stood and withdrew the glowing hand he had held pressed against the forehead of the leader of the attackers. The man watched him with a terrified expression.

"I find no mind traps on these men," Harafin said. "I don't believe they'll die under questioning."

"What do you mean, die?" the prisoner asked.

"I'll ask the questions, young man," Harafin said. "If you answer truthfully, you might even live out the night."

The man gulped and shared a fearful look with his companions. "What do you want to know?"

The heavy oak door banged open and Ah'Shan strode into the room.

Harafin nodded a greeting. "Thank you for coming quickly. I was just about to begin the interrogation."

Ah'Shan gave the fearful prisoners a dismissive wave. "Leave that rabble. We need to talk. Now."

"Hold on a minute," Kevlin said. "I want to know why they tried to kill me."

Ah'Shan didn't bother looking at him. "They can wait. You'll want to hear this too."

They left the prisoners in the large cell under the watchful eyes of a pair of soldiers and followed Ah'Shan into a nearby circular guardroom. The empty room held nothing but a small table, half a dozen chairs, and a weapons rack along one wall.

The door on the far side of the room opened just as they entered, and Gabral strode in. He was still dressed in his party finery. "Why was I not informed of this interrogation?"

"Why should you be?" Jerrik asked.

"I'm the emperor's champion." Gabral drew himself up to his full diminutive height. "I'm personally responsible for security arrangements tonight. Any breach was to be reported to me immediately."

"So you're the one who gave the asinine order banning all long weapons tonight," Drystan said.

Gabral glared and pointed a finger at Drystan. "Watch yourself, soldier. I will not tolerate insubordination."

"I nearly died tonight because I didn't have my sword," Kevlin said.

Gabral gave him a withering look. "I have bigger concerns than your safety, mercenary."

Kevlin really disliked this man. The little colonel had made it clear from the first day they met that he considered Kevlin a second-rate soldier. He hadn't revised that opinion, despite all they'd been through.

Then again, Kevlin had disliked him from day one. He still did, but it was deepening, like rotting cheese.

"Enough bickering," Ah'Shan snapped. "We have important things to discuss." He made a sweeping motion with one hand, and the walls began to glow with amber light, similar to the shielded spheres Harafin had used during Kevlin's training sessions.

Harafin raised an eyebrow. "Is that necessary? We're in the most secure wing of the dungeons already."

"We cannot be too cautious."

Leander took a seat. "I admit, the theatrics make me curious."

"I just completed probing the minds of the men captured in the assassination attempt on the emperor," Ah'Shan declared.

"Who wanted the emperor dead?" Drystan asked.

"That's the surprise. The entire attack was a fraud. We were all duped."
Ah'Shan pulled a chair around and sat down with his arms draped across
the back. "Two of the men died before I learned the true secret."

"You're enjoying this, aren't you?" Leander asked.

"What secret?" Harafin urged.

"The emperor was not the ultimate target."

Gabral huffed. "Impossible. We were there. Without our intervention,
without the Mace to drive them off, the emperor would have died."

"That's what you were meant to think. The truth was buried deep,
protected by no less than three mind traps. Kevlin and Drystan were
the targets. They were to be taken alive and delivered to the attackers'
master."

Keelin had been right when she questioned the attackers' motivation.
The assassins hadn't made a sloppy tactical error. Well, other than
attacking the company in the first place.

Ah'Shan continued. "The attack on the emperor and the ambassadors
was nothing but a diversion, an attempt to mask the real mission."

"Impossible," Gabral protested again. "No one tries to assassinate the
emperor as a cover-up. There's nothing more important."

Ah'Shan's voice turned grave. "There is. Harafin, they seek your
secret."

"What secret?" Gabral demanded.

"They seek to know who is bearer of Oris," Harafin said.

"And the location of the stone, no doubt," Leander added.

"Who would go to so much trouble to hide their intent?" Drystan
wondered.

"Tanathos." Harafin's word confirmed what Kevlin already suspected.

"That's the biggest surprise," Ah'Shan said. "Hidden in the mind of
the leader of those men, even more heavily guarded than the true purpose
of their mission, was the secret of their employer. It was not Tanathos,
but someone named Masego."

"Masego?" Kevlin exclaimed. "That's the name of the guy Rhea said
she was working for."

"That is a very interesting connection," Harafin said.

"And here in the palace," Leander added.

"So Masego's a player," Ah'Shan said. "One we haven't met yet."

"But one who's been after Oris from the beginning."

"Could he be working with Tanathos?" Kevlin asked.

Harafin said, "There's no way to know, but perhaps it was this Masego who tampered with the shield matrix."

"I'm wanting to meet this person more and more," Ah'Shan said.

"Me too," Jerrik said, patting the hilt of his sword.

"This Masego has good intelligence," Gabral said. "He knows we were there at Il'Aicharen. He suspects we know the secret, even though Harafin has kept even us ignorant of the truth."

"He'll likely attack again," Drystan said.

Jerrik grinned and flexed his huge arms. "I hope he doesn't wait too long."

Harafin said, "He already has."

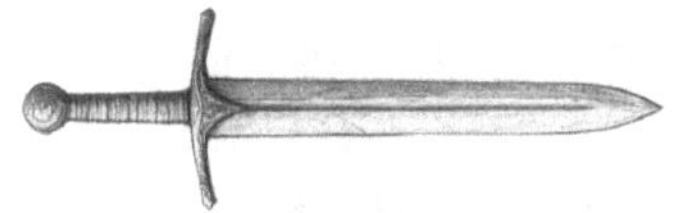

"You are licensed fugitive hunters?" Harafin asked the leader of the men who attacked Kevlin in the sunken garden.

The man gestured with the papers he held in his hand. "We are. We have all the right permits, so let us go."

"If only it were so easy. Who hired you?"

The man shrugged. "I don't know. I got a letter this morning with the job."

"Do you often take jobs by post?"

"First time. But there were one hundred gold crowns with the letter, so we weren't asking lots of questions." The man spoke with a Hallvarri accent.

Harafin nodded. "Do you have this letter?"

The man shook his head. "Strangest thing happened. I put the letter down on my desk and it caught fire."

"That does seem strange, and still you proceeded with the mission?"

"Seemed like the right thing to do. The letter promised another hundred in gold upon delivery."

"What were the terms of the engagement?"

The man pointed at Kevlin. "Take that man alive and deliver him at midnight to the catacombs for payment."

Gabral took a step forward. "You're supposed to deliver prisoners to the Department of Justice, Fugitive Recovery Office to collect bounties."

"Normally, that's what we do," the man said, unfazed. "But this was a non-sanctioned hunt. We was told the target stole from a high nobleman and he wanted justice." The man shrugged. "Seemed reasonable at the time."

"You'll lose your license for this," Gabral threatened.

The man barked a laugh. "Lost half my team tonight. You think I care naught for your permit?"

Back in the guard room, Harafin said, "Masego has indeed struck again."

Jerrik frowned. "How do you know it's Masego? They don't even know who they're working for."

"It has to be. And tonight we're going to meet him."

"How do you plan to do that?" Gabral asked.

Harafin smiled. "Weren't you listening? Masego is expecting mercenaries to deliver Kevlin to the catacombs at midnight. We have just enough time to make it."

"Do you really think it could work?" asked Leander.

"We cannot afford to miss the opportunity." Harafin's face turned hard and his eyes sparkled with power. "Come, my friends. Tonight we begin the hunt."

38

CATACOMBS

A frantic half hour later, Kevlin marched in the midst of a group of half a dozen phony mercenaries, hands held behind his back as if tied. The operation felt rushed, and that made him extremely nervous.

The black-clad soldiers, led by Jerrik, checked weapons and armor as they skirted the Sentinel Tower. They rounded a long, low cedar hedge, barely visible in the darkness.

Kevlin wished he had his sword. When they sprang the trap on this Masego, he planned to lead the charge. He hated doing that without his sword.

Bright lights blazed along the nearby Port Spoke, illuminating the steady stream of partygoers returning to their homes. Distant laughter echoed through the darkness, but seemed foreign to Kevlin. Those people had no clue about the danger lurking among them while Kevlin and this tiny group prepared for battle.

Jerrik, dimly lit by the shuttered lantern he carried, still smiled. He'd convinced Harafin to assign him to the party, but Drystan hadn't been so lucky.

They'd laid their plans quickly, with heated debate. The plan called for Jerrik's small company to lead Kevlin to the rendezvous point in the catacombs. Reinforcements would move into position exactly two minutes later. They would secure the subterranean burial ground and cut off any chance of escape. If Masego had spotters watching for a trap, their warning would come too late.

Every one of the soldiers tapped for the mission was hand-picked by Jerrik or Drystan and looked similar to the captured mercenaries. Jerrik stood out as an exception, but he successfully argued that in the shadows the difference was not enough to matter.

Kevlin had argued for Drystan's inclusion, even though his lanky brother resembled none of the attackers. Kevlin would have felt more confident with both of his brothers flanking him tonight. Still, Drystan would lead the company of reinforcements, along with Harafin and Leander.

Leander had tapped a full score of his Stalwarts to assist, and one of them marched with the phony mercenary group. Harafin refused a general call to arms. The risk was too great that Masego would realize the danger and flee.

Ah'Shan had left to summon Felix, and the two would remain outside the catacombs with Gabral, ready to call up more reinforcements if needed. Ah'Shan had argued that a Sentinel should march among the phony mercenaries, but Harafin refused to allow it. Sentinels might be sensed by one of the watchers.

Gabral was furious at his support role, but he was too well known. Kevlin was mightily tempted to rub it in, but realized he didn't have to. Gabral was working himself into a rage all by himself.

The company approached a simple stone building in a small courtyard. Inside it contained only a stone stair leading down into darkness. Without hesitation, Jerrik led the company down.

The air grew chill as they descended one hundred and seven steps into the earth. Jerrik opened the lantern wider, and several soldiers lit torches. The light illuminated unbroken walls covered with simple drawings depicting the afterlife as taught by the Stalwarts of the various gods.

Serigala welcomed home blessed children bearing yew and stone, while Asherah drew sailors down into the depths of her eternal kingdom beneath the waves. Salawin divided the just from the unjust with his great sword, while Kamen feasted with fallen warriors. En'Lil galloped the endless plains on the Fravashi spirit horses, hunting fleet-footed antelope with his Einarri children.

Kevlin averted his eyes whenever he caught glimpses of Akillik and his Wheel, and even avoided studying images of Tikir showering the faithful with riches. He couldn't afford to trust either form of Karakol right now.

He was surprised to see images of Savas feasting with his chosen ones between battles of their eternal warfare. He hadn't expected Blade Stalwarts to show a presence here, and the knowledge that they had tread these same dark steps made him shiver.

Kevlin welcomed the sight of the narrow, winding passage cut into the earth at the bottom of the stairs. Jerrik went first and his huge shoulders nearly scraped the earthen walls on either side. The low, uneven ceiling forced him to crouch to avoid cracking his helmet against protruding rocks.

The rest of the company followed single file behind him. As they passed deeper into the catacombs, Kevlin wondered about the dead buried within arm's reach on either side. Tiny plaques marked many of the graves stacked four high every ten feet along both walls. He was tempted to try reading the names and dates of those buried there.

In his travels, Kevlin had seen many comrades die and had helped bury more than he cared to remember. He had participated in burial rites of believers of all the gods, but had never thought to walk under the earth among the dead.

The thought settled heavy in his mind, and he shivered from more than the pervasive chill filling the stygian passage. They marched to meet a mysterious, deadly enemy. Before the torches burned out, some of them might take up permanent residence here in the halls of the dead.

Kevlin focused on the man in front of him. They might die tonight, but dwelling on it wouldn't help. Better to focus on the goal to send Masego to whatever god he worshipped.

They followed the twisting passages for ten minutes, and Kevlin was grateful that Harafin had insisted every member of the company memorize the route through this underground maze. The palace complex above had been laid out with exquisite care, but the catacombs showed no such planning. Passages peeled off at random intervals and intersected at odd angles. In one intersection, no less than seven passages converged.

It would be far too easy to lose one's way down here, left to wander the impenetrable darkness until they succumbed to exhaustion and joined their dead brethren. He broke into a cold sweat as an unfamiliar fear weakened his resolve. He felt the sudden urge to turn and rush the other way and not stop until he stood beneath the stars again.

Kevlin had never liked deep, closed-in places, but had never felt anything like this. He tried to breathe steady and focus on the torches held by soldiers in front of him. It helped, but only a little.

Finally, they entered a wider passage where they could walk four abreast. That helped ease his fear, even though the earthen ceiling still hung ominously low over their heads. The men of the company surrounded Kevlin and re-checked weapons and equipment.

Jerrik sent a scout ahead. The soldier slipped forward into the darkness carrying a shuttered lantern that allowed only the tiniest hint of light to seep through. The rest of the company followed a moment later. Kevlin found his pulse quickening and in his mind he practiced drawing his concealed daggers.

The scout returned a minute later. "We're almost there. I heard movement."

Jerrik grinned. "Stay tight. It's time."

Soon they reached a thick wooden door that hung open. They stepped through into a large room. It had to span at least fifty paces, but their lights failed to illuminate the far side. The soft clang of metal on metal sounded from the darkness.

Someone was waiting for them.

39

TRAPS WITHIN TRAPS

Shadows moved on the far side of the room, and the company shifted into battle-ready stances. Masego was not alone.

At Jerrik's whispered command, the company formed into two rows, with Jerrik, the Stalwart, and another soldier in the lead. The other three soldiers formed a tight rank behind Kevlin.

A rough voice called out of the darkness. "Show us the prisoner."

Jerrik pulled Kevlin forward. "Show us the gold."

In answer, the room rang with the twanging of bows being fired. The deadly sound was loud in the enclosed space.

"Look out!" Jerrik yelled as arrows shot out of the darkness. He pushed Kevlin behind him.

Kevlin stumbled, and in the flickering light of their torches, witnessed arrows driving into Jerrik and the other men in the front rank. Some clanged loud against the steel of plate and chainmail armor, but some sank deep, with the sickening sound of steel driving into flesh.

Jerrik roared in pain and staggered. He tripped over Kevlin and fell hard on his back. Beside him, the other two men toppled to the ground.

Kevlin couldn't catch Jerrik's massive bulk. Four arrows stood out from Jerrik's torso. The sight filled Kevlin with cold dread.

Jerrik's face twisted in pain and he gasped with each breath.

The enemy on the far side of the room un-hooded several lanterns that now illuminated a dozen black-clad men who had stood hidden in the shadows.

A blond-haired fellow with wide shoulders and a heavy, single brow pointed at Kevlin. "Take that one alive. Kill the rest."

His men dropped their bows and drew swords. The steely hiss raced down Kevlin's spine like ice.

The attackers charged.

Kevlin glanced down at Jerrik, who was pawing weakly at his huge broadsword. The sight filled Kevlin with a towering fury. He brushed Jerrik's hand aside and drew the massive blade.

Kevlin hefted the sword and turned toward the attackers, a snarl on his lips. This weapon would do. Jerrik had always stood by him, an indomitable force who had saved Kevlin's life more than once. That the big man's last act had been to protect him filled him with rage.

"I'll be back in a minute," he growled.

Then he turned toward the charging men and howled a wordless battle cry so loud it strained his voice.

Kevlin charged.

He raced to meet them, Jerrik's huge sword held high. He didn't know if one of them might be Masego. He didn't care.

He planned to kill them all.

Kevlin's arms burned with the need to kill as battle fury swept over him. He poured on more speed and closed the distance. The earthen floor was hard underfoot, and dust coated the inside of his mouth.

Kevlin met the center of the attacking line with a mighty sweep of Jerrik's sword that beat aside one man's blade and carved through his shoulder. Kevlin ducked another sword, and slammed his shoulder into the next man's chest, driving the man from his feet.

Then he burst through the attackers' line. The men had spread out as they charged, leaving their line thin and ragged. Kevlin wheeled left and sped across the back of their line, slashing at surprised soldiers, but not slowing.

Several men in the center of the line had halted to face him, but he left them far behind and ran down the men still charging at his last two standing companions.

One man tried to spin to face Kevlin, but tripped and fell. Kevlin took off his head, then struck down the man's companion as he prepared to attack the men of Kevlin's company.

Those survivors had formed a protective circle around their fallen comrades. They beckoned him to stand with them, but he kept running. They could hold their line for a time. He needed to harry the attackers and keep them distracted.

It was a suicide tactic, but he only needed to stay alive another minute until reinforcements arrived. The sound of battle would draw them on, but he planned to do a lot of killing before they arrived.

So Kevlin moved fast. Enemies fanned out to cut him off, and he barreled through their lines, slashing where he could, but lacking time for focused thrusts.

Several of the attackers moved against Kevlin's three companions, who fought valiantly to protect the fallen men of their company. For now, they held their own.

Kevlin ranged across the room, drawing more enemies after him. He was soon panting, and his arms ached from swinging Jerrik's massive sword, but he couldn't slow. One misstep, one moment of hesitation and they would box him in and slaughter him.

These men hadn't worked together before. That much was obvious. Had they functioned as a close-knit unit, they'd have cut Kevlin down quickly. Instead of anticipating each other's moves and working together to tighten the ring of steel around Kevlin, they mis-judged each other's moves, stumbling into each other, and leaving avenues open for Kevlin's escape.

Kevlin took advantage of every mistake. He slipped through openings in their ranks, slashing at arms and legs and faces, trying to add to their confusion and to stay one step ahead.

As the fighting ranged close to the far side of the room, Kevlin caught sight of two doors there. A shadowy figure stepped through the right-most door. Kevlin hoped it might be the blond-haired leader who he'd lost sight of during the fast-paced battle.

It was not the blond soldier.

It was Tanathos.

40

PLANS GONE AWRY

S itara hurried along one of the narrow earthen passages of the catacombs, fear a heavy weight on her shoulders. She should have already reached the side tunnel that would take her around the area where Masego had set his trap.

The sharp sounds of battle rang out in the distance, adding to her desperation. She was late. She'd left Tanathos near the large room where they were to spring the trap and take the man Kevlin. The Shadeleech thought he'd get Kevlin, but Sitara expected Masego to twist the encounter to his benefit, leaving Tanathos as the scapegoat.

If she didn't hurry, they'd leave her behind. She was apprehensive to finally meet her faceless employer, but knowing him would grant a huge advantage. She'd have to exercise extreme caution. He wielded tremendous influence from the shadows. No doubt he'd prove even more dominating in person.

Sitara picked up her pace, wishing she dared allow more light from her shuttered lantern. The tiny beam barely illuminated her path enough to keep from running into the twisting walls. She might easily have missed her turn.

No, this had to be right. The alternative was too terrifying to dwell on.

So engrossed was she in watching for the expected turn that she rounded a corner and collided with a soldier wearing the uniform of the elite guard of Einarr. He was tall, broad-shouldered, with typical close-cropped blond hair.

"I'm so sorry," Sitara stammered.

The soldier smiled at the sound of her voice. "Here now, little lady. What are you doing down here in the catacombs?"

Sitara tried to pull away, but he grabbed her arm. She said, "I was looking for my grandfather's tomb to lay some flowers on his grave to mark his birthday, but I'm afraid I lost my way."

"It's easy to do down here." He released her arm, his suspicion fading under the influence of her sweet voice. "It's not safe here tonight. I'll escort you back to the surface."

"That's not necessary," Sitara protested.

"It's no bother." He took her hand and led her along the passage. "I'm happy to help."

After no more than ten steps, the right-hand turn Sitara had been looking for came into view. She pulled the soldier to a stop. "Oh, here's the tunnel I was looking for. I wasn't lost at all. Thank you so much for your help, but I must be going now."

The soldier frowned. "I'm sorry, miss, but I'm afraid no civilians are allowed down here tonight. You'll have to leave your flowers tomorrow."

He glanced down at her hands and his frown deepened. "Where are your flowers, miss?"

This distraction was wasting too much time. Sitara opened herself to the power of darkness. Here in the bowels of the earth, surrounded by the dead, the sickening power exploded into her with exceptional force. It filled her with strength and clogged her innards with its filth. She gagged with revulsion.

"Are you sick?" The soldier leaned closer.

She clubbed him in the head with an invisible fist of air.

His cry of alarm cut off as she crushed him against the wall of the passage. He slumped to the ground, unmoving.

Sitara left him and raced down the side passage. She hoped no one else patrolled this section of the tunnels. She couldn't afford any more delays.

As she rounded the next bend, she caught sight of flickering torchlight. She whispered the keisara's favorite curse and shuttered her lantern again. Then she crept forward, extending her senses like feelers. Whispered voices echoed down the passage, clear to her enhanced hearing.

"You two, stand guard here," said one voice. "Report any intruders."

"I can hear battle," a second voice said in an eager whisper. "We should go help."

"You have your orders," repeated the first. "Harafin and the others can take care of that rabble. We're to watch for stragglers."

"And what am I supposed to do if we run into a rogue Sentinel down here?" the second voice asked.

A third voice joined the conversation. "Don't worry, my friend. Sentinels have no power over my brotherhood."

"Right," the second voice said. "Forgot that. I'll do the bladework, and you knock out the gifted."

"Deal."

Sitara backed away. There would be no easy passage this way. She would have struck down the unsuspecting guards, but her powers would have no effect on the Stalwart.

Then her enhanced senses drew her attention back the way she had come.

A deep but surprisingly gentle voice spoke. "Ho there. What happened, my friend?"

The voice of the soldier who had tried to escort Sitara out of the catacombs sounded groggy. "A girl hit me."

A quiet laugh. "Better be careful who you tell that to, friend."

"No," the soldier protested, his voice stronger. "I didn't see the blow. It came out of nowhere and clobbered me. Felt like a hammer-strike."

"Can you describe this girl?"

"Aye."

Sitara panicked. Her face was not unknown in the palaces. Tonight's plan was to flee the capital as soon as Masego learned the location of Oris from the man Kevlin.

The mention of Harafin's name by those other soldiers now cast a dreadful doubt over the success of the mission. Even if they took him, Sitara had no idea how long it might take to steal the stone. She had survived this long only through her secret anonymity.

The soldier must die.

41

OLD ENEMIES

Kevlin slid to a halt, staring but not believing his eyes. Even though they had suspected Tanathos hid in the city, he hadn't expected to confront the Shadeleech in the catacombs tonight. Didn't Harafin's shields prevent Tanathos from slipping into the city?

Tanathos stepped into the room, smiling. He wore a crimson silk shirt and a black cloak thrown back over one shoulder. Roiling darkness covered his eyes as always, and the wave of nearly palpable evil he radiated drove a dagger of terror deep into Kevlin's soul.

Tanathos threw out a hand, casting a bolt of pure darkness.

He missed Kevlin.

The bolt swept past and someone screamed. Kevlin spun to see a soldier who had been closing on him from behind writhing in the midst of clinging black shadows. The sound trailed away into a wet gurgle as his form shriveled in on itself.

Other nearby soldiers backed away and made signs to ward against evil. Tanathos's smile grew as he leeched out the soldier's life. The sight triggered an avalanche of memories for Kevlin.

Again he saw Tanathos attacking the sentinel fortress of Il'Aicharen, witnessed the tornado shredding buildings. He was swept with remembered awe as the tidal wave crashed into the battered fortress, shattering most of the remaining buildings and sweeping defenders from the walls.

Again he watched in helpless horror as Tanathos used his dark powers to form a monstrous Halimaw from Antigonus. Then he felt again the disgusting sensation of a Makrasha's face melting under his hand as Tanathos leeched its life just as he now took the life of that nameless soldier.

If only he possessed magic. He could rip out the life of his most hated enemy.

Steel would do.

He hefted Jerrik's massive blade and charged. Tanathos stood barely twenty feet away. Nothing would stop him from delivering the killing blow.

A howl of inhuman rage echoed through the room.

Leander

The Stalwart had arrived with the reinforcements, who were already swarming over the remaining attackers. Leander, his face white with rage, had noticed Tanathos. He now charged across the room in a blur of speed. He extended his right hand and his mighty war hammer, already burning with blue fire, appeared in his fist.

Tanathos's smile evaporated, replaced by open fear.

He should have kept running instead of drawing fatally close to Leander and his century of vengeful rage.

Before Kevlin could close on him, and while Leander had barely crossed a third of the long room, Tanathos threw his arms out wide. He shouted a word of power that tore at Kevlin's ears like a thousand wasps.

Kevlin stumbled, dropped his sword, and covered his ears with his hands. The ground rumbled, and the room shook.

That was very bad.

Kevlin was swept by a resurgence of panic, far stronger than the simple fear of getting lost. The thought of being trapped underground, buried alive in the chill darkness, drove him back from the Shadeleech.

Leander continued his advance, unfazed by the danger.

Tanathos pointed. Directly in front of Leander, a pillar of earth reared out of the ground and smashed into the ceiling. The entire room shook with the movement of the heavy earth.

Half a heartbeat later, the pillar of earth exploded. Leander charged through the center of it, his burning hammer held before him like a battering ram. Dust billowed out across the room and covered everything in a deep haze that dimmed the lights and plunged the room into twilight.

Tanathos spun his arm over his head and an invisible wind tore through the room. It whipped the dirt and dust into a blinding whirlwind.

Kevlin shouted a warning, then gagged as his mouth filled with dirt. He turned his back to the wind and covered his face with one arm. The roaring of the wind drowned out all sound, and it pelted Kevlin's skin like sandpaper. Kevlin tasted dirt, smelled dirt, was completely encased by it.

It felt like drowning.

Kevlin expected the amulet to capture the magic for him, but nothing came. He cursed, then spat out more dirt. The magic was not directed against him, so there was nothing for the amulet to capture.

All light vanished as the dirty whirlwind snuffed out torches and lanterns alike. As Kevlin peered vainly into the darkness, he caught a glimpse of a blue light.

Leander still advanced.

That knowledge bolstered Kevlin's flagging courage. Kill Tanathos and end the threat. He could do that.

Kevlin drew his belt dagger and crept in the direction he thought Tanathos lurked, feeling his way like a blind man. He shielded his face with his other hand, trying to breathe through the dense sand cloud, hoping to glimpse Tanathos before the Shadeleech spotted him.

The ground shook again, then the heart-stopping rumble of falling rock echoed through the room. The sound came from just ahead of him, and he felt as much as heard the closest passage collapsing in on itself.

Kevlin couldn't help but retreat from the danger of being caught in the cave-in. If it spread, they'd all die.

Then blinding white light burst into life right in front of him, blinding him worse than the darkness had.

Something struck him in the chest. The blow wasn't powerful, but Kevlin dodged in case the surprise attacker struck again. The amulet hidden under his shirt began to glow warm and pour magic into him.

Had Tanathos discovered his location? He should have known better than to attack with magic. Kevlin welcomed the inrushing power and raised the reinforced battlements to ward his mind.

Fire erupted around Kevlin, vaporizing the dirt and roaring with insatiable hunger. It encased him in a solid wall of crimson, flames licking hungrily at his body and roaring in his ears.

The amulet captured more magic, sucking the life out of flames that touched him. It protected him from burning, but could do nothing to ward off the intense heat that sucked all moisture from his mouth in an instant.

Sulfur and ash filled Kevlin's nostrils, but he snarled against the heat. Tanathos knew better than to try these tactics. It had to be Masego.

Kevlin didn't fear fire. It was the one element he felt confident controlling. Kevlin extended a thought to the flames burning all around and commanded them to subside.

The flames soared higher and Kevlin's skin cracked from the intense heat. His clothes, protected from the direct fire, still blackened under the close proximity to the inferno.

Kevlin touched the flames again, driving thoughts into the raging fire.

Rogue Fire.

Harafin's description of it finally made sense. Individual tongues of fire usually burned in time with the rhythm of life, which was how he controlled it. This fire burned in the exact opposite to the normal rhythm, so his attempt to quench the flames had only reinforced them.

If not for the amulet, he'd already be dead.

Kevlin tasted ash when he tried to breathe. The air lacked substance and left him feeling light-headed. If he didn't escape quickly, the fire would still kill him.

He threw his will again into the flames, setting his power to the inverted rhythm of this rogue fire, and connected with it.

Be gone, he ordered.

The flames flickered once and disappeared. Kevlin sagged with relief, breathing deep. Wind rushed in where fire had ruled, and the dust-laden air scraped across his raw skin. Kevlin only cared about how deliciously cool it felt after the terrible heat.

Through the blinding light that still illuminated the dust storm, Kevlin made out a shadowy form. He called upon his magic, willing it into a living spear he could use to destroy the enemy.

It revolted.

Rebellious magic crashed against his mental defenses. His shields wavered, his outer walls overrun. Kevlin sank to one knee under the onslaught, grimacing at a sudden headache as he fought to reinforce his defenses.

Waves of magic crashed against the bulwark of his shields, but he fought it down, bringing his invisible army of valiant defenders into sharp focus on the battlements of his mind.

Then he didn't want to fight it any more.

He'd experienced the devious hunger of the Trembling Madness enough to recognize the signs. He barely resisted the urge to cast himself into the raging torrent that sought to destroy his mind. Part of him yearned to embrace the chaos. He could be one with the magic, if only for a moment.

What a moment he could make of it!

He could really live, finally reach his full potential. All he had to do was let go, throw away his foolish desire for control. If he dared embrace this power at his fingertips, he could rival the very gods.

Kevlin lacked the willpower to connect with his brothers and draw upon their strength again. His thoughts wavered and his defenses faded. In a moment, he'd be swept away by the *Tai Pari*. He focused on the one thing that centered his thoughts and gave him hope.

Indira.

He formed an image of her flawless face in his mind and lost himself in the dark pools of her eyes. He remembered kissing her full lips and sliding his fingers through her silky, hair.

Using memories of Indira like another layer shielding for his thoughts, Kevlin regrouped and strengthened his will. The unruly magic sensed the change as he drove back the madness, and it relented, submitting to his will one more time.

Kevlin stood, his muscles shaking with fatigue. Sweat ran down his burned skin in searing lines.

A hand grabbed Kevlin's collar and yanked him off his feet. He flailed out when he struck the floor, and one hand closed over the hilt of the dagger he had dropped a moment ago.

Someone began dragging him across the floor and a deep, rough voice spoke. "You're a puzzle, Kevlin. I will know your secrets."

Not Tanathos, but a voice of evil. It had to be Masego.

Kevlin tried to open his eyes, but the blinding light shone right in his eyes, as if stationed in front of his face.

He didn't need to see. He shouted, "I'll share this secret for free!"

Water.

This time, the magic obeyed. A spear of water as thick around as his thigh and as hard as steel blasted up from his open left hand and struck the mysterious attacker. The man cried out as he was knocked off his feet.

His hold on Kevlin's collar broke, so Kevlin rolled away and leaped to his feet. He still couldn't see, but he could hear where the enemy had fallen.

Masego liked fire. Kevlin would defeat him with water.

A wave of water erupted out of Kevlin as he spent his magic to fuel the spell. It tumbled Masego through the nearby passageway door. The blinding light winked out and Kevlin caught a glimpse of dark robes and flailing limbs before Masego disappeared into darkness.

Before Kevlin could pursue, the water he'd just conjured flowed back into the doorway and solidified into a thick sheet of ice.

The dust-laden whirlwind also ceased, and dirt rained through the room. Sentinel lights illuminated the room. Leander stood near the caved-in passageway to Kevlin's right, hammer raised as if he planned to plow through solid earth. Soldiers guarded the captured attackers, who were huddled against the far wall.

Harafin stood at the entrance to the room, hands raised, bright blue light radiating from him. He'd probably quenched the whirlwind, and the sight of him filled Connor with renewed hope.

In the center of the room stood Tanathos, his expression desperate, hands raised high, glowing with crimson power.

He clapped his hands together with the sound of thunder.

The ceiling collapsed.

42

TROUBLE WITH STALWARTS

Sitara considered pushing thoughts into the soldier's mind to convince him to conceal their encounter, but it was too late for that. She should have thought of it earlier. Her only option was to kill him before he could reveal any more information.

Sitara crept toward the fallen soldier until she caught a glimpse of flickering torchlight around the corner. She leaned against the cold earthen wall and cast out tendrils of thought.

Her heightened senses flowed around the corner like fingers sliding along the chill earthen walls. The earth was damp in places, covered in others with moss. The musky air, long-undisturbed, tasted stale and dirty.

As the soldier sat up, her fingers of thought flickered along his form until she could picture exactly where he sat. With darkness filling her soul, she felt a bond with the dead lying all around, as if the filthy power drew strength from the old bones rotting bare inches from her face.

Sitara shaped fingers of invisible power and drove them into his soldier's chest. She wrapped them around his heart, and squeezed. Hard.

The soldier's gasp rang loud in the darkness. Sitara squeezed harder, fighting to still his powerful heart and end the struggle before her nerve broke.

She'd done this once before and still hated herself for it. She saw no other option, so she could do it again, despite the cost.

The man staggered to his knees, clutching at his chest. His panic radiated through her conduit of power. His death was sure, but he was strong. His heart fought valiantly against the invisible tendrils of her power, but it slowed.

She bit back a squeal of horror and shook out her hands against the sudden sensation of his blood spurting between her fingers. Tears she couldn't suppress moistened her cheeks as she tightened her grip.

The second man, who she had ignored, placed hands on the soldier's chest and began chanting softly. An invisible blade shattered her power and wrapped the soldier's heart with a protective barrier.

A Stalwart!

Sitara shook with fear. One Stalwart already blocked the other direction. If the two of them converged, she'd be caught in the middle with no escape.

She had little experience with Stalwarts. The old Fire Stalwart who had lived in her village had terrified her as a little girl. She had avoided all the orders residing in the palaces. She always felt exposed around them, as if standing in their presence would peel back the layers of illusion she concealed herself with.

She had to get away. And yet, if she didn't finish off the soldier, they could still track her down. The thought of being unmasked in the light of day, her lies laid bare before the keisara, filled her with more dread than the thought of the Stalwart crouched barely thirty feet away.

Sitara gritted her teeth in a silent snarl. Why did this have to be so difficult? Why couldn't she just meet with Masego before these meddlers intervened? She didn't want to kill them, but they left her no choice.

The distant Stalwart asked the soldier in his surprisingly gentle voice, "Tell me about this woman, quickly."

Sitara lashed out at the Stalwart, but her power slid off him like water from a rock.

"Ah, she was young, pretty." The soldier spoke between labored breaths as he recovered from her assault.

Sitara slammed her fist into the earthen wall, barely holding back her panic. She needed a way to strike these men down, but she carried no weapons.

Sitara cast her senses in every direction in a desperate attempt to find something, anything to use as a weapon, even though she knew the passages were empty.

Then she opened her fist where it rested against the chill catacomb wall. She sucked in a sharp breath as realization struck, followed by a wave of horror that made her recoil across the narrow passage.

No. She couldn't do it. She shook her head in silent denial while tears of frustration filled her eyes. There had to be something else.

The soldier said, "And her voice."

"What about it?" the Stalwart asked."

There was no time. She had to do it.

She gritted her teeth and drove fingers of power into the walls on both sides of the men. She allowed herself one deep breath to still her shudders of revulsion, but they tasted like rotting meat to her. She wrapped those fingers of power around the only weapons she could use, and unleashed them together.

The graves along both walls of the narrow passageway burst open, raining dirt and decaying debris. Bones, still hard despite years interred, hurtled out like makeshift spears.

The soldier cried out in fear, trying to shield his face with his hands. Bones, some with bits of rotting cloth still clinging to them, smashed into him.

A new sound echoed through the close confines of the passage. It sounded like steel striking wood. Sitara flicked her senses over the two men and found that the Stalwart now bore a heavy war hammer. With amazing skill he struck her grisly missiles out of the air, shattering them into bits of harmless dust.

Sitara grimaced and reached for more bones. No longer caring what they represented, she hurled them at the two men with growing desperation. Why wouldn't they just die and let it end?

It wasn't enough. The Stalwart deflected too many of the missiles. The barrage had managed to bruise the soldier and cut his exposed skin in several places, but that wouldn't kill him.

Voices called out questions behind Sitara. The men stationed at the next intersection were drawing closer, alerted by the sounds of conflict. She was nearly out of time.

Sitara reached farther and bared her teeth in a silent snarl of hatred for what she had to do. She cursed Masego for leading her down here to her death, then threw every ounce of power into one final assault.

From the wall of the passageway behind the soldier erupted half a dozen skulls from a single grave where an entire family had been buried together. The Stalwart stood on the far side of the man, still facing the direction of the last attack. He could do nothing but spin at the sound and reach a single hand toward the soldier in silent, helpless support.

Thunk!

The terrible meaty sound of skulls cracking into the back of the soldier's head, one after the other, reverberated through the passage. The soldier crashed to the ground, his body rigid, mouth open in a silent scream as his spirit fled to the afterlife.

Her goal accomplished, Sitara severed her extended senses and huddled against the chill grave wall. It took all of her willpower to fight down the bile that rose into her throat. She swallowed a cough and sagged to the floor, wrapping her arms tight around herself. Silent tremors racked her tiny frame.

She couldn't lose control, couldn't deal with the horror of what she'd just done. Not now. The big Stalwart would hear.

Sitara drew down the power of darkness that filled her like sludge until only a little clung to her innards like old vomit. It wouldn't help her against the Stalwart if he discovered her, and its filth was making her sick.

Footsteps rang through the passage from behind, and torchlight flickered closer. Only seconds remained before they would discover and kill her.

Sitara stood with renewed determination. She would not fall here in the darkness of the tombs. She couldn't.

She reached out with a tendril of thought, caught up a fragment of bone lying in the passage near the dead soldier, and flicked it down the passage behind the Stalwart. It made a tiny sound when it struck, barely more than a whisper.

It was enough. The Stalwart lunged after the sound with alarming speed. He cried, "I swear to deal justice for this murder!"

The men behind Sitara picked up their pace, calling out with questions about what was going on.

Sitara sprinted back to the intersection with the dead soldier. Despite the danger, she had to pause and stare at the grisly sight illuminated by the flickering torch the Stalwart had left behind. Tombs gaped open like rotting mouths, their recently disgorged contents scattered around the fallen soldier. The air reeked of death.

The Stalwart, bigger in person, stepped out of the darkness on the far side of the torch. He looked angry and pointed his deadly hammer at her. "Justice."

Sitara fled.

She ran in the only direction left to her, back toward the wide room where battle still raged, where Tanathos sought to take Kevlin, and Masego sought to double-cross him.

Harafin might already have arrived.

The huge Stalwart gave chase. He was fleet for a man his size and closed quickly. He made no sound, and his silent pursuit terrified her more than shouted curses. Other soldiers joined the chase, but none of them would matter.

Sitara applied her power to strengthen her legs and increase her stride. She managed to keep about twenty feet ahead of the Stalwart and his terrible hammer, but couldn't draw farther away.

Sitara screamed, and the echoes mocked her as she fled in panic.

Then the ground shook and the heart-stopping sound of falling earth filled the passage, followed a moment later by a blast of dust that choked and blinded her. Sitara ran on, and in desperation directed her power into the ground under her feet.

She drew water out of the air and out of the clammy walls and poured it into the hard-packed earthen floor. Within seconds, a long stretch of ground dissolved into deep mud.

The Stalwart shouted in frustration as he stumbled into the mud and fell sprawling. The men trailing him, blinded by the cloud of dust, fell right on top of him.

Sitara sprinted on, toward the growing sounds of the cave-in. To slow meant certain death. To advance might mean becoming entombed.

The earth shook again and she stumbled, falling to one knee. She glanced back.

The Stalwart shouted words lost under the rumbling of the earth. Then something whipped past her face, scraping her cheek.

Sitara bit back a scream and touched her burning cheek. She couldn't see in the darkened passage, but her fingers came away wet.

The Stalwart had thrown his hammer. Her heart quailed to think how close he'd come to killing her even when throwing blind. If she hadn't stumbled, his hammer would have blasted her into the next life.

Sitara scrambled forward on hands and knees, but the ground shook harder, and she realized the entire passage was about to collapse. She opened herself to the power of darkness and barely noticed its corrupted filth as it crawled into her soul. She threw out tendrils of power and spread invisible fingers along the ceiling.

There! The ceiling began to crack.

Sitara summoned fire and crimson flames roared all along the section of roof above her, fusing the earth in an instant.

A shout drew her gaze back down the passage. The Stalwart had traversed the mud pit and now stood in the passage, dripping with filth. Somehow he had retrieved his hammer. With the passage illuminated by her fire, he found his prey and cocked back his arm to throw.

Sitara drove daggers of energy into the ceiling between them, and pulled.

It collapsed.

43

Picks And Shovels Of The Mind

Kevlin dove toward the ice-blocked passageway as earth and stones cascaded down. The avalanche started in the center of the room and rolled outward to consume them all.

Panic overwhelmed his ability to think, let alone focus the little bit of magic still available to him. As the cave-in spread, he screamed and lifted his hands in a futile gesture of defense.

Then Leander arrived.

The old Stalwart yanked Kevlin to his feet and shouted, "Help me! We have to hold this back. We need to help Harafin get everyone out."

Leander's words pulled Kevlin from his panicked daze, offering a slender tendril of hope. He could do more than die like a trapped rat. Leander planted his feet and raised his burning hammer toward the falling debris that already filled most of the room.

Blue fire lashed out in a wave, consuming earth and fusing boulders as he transformed tons of collapsing debris into thick support columns.

"Follow my lead," Leander said, burning hammer raised like a talisman. "We can't hold it for long, but we can slow it."

"What do I do?" Kevlin asked. As much as he wanted to help, this was so far beyond anything he'd tried, he couldn't imagine how to help.

Leander took his left hand off his hammer and slapped his palm to Kevlin's head. "Sorry, but I don't have time to be gentle."

Knowledge blasted into Kevlin's mind like a blow from Leander's hammer. He rocked back into the wall, and it was all that kept him from falling. His vision darkened, and his head felt like it had been dunked in a bucket of fire.

The sensation passed quickly, and Kevlin blinked away remembered agony, muttering, "I hate magic."

Leander wasn't listening. Hammer raised and pouring out blue fire, he moved around the narrow remaining perimeter of the room.

Kevlin stumbled after him, legs weak, muscles uncoordinated from the painful lesson. His thoughts moved like molasses in a winter gale. The new knowledge Leander had shoved into his mind settled over him and he worked on assimilating it.

Dozens of questions tried to distract him, but if he thought about them, he'd lose any chance of applying the new knowledge. The ground shook again. The danger was all too real. He needed to move or he'd have eternity to ponder while entombed here forever.

Leander's blue fire intensified and he snapped, "Kevlin, I need you now!"

The temperature had risen from the constant chill of the catacombs to uncomfortably warm, driven by the intense flames. It smelled like charred earth, and surprisingly like his mother's apple crisp.

Kevlin reached for Oris with a thought and connected with the essence within the stone. Power and confidence filled him like a bucket. He just hoped he didn't leak. He stood taller, grinning from the exhilaration of feeling the mighty rock's power, despite the danger.

Kevlin focused the thrumming magic and raised his hands toward the fused debris. Cracks had already formed along the temporary wall, and the entire structure vibrated as if about to implode.

He drove a whisper of thought into it, and he shuddered at the immense weight of earth threatening to collapse onto them. The magnitude of it dwarfed him, and inside the bubble of peace that rested over his mind from Oris, he shook with fear. He wasn't sure they could do this.

Leander had shared with him the knowledge of how to fuse the earth, but he could already see that approach was failing. He drew heavily from Oris's power and threw his will into the battle to save their lives.

Green light erupted from Kevlin's hands and spread over the nearby wall. He distributed it across a ten-foot span, from floor to ceiling. Then he solidified the column of power and reinforced it until it stood a full span thick. It consumed staggering amounts of power, but Kevlin drank more deeply from the well of Oris. He had the power. For right now, he didn't care where it came from.

He left the pillar of magic there, free-standing, buttressing the fused earthen wall Leander had created. Then he moved to the right a dozen steps and repeated the process. The unfamiliar effort soon left him panting, and sweat dripped down his skin.

Leander glanced a couple of times at his work, but didn't spare the effort to comment on it. That he didn't order Kevlin to try something else was a good sign.

Then the ground shook again, somewhere off to their right, and the tremor sent cracks rippling through Leander's temporary wall. It gave way, and tons of earth shifted just a little before Kevlin's magical pillars caught them.

Kevlin shared a scared look with Leander.

"Good thinking, lad," Leander said. "Let's get out of here."

"How?" They were out of open space. The cave-in blocked their path, having filled the next entire section of the huge room.

"The only way out is through." Leander pointed his hammer like a lance at the blockage. Earth geysered from the center of the obstruction as if he carried an invisible drill instead, and he bored a hole large enough for them to walk through.

Kevlin followed, creating a series of glowing support pillars to help keep the area secure. The effort consumed vast amounts of power, although not as intense as the inferno he'd wielded around the keep of Il'Aicharen.

A flicker of longing tugged at his resolve. He could re-live that moment again. He could blast an opening all the way up to the open air. All he had to do was embrace the magic, give himself to it.

"Hurry," Leander called.

Kevlin pushed the insidious thoughts aside. He'd become so distracted by them that he'd stood unmoving for several seconds. He couldn't afford to delay, or they'd die.

With steady effort, they drilled through the collapsed earth for several minutes, slowly circling the room. On the far side, they emerged from the cave-in into an open space, encircled with pulsing amber light.

Harafin stood in the center, arms raised, a dozen men huddling close around him. Directly above him, a passage bored into the ceiling all the way up to the open sky far above.

Harafin gave Leander a single nod of greeting, then pointed to the nearest soldier. The man stood directly under the opening, with a wounded comrade over one shoulder. At Harafin's gesture, he shot up into the tunnel and disappeared from view.

A few seconds later, Ah'Shan's voice called down from above, "Good shot, Harafin. Send the next one."

One by one, each soldier or Stalwart whisked up out of the depths, thrown by Harafin's power. Kevlin didn't see Jerrik. Drystan was helping a wounded soldier limp toward the escape tunnel, his face covered in grime.

"Where are the others?" Kevlin asked.

"Harafin saved the entire group caught on this side," Drystan said. "Everyone else is already up."

Kevlin wondered how many men had been caught farther out in the room. His earlier fear had been realized. Some of them had taken up residency here among the halls of the dead. He still shuddered to think how close they'd all come to dying.

Harafin threw Drystan and the wounded soldier up and out of sight. Eventually only Kevlin, Leander and Harafin remained.

"That could have gone better," Harafin said with a tired sigh.

"Masego was here," Kevlin said. "He's a Sentinel."

Harafin nodded. "Given the situation, I'm not surprised."

"He attacked me." Kevlin pointed toward the far side of the room, concealed by tons of fallen earth. "He escaped down one of the far passages."

Harafin sighed. "Then we've lost both of them."

"What of Tanathos?" Leander asked. "Did Ah'Shan take him?"

"I haven't heard, so I don't think so. Come, let's find out."

He glanced upward and frowned. "Kevlin, I want you to form a thin layer of air all around yourself. Can you do that?"

"I think so." Kevlin focused, but found the effort far more difficult than anticipated. Why hadn't Harafin asked for a layer of water? He could have done that in a heartbeat.

After his third failed attempt, Kevlin asked, "Why do you need me to do this?"

"I need to push you with air to get you out, and Ah'Shan will do the same when you reach the top to help you land. Unless you want to remove that amulet of yours, the cushion of air will provide a buffer we can push against without alerting Ah'Shan."

"Doesn't he know already?" Kevlin asked.

"He knows you are Bearer, but I have not shared with him the full powers of the amulet."

"Why not?"

"Trust me," Harafin said with a hint of a smile.

Kevlin sighed. Even if he could somehow become Actinopathic, he'd never agree to become a Sentinel. He didn't have the temperament to adopt their cryptic ways.

It took another minute to create the cushion of air to Harafin's liking. The old Sentinel pointed at Kevlin, and a column of solid air formed under his and whisked him up the escape tunnel.

He emerged in an open field filled with cattle and scattered soldiers. Torches bathed the scene with flickering light. Ah'Shan, who stood at the lip of the opening, scowled as Kevlin appeared, and made a flicking gesture with his hand. New currents of air yanked him sideways and dropped him rather hard onto the earth.

A group of Pallian Stalwarts arrived at a jog and immediately moved to help the wounded soldiers. Kevlin caught sight of Jerrik being tended by three of them.

Leander leaped up out of the hole next and landed with a thud next to Kevlin. Without preamble, he demanded, "Ah'Shan, what of Tanathos?"

Ah'Shan pointed toward the east where the inner city wall blazed with lights and soldiers crowded the battlements. "We were situated farther to the north. Before we arrived, he tore the life out of a pair of lovers he found at the edge of this field and used their life forces to launch himself right over the wall."

"Was there no shielding to prevent him?"

"Shields are designed to keep things out," Ah'Shan said.

Leander growled and raced toward the distant wall. Half of the nearby Stalwarts instantly gave chase.

Ah'Shan shouted after him, "A general call to arms has been issued. We already have patrols with Sentinels out searching for him."

Leander didn't respond, but disappeared into the darkness.

Harafin rose at a more stately pace from below and settled to the ground next to Ah'Shan.

"What happened?" Ah'Shan asked.

Harafin surveyed the field filled with wounded and shaken soldiers. "The meeting proved to be a trap within a trap."

The obese Sentinel Felix huffed up to them and wiped dirt from his face.

"Where have you been?" Ah'Shan asked.

Felix grinned. "At the first sign of trouble, I descended into the catacombs to try to cut off anyone fleeing that way. Good thing too. When the cave-in started, we nearly lost another score of men."

The Stalwart Basak followed Felix into their light. "We're grateful to you." The thick-chested Stalwart was covered with mud.

Felix grinned. "I had to dig this one out. Nearly got entombed down there."

"At least one of the conspirators died," Basak said.

"Who?" Kevlin and Harafin asked together.

The huge stalwart shrugged. "An unknown. A young woman. She killed one of our men down there, and called down another cave-in to try to escape justice." He looked down at the ground as if trying to see through the tons of earth. "The entire passage caved in. There's no way she survived."

Felix clapped the Stalwart on the back and asked Harafin, "So, what happened?"

"We missed a great opportunity, my friend. Let's clean up this mess and see to the wounded." He pointed at the small group of attackers they had captured, including the blond-haired leader. "Then we find out what these men can tell us."

44

LAYERS OF GUILT

Sitara grabbed the upper edge of the escape tunnel and clawed her way to the top. She didn't dare use the power of darkness here aboveground, and her Actinopathic gift had abandoned her after the cave-in.

She rolled onto her back in the grass at the edge of the vertical tunnel, trying to catch her breath. She glanced back down once and shuddered. She almost hadn't escaped. The cave-in that had destroyed that vengeful Stalwart hadn't spread to the area where she had fused the roof. It had cracked and groaned, but held.

At the far end, closest to the big room where the fighting had been, the passage had been sealed by fallen earth. She had driven feelers of power through and chanced upon a passage bored through the cave-in not far away. She'd used her powers to dig to it and found it supported by strange magical pillars. Whoever left it had saved her life. She never would have found her way out without it.

Dozens of people still moved toward a distant gate of the field. If she'd escaped the catacombs any earlier, she would have climbed right into their group.

She rose to a crouch and trotted into the darkness to a remote section of fence, happy for the concealing cover of heavy clouds. Every muscle ached and lingering terror set her hands shaking.

What had gone wrong? Had Masego succeeded in taking Kevlin, or had Harafin killed him? What about Tanathos?

Before she could find answers, she had to get cleaned up and return to her rooms. The hour was late, well past midnight, and the brilliant lights that had lit the central palace were mostly dimmed. A few party-goers hurried away from the palace along the distant spokes now crowded with soldiers. Soon anyone moving around would draw attention.

It took an hour for Sitara to slip past patrols, enter the palace, steal a dress, and take a bath in an empty bath-house in one of the lower levels. She scrubbed her skin raw, but couldn't remove the lingering feeling of filth.

When she finally slipped into her own small room in the Keisara's Tower, she huddled under her blanket. While hugging herself, she sobbed while memories of defiling graves and committing murder played again and again through her mind.

45

A Bit Of Healing

By first bell in the morning, Kevlin arrived in the hospital wing to check on Jerrik. He had been in critical condition the night before, and the Healers had ordered everyone to leave them alone to work. Now Kevlin entered Jerrik's room, worried about what he'd find.

Jerrik was sitting up in bed. Marjani was feeding him a bowl of soup. He looked pale and weak, but extremely pleased. Indira stood on his other side, one glowing hand resting on his shoulder.

Kevlin drank in the sight of her. She wore her normal Healer's robes, with her long, midnight hair hanging in a loose twist down her back. She stood profile to him, and her face glowed in the early morning light that streamed in through an open window.

The impact that the simple sight of her had over him worried him. He was becoming a lovesick fool. With Tanathos free in the city, he couldn't afford any distraction.

Jerrik glanced up and grinned. "Brothers, come in."

"If Kevlin will get out of the way," Drystan said, pushing past.

Keelin followed Drystan into the room. She again carried the baby in the pack on her back, and smiled in greeting.

Kevlin followed the couple into the room and joined Indira on the left side of the bed. She smiled, and he dearly wanted to kiss those full lips.

Later. Maybe they could slip away for lunch together and actually spend some quiet time together. Their date had been interrupted, but maybe they could salvage something today.

He took her hand, about to ask her if she'd join him, but the touch of her skin triggered an intense desire to force her to give him magic. His hand shook as he fought the unexpected urge to grab her by the throat and demand it.

He closed his eyes, fighting for control. Since he'd beaten the Trembling Madness just yesterday and had his fill of magic, he had expected easy sailing today. He hated how it tempted him to hurt Indira. She was the last person he'd ever hurt. He couldn't allow it.

Indira slipped her hand out of his and retreated a step, her expression pained. "I'm sorry. I can't protect you."

How could he show her he cared, reassure her that he'd keep her safe? He knew so little about magic, he didn't know if his magic would kill him or force him to hurt others around him.

Adalia sat on a stool nearby. He hadn't noticed the petite archer before. "Kevlin, you shoulda sent for me."

"What?" She was dressed in her normal woods garb, and her bow leaned against the wall in the corner behind her. How could she help him with Indira?

Adalia scooped up her bow and held it high. "You shoulda called me ta help last night. I coulda shot them cowards afore they shot Jerrik."

"You probably could have."

Adalia hopped off the stool and faced him. "Are ye doubtin me?" The look of offense would have worked better if she stood even as high as his shoulder.

Kevlin held up his hands in surrender. "Of course not, Adalia. I saw you shoot in Hallvarr. How could I doubt you?"

"You'd find a way," Ceren said with a smile to lessen the sting of the insult. She entered the room wearing a dark blue dress. Her auburn hair cascaded in loose waves over her shoulders.

Jerrik threw his arms out wide, almost knocking Marjani from her perch next to him. "I'm honored you've all come. We should celebrate."

"Oh, no," Marjani said. "Soup for you, not ale, m'lord."

"Looks like we weren't really needed," Keelin said. "Looks like this young woman has things well in hand."

Marjani blushed, but scooted a little closer to Jerrik.

He grinned at her. "Aye, she was already here when I woke up this morning."

"Well, my lord Jerrik, last night you insisted I take care of you. What do you expect?"

Kevlin moved to the foot of the bed, giving Indira some space. Frustration at his inability to spend time with her stoked a growing anger. Tanathos was in the city, Masego had caused death and destruction, and his brother lay badly wounded. He needed to hit something.

If only it were so simple. Instead, he was forced to fight with tools of magic, tools he scarcely understood and barely controlled. The enemy appeared to have every advantage. Even when he could face them, like last night in the catacombs, the Trembling Madness robbed him of strength in critical moments, and the *Tai Pari* threatened to destroy everything he held dear.

Kevlin burned the image of the wounded Jerrik into his mind. He would find these hidden enemies, and they would not escape again. They wanted to make this personal, so be it.

Ceren moved to take Jerrik's hand. As she passed Kevlin, she glanced at him and raised one eyebrow at him. She ended up between Kevlin and Indira as she wished Jerrik speedy recovery.

What was that look for? He squashed a surge of irritation. Ceren could be difficult to understand, but she was helping him learn things about his magical dangers that Harafin didn't seem willing to share.

Jerrik took Ceren's proffered hand and thanked her for coming. Then he looked from Kevlin to Drystan and said with a rueful grin, "We made a mess of it, didn't we?"

"It could've been worse," Kevlin said.

"They knew we were coming," Drystan said. "It was a trap all along."

Keelin placed a hand on Drystan's arm. "It couldn't have been, love. Not until we intervened and saved Kevlin in the garden." They shared a look and she added softly, "That means . . . "

"They were watching us," Drystan finished for her.

"More likely they were watching Kevlin," Ceren said. "Probably even before he went to the garden."

"Why did you go there, Kevlin?" Keelin asked.

He shrugged. "I was looking for Harafin, and a servant . . . " He trailed off and frowned as something clicked in his mind.

"What is it?" Ceren asked. She and Indira took identical steps toward him.

"The servant who sent me to the garden, I've seen him somewhere before."

"Where?" Ceren asked, placing a hand on his arm, and leaning close enough to be distracting.

The memory flitting at the edge of his thoughts faded away. "I nearly had it, but I can't remember."

"It'll come," Ceren said. "Trying to force it never works."

"You're the expert at mind games."

She looked surprised, and then hurt, and he regretted the words instantly. He wanted to apologize, to comfort her, but couldn't figure out what to say without making matters worse. Indira stood nearby, and her gaze only flustered him more.

"Tell us when you think of it, Kevlin," Keelin said before giving Drystan a little kiss. "Go, love. Harafin's waiting."

Drystan rolled his eyes and said in a tone of mock annoyance. "Love, we're not supposed to talk about that."

She raised a hand toward him. "Strike hard."

He gripped it. "Leave none standing."

Kevlin followed him out the door.

46

FRIENDS AND ENEMIES

Kevlin, once again dressed in the crimson and white uniform of the emperor's guard, stood at attention inside the emperor's council chamber as the ruling council met. Harafin, Leander, Felix, and Ah'Shan all sat with the council. Ambassador Damarist had sent word that he would be late, but the other members of the council were present. No replacement had yet been announced for the obese Ambassador Gwyre from Meinarr.

Harafin had reported on last night's botched attempt to take Masego. It seemed to bother the emperor more to learn the recent assassination attempt was nothing but a diversion to learn the location of Oris.

Now Harafin reported that the men captured in the catacombs knew nothing of their employer. These latest prisoners had been hired through a middle-man in a tavern in the inner city just the day before. When members of Ambassador Kescog's personal guard had sought out that middle man, they found him floating face down in a pool in one of the sunken gardens. The report stated their belief that he had fallen over the rail from a higher level while drunk during the party.

Emperor Tegnazian slammed a fist on the table. "Confound it, Harafin. Are you telling me we still have no idea who's behind these attacks?"

"Not at all. We know this Masego is responsible for most of them."

"And he's a Sentinel?" Ambassador Janezeko from Freyarr asked.

"Yes, we believe so."

"It also appears Masego is working with the ShadeLeech Tanathos," added Leander.

"Who you also failed to capture last night," added the emperor.

Sentinel Felix piped in, "We believe one other Sentinel was involved in the attack last night and died in the cave-in."

"That's hardly good news," Ambassador Janezeko said. "We have no leads, no idea how to pursue these hidden traitors."

"Not so," Leander declared. "We know beyond a doubt that Sentinels are working with Tanathos. It's time to cast Truth on every Sentinel in the palace and root out the traitors. We could hold executions before sunset."

Leander's proposal rocked the assembled ambassadors, triggering heated arguments.

Emperor Tegnazian pounded his gavel on the table and called for silence. "Gentlemen, remember yourselves." He turned to Leander. "Your proposal is highly unusual."

"It's the best option," Leander insisted.

"What objections are there to this proposal?" the emperor asked the council.

Sentinel Durgesh, the Kestrel assigned to the emperor's security detail, spoke up immediately. "The proposal is ridiculous. Why not suggest we cast Truth on everyone in the entire inner city?"

"Why not?" Leander shot back. "Stop tip-toeing around and give everyone a chance to stand up and declare their true allegiance."

"It's difficult to see you fallen so low," said Durgesh.

"I've fallen nowhere," Leander stated.

"Who can blame you?" Durgesh continued. "Your family's murderer is at large and you failed yet again to bring him to justice. Any of us would be devastated."

"Watch where you tread, Sentinel," warned Leander. "I don't want to dislike you."

Kevlin wanted to punch the man.

A couple of the ambassadors nodded as if approving Durgesh's manipulation of the conversation.

The fat Sentinel Felix waved Durgesh to silence. "That's enough from you, young man. Show some respect to my old friend."

Sentinel Durgesh made a little bow. "No disrespect was intended."

Sentinel Ah'Shan spoke up for the first time, his deep voice calm and reasonable. "I must concur with Sentinel Durgesh. Casting Truth on every Sentinel is tantamount to accusing them all of being traitors. That's the worst thing we could do for morale. Many of them have spent the entirety of last night scouring the city for the Shadeleech. Forcing Truth on them would be the deepest of insults."

Ambassador Janezeko said, "Perhaps, but I believe Stalwart Leander has a point. If we want results, this might be the necessary tactic, no matter how difficult."

"I disagree," Sentinel Ah'Shan argued. "The enemy must be prepared for such an eventuality, and would have taken steps to avoid it."

Ambassador Janezeko leaned forward. "It appears you've given this subject a lot of thought. Has the idea been worrying you? Is there something you fear in Truth?"

"Don't be daft, man," Ah'Shan snapped.

"Then why not support the idea, for the good of the empire?"

Ah'Shan shot back, "For that matter, why not submit this council to Truth? Some information has clearly been provided to this Masego from someone in a position of power." He fixed Ambassador Janezeko with a hard stare. "Will you submit to Truth, Ambassador?"

Ambassador Janezeko waved off the suggestion with a smile. "I appreciate the attempt at levity, Sentinel Ah'Shan, but let's stay focused on the proposal at hand."

"I jest not. In full sincerity, I ask you again, will you submit to Truth?"

Kevlin watched the conversation with interest. Several of the ambassadors looked more than a little nervous, although Ambassador Kescog from Donarr was nodding his head in agreement, and Ambassador Talamantez of Einarr was leaning back in his chair, his face thoughtful.

"Ludicrous," Ambassador Janezeko said. "None of us here are under suspicion. It would serve no purpose."

The council chamber door banged open and Colonel Gabral marched in. He was dressed in his full battle armor of silver-trimmed plate, with the emperor's crest flashing bright on his right breast.

He saluted smartly and declared, "Your excellency, I am here to take over the investigation and bring these traitors to justice."

Kevlin nearly laughed aloud. Harafin raised one eyebrow in surprise, and Leander sat back in his chair, an incredulous expression on his face.

Emperor Tegnazian only said, "I appreciate the offer, Colonel, but what makes you feel you're best qualified to take over this investigation?"

"The raid last night was botched from the beginning, your excellency." Without looking at Harafin he continued, "Master Harafin made several tactical errors. It's clear this mission needs a military man in command."

Kevlin hooked his thumbs into his sword belt to keep from reaching for his sword. He felt an overwhelming urge to punch Gabral in that self-righteous mouth of his. He was having trouble convincing himself it was a bad idea.

"What errors are those, specifically?" Harafin asked calmly.

Gabral finally met Harafin's eye. "First and foremost, your decision to bar me from participating in the attack doomed it to failure. Had I been there, I would have captured these traitors instead of letting them desecrate half the graves in the catacombs."

Kevlin wasn't really supposed to talk in the council chamber, but said, "You've hit yourself in the head with the Mace a few times too many today."

Gabral scowled. "You dare speak, mercenary? You led your team into a trap and men under your command died because of your incompetence."

Leander spoke up. "You can't blame Kevlin for that."

"I can," Gabral said, not breaking eye contact with Kevlin. "You want to be a hero. You're 'The King's Avenger'. You are responsible."

"You're a fool," Kevlin said, forcing calm into his voice despite a flash of anger. Let Gabral keep talking. The man was digging his own grave here.

"You're a danger to everyone who knows you," Gabral said in a venomous tone. "Just ask Jerrik."

That was too much. Kevlin went for his sword.

Gabral reached for the Mace.

"Enough!" Harafin's voice cracked across the room like a whip and stopped them with weapons half-drawn.

Emperor Tegnazian frowned. "Stand down. If you two cannot control yourselves, I'll have you shackled in the lowest dungeon for a month."

"I am deeply sorry," Gabral said, turning his back on Kevlin.

"Wait!" Harafin shot to his feet and threw up one hand, his gaze turning east. "The Shadeleech just crossed the Iron Spoke."

Leander leaped to his feet as several ambassadors shouted questions. "Where?"

"Just past the Way of the Wall."

"Can you detain him?" asked Ah'Shan, who leaned over the table, his face eager.

"No," Harafin said. "But after last night, I enhanced the shields. He's marked for any Sentinel to see. Look for the red beacon above him."

Leander bolted for the door, followed closely by Ah'Shan.

Felix slapped one meaty hand on the table. "Finally, the break we've been looking for. I'll alert the patrols." He leaned back in his chair and closed his eyes. The silver glow of Mindlink settled over his face.

Kevlin cursed the fact that he was shackled to the emperor's service so couldn't abandon his post to chase Leander. The emperor was already displeased with him. Such dereliction would not be tolerated.

So he silently urged Leander on.

Find Tanathos and crush his skull.

47

A Flash Of Memory

"The patrols are mobilized," Felix reported a moment later.

Ambassador Kescog pounded a fist on the table. "I wish I was in the hunt with them."

"You'd only slow them down," Ambassador Talamantez said with a grin. "You eat too much."

Ambassador Kescog slapped his paunch and laughed. "I can still beat any man in this room."

"We all wish the hunters gods speed." Emperor Tegnazian raised a fist. "A successful hunt."

Every fist raised and they all joined the chorus, "A successful hunt!"

"Now, what of this Masego?" Emperor Tegnazian asked, turning to Kevlin. "You encountered the man. Can you describe him?"

"No. He blinded me with bright lights, but I'd recognize his voice."

Gabral dropped into the chair recently vacated by Ah'Shan. "Describe it."

"Cruel. Harsh."

Harafin shook his head. "No Sentinel in the palace speaks with such a voice."

Sentinel Felix added, "No doubt he masks it around others. Evil prefers to remain shrouded in a cloak of innocence until it's ready to strike."

"What I don't understand is why they didn't attack in Diodor," Kevlin said. "They could have easily remained unseen with all the visitors arriving for the funeral and coronation of Prince Lievin."

"That would only work if they were in Diodor," Gabral said.

"Exactly," Harafin said. "Whoever they are, they must be situated here. This Masego could not come to Diodor for some reason, so he orchestrated the need for us to come to him."

"And he's proven he's highly placed in the leadership," Ambassador Talamantez added.

Ambassador Janezeko barked a laugh. "So maybe one of us is involved after all?"

No one else laughed.

Harafin said, "It is no laughing matter, Ambassador. There are questions that remain to be answered. I think now is the perfect time to seek those answers."

"What do you wish to know?" Ambassador Kescog asked. The big Donarri spread his hands wide. "Ask any of us anything you like."

"I will, my friend," Harafin said. "But first I must speak with our delinquent Ambassador Damarist."

Mention of the Ambassador's name sparked a memory in Kevlin's mind and he snapped his fingers. "Of course! Ambassador Damarist. That's where I saw that servant."

48

ANOTHER PIECE OF THE PUZZLE

Sitara struggled to maintain a calm façade through the morning as she waited on the keisara. She'd been forced to murder that soldier, but that truth did little to help ease her mind. Worse, she kept re-living those terrifying moments when she thought she might be trapped underground, entombed and condemned to die a slow, lonely death.

She stood behind the keisara's padded chair in the highest room of the tower while her mistress met with Lady Ceren. Lady Ceren was dressed tastefully in a simple blue dress with a high collar. Thankfully, no one needed Sitara's assistance. The keisara called upon the blond Sentinel Omolara to fill most of the duties. Sitara suspected it was a gesture designed to impress Lady Ceren. She didn't care. The less she had to do this morning, the better.

Lady Ceren reported on efforts to track down the traitors hidden in the palace, and she gave a brief description of the battle in the catacombs. It didn't help Sitara relax.

"It sounds terrifying," Keisara Fideima said as she sipped a mild fruit drink. "Were you there?"

"I'm afraid not," Lady Ceren said. "There was very little time to assemble the team, so I didn't hear of the battle until this morning."

"You sound disappointed."

"Not really. The catacombs give me the shivers."

If she only knew.

Keisara Fideima nodded. "I can't imagine going down there with Shadeleeches and cave-ins. It must have been terrifying."

"They nearly caught one of the suspected ring-leaders of the traitors, a man named Masego."

Sitara started. They knew his name. What more did they know? All the fears she'd been trying to suppress rose into her mind like a blizzard.

"What do you know about him?"

"Very little, I'm afraid," admitted Ceren. "He attacked Kevlin but escaped during the cave-in."

"The man Kevlin seems to be involved a great deal," Keisara Fideima commented.

"Yes, ever since conflict first began in Hallvarr. He helped rescue Antigonus from Rhea when Bajaran first struck."

Bajaran. Sitara expected a renewed wave of anguish at the thought of her dead lover, but the pain seemed muted today. Could she be losing touch with him so quickly? The thought left her feeling ashamed.

"I don't think you ever told me who killed that traitor, Bajaran," the keisara said. "I'd like to reward them for the deed. Was it the man, Kevlin?"

Sitara tensed. She had vowed to avenge Bajaran, but from the accounts she'd heard, Rhea had killed him, so her lust for vengeance lacked a target. Now she feared to hear the answer. She had plans for Kevlin. He'd saved her life and proven himself a hero. She didn't want to hate him.

"No," Ceren said. "Although he helped a great deal. The Sentinel Rhea actually murdered Bajaran."

"I thought they were working together," the keisara said.

"Apparently so did Bajaran," Lady Ceren said with an evil little chuckle that made Sitara want to slap her across the face. "But it turned out Rhea had a different master, one none of us knew."

Sitara perked up. This was new information.

"What master?"

"Masego," Ceren whispered. She sat back, an expression of surprise on her face. "Masego. I knew I'd heard the name somewhere before. Masego's been involved since the beginning and none of us saw it! Masego set things up so Rhea could murder Bajaran. He's been pulling the strings all along."

Sitara gaped, legs trembling from shock. Could it really be true? The words pounded into her like blows from a fist. She was grateful no one noticed.

Masego was responsible for Bajaran's death?

Lady Ceren leaped to her feet, her face flushed with excitement. "I have to share this information with Master Harafin. Please excuse me."

Keisara Fideima motioned her toward the door. "Go with all speed, Lady Ceren. You are a wonder."

Sitara seized upon the opportunity and said, "I'll escort you out, my lady."

No one questioned the offer, and Sitara led Lady Ceren down the tower toward the outer exit. After they descended to the main level, Sitara risked opening herself to the gift of darkness, hoping she was far enough away from Omolara. The filthy power clawed into her soul, but she allowed only a whisper of it in before sealing off the rest.

Lady Ceren walked so fast she passed right by Sitara in her haste to reach the exit. She seemed to have forgotten Sitara was even with her, so caught up in her thoughts had she become.

Sitara focused the tiny amount of power and reached out with a flicker of thought to Lady Ceren's mind.

The woman's natural shields were in terrible disarray as her mind raced with the ramifications of her discovery. Sitara slipped through with barely a pause. It took only a moment for her to unearth the memories of that first night when Bajaran had attacked.

She filtered through them until she found the one she wanted and embraced it. She stepped with Lady Ceren out of the darkened forest into a burned-out clearing. Antigonus lay wounded, and Bajaran lay dead with a dagger sunk to the hilt in his eye.

Sitara choked back a wail of grief as she matched her pace with Lady Ceren. In the memory, Kevlin talked about Rhea killing Bajaran. There was no mention of Masego.

Sitara tore through Lady Ceren's memories, searching for the one that confirmed Masego had sent Rhea, but couldn't find it.

Lady Ceren stumbled and clutched at her head. Sitara withdrew. Lady Ceren might not be gifted, but she worked as an intelligence operative. She might be trained to recognize Actinopathic meddling.

"Are you all right, my lady?"

Lady Ceren squared her shoulders. "Just over-excited, I suppose. I got a terrible headache, but it's already gone."

Sitara didn't dare re-enter Lady Ceren's mind again, and the noblewoman soon disappeared down the hall. Sitara closed the outer door, considering everything she had just learned.

Rhea had killed Bajaran, there was no doubt. But the memory she'd just experienced, the sight of Bajaran's corpse gave new fuel to the fires of grief and lust for revenge that had simmered low in recent days. She had to know who was responsible.

Masego had proven himself cold and cruel and incredibly powerful, but the fiasco last night proved he was not beyond failure. Resolve firmed in her mind, and Sitara decided she had to act. She had to take the risk to know the truth.

She sent for Remiel.

49

BEACONS

Leander slowed to a halt just outside the outer gate of the high wall surrounding the upper city. Sentinel Ah'Shan caught up with him there. The powerfully built Sentinel was breathing heavily from the long run, but his face was flushed with excitement.

"See anything?"

"No." Leander scanned the crowds moving along the wide boulevard that circled the city just below the wall. Known as the Way of the Wall, it was one of the main thoroughfares crossing the Spokes.

On the far side of the Way, the slope leveled out into the wide plain of Tamera. The city's central marketplace began there and stretched for two miles. It was a maze of permanent shops and temporary tents teeming with people from the farthest reaches of the Six Kingdoms. It even included traders from Nedikat and Raghneidur.

Leander looked past the riot of colors and ignored the tumult of voices shouting deals and calling their wares. He looked just above the crowd for the telltale crimson glow marking their target.

"I see nothing," Ah'Shan said after a moment. He started forward. "Come on. Patrols are pushing into the area from all across the city. If we don't catch him, one of them will."

"He's mine," Leander said. "Justice will be done, and my hammer will deliver it."

"Only if you catch him first."

The two skirted the upper edge of the marketplace along the Way. If Tanathos had stayed on the Spoke, Harafin would have gotten a much better fix on his position, so most likely he had moved into the market.

Leander searched until his eyes began to ache, but he barely dared blink for fear of missing the sign. He'd yearned to bring his family's murderer to justice for over a century. The prospect of finally catching up with the elusive Tanathos set his blood pumping with battle fury.

The man, under the name Abaval, had committed the most atrocious murders. The gory scene of destruction in Leander's small village still burned vivid in his mind. He had never seen anything to rival the barbarity unleashed upon his town.

Now he knew the author of that atrocity. Abaval and Tanathos would die together today. The recent close encounters with the Shadeleech had only served to sharpen Leander's thirst for vengeance to a razor edge. He tried to stay objective, to focus only on dealing justice, but the thirst for revenge burned so hot he barely restrained the urge to reach for his Sentinel power.

That road led to madness and destruction.

After nearly a quarter mile, Leander's breath caught in his throat. There! Deep in the tangle of the marketplace, a crimson marker that looked like a slowly pulsing flame, peeked above a row of tents.

"There, I see him," Ah'Shan called out at the same time. The Sentinel closed his eyes, and the telltale silvery glow of Mindlink settled over his face.

Leander didn't wait for him to signal the other patrols to close in. They wouldn't be needed.

He surged off the Way and into the crowded marketplace. He resisted the urge to plow through the crowds as he wove through the press. As he moved into the maze of streets and alleys, he occasionally lost sight of the marker. His anxiety grew every second until he picked it up again.

The marker moved through the marketplace at a steady pace, but Leander closed on it. Within five minutes he had drawn close and rarely lost sight of it. It was weakening and would dissipate within moments. If they hadn't caught sight of it so soon, they would have lost this chance to destroy evil from among them.

Leander clenched his fist at his side, eager to call forth his mighty hammer. Soon the hunt would be over. He turned down a narrow alley flanked with brightly colored tents. This entire street sold cloth and leather goods from all across the Six Kingdoms. Bolts of cloth were piled high on tables along the edge of the alley, and people packed shoulder to shoulder filled the narrow street.

Leander groaned. People were haggling fiercely and crowding around the shops. There must be some sort of special deal today. He tried to push through the crowd, but could barely move.

"Leander, this way!"

Ah'Shan had caught up with him and jerked his thumb to the left where an alley barely wide enough for a single person passed between nearby tents.

Leander followed Ah'Shan down the alley. The ground was littered with filth, and it stunk like a cesspool. He chafed at the fact that Ah'Shan had managed to get ahead of him. They would have a serious disagreement if the Sentinel tried to take Tanathos.

They emerged into a wider street flanked by stone buildings and far less crowded. Leander scanned the area and almost missed the signal beacon. There, at the far end of the street, the beacon flared a final time before winking out.

It was enough.

The beacon had hovered over a figure cloaked in black who was just disappearing down a distant alley.

"I see him," Ah'Shan called.

Leander sprinted up the street without answering.

Ah'Shan muttered a curse and gave chase. He might be a master Sentinel, but Ah'Shan couldn't run nearly fast enough.

Leander sprinted up the street. People noticed him coming this time and cries of surprise spread the alarm. People wisely moved out of the way.

As Leander closed on the alley, he extended his right hand and snapped his fingers, calling forth his mighty hammer. He didn't yet release its blue fire. He refused to grant Tanathos any warning.

Leander raced into the alley. The buildings on either side reared three stories, so the alley huddled in deep shadow. He stumbled over a broken crate, but recovered his balance and vaulted it.

A man walked toward him in the alley, and for a split second, Leander could *see* Tanathos standing there. He drew back his hammer to deliver a deathblow, but his vision cleared. Instead of Tanathos, a dark-haired youth dressed in a palace uniform stood there, staring fearfully at the mighty hammer.

"Get out of here," Leander snarled and shoved the lad behind him. The youth didn't need further encouragement, and he bolted from the alley and disappeared into the crowd.

Debris littered the alley, forcing Leander to slow to a jog. He scanned the shadows eagerly, hoping to find Tanathos attempting to take refuge in the darkness.

Nothing.

Ah'Shan entered the alley, his breathing like a bellows. He stumbled over the same crate and the noise echoed in the alley.

Leander picked up his pace and raced for the far end of the alley. He leaped into the next street, hammer raised to strike. The Shadeleech couldn't be more than a few paces away.

The street was nearly deserted. It looked far older than most of the marketplace, with brick buildings housing high quality items for rich patrons. Few people walked the street, and none looked like the black-robed Shadeleech.

Ah'Shan joined Leander and together they scanned the street in vain for several heartbeats.

"Where'd he go?" Ah'Shan asked.

Half a dozen white-robed Sentinels rounded the corner a block away and fanned out through the street.

Ah'Shan grunted in approval. "They made good time."

Leander noticed for the first time that the newcomers all wore the black band of Kestrels. These were Ah'Shan's forces. The Kestrels, four men and two women, caught sight of Ah'Shan and jogged over.

"What have you seen?" Ah'Shan asked.

"Nothing, master," one burly Sentinel with a closely trimmed beard reported. "We saw a glimpse of the beacon a few minutes ago and moved to intercept, but have seen nothing since."

"Spread out," Ah'Shan commanded. "We chased him down this alley. He must be close." He pointed to one of the women, and then to the man standing beside her. "You two, mental scans of the area. Search for Sthenic signatures."

The two nodded and closed their eyes. A soft blue glow radiated from their faces as they extended feelers of thought through the surrounding area. Leander stood nearby, watching them closely and ready to intervene to help.

The discipline of these Kestrels, and their bravery, impressed Leander. It was no simple thing to scan an area for a hostile Shadeleech. The effort could cover lots of ground, but left the Sentinel open to a counter-attack that could easily prove fatal. Yet these Kestrels didn't hesitate or show fear.

These were worthy companions to take down such a foe.

After two minutes, the Sentinels opened their eyes, and the blue glow dissipated from around their faces. The woman said, "We find no gifted minds anywhere nearby, master, not until we reached the next patrol three blocks over."

Ah'Shan muttered a curse and turned a full circle. He raised his voice and shouted, "Search every building."

The Sentinels split into pairs and moved into nearby buildings. Ah'Shan pointed to the far end of the street, opposite the direction the Sentinels had approached from. "I'm going to search in this direction."

"Good," Leander said. "Notify me if you find anything."

"You're not coming?"

"No." He gestured back at the alley they just ran through. "I'm going to double check in here."

"The alley was empty."

"I know, but I feel like we must have missed something."

Ah'Shan shrugged and jogged away.

Leander dropped his hammer and it disappeared. After a final scan of the empty street, he turned and slowly walked back down the alley, deep in thought.

How could Tanathos have disappeared? They were so close. He forced down a wave of frustration. It wouldn't help, and he needed a clear mind.

Leander sat on an overturned crate and considered the situation. If the beacon had lasted even another moment, they would have caught up with Tanathos. They shouldn't have needed it. The Shadeleech was in sight, and this alley only had one exit. There was no way they should have lost him.

Leander rose and paced down the alley.

"We're missing something," he muttered. "But what?"

50

MASTER OF EVIL

Sitara stopped before a simple wooden door. It was identical to every other door in this seldom-used section of the lowest level of the underground palace, not far from where she and Remiel often met. She took a deep breath to steady her nerves, and then pushed the door open and stepped inside.

A large figure stood across the small room, cloaked and hooded. Sitara pushed the door closed, irritated at the concealment.

"Master," she said with a little curtsy. "Can I help you with your cloak?"

"Nice try," he mocked. "You haven't earned the right to see my face."

Of course he wouldn't reveal this most important secret easily. She yearned to demand the truth, but facing him, she realized she'd been a fool to think this would work.

"Thank you for coming," she managed.

"It made sense," he said, his voice lacking its normal mockery. "We need to talk, but maintaining a fully shielded Mindlink is becoming increasingly dangerous."

"What happened last night?" Sitara asked.

Masego made a dismissive gesture, never revealing his hand. "Look to the future, girl, not the past. Last night proved a setback, but I learned one useful thing. I know who killed Bajaran."

How could he know this was her purpose for requesting the meeting? He commanded a vast web of information, but had he learned that she'd discovered the truth?

"You look surprised," he said.

"I . . . didn't think you cared about Bajaran."

"Bajaran was a fool, but you're proving useful and this information is important to you, is it not?"

"It is."

"Then you'll be happy to know the man Kevlin killed Bajaran."

"I thought Rhea killed him." *And you ordered her to do it.*

Could he be speaking the truth? Ceren's memory had been so clear, but Kevlin alone had stood over Bajaran's body. Had Lady Ceren lied to the queen?

"Rhea was a useful tool," Masego said, "but the man Kevlin is the one responsible for everything that went wrong there."

"So you were Rhea's master?"

"Of course."

Could she believe him? This was too important for doubts. She wanted to avenge Bajaran's death, but she needed Kevlin for other things. She couldn't work with him to bring about the same revolution he'd killed Bajaran for starting.

Lady Ceren had no reason to lie about this, did she?

Masego did.

She knew the truth about him. His cruelty and his manipulations served only his good. His actions were not those of a true patriot like Bajaran.

He allied with Shadeleeches. That was really all she needed to know. This confirmed the rightness of her plan to destroy him in the moment of his victory over the current corrupt regime.

She needed Kevlin's help. She needed Ceren's help. She even needed Remiel's help.

Masego was responsible for Bajaran's death. It was his plan that put Rhea and Bajaran together that night in Hallvarr. Everything she'd done since first accepting Masego as her new master had been a mockery of Bajaran's death. She'd only wanted to avenge him and fulfill his vision of a better world. Instead, she'd allied with his murderer.

She should wait, bide her time, destroy him at the moment he was about to claim victory, but she couldn't. She couldn't keep up the lies.

Sitara opened herself to the power of Darkness. This time as its filth crawled into her body and stained her soul, she welcomed its power.

Masego started, as if sensing the sudden influx of power.

Sitara struck.

She formed an invisible blade of air and slashed at Masego's masked form. He cried out and staggered against the wall. The front of his cloak parted as her blade bit deep. Blood spurted across the room as a wide gash ripped open across his chest.

Masego clutched at the wound and it began to close. Before Sitara could strike again, he threw out a hand, and thick blocks of ice materialized around her feet and legs.

Sitara gasped as the ice grew up to her waist and deadly cold seeped into her legs. Her muscles cramped and she lost control of her blade of air.

Masego snarled a word she didn't understand, and an invisible force smashed her across the room against the far wall. She struck with terrific force and the blocks of ice encasing her lower half exploded on impact.

As Sitara fell to the floor, she used fingers of power to collect those tumbling fragments of ice. She hurled them at Masego just as she had struck at that soldier in the catacombs with pieces of the dead.

Masego had started to cross the room toward her, but the shards of ice slashed into him and knocked him back again. He raised a hand, and fire encircled him, consuming the ice in a flash.

Masego pointed at her and shadowy fists of air pounded into Sitara from every side. She screamed as her body lifted into the air, pounded as if from a hundred iron-hard hands. Agony scattered her thoughts and she lost her grip on her magic. Blood sprayed from her nose and mouth, and she writhed helplessly within the deadly barrage.

Then Masego struck at her mind. His will struck her shields like an avalanche, but even in the midst of the beating she hadn't dropped her mental shields. They shook under the blow, and her outer shields shattered. He drove toward her mind, but her second layer of shields broke his attack.

Despite the brutal beating, Sitara shifted her mental shields. Nothing mattered but preserving the sanctity of her mind. She would die before allowing him to possess her again.

A second blow struck, but her shields held and she shifted the multi-faceted walls around her mind in preparation for the next blow.

It never came. Instead, the beating stopped and Sitara fell to the floor. She groaned and struggled to sit up.

Masego yanked her up by the hair. She screamed as the pressure tore at her head, her feet kicking uselessly at the air as he lifted her clear of the ground.

"You stupid girl." Even hanging so close to him, she couldn't see through the darkness cloaking his face.

He shook her like a rat. "Why did you do this?"

"You did it," Sitara whispered through broken lips. She tried to spit blood at him, but lacked the strength. It only dribbled down her chin. "You killed Bajaran."

Masego threw her from him. She struck the wall and fell in a crumpled heap. "Of course I did. Bajaran was an idiot, and he made it all too easy for Rhea to murder him at my command."

He actually admitted it! Rage gave Sitara the strength to sit up.

"You think Bajaran was some kind of saint?" he demanded. "Far from it. Rhea took him to her bed and she controlled that idiot and everything he did."

"You lie!" Sitara reached for her gift, but nothing came. Why would the Sentinels block her now when she needed her gift the most?

"Believe what you want, but know this. You've outgrown Bajaran's memory. He lacked vision, but you have real potential."

Sitara couldn't believe it. He was complimenting her? He hurt too much to keep up.

Masego took a step toward her. "You have discipline. You have drive. You could be so much more than Bajaran set you up for."

"I'll kill you," Sitara said. Somehow she found the strength to struggle to her feet and face him.

"No. You will serve me."

Masego pointed at her and a mighty whirlwind erupted into the room. The wind tore at her hair and lifted her from the floor. Sitara struggled within the wind, but it held her fast.

The wind grew dark until she could barely see Masego. Then it condensed around her and began crawling under her skin.

Sitara screamed and thrashed within Masego's power as the darkness bored into her, all the way to the center of her bones. It felt like thousands of worms crawling through her skin until they writhed in the very center of her being. Sitara screamed again, and madness tore at her mind as she struggled to fight against the torture.

The sensation abruptly faded, as if the worms had found new homes and bedded down to stay. Sitara ripped at her skin with her nails and drew bloody gashes along her arms as she vainly tried to dig out the horror that consumed her.

"Get it out!" Sitara shrieked, slumping back against the ground. Tears burned her eyes and sobs wracked her petite frame.

Masego took a step closer. "You are bound to me now, just as Rhea was. You will do my bidding, just as she did."

"Never!" Sitara reached again for her gift, and this time she connected with the power of darkness. She drank in its filth greedily and focused the power on Masego.

As she drew in her will to strike at him, every bone in her body burst into agony. Sitara screamed and writhed on the floor, but still tried to direct an attack against Masego.

The pain intensified until it felt like her bones were burning. The horrifying feeling of darkness worming through her body commenced again, and it felt like the worms of dark magic were crawling toward her mind.

She couldn't hold her will any longer. Her power bled away and she tore at her chest and throat with her fingers until blood ran freely. As madness yawned before her, she yearned for death to stop the agony.

Then the pain stopped.

Sitara sobbed, hugging herself. She couldn't feel anything, as if her skin had turned to ice.

Masego stood over her. "You cannot attack me, slave. You are mine, body and soul. Should you attempt to betray me, you will die before you can speak my name."

Sitara looked up at Masego through her tears and managed to ask, "What do you want from me."

"Everything."

He leaned over her. "Know this. Should you attempt to betray me, or should you fail me again, you will die. It won't be a quick or an easy death. You have tasted a fraction of the pain you'll suffer before I release you to the eternal worlds."

What could she say? She had failed, so completely she couldn't yet grasp the magnitude of what had just happened to her. She cast her thoughts wide, trying to figure out a way to escape this nightmare.

"Kevlin," said Masego.

"What?" Had he been reading her mind again?

Masego motioned for Sitara to rise. It took several tries before she managed to stand.

"We must take the man Kevlin. Through him we can obtain the stone. He must have it."

"How can you be so sure?"

"It has to be him. He is protected in a way I've never seen before. It can only mean he's somehow still important, even though he's no longer Steward."

"What are you going to do?"

She didn't want to kill Kevlin. Masego hadn't been reading her thoughts after all, but had he provided the answer unwittingly? He was right. Kevlin was the key. If she could win him, she could escape her slavery and defeat Masego. Kevlin could bring so many forces to bear for her, if she could but explain the truth to him.

"I'm going to teach you two new spells," Masego said, "and you, my slave, are going to take the man Kevlin."

"Why don't you take him?"

"Consider it a final test to prove your worth. Time is short. You have twenty-four hours to bring him to me."

"How can you demand this?" Masego had failed after days of planning. She needed more time to orchestrate Kevlin's conversion.

"I have no use for unprofitable servants. Do this for me, and you may yet win a seat of glory with me."

The arrogant fool. He imagined she would willingly obey? She would do what she had to, but she would bend her entire will tirelessly into efforts to bring him down.

"Now," he continued brusquely. "On to the lesson. Today I will teach you how to force your will onto another."

"Then I will teach you Rogue Fire."

51

STRANGE BEDFELLOWS

Sitara startled awake when a damp cloth was pressed gently against her face. She lashed out blindly while reaching for her actinic gift. It didn't come.

"Easy, Angel." Remiel caught her hand and massaged her palm while she came fully awake.

Sitara lay back on the cot, relieved that it was only Remiel and not a Sentinel come to take her for execution as she'd been dreaming.

"Are you all right?" he asked, again dabbing her face with the damp handkerchief. The other side of it was stained pink. She glanced down at her arms where dried blood had been wiped away. She hadn't felt him do that.

The lesson with Masego had been brutal. He hadn't granted her any mercy or shown any patience with her while he taught the new spells, despite the recent beating he'd given her. After he had left, she'd collapsed onto the cot, quivering with exhaustion and terror.

She didn't know how Remiel came to be here, but she sat up and wrapped her arms around him. She needed normal human company. Well, as normal as any she could find in her current twisted world. He held her gently, and the warmth of his touch broke through her façade of strength.

"No," she sobbed. "I'm not all right."

"What did he do to you?" Remiel asked.

"I don't want to talk about it. Just hold me."

He did.

His unusual consideration startled her again. Suppressing a shudder of revulsion, she embraced a tiny thread of Sthenic power and slipped her thoughts into his mind. She needed to understand this man who was making it too difficult for her to keep hating him.

While he stroked her hair, she sank into his memories.

She found truth and despair.

Remiel had grown up in Tamera as he'd stated. He hadn't mentioned that his father's death had been an execution. He'd been wrongly convicted of stealing from a high lord. Remiel had worked hard as a boy, trying to help support his mother and sickly younger sister, but life had beaten him down at every turn.

Then Masego had found him. He'd recruited Remiel with promises of wealth and chances at vengeance against the cruel lords who kept him trapped in poverty. He had embraced that life and for a time been blinded by the fabulous riches and access to important people who, for the first time in his life, treated him like he mattered.

He'd proven himself adept at his new life and Masego had pushed him into greater crimes, from blackmailing nobles to seducing ladies. He had started to resist. That's when he learned the truth about his gilded cage. Masego owned him, and if he didn't continue operating with enthusiasm and success, his master would punish his family.

Bound to his master's word, Remiel had convinced himself it was better to hurt those who had hurt his family. Better them than risk the lives of the ones he loved to protect men and women who had never cared about them.

Then he'd met Sitara. At first he'd approached the relationship like all the rest, but she had affected him more than any other woman, and new doubts had begun to surface.

Sitara withdrew from Remiel's mind. She'd seen more than she'd intended. Remiel was enslaved as thoroughly as she. He had taken advantage of her. That truth could not be ignored. And yet, she saw much of herself reflected in his pitiful life.

He hated the injustice of the world and had hoped to change it before his life had been twisted by their master. He knew the current system top to bottom, better even than Sitara.

Together, they might be able to do what neither of them could hope to do alone. She leaned back to look him in the eye, searching his face for reflections of the secrets she'd pulled from his heart. Could she really step beyond their painful past?

Remiel touched her cheek. "I'm sorry this has happened to you, Angel."

"It was my fault. I challenged him too soon."

He cupped her face in his hands. "Why did you come back? You were free of all this! I was happy to see you return, but I would've been happier knowing you had escaped."

"There is no escape. Not until we win."

"It's impossible." He dropped his hands and leaned his forehead against hers. "Oh, Sitara, what a pair we make."

There, he'd said it. He'd identified himself with her.

"We do."

"We do what?" he asked.

"We make a pair," she said, taking his hands in hers and sitting taller. "Together we know enough to break out, to finally make real changes."

"He'll never let us."

"He can't stop us if he's dead."

Remiel cringed and glanced around nervously. "You can't say things like that."

"Our lives are forfeit already, but we have a choice. We can let him decide when and how to kill us, depending on his will and pleasure." She gripped his hands tight. "Or we can work together and bring him down."

"How?"

"Do you trust me?"

"I don't trust anyone."

She couldn't argue with that, but there had to be a way. "Are you willing to try?" She touched his cheek. "Do you believe that even broken lives can become something better?"

"I don't think it's possible."

The same terror she struggled to control shone in his eyes. He'd been enslaved to Masego longer than she. He'd been conditioned to this life, but she felt the spark of hope in his soul.

"I'll show you it can be done," she said.

"How?"
"We just need a little more help."
"Who?"
"Kevlin."

52

BABY STEPS

Kevlin threw open the door to High Lord Damarist's office in the Hallvarr Palace. It banged loudly against the stop.

Ambassador Damarist jumped and cried, "I thought I made it clear I am not to be disturbed." He recognized Kevlin and stammered, "I'm sorry, my Lord Kevlin, now's not a good time . . ."

His voice trailed off as Harafin followed Kevlin into the room.

"Make it a good time," Harafin said. He waved one hand and the door slammed itself closed.

Ambassador Damarist leaned back in his padded leather chair, his face losing what little color remained. He glanced around the room and even looked over his shoulder at the large window overlooking the Einarri field. For a second, it looked like he considered trying to escape that way.

He composed himself as Kevlin advanced. "Of course, Master Harafin. You're always welcome." He motioned toward chairs situated in front of his desk. "Please sit."

"Skip the pleasantries, Ambassador. You lied to me. This is your chance to revise your statement. I recommend you do it promptly."

Ambassador Damarist assumed an expression of outrage. "I will remind you that I am a sitting ambassador, Sentinel Harafin. Such accusations . . ."

"I haven't accused you of anything yet, Ambassador," Harafin interrupted. He leaned over the desk, "But if you don't answer my questions truthfully, I will accuse you before the emperor himself if need be." Ambassador Damarist cringed away and he added, "You will tell me the truth, or I will command Truth from you."

Kevlin shivered at the mention of Truth, even though he supported Harafin in this interrogation. The memory of being tortured by the faceless Sentinel with Truth as a boy flashed into his mind. The old memory still terrified him. The feeling of absolute helplessness triggered a sense of panic similar to what he had felt in the catacombs last night.

Ambassador Damarist straightened and tried to maintain his dignity. "Exactly what information are you seeking?"

Kevlin spoke up. "You have a servant. Young, dark hair."

"I have many servants, Sir Kevlin."

"You were meeting with him the last time we came to speak with you."

The patronizing smile that had started to spread across Ambassador Damarist's face faded.

"We believe that man is one of the conspirators. We wish to speak with him."

"Immediately," Harafin added.

"I don't know anything," the ambassador stammered.

"Then stop playing games," Harafin snapped. "Where do we find this man?"

Ambassador Damarist leaned back in his padded chair and sighed. He ran a shaking hand across his forehead. "Very well, Harafin. Be it upon your shoulders the consequences."

"Explain yourself."

The ambassador looked down at his hands. "I know nothing of these traitors you hunt. The young man you describe is in league with evil forces, but I don't know who they are or what their agenda may be."

"What do you know?" Kevlin asked.

Ambassador Damarist sighed again, and actual tears glistened in his eyes. That surprised Kevlin. This was not the reaction he expected from a conspirator.

"His name is Remiel. He approached me almost a year ago and demanded I offer him employment and access to certain restricted areas in the palace. In return for this, and a promise of absolute secrecy, he guaranteed the safety of my family. If I refused, his master would destroy them."

"Why didn't you tell us?" Harafin asked. "We can protect you. That's why . . ."

"You can't," Ambassador Damarist cried. "I kept hoping someone would discover what was going on, but no one did." He scrubbed his face with both hands. "I tried to deny them. That very day I ordered the fellow arrested." He shuddered. "Before I could even summon a Salawin Stalwart to interrogate him, I received news that my youngest son had just broken both legs in a freak riding accident."

"I remember hearing about that," said Harafin. "All the more reason to come to me for protection."

Ambassador Damarist leaped to his feet. "You blind, arrogant fool! They hurt my son the very same day. Do you really think I'd risk my family?"

Harafin met his gaze, unflinching. "I do. You're an ambassador, a member of the ruling council."

"I'm a husband and a father."

"You have a responsibility to every citizen in your kingdom."

"I have a responsibility to my family."

"You betrayed your oath."

"What about the oath I took to protect my wife and children?"

"Who knows how many innocents have been hurt or even killed as a result of your cowardice?"

"I don't know," Ambassador Damarist said, sinking into his chair, deflated. He whispered, "But I know the names and faces of the ones I've saved."

Harafin said, "Be that as it may. We will shatter this conspiracy. You're a fool, but we'll protect your family. The emperor will decide what happens to you."

Kevlin considered this man he had once held in high esteem. No veneer of greatness remained. Ambassador Damarist looked broken, afraid, cowering in his expensive chair. Now all he felt was pity for the man.

Would he knowingly endanger Indira? Was he already endangering her by insisting on keeping her so close?

He couldn't process that idea right now, so he focused on the conspirators. Finally they were taking a step forward. They knew a name. They would root out this band of traitors and destroy them all.

"Where is Remiel?" Kevlin asked.

"I have no idea. He poses as a servant in the acquisitions department, but he comes and goes at will."

"We will watch for him," Harafin said. "Notify us if he contacts you."

Ambassador Damarist nodded, gaze locked on his hands clasped on the desk. He said softly, "I'm not a traitor, Harafin."

"Perhaps not," Harafin admitted after a moment. "We won't know until we question this Remiel."

"If we can find him," Kevlin said.

53

A Dangerous Game

Someone knocked on Tanathos's door.

He stared at it, fighting down a surge of panic. His room in the quiet inn was situated on the top floor in a corner, with few passers-by and no interruptions.

He had barely escaped the hunters today. The sight of the Hammer Stalwart had nearly sent him into a panic. If they found him now, he was already dead. If they had found him, they wouldn't bother to knock.

"One moment," Tanathos called out in the feeble voice he used in the city.

He donned the blue-trimmed silver robe and wide-brimmed hat with veil he wore most often as his disguise. It proved exceptionally effective. Few people bothered a near-blind lesser nobleman who possessed just enough coin to pay for what he ordered, and not enough to encourage bothersome salesmen

Once concealed, Tanathos made his slow way to the door, tapping a walking cane as he moved. He fought the urge to embrace his Sthenic powers. Only in a moment of critical need could he risk it.

He didn't fully understand the wards placed in the city and still didn't know how the Sentinels had tracked him down earlier. Not knowing was scarier than anything else.

Tanathos pulled the door open. A dark-haired youth dressed in a palace uniform stood in the doorway. After a surprised second, Tanathos remembered his name. Remiel.

"May I come in?"

Tanathos stepped aside to allow Remiel to pass. He glanced down the hall but saw no one else. The youth came alone. He slammed the door and, despite the danger, embraced his Sthenic powers. Darkness roared into his soul and Tanathos breathed easier with the return of power.

He knew this man. Remiel, one of Masego's hirelings. He had just caught up with the young fool earlier in that alley just before he caught sight of the Stalwart closing in. If not for that, he would have already exacted his revenge.

He couldn't imagine why Remiel would come to him here, or even how he knew where to look. It didn't matter. Masego may have escaped, but this fool would suffer for his master's deception.

Tanathos struck a mighty, invisible blow at Remiel's mind. To his amazement, the blow deflected away. He slashed mental fingers across Remiel's mind and encountered heavily reinforced shields.

Surprising. Remiel's master expended great energy protecting his servant. The youth stood silent and unmoving, as if he expected the attack and waited for Tanathos to fail.

The thought enraged him and Tanathos drove a dagger of power against the shields again in an attempt to shatter them. The fool would know pain for this insolence.

Instead of shattering, the shields around Remiel's mind compressed under the blow and then exploded outward. A brilliant flash of light blinded Tanathos.

He cried out and flinched back. Full daylight was painful to his Sthenic-enhanced vision, and this light burned like living fire. The light drove into his brain and, despite his heavy shielding, it left him rattled. If not for the blind-man's cane, he would have fallen.

While he was distracted, Remiel lunged and grabbed his hand. Lightning-like power ripped up his arm and his body spasmed, every muscle locked rigid and unmoving.

Tanathos tried to speak, but couldn't move. He had never experienced anything like this. How could a powerless slave unman him so easily?

Remiel, who looked afraid but determined spoke. "While I have your attention, please hear me out."

Masego was truly a gifted double-crosser. He rivaled the Sigrun for cunning and surprise attacks. Tanathos swore to learn the secret of this spell. It would prove most helpful.

Remiel didn't bother waiting for a reply. "I bring a message and an offer from my master. He knows where you hide. He wishes to meet with you."

Remiel then waited half a minute while Tanathos worked to overcome the crippling paralysis. Slowly his muscles thawed and he managed to move his jaw.

"Your master betrayed me," he croaked when he could form a whisper.

"No, I mean my other master."

That was entertaining. It reminded him of the cutthroat circles of the Sigrun capital. "No man can serve two masters." *At least not for long.*

Remiel shrugged, "You can if neither master knows about the other."

The last vestiges of the temporary paralysis faded and Tanathos rolled his shoulders. Remiel played a dangerous game, one that even Tanathos would approach with extreme caution.

"My master who is not Masego wishes to meet with you to assist in destroying the man Kevlin."

"You offer too much too soon, fool. I should just kill you now."

Remiel swallowed and for the first time looked genuinely nervous. He quickly stammered, "If you do, my master will take that as a rejection of his offer, and will reveal your location to the Stalwart Leander. Your choice."

Tanathos cast a nervous glance from the door to the single, barred window. He'd managed to elude the old Stalwart so far, but could he do so again? The old man terrified him. He couldn't call Remiel's bluff, not yet.

"Very well. Take me to this master of yours."

54

FRIENDS IN NEED

Ceren sat by the large window in the ornate, if small, quarters assigned to her in the Freyarr Palace. She brushed her auburn hair as she considered all the various angles of the situation. If she played the game right, she could both secure the keisara's patronage and steer Kevlin's course.

She gazed out over the manicured lawns and the Tamarr Palace beyond, her thoughts turning to Kevlin. He was the key. Events were moving fast, and the thought of helping shape the future of the empire thrilled her. She couldn't be in a better position. Success would depend on some careful planning and perfect execution, but she would make it happen.

A soft knock on her door pulled her out of her reverie. She didn't have any full-time servants here, so she rose and crossed the small sitting room to her outer door.

Sitara stood in the hall, her face streaked with tears, blood caking her arms and neck.

"Sitara, what happened?" Ceren exclaimed and drew the young servant into her rooms. Could something have happened to the keisara? Could the enemy have attacked again? Dozens of questions clamored through her mind.

Sitara entered the room and swayed, as if exhausted. Ceren led her to a soft couch.

"Lady Ceren, you're the only one I can turn to for help."

Ceren sat beside Sitara. "You know I'll do anything to help." What could have happened? How could she capitalize on the situation, whatever it was?

Her thoughts scattered like a flock of birds when she met Sitara's gaze and noticed that her eyes were completely black.

Sitara clutched Ceren's arms. "I knew I could count on you."

The darkness in her eyes erupted into the room and consumed Ceren.

55

A Painful Message

Tanathos stepped through a thick wooden door into the rear entrance of a large building in the north end of the central marketplace. Remiel had chosen a convoluted path. Tanathos had no idea what merchandise might be sold here.

They passed through a storage room filled with blank boxes that revealed nothing of their contents. They entered a huge showroom that filled most of the main floor. The front door was locked, and shutters covered all the windows. The only light came from a small lamp sitting on a table beside a hooded and cloaked figure who sat in a comfortable, padded chair. Two other hooded figures flanked the seated person.

Tanathos followed Remiel toward the trio. The floor of the showroom was laid in glistening hardwood, and display cases were situated at staggered intervals throughout the room. Every case was covered with black velvet, concealing their wares.

The seated figure motioned toward a polished wooden chair that faced him.

"I will remain standing," Tanathos said.

Did the fool think to so easily subject him? Tanathos held close his anger. It gave him strength. He would show this fool very soon who was master here. First, learn what they had to offer, then consume their essence.

The seated man said nothing, so Tanathos goaded him a little. "Are you a coward to hide your face from me?"

The man chuckled and said from under the hood, "We both wear necessary disguises for now."

"Your slave informs me you wish to make an offer."

"I do."

"How can you serve me?" Tanathos asked.

The man chuckled again, his voice strong and cultured. "We cannot learn to trust each other unless both benefit from the arrangement. My offer allows us to serve each other."

"You wish to trust me?" The man was a bigger fool than he thought.

"Perhaps. But first you will trust me."

Tanathos remained silent. He could never trust anyone in this city. Masego had proven that.

"I bring word from the Sigrun," the man said, as if reading Tanathos's mind.

That was a surprise. Could he be telling the truth? Tanathos had felt no mental contact. An attempt to communicate over such vast distances would have consumed many lives.

The man continued. "I can prove the veracity of my words."

"How?" Tanathos felt intrigued despite his caution.

There was a slim chance the man might be telling the truth. The Sigrun surely controlled other spies in the city. Tanathos had wished in recent days that he knew their identities so he could contact them.

The man made no move, gave not the slightest indication that he wielded power, and suddenly a vision poured into Tanathos' mind.

It was a sending from the Sigrun council.

He knew the Sigrun from over a century serving them. The sight of them thrilled him with eager anticipation to join their ranks even as familiar fear chilled his soul.

Nyyrrikki, one of the twin leaders of the Sigrun, spoke. "Command Tanathos to complete his mission. He must return with the stone before the snows. Success will earn him a seat on this council." Then he faced Tanathos. "Fail us again, and you will suffer the fate of all the unworthy."

Tanathos shivered with eager anticipation. They still offered him the coveted seventh seat on the council. They didn't know that he had nearly succeeded in his plan to supplant them all and wrest all power from them into his own hands.

The seated figure must have used Sthenic energy to push that sending to him. His identity didn't matter, only that the Sigrun had sent another servant to support him. If they knew what he had attempted to do, they would have sent this man to kill him.

Pain so severe he could scarce comprehend it exploded through Tanathos' entire being. It ripped through his body and unprotected mind in a single overwhelming blast. Tanathos collapsed to the floor and his limbs shook with agony. He tried to shut out the pain, but it raked through his soul like nails.

It denied him the capacity to scream.

After seconds that felt like hours the pain faded, leaving him quivering on the floor. The others watched, silent and unmoving.

After a few minutes, Tanathos regained enough strength to climb into the wooden chair the seated man had first offered.

"That last part of the message was a subtle motivation to stay loyal and not fail again. Your ambition is commendable, but don't stray from the path appointed to you."

Despite the risk, Tanathos reached for his gift and shielded his mind. Either the house was shielded from the wards placed around the city, or this house was not actively monitored.

The influx of strength calmed and centered his mind. If only he had a slave available so he could feed on its life force. He yearned to reach beyond the edge of the city to where his forces remained concealed.

Tanathos tried to speak, but his throat was dry as aged parchment and painful as if scraped raw with sand. It felt as if he'd managed to scream after all. Finally he managed to croak, "The message is clear. Now tell me how you can help me take the man Kevlin."

"I will provide a way for you to enter the palace complex undetected."

As the man explained the plan and the resources at his disposal, Tanathos forgot his pain and smiled for the first time in a long time.

56

SOME FRIENDLY ADVICE

Indira stopped outside the Freyarr Palace to gather her courage. Her pulse raced and she rubbed her face to ease the heat in her skin. A hundred reasons why she should turn around and return to the safety of the hospital flitted through her mind, but for once she chose to ignore them.

Her motivation carried more weight than all her doubts, all her fears. Kevlin.

Holding an image of his face in her mind like a talisman, she strode up the wide steps into the Freyarr palace. She had to speak with Ceren or she feared she might burst.

She reviewed her interactions with Kevlin, from the first day they met when he had impulsively kissed her to the night after the battle at Il'Aicharen. She had followed her heart and kissed him back. He was such a complex man, and somehow he'd walked into her heart.

That was the problem.

She hated to see him suffer, but how could she respond? For once, helping Kevlin might mean doing the opposite of what she yearned to do. She longed to protect him, to shield him from harm, and yet the very act of trying to help might prove his destruction.

The unfamiliar frustration left her feeling unsettled and doubtful. For once in her life, she could do nothing to help. The man she was falling in love with couldn't stand in her presence without suffering the terrifying Trembling Madness. Even if it would help, she had begun to doubt her ability to shield him, or anyone, with her Faith.

For the first time she could remember, Indira didn't know what to do.

So she came to speak with Ceren, the only friend who might be smart enough to guide her. Ceren was already helping Kevlin, so she made the most sense.

Indira paused to compose herself before knocking. She waited breathlessly for a long moment, but no one came to the door. She hadn't considered what to do if Ceren wasn't in her quarters. Ceren could be anywhere. In fact, it was foolish to assume she could find Ceren at all, with everything Ceren had going on. The woman always appeared so busy.

Then the door opened. Ceren stood there, her hair disheveled and clothes rumpled as if she had been sleeping.

"Oh, I'm so sorry," Indira said. "Did I wake you?"

Ceren stared past Indira and spoke in a distracted tone of voice, "No, I don't think so."

"Can I help you? Are you all right?"

Ceren scrambled back, fear on her face.

Indira followed her into her quarters. "What's wrong?"

"Nothing. Just . . . don't touch me."

Despite the hurtful comment, Indira gently closed the door. Now that she was inside, she had to share her concerns, even if Ceren seemed to be having a bad day.

"Now isn't really a good time," Ceren said as she drifted across the living room and sank into a plush couch.

Indira followed and sat beside her. Ceren shifted away, but Indira didn't care. "I need to speak with you about Kevlin."

Ceren perked up. "What about Kevlin?"

"I don't know what to do." It felt so good to get the problem out in the open. "How do I help him?"

"What do you think is wrong with him?" Ceren asked slowly.

"Oh, nothing new," Indira said. "But he already has so much to worry about."

"Indeed," Ceren said. Her eyes wandered past Indira, and she massaged her temples.

"Are you sure you're all right?"

"I'm fine," Ceren snapped. "Just busy."

Indira clasped her hands together and said softly. "You know I . . . care for Kevlin. I'm just not sure how to help."

It felt good to speak with Ceren. The two of them had formed a tight bond of friendship in Hallvarr. Kevlin had been the one topic that Indira had hesitated to broach. Ceren had made it clear she felt Kevlin was the wrong choice for Indira, and she had tried at first to keep them apart. Lately though, she'd done so much to help him, who better to turn to for help?

"You can best help Kevlin by staying far away from him."

Indira sagged back in the couch. The courage she'd gathered to come here fled and she felt lost. She'd feared Ceren would advise her to stay away, but wasn't sure she believed it was the right choice.

Ceren patted her knee. "I know you care for him, but he'll break your heart."

Indira smiled. "I don't think . . ."

"Trust me, Indira," Ceren cut her off. "It's not safe for either of you to be together right now."

Indira slowly nodded and faced the hard truth. Kevlin seemed far more susceptible to the Trembling Madness in her presence. If he somehow succumbed to it, he might fall prey to another *Tai Pari*. If he did, he could unleash widespread destruction on the capital. Thousands of people could be hurt or killed.

Could she justify staying close to him despite such a risk? If she did trigger his destruction, she would contribute to so much pain and suffering. It would make her entire life's work a lie.

Fighting back tears, Indira whispered, "There has to be some way . . ."

"No, there's no way. If you care for Kevlin, stay away. Give him some time."

Indira hesitated, torn by conflicting needs.

"Please trust me," Ceren added.

"I will." What else could Indira say?

She rose and Ceren gave her a hug before leading her to the door. Indira walked slowly away, still wrestling with the right course.

For the first time she could remember, the choice to place the needs of others first was a difficult one. She wasn't sure what she was going to do.

57

BOUND FOR TROUBLE

Kevlin exited the Tamarr Palace into the cool night. He descended the stone steps and paused in the shadows between torches set in ornate sconces along the nearest walk. It felt great to be outside and feel the light breeze on his face.

He glanced back at the Tamarr Palace. Despite his personal dislike for Gabral, the short colonel did have a sound mind for strategy. He commanded an extensive knowledge of the greater palace compound and its security forces.

In the just-concluded meeting, they had set up a plan for taking the elusive Remiel when he appeared. Kevlin would prefer cornering Remiel with his brothers and beating the truth out of him, but he had to admit the plan was a good one.

Maybe Remiel would resist when they captured him. The thought was promising.

Kevlin crossed the Silver Spoke and followed a secondary walk paved with cobblestones around the front of the ornate Freyarr Palace. He passed few people. This time of night, most people seemed to prefer staying in the lower levels to coming out in the cool air. Jerrik and Drystan had both decided on that route, but Kevlin was glad he chose to walk aboveground and take the long way around. It provided uninterrupted time to think.

The Trembling Madness was barely discernible, and the constant craving for magic well contained. Tomorrow, he'd have to seek out

Harafin to get some magic, but for now he enjoyed feeling normal and free of danger.

Leave until tomorrow the next battle with unruly magic. Would it ever submit willingly to his control again? If not, how long could he continue to conquer it? How long before his concentration slipped or his will wavered?

Kevlin glanced forward to the statue of Akillik that stood bathed in bright lantern light. He skirted it and kept his gaze averted. The last person he wanted to see was the fickle god. Could he really avoid ever spinning the Wheel again? What would happen if it spun against him?

Kevlin shivered.

When he reached the blocky, granite Meinarr Palace, Kevlin paused in front of the towering statue of Asherah in her flowing blue robes. He should have brought some money to leave a donation. Now might be a good time to start returning to her good graces. He no longer doubted that she existed. It would be nice to convince one of the gods to remain on his side.

As he stood there contemplating the statue, a wave of dread crept into him, like a chill on a winter's night. It felt almost tangible, a palpable wave of terror. He'd only ever felt such a thing in the presence of . . .

Kevlin spun and grabbed for his sword. He also snapped his left hand down to unsheathe hidden stiletto from his wrist guard.

Dozens of heavy ropes whipped out of the shadows on the far side of Asherah and wrapped around him like living snakes. With startling speed, the ropes bound him from neck to ankle and pinned his hands to his side. All he managed to do was extend his stiletto between layers of encircling rope.

Bound so tight, Kevlin slowly tipped sideways to the ground. A hooded figure stepped out of the shadows and approached. Kevlin didn't need to see their face to know them.

Tanathos.

The Shadeleech carried a two-foot, intricately carved wooden rod that looked vaguely familiar. He had been pointing it at Kevlin like some kind of weapon, but now tossed it aside.

Kevlin tried to shout for help, but Tanathos lunged and shoved a rag so far into his mouth it started choking him. He tried spitting it out, but

Tanathos tied it in place with a wide strip of black cloth. Kevlin fought a growing sense of panic. He could barely breathe.

Tanathos punched him in the side of the head. Lights danced behind his eyes, but anger burned away some of the fear. The Shadeleech leaned over him and pushed the brim of the wide had he was wearing far enough back for Kevlin to see the roiling blackness covering his eyes.

Tanathos smiled down at him. "Hello, Kevlin. Your soul belongs to me."

58

CHAOS

A dozen heavily cloaked figures stepped into the center of the Silver Spoke at the edge of the central marketplace. Other pedestrians flowed around them without paying much attention. Now that evening had settled over the city, the shops were closed, but the taverns and other entertainment houses were in full swing, and crowds thronged the boulevard.

One wealthy merchant, mounted on a huge roan stallion who clearly expected pedestrians to move out of his way, hauled on the reins to keep from trampling the hooded figures. He cursed down at them, "Watch yourselves, fools! You're going to get hurt if you don't look where you're going."

The closest figure, much smaller than the others, threw off his cloak to reveal blood-red robes. He said, "I'm not the one you should be worried about."

The merchant gaped as the Shadeleech pointed at him and a wave of pure darkness rolled over him and his horse.

The Shadeleech grinned as he sucked the lives out of the fat merchant and his horse. He took his time. No need to hurry.

This way, they had more time to scream.

The agonized wails from the doomed merchant and his horse carried over the crowd and drew the attention of hundreds of eyes.

They all witnessed the impossible.

Makrasha in Tamera.

The monstrous creatures threw off their cloaks, roared blood-chilling battle cries, and fired small crossbows into the crowds. Men and women fell under the volley, and dozens of voices screamed in pain and fear.

The Makrasha drew swords and leaped into the crowd on all sides slashing down the shocked ranks of unarmed civilians. Blood sprayed far out over the crowd, but the screams piercing the early evening darkness drove farther still. People tried to flee, but many were trampled in the press.

Some of the crowd were armed and tried to defend themselves. The Makrasha cut them down and howled louder with bloodlust.

The Shadeleech targeted half a dozen panicked civilians and caught them in his Sthenic power and sucked out their life forces. If only he had time to torture their souls before releasing them to the eternal worlds.

No matter, they served well. He used the pure strength of their souls to conjure crimson fire that he unleashed in rippling sheets through the crowd.

The horrible shrieks of people dying under his power mingled with the agonized screams of those consumed by fire. The Shadeleech tossed balls of fire into nearby buildings and the flames spread quickly, as if the market had been eagerly waiting an excuse to burn.

Panic spread faster than the flames.

The Shadeleech grinned and began systematically targeting as many people as he could, until their soul fires filled him to the uttermost. He fought to contain the tremendous quantity of magic and turned to face the inner city.

Soon the Sentinels would come, and he would destroy them.

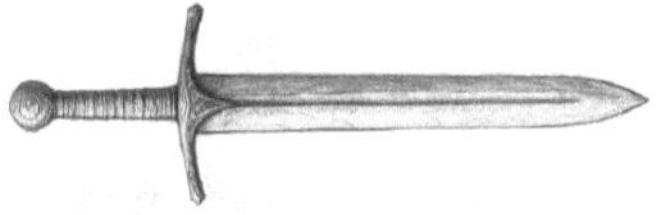

At exactly the same time, at the southern end of the central market, a second Shadeleech and his dozen Makrasha stepped into the Iron Spoke and announced their presence by consuming an entire portable stage with fire.

Thirty actors, who had been taking a final bow, burned along with two hundred spectators crowded into the small, wooden structure.

The Makrasha waded into the nearby crowds, slaughtering everyone who got in their way while the Shadeleech spread burning destruction in an ever-widening circle.

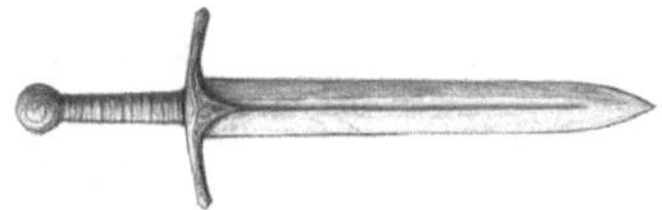

In the outskirts of town, dock workers lived in a decrepit section of town made up of a warren of narrow streets, crowded with wooden buildings. The ramshackle buildings only remained standing because they were packed in so close to their neighbors they lacked space to fall.

A third Shadeleech and his Makrasha stepped into a rare open park in that poor section of town, surrounded by narrow streets and crowded houses. They struck first at a group of dock workers and their families celebrating the emperor's return to health.

Fire spread so fast in that part of town that it consumed the attackers along with everyone else.

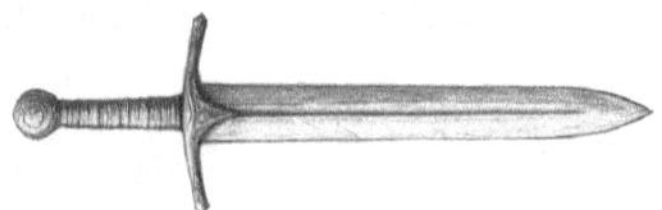

Ten more groups of Makrasha attacked important intersections scattered throughout the city. Each group of half a dozen Makrasha threw off cloaks, howled blood-curdling battle cries, fired small crossbows, and attacked everyone that moved.

Panic spread through the city of Tamera faster than the flames fanned by the gentle evening breeze. Wildly conflicting accounts poured in and soon overwhelmed the under-manned city watch. Rumors ran rampant that they were under full-scale attack. Panic ran out of control and the watch proved incapable of maintaining any semblance of order.

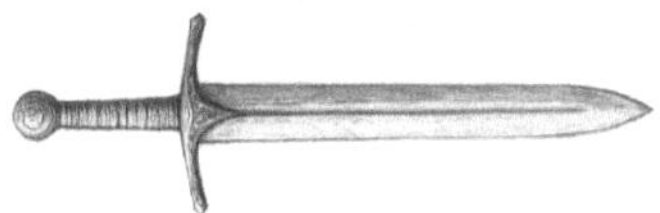

In his tower room, Harafin ran to the wide window overlooking the city. He couldn't see down the spokes, but he felt the attackers releasing their deadly powers. Surprise and fear for the population rattled him for a single heartbeat before he pushed focused on responding to the crisis.

Harafin rushed to the ornately carved stone column in the corner of the room and placed a glowing hand on the emperor's seal. He closed his eyes in concentration.

Throughout the palace complex, through every building and down every hall, Harafin's voice boomed impossibly loud. "To arms. The city is under attack by Shadeleeches and Makrasha. This is not a drill. To Arms!"

Soldiers boiled out of barracks and raced for positions along the wall while still struggling to don armor. Many Sentinels rushed along with them. Others released hawks and bonded with the birds to use their senses to scout for enemies. Within seconds of taking flight, they located the burning sections of the city or areas where blood flowed freely down the streets and people fled in panic from Makrasha.

Information began flowing to Harafin, who had leaped from his tower window and slid down a ramp of hardened air. The invisible slide deposited him at the base of the inner city wall. Within minutes, he marshaled the troops and sent companies charging through the upper city toward areas of conflict.

Leander moved faster.

Less than one minute after the alarm sounded, Leander charged through the inner gate of the wall along the Iron Spoke with threescore armed and armored Stalwarts at his heels. His mighty hammer led the way, already burning with blue fire.

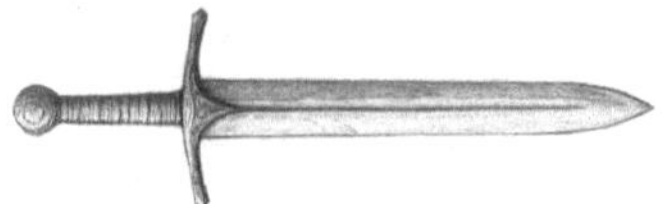

Adalia stood on the gentle slope of the Iron Spoke, not far from the outer city wall. One hand clenched her bow so hard her slender fingers showed white against the polished wood.

Facing her, a middle-aged nobleman of a major Meinarr trading family, flanked by half a dozen of his guards, barked a laugh. "It doesn't really matter how good you are with that bow, young lady. My guards need to strike fear into the hearts of would-be robbers *before* they attack." He pointedly looked down at her tiny frame. "With you along, they'd only be encouraged."

Before Adalia could deliver a withering reply, half a dozen cloaked figures who had been approaching quietly from down the street threw back their hoods and roared blood-chilling battle cries.

Makrasha.

The lord and his men all turned to stare just as the Makrasha fired their small crossbows.

Adalia was already moving. Even as the terrifying sounds registered, she dove to the side, and settled in a firing stance on one knee.

The crossbow bolts slammed into the lord's guards. Two of them fell to the ground, screaming, with bolts sunk deep into their torsos. The other guards' cloaks flashed with light. Although they suffered no visible harm, they stumbled back in confusion and fear.

Adalia grinned as she settled into her hunting calm and drew the already-knocked arrow in a single, fluid movement. She didn't care how Makrasha came to be in Tamera, refused to acknowledge the fear that could threaten to set her arrow trembling. All she cared about was that she finally had a worthy target to shoot.

So she did.

The lead Makrasha's center eye exploded in a burst of green liquid as her arrow punched through and sank deep into its brain. It fell dead before it took its first step forward.

The other five Makrasha charged past their dead companion, howling with blood lust. The lord's guards cried out in fear, and retreated, dragging their employer with them. Only their captain had drawn his sword.

Adalia shot the second Makrasha at ten yards.

She dropped the third at five.

With practiced motions, she reached for the next arrow.

The Makrasha recognized her as the primary threat, and focused their charge at her, swords raised to strike her down. The closest Makrasha leaped the last three yards in a single bound, sword already swinging in a mighty overhand blow that would split her in two when it fell.

It never did.

Adalia shot the beast in mid-air. Her arrow drove right through its open maw and punched through the back of its head. She rolled to the side to avoid the corpse that crashed onto the spot she had been kneeling.

The fifth Makrasha leaped over her latest kill, too close for her to shoot. That could be a problem.

The captain of the foolish lord stepped in front of her and shouted defiance as the monster closed with him.

Idiot, Adalia thought as she scurried to the side to get a clear line of sight. Hopefully she could kill the monster before it slaughtered the gallant fool.

The Makrasha crashed into the soldier who didn't try to dodge, and didn't even raise his sword to block. Adalia cringed as she expected to see the much smaller soldier smashed from his feet.

The captain's cloak flashed with blinding light, and it was the Makrasha, not the soldier, who recoiled as if it had collided with a brick wall.

The captain struck, slashing all three of the creature's eyes in a single blow. It howled with pain, and the captain plunged his sword up through its open maw, between its long fangs.

The last Makrasha lunged at the captain, from the opposite side from where Adalia stood, so she had no line of sight.

The Meinarri lord charged into view, flanked by two other guards. He held an ornately carved wooden rod in front of him like a lance.

The rod flashed with white light, and dozens of thick ropes whipped around the monster, tying it up in a double heartbeat. Even as it toppled, the other two guards fell upon it and, with two might blows, decapitated it.

Adalia surveyed the area but found no other threats. She turned to the Meinarri lord, who was standing with his guards, staring at the dead Makrasha in mute astonishment.

"Good tool, that," she said, nodding toward the wooden rod he held loosely in one hand.

The lord hefted it. "Latest Kedo talisman. My men's cloaks too. Best money I ever spent."

The captain dropped to one knee before Adalia and banged a fist to his heart. "My lady, you inspire me."

He was quite handsome. Not a total waste after all. She grinned. "Good thing too. You lot woulda been dead afore now if'n I hadn't been around."

The lord pressed his full purse into her hands. "That was the most amazing display of courage and skill I've ever seen. You're hired."

Adalia took the heavy purse. "Thank you, my lord." She cocked her head to listen to the growing tumult from the center of the city. Then she turned uphill at the sound of many booted feet running on the paved thoroughfare.

Stalwart Leander, his mighty hammer burning with blue fire, appeared out of the darkness at the head of threescore battle-ready Stalwarts.

"Are you all right?" he called.

"Took care of this lot already."

Leander saluted and pounded past without slowing.

Adalia turned back to the Meinarr lord. "I'll have to get back to you on that job. I have to check on me friend. She's always getting into trouble, and she can't take care of herself."

The soldiers gave her crisp salutes, and she smiled as she trotted uphill toward the inner city.

She muttered as she ran, "Indira, I bet this entire purse you're caught up in this somehow."

59

A Long Drop And A Quick Stop

At the first sound of Harafin's voice booming across the palace complex, Kevlin rejoiced. Of course Harafin knew what was going on. He monitored the shields covering the entire palace. Somehow the wily old Sentinel had orchestrated this whole situation to capture Tanathos.

Then the full impact of Harafin's words sank in and stomped his hope down to a dark place in the pit of his stomach.

Tanathos grabbed him by the collar and dragged him into the deeper shadows. Within seconds soldiers, Stalwarts and even Sentinels raced past, almost close enough to touch. None of them so much as glanced at the shadows where the two hid.

Tanathos leaned over Kevlin and whispered, "No one will even know you're missing for hours. We're invisible here. We have all the time in the world."

His words beat the tiny flicker of hope into tiny pieces. Tanathos was right. No one was going to come to help. Somehow, impossibly, Tanathos had evaded the guardian wards protecting the palace.

Who was attacking the city?

A wave of helplessness and fear washed over Kevlin. He fought to hold it back with sheer obstinacy, with only a little success.

Tanathos reached under the ropes encircling Kevlin's shoulders and drove his hand down under Kevlin's shirt. His skin crawled at the contact from this evil creature and he tried to struggle, but only managed to flop a little like a gutted fish.

Tanathos clubbed him in the side of the head with one fist. Shadows closed over his vision, and his ears rang from the impact. While he lay stunned, Tanathos pulled from under his shirt the amulet on its silver chain.

Kevlin tried to scream defiance as the Shadeleech slipped the chain from around his neck and, with a grin of victory, draped it over his own head. The effort only wedged the gag in deeper, and for a second Kevlin couldn't breathe at all. Only by relaxing and focusing on shallow breaths did he manage to keep from asphyxiating.

Tanathos stood over him, gloating, and Kevlin could do nothing to resist. Tanathos had the amulet. How soon until he destroyed Kevlin?

He hadn't felt so helpless since the first time Tanathos had captured him, deep in the forest of Hallvarr when he had infiltrated their secret fort. At that time, he had known nothing of the protective powers of the amulet and he'd nearly died from that ignorance.

Now, despite everything he knew, despite all the skills he'd developed, despite the fact that almost unlimited power lay hidden in his boot, he was powerless. He trembled as the sense of complete helplessness drew from the bilges of his memory his darkest fears. He again re-lived the moments of torture at the hands of a Sentinel on his father's ship. He'd fought his entire life to never be helpless again.

He'd failed.

Now, even if Harafin somehow appeared to help, Tanathos possessed the amulet. Not even Harafin could overwhelm the mighty talisman.

Tanathos dropped to one knee beside Kevlin and asked in a low hiss, "Where is Oris?"

Kevlin tried to tell him to go burn in EnKur's chains, but he only managed to make a muffled grunt. Tanathos yanked the gag out and repeated, "Tell me."

Kevlin screamed for help as loud as he could.

Tanathos punched him in the face. Kevlin tasted blood, his eyes watered, and his entire face felt on fire. He coughed, and Tanathos shoved the gag back in. This time he managed to close his mouth around it and prevent it from driving in as far. That strange smoky taste he always got when punched in the mouth returned.

"What's going on over there?" a gruff voice called.

Tanathos rose and spun toward the voice. Kevlin's only view, between Tanathos' legs, was of a pair of military boots circling the statue.

Tanathos yanked another wooden rod out of the folds of his cloak and ropes whipped out to encircle the surprised soldier. The man fell to the earth with a muffled curse. Before he could cry out for help, Tanathos leaped upon him and beat him in the head with the rod until he stopped moving.

Tanathos dragged the unconscious soldier into the shadows next to Kevlin. With a casual flick of his wrist, he slit the man's throat with a small dagger.

Hot blood gushed out and splattered all over Kevlin. The coppery stench of it filled his nose, and the sound of it splashing all around him filled him with horror. The casual murder drove home the desperation of his situation.

He would join the soldier in death all too soon.

If only it could be so clean.

As if reading his mind Tanathos said, "What a pity to waste a soul like that." He crouched beside Kevlin and tried patting him down, searching for the stone. The layers of rope encircling his torso made that effort all but impossible.

Tanathos straddled Kevlin and draped his cloak over both of them, plunging them into complete darkness. His voice whispered from just above Kevlin's face, "Better idea. I'll use the direct method."

A cold hand grabbed Kevlin's face in a rough grip, and pain lanced into his head. It felt like five daggers drove through his face simultaneously and sank into his brain.

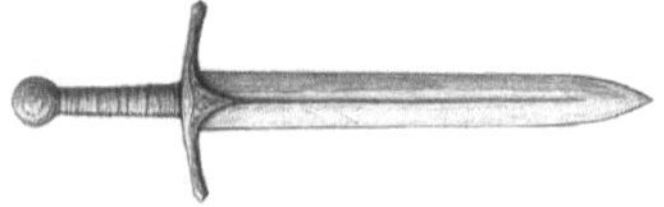

Harafin paused in mid-sentence and whirled around to face the palace. From where he stood atop the inner city wall, he could see over most of the supporting buildings to the individual kingdom palaces. The Great

Dome rose high above them all. Sentinels stood beside him, and Colonel Gabral had just pushed his way through the crowd.

Harafin glanced back at the city where he could easily make out many fires. In the last frantic minutes, he'd coordinated dispatching teams of soldiers, Sentinels, and Stalwarts to destroy those pockets of attackers.

Already it seemed clear they faced scattered attacks designed to strike panic into the hearts of the citizens, not a full-scale assault on the city. The suicide attackers might kill ten times their number due to the surprise nature of the assaults, but the entire effort would prove fruitless.

Now he knew why they did it. Their efforts were but a feint designed to draw his attention from the real danger lurking in their midst.

It had worked.

"Felix, take over here," Harafin ordered.

"I demand to know what's going on," Gabral said.

"Come then," Harafin said.

He grabbed Gabral by the arm and leaped off the inner side of the wall, dragging the surprised colonel with him over the edge.

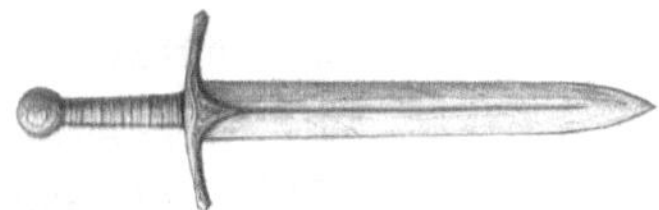

Kevlin screamed and writhed under Tanathos' hand, but the gag muffled everything.

Tanathos slammed a knee into his chest to hold him still, and the pain in his head intensified. Thought scattered and madness chased him through the halls of his memory. Kevlin found himself laughing into the gag along with the memory of Akillik.

Should he spin the Wheel?

What did he have to lose?

Even in the depth of despair, wracked with torment to the brink of sanity, Kevlin couldn't throw his fate into the void controlled by the fickle god.

Then Tanathos shouted with victory, and a lightning-like wave of magic rippled down through Kevlin's torso. Every muscle convulsed, and he screamed so hard he tasted blood.

Without the amulet, he had no defense. He also had no way to capture the magic. As the ripple of agony burned through him, the Trembling Madness awoke. Kevlin howled against the gag and his arms and legs writhed against the restraining bonds as he fought to hold onto even a fraction of the power that tore at him.

He had to have it! He couldn't let it all escape. Kevlin screamed at the torment, his hands clenching in the vain attempt to physically grab the magic. He sawed at the ropes with his little stiletto, but the rope parted too slowly.

As the magic subsided, the torment proved too much and Kevlin's scream changed to hysterical laughter. He embraced the memory of Akillik and laughed along with the young god as the magic he yearned to feel drained out of him. Then it was gone, and Kevlin lay panting on the ground, exhausted. Tanathos stood and flicked his cape away.

He frowned down at Kevlin. "What madness is this?"

Kevlin lunged against the ropes and managed to lift half his body off the ground before falling back. He tried again. If only he could reach Tanathos's throat. Even with the gag, he'd rip the Shadeleech's head off to get the amulet back, to restore the route to power.

Tanathos kicked him back down. "You don't suffer as well as I'd like. No matter, there will be plenty of time to perfect the right torture."

The Shadeleech scooped Kevlin up and threw him over one shoulder. Kevlin tried to bite Tanathos's back as his head bounced along with the Shadeleech's stride, but the gag prevented him from doing more than bruising his lips.

Tanathos skirted the southern end of the central palace and walked west. That direction made no sense.

Then Kevlin understood. Tanathos made for the high cliffs above the Tamerlane Sea. There was no exit that way, no way down. Tanathos meant to throw him off the cliff.

Kevlin struggled harder, but Tanathos merely shifted his grip and kept walking. The man's strength proved far greater than Kevlin would have imagined. Nothing he tried so much as caused Tanathos to stumble.

They passed through an orchard and then crossed a pasture filled with sleeping cattle. The distant crashing of waves reached Kevlin's ears. As Tanathos twisted to cross a fence, Kevlin caught sight of the cliff edge, barely fifty yards away.

This was it, the end of all things for Kevlin. In his mind, he heard Akillik laughing, but his thoughts focused on the Wheel burning in the young god's hand.

Time to spin the Wheel.

Kevlin laughed into the muffling gag. He would call upon Akillik's fickle luck.

A wall of flame erupted out of the ground directly in front of Tanathos. The heat beat upon the back of Kevlin's legs like a hammer.

Tanathos threw Kevlin from him. Kevlin tumbled to the ground in a heap and stared in amazement at the fire. He'd expected the Wheel to come up against him, but he never imagined Akillik would attempt to roast him alive.

Wait. He hadn't actually spun the Wheel. Now he never would.

Tanathos spun back the way they'd come and raised hands already glowing with crimson power. Lightning-like magic slammed into him again and again, so fast the multiple bolts fused into one.

Kevlin clenched his eyes shut against the blinding light, but the after-images burned in his eyelids. Tanathos cursed as his cloak burst into flames and fell away from him in tattered, charred pieces.

"I think you've gone far enough tonight."

Kevlin forced his eyes open at the sound of the familiar voice. Sentinel Ah'Shan strode out of the darkness toward them.

Tanathos beckoned Ah'Shan forward and made a sweeping bow. "Excellent timing, Sentinel. Had you waited a moment longer, you would have lived out the night."

Ah'Shan smiled. "You're unusually confident for one trapped behind enemy lines."

"I am far from trapped," Tanathos said. He lowered his hands and spread them wide. "See for yourself. Your magic has no power over me."

Ah'Shan glanced at Kevlin, looking a little less sure of himself. He took a single step forward. "I'm surprised one of your kind bothers to take prisoners. Why not kill this one now?"

Kevlin tried to shout. He needed to warn Ah'Shan about the amulet, but the gag still remained tightly wedged in his mouth.

Tanathos said, "This man's death is already scheduled, in my good time."

"Late night snack, eh?" Ah'Shan asked. He whipped his hands up and they flared with white light.

Tanathos did the same, his hands glowing crimson.

Flames leaped out of Tanathos' hands in a horizontal sheet toward Ah'Shan. The Sentinel flicked his wrist, and a whirlwind of air caught the flames and dispersed them in all directions. Then Ah'Shan threw his hands forward and a bolt of pure white light leaped between them and struck Tanathos.

It blasted him from his feet.

Tanathos rolled several times before landing in a crumpled heap on the ground. He groaned and staggered back to his feet. As he rose, he pawed at his collar, drew the amulet forth, and stared at it, clearly confused.

Kevlin snarled to see the amulet around Tanathos' throat. The fool broke it! He threw himself against his ropes and started rolling toward the Shadeleech. He had to get it back. Nothing else mattered.

As he rolled, a lance of pain in his left wrist snapped him out of his crazed rage. His hand was twisted at an uncomfortable angle, still clutching the stiletto. He had cut a couple of ropes earlier, granting him a tiny bit of movement.

Kevlin sawed against the ropes with frantic intensity.

Ah'Shan chuckled. "Your failure is astonishing. Clearly you intended to capture Oris, but all you found was a broken amulet and a Steward who no longer possesses the stone."

Tanathos let the amulet to fall to his chest and, with a snarl, threw out a hand toward Kevlin, who lay barely ten feet away. Fingers of pulsing fire encircled him and sank into his chest.

Kevlin screamed and writhed inside the flames. He decided he didn't like torture. Only minutes in Tanathos's power was more than enough.

He continued to saw frantically at the ropes, but couldn't tell if he was making any headway. He should have been rolling toward Ah'Shan and safety.

"You've proven yourself a fool twice over," said Tanathos. "Choose your next move carefully. I'm linked to the Steward now. Any attack you direct at me will be passed to him. He will die first, I guarantee it."

That was bad. What a coward.

Ah'Shan shouldn't have wasted all that time talking. Why would he do that? Now Tanathos had turned the tide against him yet again.

Tanathos grabbed Kevlin by the collar and yanked him to his feet. He held Kevlin before him like a shield and started dragging him toward the cliff.

Heading for the cliff made no sense. He and Tanathos shared a mutual hatred, but he would have thought the Shadeleech wanted to survive the encounter. If he threw Kevlin off now, he'd lose his defense.

Tanathos wasn't a quitter, and he wasn't stupid crazy, so he had to have a plan. His arrogance was only rivaled by the depth of his evil.

Kevlin sawed harder at the ropes. One severed, granting him a little more room, making it easier to saw at the next one.

Ah'Shan paced them, thirty feet away, hands half-raised to strike again. "Why should the life of this man concern me?"

"Because he is the only one who can reveal the stone."

Ah'Shan frowned, "You lie."

"Not in this. I see you too wish to know the secret. I know it, and this man is the key."

They now stood barely three paces from the edge of the cliff. The pounding of the waves crashing against the rocks far below rang loud in Kevlin's ears. He vainly tried to dig his heels into the soft earth to slow their progress toward destruction.

A chill breeze blew off the water, filled with the salty tang of the sea. It brought back memories long forgotten of his earliest years aboard his father's ship. For the first time in a very long time, he yearned to see his family again, just one more time before he died.

"You've reached the end of your path, Tanathos," said Ah'Shan. "You cannot hope to win this fight."

"Perhaps not, but I guarantee you will lose it."

Movement to the right of Ah'Shan drew Kevlin's gaze. His heart leaped with hope at the sight of Harafin and Gabral racing toward them.

Gabral pointed the Mace at them. From fifty yards away, the top spike fired off with a loud snap. It ripped through the air faster than an arrow, headed straight for Kevlin.

The idiot was supposed to be saving Kevlin, not trying to execute him.

Tanathos hissed and jerked Kevlin to the side. He extended his other glowing hand toward Gabral. The spike deflected just a little and streaked past Kevlin's right arm.

The stiletto cut through another rope. Kevlin finally managed to slip his left arm out of the constricting loops. He spun the blade in his hand and drove it backward. It sank to the hilt between two of Tanathos' ribs.

Tanathos gasped, and his hold on Kevlin's collar eased. Half a heartbeat later, agony speared into Kevlin's torso between his ribs. He doubled over in pain. He had hoped Tanathos was lying about passing pain on to him.

Then the ropes binding him disappeared.

Kevlin didn't know if it was Harafin or Ah'Shan, but as soon as the ropes vanished, he lunged against Tanathos, grasping for the Shadeleech's neck.

Tanathos snarled into his ear, "Die then, knowing your life fuels my escape."

He had thought he hurt before.

Now overwhelming agony tore through Kevlin's body from Tanathos's powers. Kevlin arced away from the Shadeleech as his entire world disintegrated into burning fire.

Deep inside of him, Tanathos began ripping out his soul. Darkness descended over him, while waves of agony crashed through his head. Every inch of his skin burned as if immersed in living fire, and he could no longer breathe.

Then the pain disappeared.

Kevlin clutched at Tanathos as his legs buckled. Tanathos looked as surprised as Kevlin did that the pain had stopped.

Someone had interfered.

Kevlin wasn't about to give him a chance to figure out how to restart the torture trip. He lashed at Tanathos's throat and his hand closed around the amulet. He shouted with exultant victory.

Tanathos wrapped his arms around Kevlin and threw himself backward. Together, they toppled off the cliff.

The insane Shadeleech didn't even say anything profound when he consigned them to death. It seemed a waste of an important moment.

The two plummeted toward the jagged rocks hundreds of feet below, but Kevlin still clawed at Tanathos, trying to rip the amulet off his head. If he was going to die, he'd die with the amulet in his hands.

Tanathos bit his arm, making him release his grip. The two tumbled around each other, buffeted by the wind, bare inches from the rough stone of the cliff, punching and biting at each other.

Tanathos grabbed Kevlin's face and dug at his eyes. Kevlin beat the Shadeleech's hands away. That was all the distance Tanathos needed. He hardened the air between them like a wall.

Kevlin continued to plummet straight down as Tanathos slid along the hardened air and began circling away from the cliffs in a gentle spiral.

"No fair!" Kevlin screamed.

The rocks approached with shocking speed.

The night burst into blue-white brilliance as a bolt of lightning ripped through the air from the top of the cliff and slammed into Tanathos. The blow flung him sideways and he bounced off the cliff face. The impact threw him into a wild spin.

Kevlin laughed with terror, trying to keep his eyes focused on Tanathos's limp form instead of the fast-approaching rocks. At least the two of them would die together. He closed his eyes and waited for the abrupt crash that would rip him from this world into the next.

The loud rushing of the wind dimmed, and Kevlin glanced down. The rocks rushed up to meet him, barely fifty feet away.

He screamed. What else could he do?

The rocks slowed their advance and the wind lessened further. Kevlin's stomach lurched as an invisible force yanked against him and his body bent under the strain of conflicting forces. Waves crashed just below, and spray flung up from the rocks to splash against his face.

He stopped. Kevlin hung in the air barely twenty feet above the rocks and the crashing waves. Tanathos hung motionless in the air not far away.

They started to rise.

Kevlin's stomach roiled in protest from the unexpected change of direction as his body began accelerating up the cliff face. He fought the urge to vomit and chided his useless stomach. Why get sick when escaping danger?

He caught sight of the amulet glinting in the moonlight as it hung on its silver chain around Tanathos's neck. He reached for it, even though it hung far out of reach. He needed it. He had to have it, and he would never let it go again.

The two of them sailed over the edge of the cliff and touched down gently on the earth a dozen paces inland. As soon as he felt solid ground under his feet, Kevlin launched himself at Tanathos.

He yanked the amulet off the unconscious man's head. Then he drew his belt dagger and raised it high, intending to plunge it through Tanathos' heart.

Strong hands grabbed his wrist and yanked him off. He growled and spun. Gabral punched him in the mouth and pushed him aside. He hit the ground hard, but lunged back to his feet, dagger at the ready.

Gabral shooed him back. "Gather yourself together, man. We can't kill him yet."

"Sure we can," Kevlin protested. "It'll just take a second."

"No, we cannot," Harafin said. The old Sentinel pointed a glowing finger at Tanathos, and a bright blue prison of magic settled around the Shadeleech.

"Is he dead?" Ah'Shan asked.

"No," Harafin said, "Although he is not very alive. That lightning strike was a poor choice."

The powerful Sentinel shrugged. "It seemed appropriate. This man is extremely dangerous. I didn't want to take any chances."

Kevlin hissed, "Kill him." They couldn't risk leaving Tanathos alive.

Harafin ignored Kevlin. "You took an awful risk, Ah'Shan. You might have struck Kevlin, or you might have killed him."

"But I did neither."

"No, I suppose not." Harafin placed one hand on Tanathos's glowing prison and grinned. "Finally, we have him."

Ah'Shan said, "Bind his prison to me, Harafin. I'll see him to the secure holding cells and oversee his questioning."

"Very well. You're best qualified to extract the truth. Report your findings to the council chamber. I will assemble the council."

Kevlin sheathed his dagger and fought down a flash of irritation that no one bothered to ask if he was all right. His muscles ached and his entire body felt like he'd been keel-hauled.

Gabral returned the Mace to its curious leather sheath on his back. Kevlin loved watching it melt and flow up over the spiked ball. Why did such an arrogant fool get such an awesome weapon?

"How did you know he'd deflect that spike when you fired it?" Kevlin asked.

Gabral shrugged. "I'm surprised he did. If he hadn't, the spike would have passed right through your unarmored body and killed him too."

He clapped Kevlin on the shoulder. "Sometimes victory comes at a price. I was willing to pay it."

Then he turned and walked away.

Kevlin wanted to follow him and explain with his fists what price he was willing to pay for renewed peace of mind. He resisted the urge. Barely. Instead,, he watched Tanathos's floating prison begin following Ah'Shan toward the palace. The sight of his most bitter enemy immobilized in Harafin's power was one he wanted to memorize.

60

CRYPTIC WORDS

A muted knock on the thick, ironwood door of the prison cell broke Ah'Shan's concentration. He shouted, "Peace! I am not to be disturbed."

The door creaked open anyway and the Kestrel assigned to guard the outer door poked his head through. "I apologize for disturbing you, master, but the ruling council is already assembled and they demand an update. A servant named Remiel is here on orders to speak with you."

Ah'Shan groaned and sat back in the simple wooden chair that made up the sum of all the furniture in the small, square room. The cell was situated in the deepest level of the dungeon, its walls reinforced with magic that blocked access by any outside power.

Those magic-enhanced walls also served another, more important purpose. They slowly drained away the Sthenic energy from Tanathos's body.

The Shadeleech floated in his glowing prison. His right hand and face were free of the prison's restraint, but Ah'Shan had blocked his ability to talk to prevent him from speaking a forbidden word and triggering a mind trap to kill himself.

Remiel was a young, dark-haired man dressed in the palace livery of Hallvarr instead of the emperor's personal colors. Instead of delivering the council's request, Remiel pointed at Tanathos. "Look!"

Tanathos was writing on a parchment that floated in the air next to his hand. Ah'Shan frowned and stepped closer.

As expected, Tanathos had refused to write any responses yet. Ah'Shan hadn't expected to proceed with the interrogation until the room drained the Shadeleech's powers that still shielded his mind. At that point, Ah'Shan could batter through Tanathos's mental shields and begin the delicate process of searching for cleverly hidden mind-traps that protected the vital information he sought.

Tanathos finished writing with a flourish. Ah'Shan snatched the parchment and read the short message.

In time, you will breach my defenses, but we both know that will take days. However, leave me in solitude for two hours and I will reveal information you do not yet know enough to seek.

Ah'Shan glanced up at Tanathos and stared into the roiling blackness that still concealed the Shadeleech's gaze. "Why make this offer?"

Tanathos gestured for the parchment and wrote, *Secrets one of us yearns to conceal will soon be revealed. This is not done lightly. Time is needed to prepare for the course that must be set.*

Ah'Shan frowned. "Double-speak does not serve you now, Shadeleech." He turned to hand the parchment off to Remiel. The young man was staring at Tanathos, his face white, terrified.

"Don't worry, lad," Ah'Shan said. "He cannot hurt you."

Remiel took the proffered parchment, glanced at the written words, and his hand began to shake. "I'm sure you're right," he said in a trembling voice.

Ah'Shan turned back to Tanathos. "I will grant your request. You have two hours to prepare your mind." He paused and added, "Willing or no, at that time you will reveal your secrets to me."

Ah'Shan left the cell, followed by Remiel. The Kestrel assigned to guard the cell sealed the door with a wave of one hand. At his gesture, spikes grew out of the steel frame surrounding the heavy door and bored into the thick wood. No key could open the door, and it would take a man with an axe an hour to cut through the dense ironwood.

Ah'Shan said to the servant Remiel, "I will report to the council personally. You are dismissed."

The young man bowed and scampered away. Ah'Shan hoped future messengers showed a little more backbone. To be so unnerved by a captured Shadeleech, what would the man do when faced with a real emergency?

"What of the two Pallian Stalwarts, master?" the Kestrel asked.

"Let them join you here. That should satisfy Leander for a time."

As he began the long trek up to the emperor's council room, Ah'Shan prepared his strategy for assaulting Tanathos's mind. He welcomed the challenge. He expected the man to prove exceptionally well protected, and little pleased him more than breaking a worthy adversary's mind.

Things were working out extremely well. With the glory he would reap from breaking Tanathos, he would be positioned to take the next bold step forward.

The man Kevlin would not long bear the stone.

61

GAMES OF THE MIND

"I demand access."

Leander stood at the large round table around which the ruling council sat, along with Harafin, Ah'Shan, and Felix. Kevlin stood with Drystan, Gabral, and the Sentinel Durgesh on guard duty along the walls.

"I will not allow it," Sentinel Ah'Shan said from his place across from Leander.

Leander pounded his fist on the table. "Do not deny me this, Ah'Shan."

The outburst didn't scare the Sentinel. "Your vendetta is too well know, my friend. I cannot risk allowing you in the same room with the prisoner until I've extracted all the information I can from him. Then, my friend, you can have at him."

"After I order the execution," Emperor Tegnazian cut in.

"Of course," Ah'Shan said smoothly. "The execution of this man is a given. The only question is the timing of the event."

"Speaking of timing," Ambassador Janezeko of Freyarr said, "Why are we sitting here talking about interrogating this Shadeleech and not actually doing it?"

"I granted the prisoner two hours in solitude to prepare to answer my questions."

Leander slammed his open palm on the table, shaking the sturdy piece. "Are you insane? You cannot make deals with this man! He's too dangerous."

Emperor Tegnazian snapped, "Stop all the shouting, Leander, and don't hit the table like that again. You're hurting my ears."

Leander didn't look away from Ah'Shan.

Harafin said, "I have to agree with Leander. Tanathos has proven himself far too dangerous to grant any favors. Perhaps I should take over the interrogation."

Ah'Shan waved a dismissive hand. "You're all over-reacting. Harafin, you are unrivaled in battle prowess. This is my realm of expertise. I know what I'm doing."

"Then why not do it?" Ambassador Kescog asked.

"Very well, I will explain. Probing the mind of a Shadeleech is a very delicate, time-consuming process. When that Shadeleech is actively shielding his mind with Sthenic energy, it becomes entire magnitudes more difficult and more dangerous."

"I thought you had him in some kind of magical prison that blocked his powers," the emperor said.

"That is correct. He is prevented from directing his powers outward, but that power is still there, still available to protect his mind."

"Why not cast Truth?" Ambassador Janezeko asked. "After all the argument about wanting to cast Truth on everyone, I'd have thought you'd have done that already."

"I could, but we suspect his mind is heavily guarded by layers of mind-traps, many of which are triggered when certain words are spoken. By forcing him to speak before breaking into his mind and disabling those mind-traps, he would most likely die in the very moment he tried to speak the information we so desperately seek."

As they digested that information, Ah'Shan added, "The cell where Tanathos is held has layers of magic woven into the fabric of its walls. That magic will slowly and safely drain the Sthenic powers from him, leaving his mind vulnerable to penetration."

Ambassador Talamantez leaned forward with a nod of understanding. "So when you agreed to grant him time to prepare, you lose nothing."

"Exactly," Ah'Shan said. "I'd have to wait that long anyway. And more than just bleeding Tanathos of his powers, I gain another significant advantage that I believe he does not anticipate."

"Forcing Truth from an unwilling gifted mind is difficult, even after breaking the mental defenses and disabling any mind-traps. However, if Tanathos does indeed begin sharing information willingly, I can apply Truth in stages through that conversation. Through careful application of Truth, I can first lengthen the conversation beyond what he intends. Before he realizes what's happening, he will reveal all his secrets."

"Amazing," the emperor breathed.

"Tanathos has played right into our hands," Ah'Shan assured them. "He has no idea what I can do with Truth."

Kevlin shuddered at the distant memory when he had been tortured by Truth. He almost hoped Ah'Shan failed to pull Tanathos's secrets so easily from his mind. The process sounded far too painless. Tanathos deserved to suffer.

It seemed impossible that they had done it. Tanathos had stalked them since the first days after Rhea had turned on Antigonus and Kevlin's fate became bound with Oris. Tanathos had successfully smuggled hundreds of Makrasha and at least a dozen Shadeleeches clear across the empire undetected. Even he couldn't spin the Wheel forever.

Now he hung in Harafin's prison. Soon Leander would be authorized to execute judgment on Tanathos for all the murders he'd committed.

Too bad Leander killed so quickly. Tanathos deserved to die by inches. If he screamed once for every life he had taken, they'd have to torture him for weeks to work through them all. Even that seemed too small a price to pay.

"I want to be there when you question him," Leander said again.

Ah'Shan shook his head. "I cannot allow it. I granted your two Stalwarts to assist in guarding the cell, but I can allow no more until the interrogation is complete."

Leander clenched his right hand slowly, but finally nodded. "Be quick about it, then."

62

DINNER FOR TWO . . . AH, ONE

Marjani stopped with Jerrik beside a dark-paneled door in a side corridor in the second level of the Donarr castle. He opened it with a flourish and ushered her inside.

Marjani rounded on him when he joined her in the cozy study. "How is this a little walk to help your recovery?"

Jerrik had combed his shaggy brown hair and unruly russet beard into a semblance of order. Although he wore the brown trousers common to Donarr, he had added a fine gray silk shirt and a blue coat.

Marjani appreciated his choice. He'd asked her to come for a walk tonight and insisted she wear something other than her palace livery. She really liked the huge warrior, but he belonged to an important noble house. She felt distinctly aware of the simple peach-colored dress she wore. If he'd worn the full finery available to him, she would have felt more than a little uncomfortable.

The cozy study had a cheery fire crackling in a hearth flanked by dark bookcases. A padded sofa and two overstuffed chairs faced the fire. At the other end of the room a small table, draped with a white tablecloth and set for two, had been squeezed into the corner.

Jerrik motioned toward the table. "Join me for dinner. I promise that'll make me feel better."

A door in the opposite wall opened and a servant dressed in the Donarri livery entered with a covered silver tray.

Marjani had to admit, she was impressed. Jerrik had clearly given the evening a lot of thought when most men she'd known would just try to box her into a dark corner and force a kiss out of her. She knew just where to kick to escape those situations, although she wasn't sure anything she could do would hurt this giant of a man.

So she smiled. "If I like the food, I'll forgive you for the surprise."

No sense in making it too easy for him. Nobles rarely showed interest in serving girls for any reason other than cheap dalliances, and she wasn't interested in that kind of relationship. She enjoyed Jerrik's presence and found his attention decidedly flattering despite instincts honed by years working in the palace that warned her to be on her guard.

She allowed Jerrik to seat her at the table. As he sat across from her, she said, "I'm not accustomed to dining alone with strange men."

Jerrik lifted a glass of his favorite ale in salute. "I may be strange, but my intentions are honorable."

The servant removed the cover from the platter with a flourish and Marjani grinned at the sight of roasted spiny besofish.

"This is my favorite dish," Marjani exclaimed.

Jerrik grinned, obviously pleased with himself.

"How did you get it?" Spiny besofish were notoriously difficult to catch, and were found only in Meinarr. Rarely were they caught this time of year.

"I can't tell you all my secrets. We haven't even eaten yet."

Marjani gave Jerrik a wide smile. He intrigued her more and more. Tonight he just might get that kiss he was working up to.

Before the servant could offer her a portion of the fish, the outer door banged open. Kevlin and Drystan strode into the room, armed and armored. Kevlin was smiling, and Drystan's eyes shone with the thrill of battle.

"What's going on?" Jerrik asked uneasily. It looked like he understood his carefully orchestrated evening was about to fall apart.

Kevlin said, "Come on. We just received word that Remiel's surfaced. Ambassador Damarist arranged a meeting in his office tonight. We're going to set the trap for him now."

"Now?"

"Now," Drystan said, snatching up a piece of fish and popping it into his mouth. "Let's go." He gave the fish a closer look. "This is really good."

"This has to do with those rumors of battle last night, doesn't it?" Marjani asked, shielding her plate from Drystan.

Jerrik rose. "Unfortunately, we can't talk about it."

He looked genuinely sorry. Marjani glanced from his pained expression to the delicious dinner and made up her mind. She stood, pulled his face down to her, and kissed his cheek. She stroked his rough beard and whispered into his ear, "Thanks for dinner."

Then she seated herself, straightened her napkin, and motioned to the servant to proceed.

"You're going to eat without me?" Jerrik exclaimed.

"You didn't expect me to waste all this delicious food, did you?"

Kevlin laughed and grabbed a dinner roll. "Bye, Marjani."

She waved as the trio left and called, "Be careful, boys."

Drystan's voice echoed back down the hall, "I thought you didn't like fish?"

Grinning, Marjani dug into the most delicious fish she'd eaten in months.

63

THE HEAVY COST OF SECRETS

Tanathos hung suspended in his cell, counting the seconds until the cursed Sentinel returned. His options were limited. He held only one trump card, and if it wasn't played soon, all he could hope for was that maybe the Sentinel might miss one of the many mind-traps buried deep beneath his mental shields. He only needed to trigger one.

He hated needing them. Dying with a broken mind so close to victory was worse torture than anything the Sentinels could devise. He wanted to howl with frustrated rage, but his sealed lips blocked any sound. So he clenched his right fist repeatedly, envisioning his fingers around Kevlin's throat.

He'd held Kevlin's life in his hand, with the stone in the man's boot. Somehow, although he couldn't comprehend the reasons for it, Kevlin still carried the stone. He'd lacked time to sort through the man's memories in detail, but that one fact burned so clear he couldn't miss it.

One moment longer and he would have escaped with the prize, free to return to Grakonia and claim a seat on the Sigrun Council. Or, better yet, infiltrate the node of power in Freyarr and murder Kevlin there. He'd stood so close to limitless power, he wanted to scream his rage and wreak deadly havoc on these fools. Twice now, the man Kevlin and his companions had thwarted him. He deserved more than suicide. He deserved to rule.

Instead he hung powerless. The last of his forces were surely slaughtered, their sacrifice worthless. Soon, the dreaded Hammer Stalwart would exact vengeance and release Tanathos to endless torment in the chains of the master he'd failed. As Tanathos mulled over the infuriating situation, a distant sound echoed faintly through the heavy door barring his cell.

It sounded like a scream.

Tanathos waited, barely breathing as he watched the door and strained his ears for any other sounds. Time was nearly up.

A long minute later he smelled smoke. Only then did he notice the ironwood door had begun to glow dully. As he watched, the glow intensified. So did the smoke. Then, all at once, flames engulfed the door.

Within seconds only charred remnants of the once-sturdy ironwood door remained, clinging to the edges of the frame. Thick smoke billowed into the room, choking Tanathos and enveloping him in its sooty cloud.

A figure strode through the dense smoke into the little cell. Tanathos coughed into his sealed mouth, and his eyes burned from the smoke. Then the smoke parted to reveal the newcomer.

Remiel.

The dark-haired young man coughed a couple of times into the sleeve of his long, black leather coat and wiped soot from his face. He dropped an ornately carved wooden rod with a blackened end and kicked it into the corner.

Without a word, he produced another carved rod, this one only about three handspans long and as thick around as his thumb. He twisted the handle and pressed the other end against the glowing prison holding Tanathos immobile.

With a brilliant blue flash, the prison shattered.

Tanathos dropped to the floor and nearly fell. He caught his balance against the wall, then yanked his hand back with a snarl. His powers had been draining steadily since they had placed him here, but that brief contact with the enchanted wall chilled him to the bone. It felt as if every ounce of power and warmth was sucked out through his fingers.

Tanathos laughed, exulting in the ability to speak again. "Remiel, you don't disappoint."

Remiel shrugged. "One must protect one's secrets."

"I was starting to wonder how far you would go."

Remiel led him through the charred remnants of the door, but paused in the next room. "I do what has to be done."

In that antechamber outside the cell, a Sentinel and two Stalwarts lay in pools of blood, riddled with crossbow bolts. They lay on their backs, mouths open in silent screams. The smell of blood and smoke hung heavy in the air, and Tanathos breathed deep the satisfying aroma. Silence reigned in the short hall beyond and Tanathos grinned at the sight of fallen enemies broken and dead at his feet.

This is how things were meant to be.

"I am impressed. How did you do this?"

Remiel picked his way around the bodies and waved a hand at a simple, unadorned wooden box stained so dark it looked black. It lay in the corner, with the one open face turned toward them to reveal an empty interior. Tanathos frowned. The box was square, barely one handspan to a side. There was no way a single crossbow bolt could be stuffed in there, let alone half a hundred.

He was about to ask Remiel to elaborate when one of the Stalwarts coughed weakly.

Remiel yelped and back-pedaled, his face white with fear. Tanathos leaped upon the still-living Stalwart and reached for his gift. He lifted a hand already glowing with crimson light as he prepared to suck the life out of this man, a member of the most hated sect of Stalwarts. After the humiliation of his recent capture, taking this life would restore a little of his battered pride.

"Don't!" Remiel hissed.

Tanathos glanced at the youth, who looked more frightened than before. "This unnerves you after you committed murder a moment ago to protect yourself?"

"No, you fool," Remiel said urgently. "If you use your powers, you'll trigger the guardian shields layered all through this part of the dungeon. We'd never get out before the Sentinels arrived."

Tanathos released his powers with a frown. "Warn me next time."

"I didn't get a chance." Remiel drew from within his leather jacket a bundle of cloth. He shook it out to reveal a simple, gray woolen cloak and tossed it to Tanathos.

"This is imbued with a personal shield. Yank off the button near your collar to activate it. It'll shield you long enough to escape the inner city if you don't waste too much time."

Tanathos donned the cloak but refused to reveal to the servant how much relief he felt under its protective cover. Remiel turned and began walking up the corridor, but Tanathos lived his life by an unbreakable creed.

At any opportunity, kill.

So he drew the Stalwart's own hammer from the fallen man's belt and buried the spiked end deep into the man's skull. He left it there, standing out from the corpse, and smiled as he followed Remiel out of the dungeon.

The outer guard, wrapped in layers of rope, lay dead with a gaping wound across his throat. The wooden rod Remiel had used to capture the man lay nearby.

"You have access to powerful tools," Tanathos said as they walked past.

"I have powerful masters. Even so, you have no idea how much those things cost me."

Tanathos shrugged. "I know how much not having them would have cost you."

Without another word, they ascended to the underground palace and Remiel led Tanathos through the long twilight corridors of the lowest level. The youth chose a convoluted path that certainly took longer, but they saw almost no one during the long walk. Those few times they did encounter another person, Tanathos kept the hood of his cloak over his face and they passed without incident.

Finally, Remiel ascended a long wooden stair and led the way through a dusty warehouse filled with dark rows of wooden crates piled almost to the high ceiling. They slipped through a creaking wooden door that emptied into a narrow alley that smelled of urine.

Remiel pointed to the right. "The inner wall lies just around that corner. The road will take you to the Iron Spoke. The gate should be open. The guards there won't bother you even at this hour since you're leaving. Keep your hood up and walk at a normal pace. I suggest you leave the city."

Without waiting for a reply, the young man headed in the opposite direction and disappeared around the corner without looking back. Tanathos took a deep breath and, with a smile on his lips, marched confidently out of the alley toward promised freedom.

Already he began forming a new plan to take the man Kevlin. Next time, he would not fail.

64

GOOD NEWS AND BAD NEWS

The richly paneled door swung open in Ambassador Damarist's office high in the Hallvarr Palace. Kevlin tensed and pressed his back against the wall where he stood concealed behind the opening door. He gripped tight his belt dagger.

He risked a glance to the right and shared a fierce grin with Drystan, who stood pressed against the wall beside him. The lanky Einarri soldier's eyes glittered with lust for battle.

The two were alone in the study with Ambassador Damarist, who sat behind his long desk. He tried to look bored as he pretended to study one of the ever-present parchments bureaucrats loved so much.

A man's voice, smooth and confident, spoke from the doorway. "You'd better have a good reason for insisting I come up here so late, Ambassador. I've had a busy night."

Ambassador Damarist looked up from the parchment and frowned. "Watch your tone in my office, Remiel." His voice shook and, as he talked, his eyes flickered over to Kevlin and Drystan.

Kevlin lunged around the door. They'd warned the ambassador to keep his eyes on Remiel and not look at them.

The young man was already sprinting away through the outer office. He ran like a deer and even as Kevlin gave chase, he knew he could never catch the youth.

He didn't have to.

Jerrik, wearing a heavy coat of chain mail, stepped into the outer door just as Remiel tried to race through. The young man slammed into Jerrik and, with a loud rattle of Jerrik's armor, bounced back into the room. He crashed to the floor and lay there for a second, stunned.

Kevlin and Drystan pounced on him. Kevlin punched him in the face and Drystan wrenched his arms behind his back and yanked him to his feet. Remiel yelped with pain and struggled weakly, but Drystan held him fast. The blood dripping from Remiel's nose was a deeply satisfying sight.

Kevlin cocked his arm back, ready to throw another punch. "Sure you want to keep struggling?"

"No. I surrender."

"Of course you do," Jerrik said as he stepped into the room. "Got no choice, do you?"

Leander and Harafin entered behind Jerrik. Harafin said, "Well done."

"Told you we could handle it," Drystan said.

Jerrik snorted. "Sure. You let him get away."

"Thank the ambassador for that," Drystan protested.

"Told you he'd crack."

"I'll have you know, I didn't crack," Ambassador Damarist objected from the doorway to his office.

"Don't worry about it," Jerrik said. "Worked better this way. We got to hit him harder."

Kevlin tied Remiel's hands behind his back with a length of rawhide cord. Things were falling into place faster and faster. First they captured Tanathos, and now one of the key conspirators.

They'd have the entire conspiracy rooted out and executed by tomorrow night.

As he yanked the final knot tight, he realized he had no idea what they would do after they broke the conspiracy. Ever since he first stumbled upon Antigonus in the forest, they'd been rushing from one conflict to another, with hidden enemies lurking nearby, striking from the shadows. Maybe now he could relax, learn enough from Harafin to control the raging magic trying to kill him or drive him insane.

He could finally spend some quality time with Indira. That thought brought a smile to his lips.

"We have a great deal to talk about," Harafin said to Remiel. The old Sentinel considered the young man, weighing him like a merchant would a sack of grain.

Remiel's face paled and he refused to meet Harafin's gaze. He spoke quickly, the words tumbling out in a rush. "Before you do anything to me, I want to make a deal."

Drystan shook Remiel hard. "We don't need to make any deals. We own you now, and you'll tell us everything we want to know."

"Of course, but it takes a while. We can avoid a lot of unpleasantness. Look, I just want amnesty. There's things I can't talk about or I'll die. I know that. But I can tell you one thing right now that I guarantee you want to know."

"Tell me," Harafin said. "You've chosen not to trigger mind traps and take the coward's path. I will not guarantee amnesty, but if you cooperate, the process will definitely be less painful for you."

Remiel risked a glance at Harafin, his expression a mask of desperation. "It's not my fault. They force me to help. I have to protect my family."

"Hey," Ambassador Damarist said. "You can't claim that. You blackmailed me by threatening my family."

Remiel shrugged. "It's pretty standard. They do it to all of us."

"Tell me this information, and we will judge its worth," Harafin said.

"Very well. That Shadeleech you captured, Tanathos . . ."

"What about him?" Leander demanded, grabbing Remiel by the front of his shirt.

"He's escaped."

65

A QUESTION OF INTEGRITY

"This farce must end!"

Leander, dressed in full battle armor, paced before the emperor and the ambassadors who were assembled in a large meeting room in the Northern Kingdoms Admin Palace. They had chosen the room for its close proximity to the central courtyard and easier access from the wall and other parts of the inner city.

Through the long night and the following morning, messengers relayed updates to the command post set up nearby. Now the council sat around a trio of long, mahogany tables formed into a rough horseshoe. Harafin sat with the council at the heavy tables, and Sentinel Durgesh flanked the emperor's chair in the center.

The burly, shaven-headed Stalwart, Basak, also dressed for battle, flanked Leander. Kevlin stood to one side with his brothers, all still dressed in their mail shirts from when they took Remiel late last night. It seemed days ago when Remiel revealed Tanathos had escaped, not barely twelve hours.

Kevlin rubbed his face. His body ached all over, after-effects of the fight with Tanathos yesterday and of the long night spent scouring the city for the escaped Shadeleech. He felt dirty, tired, and irritable.

Tanathos had vanished.

Immediately after news of Tanathos' escape, Leander and Harafin had ordered all available Stalwarts and Sentinels out into the city to hunt for him. Battle-ready columns of Stalwarts had raced down the spokes while Sentinels flew upon the senses of birds and even rats to hunt. Others led columns of soldiers through the streets, searching with their minds for the dangerous, elusive prey.

Unfortunately, the very obvious presence of these forces sparked panic-driven riots throughout the city. Two full legions had been mobilized to assist the normal city watch in restoring order. The population, already in turmoil from the Grakonian attacks earlier in the evening, could barely be contained.

Some neighborhoods erupted into armed conflict, while in others people accused neighbors of being in league with the enemy and murdered each other in the streets. The attackers who struck last night had been killed to the last foul Makrasha in less than an hour. They'd kill almost five hundred people and sparked riots in four districts. Now everyone seemed ready to flee or attack each other at the barest whisper of suspicion.

After hours of fruitless searching, and as the situation in the city deteriorated, the emperor took drastic action. He mobilized the entire military might of the inner city and stationed columns at every major intersection. Companies a hundred strong patrolled the neighborhoods. He agreed with his ambassadors that Tanathos had almost surely fled the city long since, and called off the hunt.

Worse, he issued a proclamation that the final enemy had been slain, and conspirators imprisoned. The proclamation, read in every neighborhood, did little to quell the unrest, but it effectively terminated any overt attempt to hunt Tanathos.

Now Kevlin stood in the council chamber, filled with restless anger. Gabral stood nearby. The short colonel wore his silver-trimmed armor under a long burgundy overcoat. He looked decidedly grumpy about being up most of the night. As Emperor's Champion, he had played a major role in re-establishing order throughout the city, and had reported to the council only moments ago.

Ceren stood against the wall at the foot of the long chamber, covered from neck to toe in a dark green cloak. She leaned against the wall as if tired, her eyes fixed on her feet. Her expression was strangely blank, but her skin was flushed as if with excitement. Kevlin was surprised she didn't draw closer, but he never pretended to understand any woman. Ceren confused him more than most.

Not far from Ceren, although not exactly close either, stood Indira. She had briefed the council on casualty counts and work being done by the Healers in attending the sick and injured.

Kevlin's eyes kept drifting back to her. Even though she looked exhausted, he yearned to touch her tousled hair. If only he could go to her, offer his shoulder for her to lean on, inhale the gentle scent of her, and just feel her closeness.

Instead he held his ground. Their eyes had met briefly when she first entered the long council room, but she'd looked away at once. Her body language spoke louder than words. She still didn't trust him.

He wished he'd punched Remiel a few more times.

The Sentinels Ah'Shan and Felix stood off to one side, and the Stalwarts cast many unfriendly glares in their direction. Tension filled the room so thick it was almost palpable. Kevlin wanted to pace with Leander to relieve some of his impotent rage. They'd been so close to complete victory.

Now Tanathos was gone, escaped from the very heart of their stronghold. Remiel was locked in a glowing prison to prevent him from speaking a word that might kill him until Ah'Shan could dig through his mind. No less than ten trusted Sentinels stood guard, and a full dozen Stalwarts guarded the entrance to the dungeon.

It almost didn't matter. Tanathos was already gone, and the ambassadors couldn't agree on what steps to take next to protect the city. They all but admitted they planned no further pursuit of the Shadeleech.

From Harafin's face, Kevlin could tell the subject was far from dead. He expected the old Sentinel to eventually convince the emperor to launch a covert team to chase the Shadeleech down. He planned to be a part of it.

The ambassadors argued about the cost of recent unrest, about best ways to calm the city, and about a hundred other topics, most of which seemed ridiculously petty. With such important things to deal with, all of the other bureaucratic nonsense irritated Kevlin.

Leander planted his feet and faced the ruling council. "You've bickered away any chance to take Tanathos. He's gone until he strikes again."

"Watch your tone, Stalwart," Sentinel Durgesh said from where he stood behind the emperor. "You forget yourself."

"As do you," Ah'Shan said. "You're here as a protective measure, not as a participant."

"Forgive me, master," Durgesh said with a little bow. "I take my responsibilities too seriously, perhaps."

Emperor Tegnazian waved Durgesh to silence and said to Leander, "I understand your anger, master Leander, but we've already proven tonight the folly of allowing emotion to trigger hasty responses. We cannot compound those mistakes with new ones."

"Angry?" Leander repeated loudly. "I am far beyond angry, Your Excellency. Two of my Stalwarts lay dead, murdered by Sentinels."

"How dare you?" Ah'Shan called. The powerfully-built Sentinel swelled with outrage. "One of my Kestrels, a long-time personal friend, also died in that dungeon attack."

Leander rounded on Ah'Shan. "Then why not join with me in demanding Truth on every Sentinel?"

"You're mad."

"Am I? Then you explain how our men could be riddled with half a hundred crossbow bolts without enough warning to so much as draw their weapons?"

"I cannot explain it."

"Of course you can. That many men approaching would have been ample warning. Our people would have been on alert and not taken by surprise. Besides, you couldn't fit enough men in that corridor to fire so many crossbows at one time. It's not possible."

"What are you saying?" Emperor Tegnazian asked.

Leander declared in a ringing voice, "Only Sentinels could have facilitated that attack."

"I disagree," Felix said. The obese Sentinel pointed at a small table standing against the right hand wall of the council chamber upon which sat three elaborately carved wooden rods.

"The evidence recovered from the dungeon shows that the attackers had access to Kedo artifacts. Nerys has already identified these items as some of the artifacts stolen last night from their new market location when it was broken into during the riots."

"And yet none of those artifacts deliver crossbow bolts," Leander said.

"No, they do not."

"What of the final artifact?" Leander said. "I don't see that box here."

Felix said, "It was deemed unimportant."

"By who?"

"Nerys."

"What box are you talking about?" the emperor asked. "Bring it here."

While they waited for the evidence to be fetched, the ambassadors started arguing about Leander's proposal. Ambassador Janezeko strongly supported the idea and presented compelling reasons why they should adopt the plan. Sentinels Ah'Shan and Felix argued strongly against it.

Finally the emperor said, "Enough debate. Despite the strong reasoning against this course of action, I am leaning toward implementing it."

"Your Excellency, you cannot do this," Ah'Shan said.

"So you suggest we do nothing?" Leander fired back.

Emperor Tegnazian held up his hand for silence. "I agree this is an onerous plan, and one I wish not to implement. And yet we're faced with unprecedented danger. Somehow an unknown enemy has infiltrated the very heart of the inner city. The city is in chaos, and murder and mayhem are unleashed within these very walls. I will not accept a plan of action that calls upon us to do nothing."

"Therefore," he continued loudly, "I decree that if you cannot provide further information through the traitor Remiel by noon tomorrow, we will lock down the inner city until every Sentinel submits to Truth."

"And what if that doesn't uncover any more traitors?" Felix asked, his voice strained, his face angry. "Will you insist on casting Truth on this entire council?"

"Preposterous," Ambassador Janezeko called. "Stop trying to twist the conversation."

"I am not," Felix said. "Where will we stop? What line will we not dare cross once we start down this road? Once we choose to not trust each other, only anarchy results."

The outer door opened and a soldier marched in carrying a small, plain wooden box.

"Is this the artifact you found in the dungeon?" Emperor Tegnazian asked.

"It is," Leander said.

That box looked familiar. Kevlin approached the soldier carrying it. "Let me see that."

Close inspection confirmed his suspicion. "Leander, did you say Sentinel Nerys claimed this box was irrelevant?"

"Yes, he did."

"He lied."

"Explain," Emperor Tegnazian commanded.

"I recognize this box," Kevlin declared. Everyone's attention fixed on him and he felt the weight of their stares. "I stopped by the Kereskedo shop the other day and Nerys himself showed me around. In his shop I saw a box identical to this one. He said it was an experimental product. He described it as a multi . . . something. At the time I didn't pay it any mind, but I'm convinced this is the same box. I believe it was designed to fire those crossbow bolts that killed your men."

"It must have been stolen from the market location with the other artifacts," Ambassador Janezeko said.

"Then why claim it was irrelevant?" Leander asked.

Kevlin shook his head. "It couldn't have been stolen. Nerys said the box was experimental, one of a kind."

Emperor Tegnazian said, "This is a serious accusation. Summon the Sentinel Nerys to explain."

Leander said, "I will fetch him myself."

He strode for the exit with Basak on his heels.

66

ONE LITTLE KISS CAN DO SO MUCH

"Kevlin, I need to talk with you."

He was surprised to find Ceren close beside him. He hadn't noticed her approaching. Her auburn hair hung in waves down her back, and she smelled like springtime. She still looked down at her feet.

"Sure, Ceren. What is it?"

"We need to speak in private. It's confidential."

"Can't it wait? This is kind of important."

"So is this."

Ceren turned and started toward a side exit without waiting for a reply and without looking back. Kevlin glanced around. The emperor and other members of the ruling council were talking amongst themselves while they waited for Leander to return.

At the moment they were arguing over the make-up of a delegation they wanted to send to the far western border fortifications to report on the current state of defenses. Given that open warfare was expected as soon as the passes cleared next spring, they argued about whether or not the delegation could complete an inspection prior to snowfall this year.

Kevlin's swordbrothers had moved over to talk with Sentinel Felix. He didn't see Indira anywhere. It looked like no one would miss him for a few minutes. He should easily beat Leander back. So he followed Ceren out into the hall.

She led him down several long corridors filled with workers wearing the green and gold of the emperor's colors. Many people looked nervous, more looked tired. Almost everyone had spent the night awake, scurrying to fill the emperor's commands and support the massive hunt in the city.

Given the press of people in the halls, Ceren must have felt uncomfortable speaking with him because she continued walking. Eventually she led him into a sunken garden and passed through a long row of arced trellises covered with vines. The constant roar of the waterfall soon drowned out the sounds of the palace and surrounded them in a bubble of peace.

When Ceren reached the stair that surrounded the central pit of the garden, she led the way down.

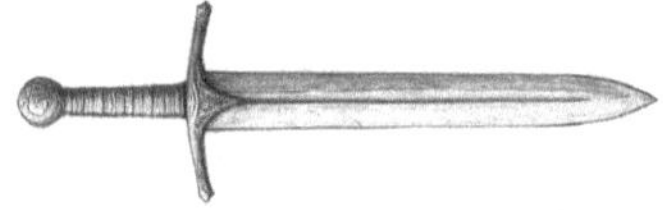

Indira paused in the entrance to the sunken garden. The hall behind her teemed with busy workers, but the garden stood empty. This one was filled with flowers and arched trellises covered with vines. The vines looked brown and dying now, but in the spring they would be filled with pretty white flowers. By high summer the flowers gave way to sweet dewberries. This garden produced bushels of the little black berries.

Indira headed through the arches toward the stairs leading to the lowest level where Kevlin and Ceren had just descended. She picked at her green robe and told herself to calm down.

She wasn't calm. She was terribly nervous. Ceren had warned her to stay away from Kevlin. She had agreed, but she couldn't do it anymore. The sight of him in the council chamber had warmed her heart. She only allowed herself to meet his gaze for a second, but that moment of eye contact had been enough.

Maybe it was dangerous to be near Kevlin. Maybe it was selfish to take the risk. For the first time in her life she felt compelled to take a step into the shadows outside of her regular, safe life. This would be the perfect chance to set everything straight with Ceren and Kevlin both.

As she approached the stairs, she slowed. The waterfall in the center of the garden roared and filled the air with glistening droplets of water. Late morning light shone into the garden from the open roof above, triggering dozens of tiny rainbows. The beautiful sight helped ease her tension, but she paused for a long moment at the top step.

Could she really take this risk? She hadn't been able to protect Adalia in the city, and that failure still haunted her. Even if she felt sure her gift would function perfectly, she couldn't protect Kevlin from the terrible dangers he faced.

She could support him, though. She could show him she cared, that she trusted him more than she feared him.

With that thought firmly fixed in her mind, she started down.

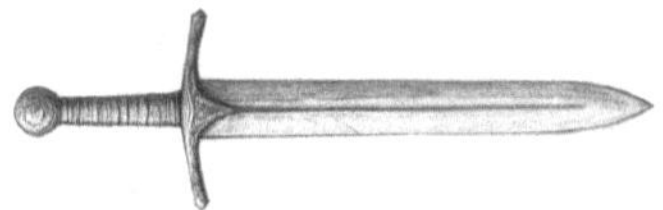

In the lowest level of the garden, Ceren crossed the close-cropped grass that carpeted the ground. Along the edges of the garden in this level stood dozens of Antalya fruit trees, heavy with their strange fruit. Kevlin hadn't seen Antalya trees since his youth. They were normally only found in wetlands of Meinarr. It looked ripe. He might just pick one after Ceren finished with this mysterious conversation.

Ceren finally stopped at a stone bench seat near the fruit trees. She had led him a quarter of the way around the garden from the stairs.

"Well, that was quite a trip." Kevlin dropped beside her on the narrow bench. "I have to admit, I'm curious."

Ceren, who sat looking down at her hands said, "Kevlin, have you ever wondered why people like us have so much wealth and so many privileges while most of our countrymen can barely scratch out a living?"

That was a strange way to start a conversation. He'd never known Ceren to flaunt her position, and she'd sacrificed much for the empire, sacrifices the rest of the world would never know about.

"What are you getting at?"

"It's a simple question. The empire is so unequal. Some like us are granted position and power through no other gift than birth."

"Did you lose to Indira at Oaths and Dares?" Kevlin asked.

He couldn't imagine Ceren would be dumb enough to play that game against Indira. The loser either had to swear an oath to serve the winner for a period of time or perform a difficult task. Or they were forced to accept a dare, which was usually embarrassing or even scandalous. He was surprised Indira would put her up to something like this.

"No, I'm serious." She sounded irritated, unlike the normal controlled persona she usually presented. Something was going on here, but he decided to play along until he learned the truth.

"Ask your questions then, but don't pretend I fall into that category."

"But you're a noble, the King's Avenger, and a hero."

He barked a laugh. "Just because Crown Prince Lievin proclaims me a lord doesn't change my life. You know my history. I grew up sailing the Six Kingdoms on a merchant ship my father could barely keep afloat. I spent years as a mercenary, eating mud more than cake. If anyone hasn't tasted wealth and privilege, it's me."

"But don't you see, that proves the system is broken."

"What system?"

"Everything." She spoke with rising passion. "The way the empire is set up with the privileged few ruling over the ignorant masses."

Kevlin chuckled, "Have you known many of the ignorant masses? I wouldn't want most of them ruling anything."

She punched his shoulder, but still didn't look up. He had been hoping to get her angry look. Her emerald eyes sparkled when she got angry, and he was surprised she didn't unleash her wiles on him like she usually tried to do.

"Kevlin, you have to admit changes are needed."

He shrugged. "Sure. Changes are always needed. That's why we do what we do."

"But we need to do more."

"All right. What do you suggest?"

She shuffled closer, her face flushed with excitement. "To effect real change, we need a powerful leverage."

"That makes sense. You have the keisara's ear. Get her to help."

"We need more than that."

"More than the keisara? What are you thinking?"

"We need Oris."

"Oh, no," Kevlin said. "Don't go messing around with that."

"We need to," she insisted. "Kevlin, I need to know who Harafin chose as Oris's new bearer."

This conversation had left weird behind and jumped right into 'time to leave'. "Ceren, you know I can't answer that. Harafin said . . ."

Ceren placed a finger to his lips, although she still didn't look up. "I know. That's not really what I wanted to talk about."

"Then why . . .?" She was making less sense than normal. That was saying something.

"Kevlin, do you remember that time we kissed in the forest?"

How could she jump so fast between topics without hurting herself? As if he'd forget his first kiss with a noblewoman.

Ceren was a complicated, driven young woman, but she was very pretty. Kevlin had worked to develop a strong friendship with her and tried to bury that memory. Talking about it made that impossible.

That night in the forest, huddled together after discovering the enemy's secret stronghold, their situation had felt desperate. Soaked from constant rain and miles from help, Ceren had kissed him before leaving to search for help. Neither of them had known if they would survive the night, and through that kiss they'd shared their yearning for life.

It was a good memory. As he considered it, Kevlin became acutely aware that here in the lowest level of this sunken garden they were very alone.

She'd kissed him again in Diodor just days ago. She'd claimed the kiss came from Indira, but that story had seemed a bit weak even then. Indira's reaction had implied she'd sent a message, but hadn't intended Ceren to take it so literally.

Had Ceren been lying to him all along? Had she been lying to Indira?

"Ceren, why did you bring me down here really?"

She shrugged out of her cloak with a single, sinuous twist of her shoulders.

Oh. That.

This woman was as complicated as she was stunning in that outfit.

Ceren wore only a thin, silky red shift that revealed far more than it concealed of her lovely figure. Kevlin tried not to stare, but wasn't very successful. She'd obviously taken great effort in choosing her outfit for the evening, and even he knew it was unwise to insult a woman's choice of clothing. Her coppery skin seemed to glow in the soft light and, as she turned toward him, it pulled the shift in all kinds of ways he shouldn't be seeing.

"Ah, I think you're going to get cold."

Eyes still downcast, she took his hands in hers. He tried to pull away, but she clung to him.

"Ceren, have you been drinking the keisara's wine?"

"Kevlin, I never told you why I kissed you."

"I don't think now's a good time."

He tried to extricate himself and stand, but she wrapped her arms around his neck and clung tighter. Her skin was soft and he didn't want to hurt her.

"I have to tell you," she whispered into his ear.

"So tell me." Maybe then she'd let him go.

"Because I love you."

"Are you insane?"

She grabbed his face and kissed him hard on the lips.

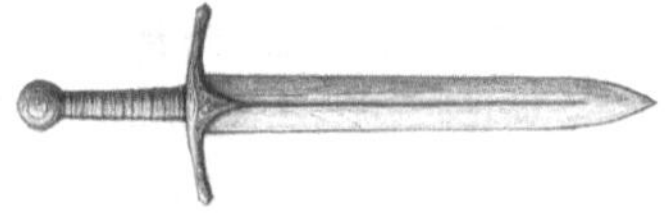

Indira clutched the inner rail of the garden stairs and gasped. Her cry was drowned by the roar of the waterfall. She stood in the shadows almost at the base of the stairs.

Ceren, dressed in a scandalously small outfit, was kissing Kevlin. The sight seared Indira's mind and left her weak. She felt sick by the betrayal.

Ceren had lied. All this time she'd pretended to be a friend, pretended to help, but all the while, she'd only been manipulating Indira. Of course she wanted Indira to stay away from Kevlin. It had nothing to do with protecting him. With Indira out of the way, Ceren could take Kevlin for herself.

That's why Ceren had kissed him in the palace of Diodor. She'd asked Ceren to give Kevlin the message that she cared for him, wanted to be with him. Instead, Ceren had kissed him and claimed it was on her behalf.

She'd been so naïve! How could she fall for such a blatant ploy?

Indira glanced back across the garden again. The two kissed like secret lovers.

Kevlin loved Ceren.

Indira turned and fled blindly up the stairs as tears burned in her eyes, not trying to swallow her sobs. Her hands shook, and her steps faltered, but she pressed forward.

She'd often drained pain out of her patients and often shared some of that pain. Always she felt confident in her strength. Pain never terrified her. She knew how to destroy it.

Now agony burned through her, so severe she could barely breathe. She'd never felt anything like it. Indira staggered out of the stairs at the uppermost level and collapsed there, weeping.

67

CRAZY ISN'T ATTRACTIVE

As Ceren's lips pressed hungrily against his, Kevlin tried to pull back. She held him stronger, her arms like iron bands. She kissed him hungrily, as if she'd yearned to do so forever. The heat of her passion was a heady thing.

Kevlin cared for Ceren. At one point he'd even fantasized about kissing her again. She should have made her move then, but she'd missed her chance. She was a trusted friend, but he didn't want her this way now.

Kevlin pushed harder. If she didn't back off, he'd have to hurt her. Her skin felt burning hot through the thin silk shift. The springtime scent surrounding her filled his nostrils, and she lunged against him, pressing him against the back of the narrow bench. Her warm lips tasted salty.

This was so wrong.

She wasn't Indira.

Indira's face flashed into his mind and he imagined what she'd say if she saw them like this. Kevlin shoved Ceren hard enough to bruise her, knocking her off the bench.

"Ceren, cut it out."

Ceren cried, "Stop thinking Kevlin and just kiss me. I need you, and together we can change the world."

"Start by changing your clothes." He tried to retreat around the bench, but she jumped into his arms and clung to him like a leech.

Ceren was many things, but she'd never acted desperate. Ceren teased or cajoled, and always confused. She never revealed her real purpose or clarified her comments when she left him confused and bewildered. She would never do this.

Kevlin forced himself ignore how she felt pressed against him, tried to tear his eyes away from that alluring outfit that acted like a visual magnet. He stumbled across the garden and finally pried her hands from around his neck. With a quick twist, he ducked under her arms and spun away.

"Ceren, calm down. You're not yourself."

Ceren stalked after him, but her gaze remained strangely downcast. Her hair hung in tangled waves across her face. It was a wonder she could see at all. "Tell me one thing, Kevlin."

"Anything you want, as long as you stay back."

"Who killed Bajaran?"

"What?" That was a stupid question. She really had gone mad.

Ceren crouched several feet away, her hands wide. "Who killed Bajaran?" she repeated.

"I told you. Rhea did."

"Who was Rhea's master?"

"Masego."

"Where is Oris?"

"You know I can't tell you."

"That's not good enough." Ceren started forward again. "I love you, Kevlin. You have to tell me. It's the only way to make things different."

Kevlin retreated toward the stairs. He needed other witnesses, although he cringed to think of Ceren walking in public in that outfit. It was her choice. He wouldn't allow her to keep him trapped down here to protect her image.

"Ceren, what's wrong with you?"

"I love you! Tell me!"

"No."

Ceren snarled like an animal and charged. Kevlin dodged her attack, but she chased him and lunged a second time.

He grabbed her arms, wrestling her for control. After a moment he managed to twist her arms behind her back. The feel of her pressed against him no longer tempted him. She must be suffering some kind of mental sickness. He hoped it wasn't contagious.

He'd look ridiculous trying to slip into an outfit like that. He shuddered to even consider it.

After a moment of intense struggle, Ceren suddenly sagged against him. She whispered, "You have to tell me. Please, you have to help me."

Kevlin was relieved that she seemed to be regaining her composure. Somehow they'd work this mess out. Crazy was definitely not attractive.

"I want to help you." Kevlin released her hands and, when she didn't lunge at him again, brushed the hair from her face. "Ceren, I don't think you're well. You know I can't tell you."

For the first time that evening, Ceren looked up and met his gaze. Her eyes, normally lovely emerald green, looked black in the twilight of the garden.

Kevlin recoiled. That was definitely not good.

Ceren lashed out and yanked his belt dagger from its sheath. She snarled, "Then the only way you can help is to die for me."

"Whoa! What are you doing?" Kevlin grabbed for the dagger.

Ceren side-stepped his hands like a cat and drove the dagger toward his heart. He twisted and flung out a hand to block the surprise attack. The dagger scraped along his forearm, leaving a trail of blood that burned like living fire.

Kevlin retreated, but Ceren gave chase and slashed the dagger across his side. It scraped along his chain mail with a wicked screech.

She was in earnest. She really meant to kill him. Whatever insanity plagued her, he had to disarm her quickly or she might really hurt him.

Kevlin blocked her next strike with his arm and managed to avoid getting cut this time. Then he reversed direction and surprised her by closing. He caught her hand and they struggled for control of the dagger.

Ceren kneed Kevlin between the legs.

That wasn't sick. That was pure evil. So much for loving him.

His vision went black and he convulsed with agony. He couldn't breathe, couldn't move. He collapsed to the short-cropped grass.

The first thing he noticed was the waterfall. Somehow he'd lost track of a couple of seconds.

Ceren stood above him, dagger raised high. With an ear-numbing shriek, she drove the dagger down at his heart with all her strength.

68

THE ALLURE OF A STRONG WOMAN

Kevlin couldn't stop her. His body still trembled with shock and his arm moved far too slowly as the dagger plunged toward his chest. Maybe he should have kissed her? That would've been less lethal.

Too late. She was going to kill him.

The blade flashed as it passed through a ray of light. Then it came to a jarring halt half an inch from his chest.

Ceren stabbed at him again. Again the blade stopped a quivering half inch from him.

"Get away from him you black-hearted liar!"

Indira?

She stood almost halfway up the curving garden stairs, barely visible through the waterfall. Her midnight hair fell about her face in a tangled mess and tears streaked her cheeks, but she glared at Ceren with burning fury.

She'd never looked so good.

Ceren moved toward the base of the stairs, and Indira started down. Kevlin tried to call out to her to beware, but only managed a cough. He tried to stand, to help, but it took all his focus just to roll over. His body hurt so deep he gasped for breath.

Move, soldier! He had to help Indira or Ceren would butcher her. On his second try he managed to stagger to his feet. He stood, feet spread wide, barely keeping his balance.

He was pathetic. The woman he loved was about to be murdered by the psycho mental case he had once though was a good friend.

As Indira neared for the bottom of the stairs she cried, "You lied about everything!"

Ceren said nothing. She held her dagger low and motioned Indira on.

She came. Indira stepped off the stairs and marched toward Ceren. Ceren lunged and drove the dagger at Indira's stomach.

Indira jumped back with a cry of surprise, but Ceren pursued and lunged again.

Indira abruptly reversed direction. Kevlin cried out a warning and staggered toward the women, although he would be far too late to help. Indira twisted at the last second, and the dagger ripped into the folds of her green Healer's dress.

She punched Ceren in the jaw.

Ceren's head whipped back and she stumbled. Indira grabbed the shorter woman and, with a cry of rage, lifted her off the ground and slammed her to the grassy soil. Ceren hit hard and air exploded out of her lungs.

Indira straddled Ceren's arms and slapped her hard across the face, leaving angry welts.

"You betrayed our trust."

"You're all dead!" Ceren shouted.

Indira hit her again, a hard backhand blow.

Ceren shrieked and writhed on the ground, but Indira kept her pinned and slapped her again and again until blood sprayed from Ceren's split lips.

Indira screamed a wordless cry as she struck. It tore at Kevlin's heart. It sounded like her heart was breaking, like she was hurting herself as much as Ceren. She didn't stop. Tears streamed down her face and her hair flew as she rocked back and forth with the effort of beating Ceren.

Kevlin finally reached them. He still walked funny, and it would be a long time before he'd consider himself okay. He grabbed Indira's arms, and shook her. "Stop!"

Indira brushed hair from her tear-streaked face and looked up at Kevlin. Her eyes looked haunted and her lips quivered. He focused on those full lips. They were so kissable, and he yearned to taste them.

Now probably wasn't a good time.

She rubbed at one cheek with a blood-stained hand, leaving a streak of read across the porcelain skin. She lifted a hand toward Kevlin and he moved to raise her up.

Ceren lunged off the ground as soon as the pressure on her arms relaxed, and tumbled Indira to one side.

Kevlin caught her and twisted the dagger from her hands. She turned on him, but he was ready for her this time and quickly pinned her arms behind her back.

Indira approached, the dagger clenched in one bloody fist. She raised it.

"Don't!" Kevlin cried. "She's not herself."

Indira glanced at the dagger, as if only just realizing she held it in her hand. She tossed it away like it was a venomous snake, and retreated a step.

"What have I done?" she mumbled.

"Help me," Kevlin called as he fought to hold Ceren. "I think she's possessed or something."

Indira half-raised a hand, but then dropped it and shook her head. In a voice barely above a whisper she said, "I can't."

"Of course you can. You can heal anything."

Indira shook her head again, harder. "I can't heal someone I hate."

"Ceren's your friend. She's not herself right now, can't you see that?"

Tears glistened in her eyes, reflecting her deep hurt. He'd give her a hug if crazy Ceren wasn't still struggling like a possessed animal.

"I don't know what's going on here, but I know Ceren is your friend. Please, Indira. Please just try. Let's find out the truth."

Indira turned and walked away. That was a first.

She moved to the fountain, splashed water on her face, and took several deep breaths. Then she returned with a purposeful stride, her expression resolute.

"I'll help until I know the truth," she said. "And if . . ." her voice trailed off, and for a moment a look of pure rage flickered across her face.

She blew out a breath and repeated, "Until I know the truth."

Kevlin reminded himself never to make her really angry. This was a side of Indira that not even those who tried cheating at cards ever say.

She closed her eyes and placed a hand on Ceren's head. Ceren screamed and convulsed in Kevlin's grasp, but he held her fast. Her wrists would be bruised from the pressure she forced him to use, but he had no choice.

Indira leaned closer, and Ceren tried to bite her. Indira grabbed a fistful of Ceren's hair and yanked her head back out of the way. Ceren screamed again, but Indira ignored her.

Several tense seconds passed before Indira's hand began to glow. Very faintly at first, the light grew slowly brighter over half a minute.

Kevlin bit back the urge to tell her to hurry. He still wasn't feeling great, and he'd love to lie down or go fall in the water for a minute or two. His arms burned from holding the still-struggling Ceren, but he gritted his teeth and held on.

Indira's hand burst into brilliant white light. Ceren screamed in agony, then collapsed against Kevlin. He nearly dropped her.

Indira frowned and began chanting. Her clear voice filled the clearing and melded with the constant roar of the waterfall. Kevlin drank in the sound, and the melody held real power. His tension faded, along with some of his pain.

This time the haunting melody carried an undertone of sadness he'd never heard before. That only made it more enchanting.

After several seconds she gasped. "You're right, Kevlin. Someone's tampered with her mind."

"Who? What did they do?"

Indira frowned, brows knit together in concentration. After another moment she said softly, "This is beyond my skill. We need Leander and Harafin."

Kevlin tried to pick up Ceren, but almost fell. Indira's voice had comforted him, but he was still not well. He decided it really was a good time to sit down.

Indira knelt beside him and he brushed the dried tracks of tears from one cheek. She leaned into his hand and sighed. Their eyes met, and he would have been happy to stay like that for hours.

He suppressed another urge to kiss her. The timing still felt wrong. He pulled the amulet up over his head and dropped it to the grass beside him.

"Got anything left?"

Indira almost smiled as she placed a glowing hand on his shoulder. He closed his eyes to enjoy the feeling of her pure healing magic, but nothing came.

He opened his eyes and found her watching him. She leaned forward, but not to kiss him, and her voice held an edge of steel. "After we see to Ceren, you're going to tell me about that kiss."

Kevlin tried to stammer an explanation, but she placed one finger across his lips. "Later. You'd better have a very good explanation."

"I promise."

He'd never seen Indira like this. He found the spark of anger in her eyes and the steel in her voice powerfully alluring. "Just help me enough so I can get Ceren to Harafin, then I'm yours."

Indira kissed his cheek and whispered into his ear, "If you ever kiss her again, I'll break every bone in your body."

69

SLIPPERY SNAKES

Leander flung open the door to the Kedo shop in the inner city and marched inside, flanked by Basak. Sentinel Nerys stood at the main counter with a richly dressed lord, discussing an ermine cape that lay on the countertop.

"Out," Leander snapped to the lord.

When the man protested, Basak laid a firm hand on his shoulder and propelled him out the door. The burly Stalwart stationed himself there to ensure no one else disturbed them.

Sentinel Nerys frowned. "By your rude behavior, I assume your visit here is not for the purpose of purchasing our merchandise."

"It is not," Leander said. He marched up to the glass counter. "By order of the emperor, you will accompany me to the council chamber to answer charges of lying and facilitating the recent attack that left two of my brethren dead."

"Calm down," Nerys said, making placating gestures. "I already explained that our market location was vandalized. Artifacts stolen there were indeed used in that terrible attack, but I bear no responsibility for those actions."

"Those artifacts are not in question. What is in question is why you lied about the box artifact found with the dead."

"I don't know what you mean," Nery said, but his expression turned nervous.

"Stop lying to me," Leander snapped. He slapped a hand onto the glass top of the counter, rattling the case. "You lied about the box and withheld evidence. Now tell me who purchased it."

"I cannot share our client list with anyone," Nerys protested. "It's confidential information. What clients choose to do with our products is not our responsibility."

Leander leaned over the case. "Then why lie about it?"

"I'll have to see this box again," Nerys said. "I don't remember any such thing."

"Sir Kevlin recognized it. He said you showed it to him in this very shop and told him it was an experimental model, one of a kind."

Nerys glanced to his right, at an empty spot on a high shelf. His face paled. "I'm sorry. I cannot help you."

"Let me make this clear," Leander said, his voice deadly soft. "You either cooperate willingly, or I'll assume you're an accomplice. You won't like that nearly as much as I will."

Nerys glared. "Do you really think it wise to threaten a Sentinel in his own shop?"

"Your powers don't concern me." Leander headed for the end of the case. "And your time is up."

Nerys snatched a short, intricately carved wooden rod from inside the display case. He pointed it at Leander and flicked a knob on one side. Dozens of thick ropes exploded out of the tip and wrapped around Leander.

Leander toppled forward against the case. "You fool," he shouted. "I'll have your head."

Basak charged from where he stood near the door. Nerys pointed the rod at him and more ropes whipped around the burly Stalwart. His legs tangled and his forward momentum toppled him hard to the floor.

Nerys bounced the rod in his hand and said in a smug tone, "I tried to warn you, old man. Only a fool attacks a Kedo on his home ground. Now, after I have you two thrown out the door, I want you to . . ."

"Enough!" Leander shouted. "Time for Justice."

The ropes binding him vaporized in a blinding flash of light. Still-burning tatters drifted to the floor around him as he snapped his fingers and called forth his mighty hammer.

Nerys scuttled back to the wall as Leander leaped the display case and advanced on him. The Sentinel touched a small figurine carved into the shape of a hand holding a key. He pressed himself against the wall and disappeared.

Leander lunged and collided with the back wall. He smashed the figurine and struck the back wall with his hammer. The wall shuddered under the blow, and one shelf to his right collapsed and dumped its contents to the floor with a crash. Nerys was nowhere to be seen.

Leander spun and surveyed the empty shop. He snapped the fingers of his left hand, and the ropes still binding Basak melted away. "Let's spread out. We'll find that traitor."

"Found him." Basak pointed out the window. Sentinel Nerys was sprinting around the corner, heading south.

Leander bolted from the shop and gave chase, with Basak close on his heels. As he ran Leander growled, "There is no escape from Justice. I will not be denied again."

70

FRACTURED CLUES

"**Y**ou are right," Harafin said. "There is evidence of mind tampering here." He knelt beside a plush couch upon which Ceren lay, wrapped in her long, green cloak, still unconscious.

Kevlin stood nearby, trying not to show how tired and sore he still felt. Indira had healed him enough to carry Ceren out of the sunken garden and back to a small waiting room near the council chamber where Harafin was still in the meeting.

The old sentinel then led them to this richly appointed meeting room. It held a huge mahogany table surrounded by ten padded wooden chairs, a fireplace, two couches, and three overstuffed chairs. Now he looked up from where he had been examining Ceren.

"Tell me exactly what happened."

Kevlin related the strange experience, but glossed over the part where Ceren threw herself at him. Indira scowled when he reached that part.

He chose his words very carefully. Indira remained motionless, her lips turned down. Could she really break every bone in his body? Would she?

Yes, on both counts. The certainty of it thrilled him. She had to really care for him. Smiling right now would be a really bad idea, though.

He finished the tale by detailing the fight and Indira's assistance. Harafin didn't seem very interested in that part, although he did raise an eyebrow in surprise when Kevlin related how Indira punched Ceren and beat her senseless.

"You did the right thing, my girl," Harafin said. "I'm impressed you had the strength for it. It must have been extremely difficult for you."

"At the moment it felt like the right thing to do."

Harafin placed a glowing hand again on Ceren's head. Indira glanced at Kevlin, and he gave her a reassuring smile. She didn't return it, but didn't glare at him either.

After several quiet moments while they watched Harafin work, the old Sentinel leaned back with a sigh. Ceren blinked and opened her eyes.

She seemed surprised to find Harafin kneeling so close to her. She looked around, her expression confused. "Master Harafin? Kevlin? Indira?" She sat up with Harafin's help. "What happened? Where are we? Why does my face hurt so much?"

As she gingerly explored her bruised cheeks with one hand, Harafin said, "Tell me what you remember, Ceren."

"I just had the craziest dream . . ."

She glanced at Kevlin and then at Indira. Her eyes widened in surprise and she peeked under her concealing cloak. Her face flushed crimson and she buried it in her hands.

"It was real, wasn't it?" She risked a glance at Kevlin. "I really . . .?"

He nodded.

She turned to Indira and asked in a tiny voice, "Really?"

"You did." Indira didn't hide her anger.

"Oh, no." Ceren turned to Harafin, her face panicked. "What happened to me? I didn't . . . I mean, I couldn't. I wouldn't!"

"Easy," Harafin said. He lay a comforting hand on her shoulder. "Indira discovered that someone tampered with your mind and forced you to those actions."

"How?"

"What's the last thing you remember from before your . . . dream?"

Ceren glanced at Kevlin again and her blush deepened. Then she looked at Indira and her face paled, and tears glistened in her brilliant emerald eyes. She scrubbed at her face and winced, and then stared at her hands. She took a few deep breaths and looked to be barely fighting back tears.

"I know this is a difficult time and a great deal to absorb." Harafin said.

"What else did they make me do?"

"I found no other evidence of tampering. However, I will want to examine you further once you feel better. Matters of the mind are very delicate. For now, I must know what you remember."

"Nothing. The last thing I remember, I was sitting in my rooms in the Freyarr Palace, and someone knocked on the door."

"Who?"

"I don't know," she wailed. She jumped off the couch and stepped toward Kevlin, her face anguished. "Kevlin, I . . ."

She realized her cloak had fallen open. Not the image she was probably trying to convey. She snatched it closed.

Indira moved protectively to Kevlin's side.

"Oh, Indira," Ceren cried.

She swayed toward the healer, as if wanting to rush to her. When Indira made no gesture of encouragement, she retreated back to the couch and buried her face in her hands again. She no longer tried to hold back her emotions, and sobs racked her slender frame.

Kevlin wanted to comfort her, but he couldn't think how that wouldn't end in disaster. Indira would flay him alive. It was clear Ceren hadn't been in control, but the emotions were too recent, too powerful.

What an insane dilemma. Ceren was a close friend, and she had been the victim of a villainous scheme that robbed her of her conscious will. She had been a helpless victim, but he couldn't comfort her. The unfairness of it made him want to hit something.

To his surprise, Indira moved to Ceren's side and sank to her knees beside the weeping young woman. Indira wrapped Ceren in her arms and said softly, "It's all right, Ceren. We understand."

Ceren threw her arms around Indira and wept into the Healer's shoulder. "Oh Indira, I'm so sorry."

Indira held her until Ceren's emotions ran their course and she regained control. Finally she sat up and wiped at her bruised cheeks.

"Harafin, who did this to me?"

"I do not know. They extracted the memories of their visit quite thoroughly. All I could sense was that your attacker was someone you knew."

"But I know everyone."

"Then that part's not very helpful."

"Why would they?"

"It appears the enemy is growing desperate," Harafin said.

"They wanted to know about Oris," Kevlin said. He didn't bother to comment on the ridiculous comments about changing the world.

"That's not surprising," Harafin said. "What I don't understand is the question about Bajaran's murderer."

"Masego," Kevlin said.

"We really should have seen that connection sooner," Harafin said.

"He's been involved from the very beginning," Kevlin said.

Ceren nodded. "He was Rhea's master. He set her up to work with Bajaran and then betray him after he attacked Antigonus."

"He's been a player since before Antigonus left on his fateful journey," Harafin said. "An enemy among us, working from the shadows. We've underestimated him."

"Why ask about it though?" Indira asked. "If he was involved, why point it out?"

"It means whoever broke into your mind was hunting for that connection too," Harafin said.

"Another faction?" Kevlin asked.

Just what they needed, more secret enemies. The capital seemed to breed them like rats.

Tanathos had escaped, Masego was attacking at will despite everything they did, and now some unknown third party was apparently involved. He wasn't sure the city could handle any more.

"What if they try again?" Ceren asked.

"Don't worry about that. I have shielded your mind. You are under my personal protection now. Should the enemy attempt to influence you again, I will know about it instantly." He gave her a reassuring smile. "Should they attempt it, they will not find you an easy target."

"Thank you." Ceren hugged him. He looked a little surprised, but held the slender woman for a moment.

"For the time being, I want you to return to your quarters and don something more appropriate."

Ceren pulled the cloak more closely around her. "Of course."

"Do you remember enough to understand the situation in the city?"

"Yes."

"Good. Once you're dressed, go to the keisara and deliver an update on the situation."

"That's it?"

"It is enough for now. Keep up the appearance of normalcy until we determine a plan of attack."

"How can we do that?"

"The person who tampered with you mind showed great caution. They implanted the powerful impulses to act the way you did, but left no trace back to them. They must be planning to meet with you again soon to see what you discovered."

"Who are you meeting with today?" Kevlin asked.

"Just the keisara, and then Ambassador Damarist."

Kevlin shared a look with Harafin, who said softly, "Again we turn to the ambassador."

"Do you think he's lying about everything?"

"Not everything. Rarely does anyone lie about everything. It's too easy to prove the fabrication. For example, I have confirmed with Ambassador Janezeko that he did, in fact, refer the Blade Stalwart Dhanjal to Ambassador Damarist."

"So, you don't think he's involved in this plot," Ceren asked.

"I didn't say that. His involvement with Remiel was foolish, but perhaps not intentionally deceitful. However, I suspect there is more he is withholding from me."

"He's not a Sentinel," Ceren said. "He couldn't have done this to me."

"No, but he may know who did."

"So what do we do?"

"Go visit the keisara. We will fashion a plan around your visit to the ambassador to ferret out the truth."

Harafin's voice took on a hard edge. "Then we hunt down whoever did this to you and we destroy them."

71

TIME FOR JUSTICE

Nerys sprinted south, faster than he'd run in half a century. His powers might be ineffectual against Stalwarts, but there was more than one path to victory. The strength he focused down through his legs enhanced his muscles until he sprinted as fast as a galloping stallion. He hadn't run like this since he was a young Accepted.

He glanced back. The two Stalwarts were giving chase, and the old man ran like a gazelle. It wouldn't matter. They would never catch him. In a few minutes, he'd reach the sanctuary of the Sentinel Tower, and even the mighty Leander couldn't drag a Sentinel unwilling from that fortress. Every Sentinel there would rise up to stop him.

Nerys grinned as he ran. What a victory! His products were now battle tested against Stalwarts. Why hadn't he thought to try this before? He'd have to figure out how to add something to the marketing efforts that highlighted that even the mighty Pallian Stalwart Leander was no match for Kedo talismans.

As Nerys raced around the rear corner of the Donarr Castle, he nearly collided with a squad of imperial guardsmen.

"Ho there," the captain called. "What's all this then?" The man was a blocky veteran with a commanding voice and a grim visage.

Nerys pointed back at the pursuing Stalwarts. "Those men are bent on murder. I'm going for help."

The captain puffed out his chest. "We'll see about that." He stepped into the street and called to his men, "Form ranks."

Nerys chuckled as he ran on. He didn't really need the help, but it amused him immensely to throw one more obstacle in Leander's way. The Stalwart was far too serious. He should learn to laugh more.

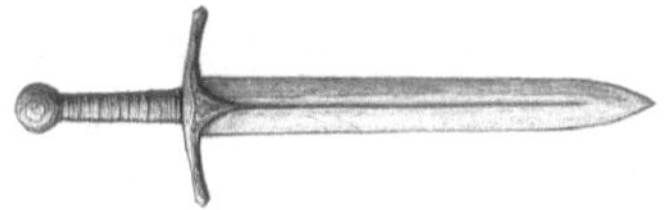

Leander frowned as a company of soldiers moved to block his path. Curse the fool Nerys for his meddling. All he had to do was co-operate and name the conspirator. Why fight so hard to protect the traitors? Maybe he really was in league with them.

Leander would find out one way or the other, and justice would be meted out for crimes committed. The simmering fury that he'd struggled to contain since learning of Tanathos' escape yesterday boiled through him now and he barely kept it in check. Restraint was proving unproductive, and he would not allow these traitors to escape. If they pushed him to the brink, they would not like the result.

The captain of the company stepped forth and shouted, "Hold, Stalwart and explain yourself."

Leander said, "Basak, run on. I'll deal with this."

As Basak circled out around the soldiers, several of them moved to intercept him, but Leander cut them off. He planted himself in the street and said, "Captain, remove your men. You have no authority to interfere with me."

The captain said, "Where is your man going?"

"To catch a criminal."

"That Sentinel who just ran past?"

"The very one. He's in league with the forces that sparked the riots last night, so get out of my way."

"He lied to me?"

"Don't take it personal. He lied to the emperor not an hour ago."

Leander ran after Basak, who had already rounded the next corner. Behind him the captain spat out a curse. "Double time, men. We'll bring that liar to the emperor in chains!"

The soldiers broke into a run, but Leander left them far behind. As he rounded the next corner, he caught sight of Nerys disappearing around the city side of the Hallvarr Palace and realized the Sentinel's destination.

If the man reached the Sentinel Tower, extricating him would waste time Leander refused to lose. So as he ran, he called forth his Actinopathic gift. The power roared into him, so intense he shook with the influx of new strength.

With the power came all the horrific memories of his murdered family and the insanity that swept over him after their death. Coupled with his already-simmering fury, he barely refrained from unleashing his powers against the distant Nerys.

Should he do that, the gods only knew if he could ever stop. Instead, Leander focused on Basak. As the burly Stalwart ran, Leander *pushed* against him with each step. Basak flew forward as each leaping stride covered first twice the distance as before, and then five times as much.

If Basak felt surprised by the unexpected help, he didn't show it, and he adjusted his stride accordingly. Propelled by Leander, Basak closed rapidly on Nerys.

It was going to be close.

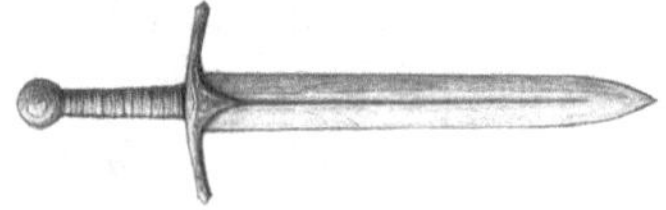

Nerys ran up the Iron Spoke and wove through the increasingly heavy foot traffic without slowing. Several people shouted angrily as he barreled past them, and he only barely avoided colliding with a courier on an imperial stallion.

He rounded the front of the Hallvarr Palace and grinned. The white walls of the Sentinel Tower, shining like a beacon, seemed to reflect and amplify the late morning light. There, sanctuary was guaranteed. He'd have all the time he needed to craft the appropriate response and deflect suspicion from the Kedos.

There had to be a way to capitalize on all the attention their artifacts were receiving. It was unfortunate their effectiveness was being interpreted in such a negative light. It wasn't the Kedos' fault someone applied their artifacts to nefarious pursuits. If only everyone could look past those deeds and celebrate together the craft so clearly displayed through the successful deployment.

He expected sales to jump next month.

Nerys glanced back and was startled to find the burly, shaven-headed Stalwart closing fast. The big man leaped impossibly far at every step. In one stride, he vaulted over a heavy laden wagon.

Nerys redoubled his efforts and focused his power to increase his speed. He couldn't falter, not this close. As he neared the tower, he spied four other Kedos exiting the building. He waved to them and caught their attention.

Even though he was still a good hundred leaping strides from the tower, he prepared to call to them and warn them of the danger. He could easily enhance his voice to cover the distance, and they would raise the alarm and provide assistance.

Before he could, something struck him in the back of the left shoulder, knocking him off his feet. He crashed to the ground and tumbled several times before sliding to a painful stop. His robes were twisted about his frame, and his skin burned from scraping against the cobbled street. His ears rang, but he heard no other sound. He tasted smoke, dirt filled his nostrils, and he sneezed.

He looked around, dumbfounded, trying to understand what had happened. His head pounded, his thoughts moved sluggishly, and everything he looked at seemed layered in thick fog. Beside him on the ground lay a Stalwart's hammer. He stared at it for two heartbeats before understanding dawned.

The cursed Stalwart.

Rough hands grabbed his shoulders and hauled him to his feet. His legs wobbled and he would have fallen if he'd been released. He blinked a couple of times before the burly Stalwart came into focus.

"Nice try," the big man said in a surprisingly gentle voice. "Not good enough, though."

The words echoed into Nerys' head as if from a great distance, and he struggled to grasp their meaning. The Stalwart retrieved his hammer and started dragging Nerys away from the tower.

The movement jolted him out of his stupor, and his head cleared. Around them, pedestrians were staring or pointing. The Stalwart Leander was approaching fast, a look of grim satisfaction on his face.

The sight of Leander drove the first spike of fear into his heart. He dug his heels in against the cobbles and pulled against the Stalwart.

"I demand to be released," he cried, his voice weak and shaking.

The Stalwart ignored him and gave a single yank against his robes. Nerys stumbled after the powerful man, unable to resist the man's iron grip.

"Release him!"

Nerys glanced back and found the other Kedos approaching. Several other Sentinels were coming behind, and more were exiting the Tower as word spread. The sight bolstered his confidence.

He yanked against the Stalwart's restraining hand. "I might have run too slow, but so did you. Now release me."

"No."

The Kedos drew close and Nerys called to them, "Help. This man is intent on murder."

"Let him go," commanded the closest Kedo Sentinel, a hot-headed young man named Yasam. He glared at Basak and moved to intercept the burly Stalwart. He stood a full head taller, and with his thick head of black hair, he towered over the shorter man.

"Move aside," Basak said softly. He kept walking, and did not slow.

"You really are stupid, aren't you?" Yasam asked. He spoke with a thick, southern Freyarr accent. People from that mountainous region bordering Nedikat often intermarried with their neighbors to the south. By his swarthy skin, it looked clear Yasam shared that mixed heritage.

Basak kept walking. Yasam grabbed Basak's arm and snarled, "I said, let him go."

Yasam's hands burst into blue fire as he called upon his powers, but the light flickered and faded away.

Basak grabbed Yasam by the front of his robes with one hand and frightening ease, flung Yasam over his head. The young Sentinel shouted with surprise before landing on his backside several strides away.

The other Kedos cried out against the abuse, but kept a careful distance. Basak kept walking, dragging Nerys after him.

Nerys started to panic. Would they really let this brute drag him away? Leander would arrive in a few seconds. He needed help.

The ground under Basak's feet erupted without warning and flung the burly Stalwart thirty feet into the air. He didn't release Nerys, and tore a piece of fabric from Nery's robes. His arms and legs windmilled helplessly as he sailed in as low arc and plummeted to the hard cobbles. He struck with a loud thud and lay in a crumpled heap.

Nerys smiled through the rain of cobblestones. He gladly accepted the supporting hands of his friends. They turned and started back toward the Sentinel Tower where twenty Sentinels now gathered to watch the unusual event. Already Nerys's mind whirled as he worked out how to spin these events to his advantage. So much publicity in one day could be a gold mine if he could direct its focus.

"Hold!"

Leander was slowing to a stop beside Basak. The burly Stalwart stood, but he limped and one arm hung useless at his side. One entire side of his face was already darkening in an ugly bruise.

"Leave off," Nerys called, "or we won't be so gentle next time."

Leander planted his feet, his expression furious. All that anger had to be bad for his heart. He pointed at Nerys and shouted, "Surrender that man to me. He is wanted for questioning by the emperor in connection with attacks in the city last night."

Yasam said, "You lie."

"Don't push me, boy," Leander growled. "I lack the patience today."

"You lack sanity," Yasam shot back. "You will not take Nerys, not today, not ever. You cannot stand against us here, so take your bulldog and be gone or we'll chase you away."

"You openly defy the emperor's command then?" Leander asked.

"I defy you," Yasam shouted. "If the emperor wishes to speak to one of us, have him send someone with authority."

"Very well. I warned you, boy." Leander started forward, his expression determined.

"Flaming chains, you senile old idiot," Yasam cried. "I told you to leave!" He flung out a hand and glittering orange light gathered around it. The ground under Leander heaved upward, just as it had under Basak a moment ago.

Leander did not catapult up and away as Basak had. He rode the column of earth up, but remained fixed to it as if glued there. It settled again, and he rode it back down. When it sank into the ground, he stamped one foot.

The ground in front of Yasam erupted in a slanted column that smashed the young Sentinel in the chest so hard his body wrapped around it and his breath whooshed out. He catapulted away, turning a slow somersault as he flew limply through the air.

Just before he slammed headfirst into the cobbled street at the foot of the stairs leading into the Sentinel Tower, the air under him coalesced into a web of rainbow strands that gently caught him and set him down.

Nerys retreated from Leander, his fear renewed. He might have been able to duplicate that feat, but he was a fully trained Sentinel. Leander was nothing but a Pallian Stalwart, wasn't he?

The gathered Sentinels shouted their outrage, and many in the group moved to join Nerys in confronting Leander. The other Kedo member, a portly, middle-aged man named Viti stepped between Nerys and Leander, who resumed his advance.

Without a word, Viti clapped his hands together. A concentrated whirlwind exploded from his extended fingers and drove toward Leander. Nerys flinched to see the powerful spell unleashed so close and against a single person. They'd discussed ways to imbue artifacts with Viti's exceptional wind powers, but had not dared trust anyone with such destructive power yet.

He expected to see Leander's body snap under the onslaught. At the least, they'd get to watch the foolish Stalwart tumble over the distant Hallvarr Palace.

What he saw terrified him.

The wind tore into Leander, but he stood in the center of the whirlwind, unaffected. The silver hairs on his head and beard did not so much as shift with the wind.

Viti grunted and redoubled his efforts. The whirlwind roared with hunger to destroy. Leander stood calmly in the raging storm while tendrils of wind tore off of the central cyclone and whipped down nearby streets. Gusts tore hats off fleeing pedestrians and even overturned a cart filled with fruit. People shouted with fear and the courtyard emptied.

A company of soldiers advanced and Nerys recognized the captain he'd sent against Leander. He snarled with frustration. Things were getting out of control. They needed to bring this Stalwart to heel before serious damage could be done.

Viti lowered his hands and the whirlwind dissipated. He shared a surprised glance with Nerys and took a fearful step back. Nerys looked around, and the sight of a score of Sentinels moving to join them bolstered his confidence.

Leander spoke. "My turn."

He snapped his fingers and a deadly war hammer appeared in his fist. He took a single step forward and *threw* the hammer. His arm moved so fast, Nerys barely registered the movement before the hammer smashed Viti off his feet.

Viti screamed on the ground. Blood already soaked the front of his robes, and his shoulder and part of his chest looked completely caved in.

Sentinels dropped to the ground beside Viti and began administering healing to him. Others moved to stand beside Nerys, hands raised in unison as they formed a shimmering wall between the group and Leander.

"Stand down," Leander said. He raised his hand, and his hammer appeared there again. He pointed at Viti. "So shall be done to any who stand in the way of Justice today. Now give me the man, Nerys."

"Be gone," Nerys said, "Or we'll no longer show any restraint. Leave, or you will die here today." Around him, the other Sentinels shouted similar feelings, or taunted Leander to step forward again.

A new voice shouted above the others. The Kestrel Sentinel Durgesh moved to the front of the group. "You've finally lost your mind, haven't you?"

"Do not trifle with me today," Leander said.

Durgesh turned to the other Sentinels. "I serve the emperor on the ruling council. This man's condition has been discussed there in depth. His paranoid ravings against the Sentinels are growing wilder by the day. He's clearly slipped over the edge into senility."

"You intend to stand against me in this, then?" Leander demanded.

"Of course. It's painful to see a man once trusted fall so low." He turned to the other Sentinels and, with a sweeping gesture of one hand added, "We should pity him, my friends."

Leander slowly lowered his hammer. "So be it."

Durgesh grinned. "The old fool is finally coming to his senses." He muttered to himself, "He won't escape consequences again."

Nerys turned to help restore Viti, once again smiling. Everything was working out for the best.

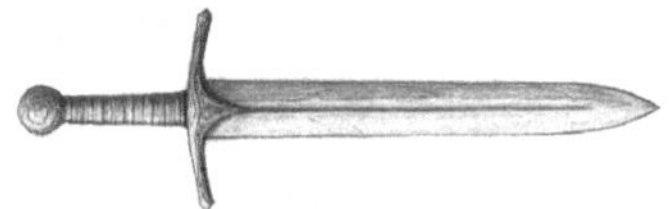

The soldiers who had chased Leander came to a halt close to him and the captain approached the old Stalwart. "Shall I arrest that man now then?"

"No," Leander said. He placed a glowing hand on Basak's wounded shoulder and closed his eyes in concentration. The burly Stalwart sighed with relief as healing magic pushed the pain away and restored broken flesh.

When Leander finished, he turned to the captain. "There is one service I need from you."

"Name it."

"Clear this area and seal it off."

The captain glanced around. "Are there more traitors?"

"There are. We will deal with them. It will get messy. I don't want any innocent bystanders accidentally injured."

"I'll see to it at once." The captain began barking orders.

Basak rolled his shoulder experimentally and grimaced at lingering pain. "What are we to do, my Styra?"

"Summon the brethren. Full battle orders."

"You mean to take the man Nerys, then?"

Leander turned to look at the Sentinels still gathered, still throwing taunts his way. "No, my friend, not just Nerys. Today we cleanse the inner vessel."

72

Never Underestimate Age And Craftiness

Sentinel Nerys was just beginning to help the still-groggy Viti to his feet when Sentinel Durgesh pushed into the center of the group of Sentinels who had all begun returning to the Tower.

"Ware! The Pallians intend to attack."

The Stalwart Leander stood alone, fifty yards away, feet planted, hands hanging loose at his side, his legendary hammer planted between his feet. His head was tilted back, as if he stared at the clouds above the Tower.

Somehow his look of calm unconcern unsettled Nerys more than his angry bluster from earlier. He looked completely at peace.

He looked like he'd made a decision and already accepted the consequences. The thought chilled Nerys despite standing surrounded by other Sentinels. He chided himself for being a fool. Not even Leander could stand against so many of them.

One of the Sentinels said, "I'll take care of him once and for all."

Durgesh snapped, "No. Do nothing."

He drew the others in closer. "Summon the other Sentinels. We have a few minutes to prepare a proper response. We'll teach these arrogant fools what it means to fear Sentinels again."

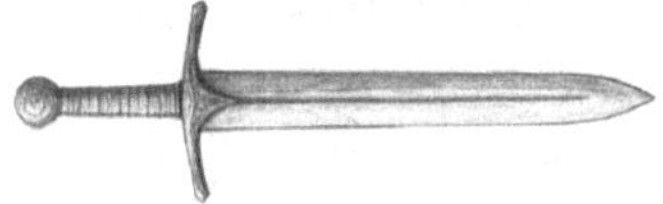

The door to the study banged open and a soldier burst in.

"Master Harafin, the emperor summons you at once."

"What developments?"

"Stalwarts are moving to attack the Sentinel Tower!"

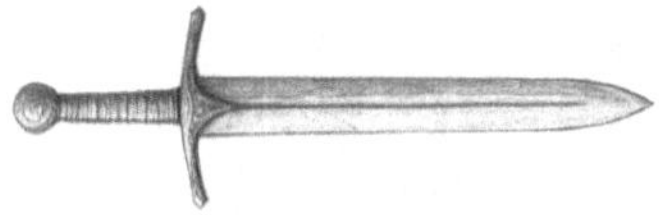

Three score Pallian Stalwarts ran in perfect step together through the streets of the inner city. They ran lightly, eagerly, despite their heavy chainmail coats, helmets, and hammers. The weight didn't matter. Their Styrskena summoned them to battle. Today Justice would be served.

Commoners and nobles alike scurried out of their path, and rumors spread like wildfire throughout the inner city. Already talk of conflict between the Stalwarts and the Sentinels had spread throughout the palaces and out into the lower city. The imperial guard had cordoned off a wide area around the Sentinel Tower, only reinforcing the rumors.

Leander turned from the Sentinel Tower as his brethren approached. He ignored the two dozen angry Sentinels gathered around the Tower. Their numbers had grown in the last few minutes, and he knew many more Sentinels watched from windows or lurked in the tower on the main floor, undecided.

They would decide soon. Today, finally, everyone's allegiance would be proven. For the first time in days, Leander felt at peace. No longer would he tiptoe around the enemy. Today everyone faced the same choice. It should be an easy one to make.

For those who struggled to decide where their allegiance lay, he hoped to provide ample encouragement to choose wisely. Mercy was always available for those who mended their ways. For those who chose to side with the enemies of the empire and come out in open rebellion, the answer was also simple.

Justice would claim them.

The Stalwarts spread out as they slowed to a halt, forming two even rows. Leander raised a hand in blessing to them. "Today we exercise the tenets of our faith."

All raised hammers together and chanted, "Mercy. Justice. Light."

Behind the Stalwarts, two hundred imperial guard had responded to the captain's call for reinforcements. They blocked the streets nearby and held inquisitive by-standers at bay.

They did nothing to block other Stalwarts. A dozen Wheel Stalwarts had gathered like vultures around a fresh kill at the first rumors of conflict. Dressed in fine silks of the latest fashions, they were easily identifiable by the images of Akillik's Wheel affixed to their backs. They moved through the crowd, loudly taking bets and giving odds.

Leander and his Stalwarts were given long odds. He toyed with the idea of placing a bet of his own. That would rattle them. It wasn't worth it. Better to stay far from the fickle god and his fickle, often deceitful Stalwarts.

Two Gurcek Stalwarts approached. As always, they walked with a stately, dignified pace, although Leander wondered if they had run through the Underground Palace to get here so fast.

They wore the customary long, black robes of Salawin's Justices, with heavy swords on their backs. Those swords, replicas of Salawin's Sword of Justice, were well used in executing the judgments the Gurcek Stalwarts issued from the courts.

Leander maintained a neutral expression as the Gurcek Stalwarts drew near. He too served Justice, but Salawin's Stalwarts left no room for Mercy in their rulings and often bordered on the cruel with decisions they handed down.

"Stalwart Leander, you dare not call upon Justice within the realm of our purvey," the senior Gurcek Stalwart stated gravely.

"You hold no sway here. Justice will be done. Do not interfere."

"You break our laws by this insurrection," the second justice said. "You will fall under the shadow of the Sword if you continue this reckless course."

"Then draw your sword and we'll see whose justice prevails today," Leander snapped. When neither of them reached for their swords, he said, "Stand aside."

"Very well," the first said. "Justice always prevails. We see and we remember."

"Do so. I act."

He spun from them and reached for the calm he had felt while he waited for his brethren. He refused to accept their words. He too served Justice. They were blind to the full facts as he understood them.

"Basak, show mercy on all you can."

"We will."

"Remove any who resist."

Leander took a step forward and the gathered Sentinels immediately moved into a long line facing him, fifty yards away. Durgesh seemed to be leading the group, and Leander hoped the man would insist on trying to stop him. Nerys stood with the group and that was surprising. The profiteering Sentinel was a coward. He must expect some gain through standing so boldly.

Good. It would make it easier to take him.

He was surprised to see Felix standing with the group. He and Felix may have disagreed on how to respond to the threat, but he genuinely respected the obese Sentinel and didn't wish to fight him.

Leander called out in a loud voice. "Fair warning. We will cull from your midst traitors wanted by the emperor. Any who resist will be subdued. Do not make this harder on yourselves than it has to be."

Sentinel Durgesh shouted, "Cross the shield barrier, and we'll consider you enemies. No quarter will be given."

Leander reached for his gift. It roared into him as if eager for release after so long. He fought to control it, to rein it in. It struggled against his control like a restless stallion too long left to run wild in open pasture.

He focused some of the power on his eyes and the shield barrier came into view like a shimmering translucent silver wall ringing the tower. The layered shields of the matrix that overlay the entire inner city shimmered all around, but Leander focused on the barrier shield around the Tower. This shield stood apart, separate.

That would prove its weakness.

The subtle changes he had made to the barrier while he waited for his brethren remained in place and apparently undetected. The Sentinels relied heavily on the shield but paid it insufficient mind.

He stepped forward until he stood just outside the shield.

Sentinel Felix moved to the front ranks of the waiting Sentinels. "Leander, do not do this. You will bring great suffering upon those who follow you."

"Surrender the traitors hiding among you, and the conflict can be avoided," Leander shouted back.

To either side of him, the Pallians stood at attention. A few shifted a bit, but that was the only sign of nervousness. Their loyalty and confidence in him was inspiring. Sentinel powers could not directly strike them through the shield of their Faith, and yet they were not immune to harm.

The Sentinels understood this. They'd had several minutes to prepare their assault. Without Sentinel powers to protect them, the Stalwarts would stand little chance in a direct, fair conflict.

Fighting fair was not a tenet of Leander's fait.

"We cannot surrender one of our own under threat of duress," Felix called. "Stand down and we will negotiate."

"Negotiations are over. Make your choice and accept the consequences."

"Very well," Felix said. He looked genuinely saddened by what was to come.

Sentinel Durgesh shouted, "We've made our choice, you crazy old fool." To the gathered Sentinels he shouted, "Now!"

All of the gathered Sentinels except for Felix raised hands in unison. Even at such a distance, Leander felt the Actinic vibration as they drew upon their powers and unleashed their carefully prepared assault.

"Stand fast and do not move," Leander called to his Stalwarts.

Two hundred thick cobblestones erupted from the ground in an explosion of earth and shot through the air at the Pallians. The volley of flying stone could have smashed the mighty gates of the inner city wall.

Leander and his brethren stood fast.

The barrage of rocks slammed into the invisible shield barrier. It flickered into view like a wall of rainbow light. Many distant onlookers exclaimed at the beautiful sight.

The stones did not pass through. Instead they bounced back the other way with twice their previous force.

Leander didn't smile to see the success of his ingenious alteration of the shields. He did not rejoice in administering pain.

Some of the Sentinels reacted quickly enough and raised personal shield barriers that cobblestones ricocheted off of.

Most did not.

Sentinels screamed as stones smashed into them like ballista bolts, shattering bones and flinging them from their feet. Their ranks disintegrated into chaos as they collapsed, bloodied and broken. As screams echoed across the open ground around the tower, bystanders gasped, and Wheel Stalwarts quickly revised odds and called out new bets.

More Sentinels boiled out of the tower, drawn by the sight of fallen friends. Leander wasn't surprised. Many of them probably assumed the Stalwarts would be scattered at the first barrage and didn't feel it necessary to participate.

Now they faced their first choice.

Leander shouted above the din. "Choose a different path so Mercy can apply to you."

Several Sentinels howled with rage, and three of them forgot the Stalwart shields of Faith and unleashed their powers in a fit of anger. Lightning raked across the courtyard toward the Stalwart lines while magical flames roared out to consume them.

Nothing crossed the line of the altered shield barrier.

Lightning bounced back, doubled in intensity and ripped into the Sentinel ranks. Fire boiled through their ranks, engulfing the entire company.

More screams, and a few shouted curses floated out of the inferno. The flames winked out quickly, but several Sentinels looked badly burned. Others had been struck from their feet by the lightning, and at least one of those unlucky ones had taken fatal wounds. The body lay amid the wounded, little more than a smoking husk.

"You bring this destruction upon yourselves," Leander proclaimed. "Do not choose to continue down this path."

"Shut up!" Sentinel Durgesh shouted. He called out to the others, "He's altered the shield barrier. Come on! We have to cross the barrier to kill them."

His face mottled with rage, the young Sentinel led a disorganized charge of furious Sentinels.

"So be it," Leander said. "My children, subdue them. Try not to kill too many."

As the charging Sentinels approached, Leander reminded himself not to kill Durgesh. The young man might be an arrogant fool, but that didn't merit death. Usually.

Leander raised his hammer and it burst into blue fire. All the Pallians lifted hammers to the ready and prepared to meet the onrushing Sentinels. Now the tables were turned. At close combat, the Sentinels would learn to fear the Stalwarts.

"Today we cleanse the inner vessel!" Leander shouted.

They charged.

73

Nothing To Lose

Ceren gratefully accepted a cup of fruit wine from Sitara as she sat with Keisara Fideima in the uppermost room of her tower. The presence of the keisara and her servant, surrounded by finery, soothed Ceren's frayed nerves. In this room, she felt a sense of solid dependability. No matter how bad things got, evil could not penetrate here.

She mentally checked her posture and facial expression, a habit long perfected in her father's court in Agoraeun. Today she needed that skill to ensure she maintained an expression of calm.

When she had returned to her rooms in the Freyarr Palace, she'd allowed herself a few minutes to weep, to shriek, and to throw things around the room. Her memories of events were cloudy, but clear enough for her to know what she had done.

The worst part about it, the thing that terrified her to the very core, was how much she had enjoyed some of it.

"Ceren, I'm so glad you came," Keisara Fideima said. "What can you tell me of events in the city?"

Ceren updated her on efforts to quell the riots and restore order. She also spoke of Tanathos's escape and the lack of success in tracking him down.

Keisara Fideima walked to one of the huge windows that looked out over the city, rubbing at her arms as if chilled. "To think such an evil man is still at large, maybe even still in the city."

"I do have one piece of good news."

"That would please me greatly."

Ceren leaned forward, and the keisara seated herself in an overstuffed chair next to Ceren.

"We captured one of the conspirators."

"Who?"

"I can't say his name, but he was hidden right here in one of the palaces, disguised as a servant to one of the ambassadors."

"No!" Keisara Fideima breathed excitedly. "To think he could."

"Oh, yes. We're convinced the young man played a key role in the conspiracy. The Sentinels are going to interrogate him later today." She leaned closer. "They expect he'll reveal names of other conspirators. This could be the beginning of the end for all of them."

"How did you take him?"

"Kevlin figured it out."

The keisara leaned back in her chair and said thoughtfully, "I must meet this man Kevlin. He sounds like a rare fellow. Do you know him well?"

Ceren felt her cheeks flush. "Yes, Your Majesty. I know him quite well."

Sitara listened to the conversation with growing panic. It had to be Remiel Lady Ceren was talking about. If he was indeed taken, then her life was forfeit. He would reveal her and Masego, unless their master's curse destroyed him first.

Worse, Lady Ceren appeared totally normal. Despite careful observation, she detected no traces of her efforts to tamper with Ceren's mind. It was as if everything had been wiped clean.

She was tempted to explore Ceren's mind again. Omolara was not in attendance, so there was little danger of being discovered. A foreboding of danger warned her against it. She'd survived this long only by obeying that sometimes-subtle instinct. No, she would not dare Lady Ceren's mind again.

What to do, though? Everything was falling apart. Masego's power enslaved her and prevented her from fleeing or turning against him. What would happen once they broke Remiel's mind?

Harafin would come for her.

That thought terrified her so deeply, she nearly forgot her place and sank into a chair. Only with a focused effort did she maintain her silent place near one of the large windows. The two ladies were so engrossed in their conversation, she might have been able to sit without either of them noticing, but she couldn't take the chance.

She had to act. Her life was in danger, but so too was Remiel's. Their fragile new understanding made her worry for him perhaps more than he deserved. She needed to believe they could escape the life of slavery they'd both fallen into.

Having learned of Bajaran's infidelity had left her feeling shaken and unsure, where before her love for him had been her one sure rock. Who could she trust? Who could she turn to now that the world was turning against her?

If only Ceren's mission had been successful. Winning Kevlin to her side would have been the key to changing everything, but had she even made the attempt? Could Kevlin still be swayed?

Sitara tried to consider the situation from every angle, tried to drain the emotion from her thoughts, with only partial success. No matter how she viewed it, she came to the same conclusion.

She had to free Remiel, or all was lost.

Sitara dismissed immediately the thought of trying to do it herself. From what Lady Ceren was saying, security was incredibly tight. Only a trusted person, a person with absolute authority could command the release of Remiel.

Who had such authority?

The answer was so obvious it took her another minute to figure it out. She turned her attention on the two chatting women. She couldn't touch Lady Ceren's mind. The more she thought of it, the more she was convinced someone had discovered her tampering and broken the spell. Worse, they might have embedded some kind of mind trap against the possibility of her trying again. Masego had warned her that such things were possible.

No, Lady Ceren couldn't help.

Keisara Fideima could.

Sitara breathed slow and deep, calming her mind. She'd gently influenced the keisara in the past through impressions and dreams. That disastrous experiment had nearly resulted in her capture. If she did this now, she'd have to run with Remiel. The truth would be revealed all too soon, and then Harafin would come. She shuddered to think of the dreadful Sentinel chasing her down.

She spent the long minutes while the ladies chatted considering her plan and trying to work out the details. She needed to free Remiel, and she needed to position Kevlin in such a way that he would be forced to help, whether or not he decided to join her revolution.

If she hesitated, death lay at the door. Again, Harafin would appear, even sooner, to take her away.

With her mind made up, Sitara opened herself to the power of darkness. It clawed into her soul eagerly and filled her with its filthy power. She drank it in. The time for hesitation was far past.

She re-filled the ladies' glasses. When Lady Ceren paused to drink, she focused her power as her master had taught her, and struck at the keisara's mind.

74

THE LINE BETWEEN PRINCIPLE AND FOLLY

"Stand down!"

Harafin's voice boomed so loud it cracked windows and lifted dust from the ground. The Sentinel charge faltered and the Stalwarts slowed to a halt.

His intervention would surely save many Sentinel's lives, but Leander wondered if his old friend would ever allow the inner vessel to be purged. A few more seconds, and justice could have been served on many.

Harafin galloped across the courtyard on an Einarri stallion and drove the animal between the two groups. He took in the scene of the battlefield with one glance and his entire body glowed with power.

He leaped off the still-moving horse and his overwhelming voice boomed again across the courtyard. "This insanity stops now, or by the seven accidental gods, I'll strike you all down where you stand!"

The Sentinels retreated from his towering fury and Harafin ordered, "See to the fallen."

Then he turned to Leander. For a moment the two old friends met each other's gaze. Leander felt the heavy weight of Harafin's anger and disappointment. He snuffed out his own raging powers, and for the first time he wondered if he'd gone too far.

Harafin turned away and strode to the invisible shield barrier. He placed a hand on it, and the entire shield flared and then disappeared.

Several Sentinels gasped and murmured among themselves.

Harafin barked, "Felix, get over here."

While he waited for Felix, Harafin turned back to Leander. "You betrayed my trust."

The simple accusation seared Leander to the core. He had feared this would happen when he had altered the shield, but he'd hoped Harafin would understand. He'd had no other choice. He couldn't allow the Sentinels to attack without defending his children.

"I acted in good faith."

"You acted in anger. Be careful, my friend. You are regressing."

"Then offer me a viable alternative," Leander said, not concealing his frustration.

When Felix approached, Harafin said, "I'll replace the shield barrier when there's time. Until then, assemble some of the Sentinels to erect temporary barriers. All classes are to be canceled."

"I will see it done."

"You could have stopped this," Harafin added.

"I didn't believe it would escalate to this point," Felix said. He looked at Leander. "Now perhaps we can use our heads and work together instead of fighting each other."

"All you had to do was surrender Nerys."

"No," Felix snapped. For the first time he looked angry. "Don't you see? You approached this as if guilt was proven, as if everyone is a suspect."

"Yes, I do."

"Then you bear full responsibility," Felix said.

"I accept what I did."

"You don't see the folly of it," Felix said. He threw his flabby arms out wide. "All you had to do was send your concerns through the proper channels and this could have all been worked out without bloodshed."

"No, my old friend. You really don't understand. Today we all faced a choice, a chance to show our allegiance."

"You chose chaos and conflict," Felix said."I chose loyalty to Justice and Truth."

"You both chose poorly," Harafin said. "Enough. Leander, you will join me before the ruling council to explain this insanity."

He turned and shouted, "Sentinels Durgesh and Nerys. Come here at once."

The two approached slowly. Nerys looked nervous while Durgesh glared at Leander as if he wanted to resume hostilities right there. Some fools never learn.

"Follow me," Harafin said.

It frustrated Leander that they all fell into line after Harafin where they had fought him, treating him like the criminal. "Basak," he ordered. "Stand the brethren down but do not leave the area. You may be needed."

"Shall we help with the wounded?"

Leander glanced at the bloody Sentinels being tended by their gifted brethren and shook his head sadly. "I fear we would do more harm than good. They see us as enemies. Wait until they request aid."

"I don't believe they will."

"Nor do I."

75

AN UNEXPECTED USE OF AUTHORITY

Ceren drank gratefully. The mild fruit wine warmed her belly, but its chill liquid cooled the fires in her cheeks where Indira's blows still burned.

Had she really tried to kill Indira? Had she really . . .? Yes, she had. She'd done all of it. She regretted some of it.

She forced herself to focus. Just then the keisara moaned and rubbed at one temple. She almost dropped her wine, and Ceren caught the glass from her trembling fingers.

"Are you all right?"

"I am . . . fine," Keisara Fideima said weakly. She closed her eyes and took a deep breath. Then she sat up and said in a stronger voice, "Just a sudden headache."

"You startled me."

"I'm all right." The Keisara looked down at her hands. "Lady Ceren, I must confess I feel useless to my husband in this time of trial."

"You mustn't feel that way."

"But I do. All of you are working so hard, placing yourselves in danger, sacrificing for the empire while I sit here and watch from my window."

"You do so much more than that."

"Do I?" The keisara's voice became angry, although she did not look up. "No, I will do more."

"What are you thinking of doing?" The keisara's abrupt shift surprised Ceren. The keisara couldn't risk descending to the streets during the chaos. That would just make matters worse.

Could she stop her?

"I will interrogate this man Remiel myself."

Ceren wasn't sure how to respond for a few seconds. That was the last thing she had expected the keisara to say.

"Your majesty, how do you know his name?"

Keisara Fideima paused before saying, "You're not the only source of intelligence at my disposal, Lady Ceren."

"But you seemed so surprised when I told you about his capture."

Another pause. "I learned of Remiel from another source, but didn't make the connection until just now. I believe I can shed important light on this investigation and speed up the process."

"How?"

"Think of it," Keisara Fideima said excitedly, "We could capture the entire group of conspirators before nightfall." She clutched Ceren's hands, but still didn't look up to meet Ceren's gaze. That odd behavior troubled Ceren. Something about it alarmed her deeply, but she couldn't quite pinpoint why.

"What do you know?" Ceren asked.

Keisara Fideima laughed. "Oh, Ceren. Not yet. I want it to be a surprise."

"If you have information, let me bring it to the ruling council."

"No. This will be my victory, not theirs. Summon the man Remiel. Bring him to me and I will reveal the secret."

"He's under heavy guard. I suppose we can bring him safely here."

"No. I will not have Sentinels in my apartments. This will be my victory and mine alone. Not theirs."

"But the man is very dangerous."

"Is he gifted?"

"No, but . . ."

"Have the man Kevlin bring him to me."

"Kevlin?"

"Of course. You said yourself he's been instrumental in our victories since the beginning of troubles weeks ago. Who better to guard this ungifted traitor?"

"I'm not sure . . . " Ceren began.

"Enough," the keisara snapped. She rose and walked to the window. "My intention is fixed. Bring the traitor to me. The man Kevlin will accompany him alone. Once I complete my interrogation, I will reveal the truth to you first."

Despite the bizarre turn of the conversation, Ceren felt a thrill of excitement. If the keisara really did have the ability to crack this case, Ceren would learn the truth first. She'd share in the victory. After everything that had gone wrong, the temptation to be a part of something so wonderful overwhelmed her worries.

"I will see it done, your majesty."

76

Infighting

Kevlin stood in the packed conference room in the Northern Kingdoms Admin Palace where the ruling council still held audience. He wished his brothers hadn't left. Gabral stood not far away, among a knot of high-level military officials.

Many other nobles, and even several Stalwarts from four orders had all pressed into the room in the past few minutes. Everyone was eager to hear firsthand about the recent conflict in front of the Sentinel Tower. One of the Stalwarts, a grim-faced Gurcek Justice, spoke quietly with the emperor for several minutes.

The excited buzz of conversation fell to muted whispers as the double doors opened and Harafin strode into the room. Leander flanked him on the left, with the Sentinel Durgesh on the right. Durgesh looked angry and spent more time glaring at Leander than watching where he walked.

For Leander's part, he looked angry but controlled. Leander's anger ran deep, but he had almost a century's practice controlling it. Kevlin hoped the rumors he'd heard about what had just transpired outside the Sentinel Tower were wrong and that Leander hadn't started slipping.

Sentinel Ah'Shan entered behind the trio, gripping the arm of a reluctant Sentinel Nerys. As the group approached the horse-shoe shaped council tables, Emperor Tegnazian slammed his open palm down on the mahogany table.

"By Gurcek's mighty sword of justice, I demand an explanation. Pitched battle in the inner city? Stalwarts and Sentinels murdering each other?" He pointed at Leander and Durgesh. "Word of your fighting is already spread into the city and threatens to destabilize the fragile peace we barely finished restoring!"

Kevlin had to admit, the emperor knew how to capitalize on moments like this. He sat tall, his eyes flashing with displeasure, his voice ringing through the room.

Leander looked surprised by the emperor's anger. Sentinel Durgesh lowered his head and assumed a humble, penitent posture. The fact that he continued to cast angry glares at Leander diluted the performance.

Leander asked, "What would you have me do, your excellency?" He pointed at Nerys, who now stood off to one side. "Would you rather I allow this man to flee Justice and your command that he answer for his lies?"

"I never commanded you to assault the Sentinel Tower."

"They interfered with the capture of the man Nerys, whose flight confirms his traitorous intent."

"I never!" Nerys protested in a display of great outrage. Had he no shame? He'd sold the tools that had allowed Tanathos to escape.

"It's your fault," Sentinel Durgesh said to Leander. "You think we're just going to sit back and watch you beat up a Sentinel at the very doorstep of our tower?"

"If that man is a traitor, I expect you to do exactly that."

"Then you're a fool."

"You and those Sentinels who chose solidarity with a criminal over loyalty to Justice got exactly what you deserved."

"I will see you dead for what you did!" Durgesh shouted. He looked prepared to resume the fight right there in the council chamber.

Leander flexed his right hand. "You really think that's wise, boy?"

"Stand down," Harafin snapped. He stood close behind Leander and Durgesh, and the weight of his glare broke through Durgesh's anger.

Sentinel Ah'Shan, who had drawn close to Nerys said, "Durgesh, remember your place."

"He started it," Durgesh said sullenly.

"Enough," the emperor commanded. "You both acted rashly, and lives we cannot afford to lose were sacrificed as a result. I will not have you fighting in this council chamber. You will both remember yourselves or by the gods I will strip you of place and powers."

Durgesh paled before the emperor's anger and turned away from Leander.

"May I remind you why we're here?" Leander asked. "The Sentinel Nerys must confess his lies and reveal the identity of the murderer who freed Tanathos."

"Don't tell me what business requires my focus," the emperor snapped. "I find your lack of remorse for your actions greatly disturbing. It reflects poorly upon your station as leader of the Pallians."

"I regret none of my actions. It's past time we cleanse the inner vessel, beginning with the inner city."

"Is that how you justify the deaths of seven Sentinels?" Ah'Shan demanded, glaring. He acted as if he'd been at the tower.

"Their deaths are the result of choices they made. You were master of several of them. I suggest you look to your teachings and instill a greater respect for Justice."

That's why he was so angry. Some of the dead Sentinels were his acolytes.

It was Durgesh who responded, though. "You lie! You incited conflict."

"I demanded Justice, no more."

Emperor Tegnazian pounded his gavel and waved them all to silence. "Master Leander, your reckless abandonment of the rule of law threatens the stability of this city. I demand an apology from you to the Sentinels, or I will remove you from your place."

Leander slowly shook his head. "I'm afraid you fail to see the truth of these events, Your Excellency. It is my dedication to Justice that demanded action."

"I'll make up my own mind," Emperor Tegnazian snarled. "You would do well to remember whose authority rules here."

Leander said, "Never before has an emperor meddled with our order."

"Never before have Stalwarts and Sentinels fought pitched battles in this city! Can you really fail to see your responsibility?"

Leander's calm expression cracked. "I stand by my actions. At least I acted. I chose not to sit in committee debating action, wasting precious time."

"Action without careful planning is folly. I thought even you saw that after the fiasco last night."

"What I see are decisions prompted by fear and hesitation. Wars are not won that way."

"We are not yet at war."

Leander shook his head, once more in control of his emotions. "That is exactly why you will fail. Our enemies are at war. They understand the stakes. You do not."

"That is enough, sir."

"No, Your Excellency. It is just the beginning."

Kevlin wanted to shout to Leander to back down. He couldn't win this argument, not now, not with so many witnesses gathered. Emperor Tegnazian couldn't back down, not while presiding in council.

As Kevlin feared, the emperor stood and declared, "I am the highest law here! You leave me no choice but to levy judgment against you."

Behind the emperor, the Gurcek Stalwart smiled smugly at Leander and fingered the hilt of his great sword.

Silence fell over the crowd as Leander raised his hands high. His voice rang through Kevlin's ears like drums of doom.

"I serve a higher authority than you, Excellency. I reject your authority."

"Don't do this," Harafin said. He grabbed Leander's shoulder, but the Stalwart shook him off, his face determined.

Leander cried, "We face a time of choices. I choose loyalty to Justice over loyalty to a fallen emperor."

Then he spun on his heel and marched from the council chamber.

Emperor Tegnazian watched him go, his mouth moving wordlessly. Several seconds of complete silence reigned after Leander's shocking choice. Then half a hundred excited conversations erupted together.

Emperor Tegnazian pounded the gavel on the desk so hard the handle snapped. He shouted after Leander while the doors were closing behind the old Stalwart. "You are hereby removed from office and banished from this city! Do you hear me? Banished!"

77

HEDGING BETS

Kevlin stood in the midst of the chaotic crowd, chilled by the unexpected turn. Why had Leander pushed so hard? Why couldn't he just hold the course?

How could the emperor do this? Leander was one of the most respected defenders of the empire alive. The last thing they needed now, at the brink of open warfare with the Grakonians, was to fracture and fight among themselves. If Tanathos accomplished nothing else by his assaults here in Tamera, he'd already done much to weaken the empire.

A hand touched his arm and he turned to find Ceren standing close beside him. Startled, he retreated, prepared to run. Only the fact that she met his gaze, her emerald eyes unclouded by darkness, helped him stand fast.

Ceren had changed into a tasteful blue dress. Her long, auburn hair fell about her shoulders in loose waves, and her face looked clean, untroubled by recent events. What a change from the last outfit she'd worn. He hated what had happened to her, but he doubted he'd ever forget either.

Ceren dropped her eyes, and a gentle blush rose in her cheeks. It looked like he wasn't the only one with an active memory.

Kevlin glanced around for Indira. She hadn't returned to the council chamber with him, but the last thing he wanted was for her to see him speaking with Ceren. Even though Ceren had been forced to do what she did, the wounds were still far too fresh to risk alienating Indira more. Besides, he didn't want that many broken bones to deal with.

"What are you doing here?" Kevlin asked. "I thought you were meeting with the keisara?"

"I was."

She took a step forward. Kevlin backed away again and bumped into Gabral.

"Watch your step, mercenary."

Ceren drew close to both of them, and Gabral gave her a short bow. She ignored him. "Kevlin, I need your help. We have a serious problem."

"I know."

"Really?"

"Everyone knows."

"They do?"

Kevlin frowned at her and swept an arm at the chaotic room. "We all heard what just happened. Leander's stripped of title and banished. I'd say we have big problems."

Ceren gasped. "What?"

"Where have you been?"

"I just barely arrived."

"Now is not a good time."

Ceren grabbed his arm. "Listen to me. The keisara just ordered us to fetch Remiel from the prison. She wants you to deliver him to her quarters for questioning."

"She did what?" Kevlin drew Ceren out a side door, with Gabral in tow.

"Why would she do that?" Kevlin asked.

"She claims that she has more information, information to help force Remiel to confess."

"Excellent," Gabral said. "I'll inform the emperor at once."

"No." Ceren grabbed the sleeve of Gabral's coat and pulled him back. "The keisara forbids it."

"Why would she do that?"

"That's the problem. She said she feels useless, that she wants to participate in breaking this conspiracy. She insists that we do this at once, and that no one interfere. She means to interrogate Remiel personally."

"We must fetch him," Gabral said.

Kevlin asked, "Are you insane? Ah'Shan hasn't interrogated him yet. He's locked in the dungeon under the heaviest possible guard. No one's getting him out of there."

Gabral gave Kevlin a disgusted look. "I forget sometimes how lacking your education is. When the keisara issues an order, it must be obeyed."

"But this is madness."

Gabral gestured back at the council room where the emperor was calling for order. "Leander forgot that and rebelled against the emperor. Look what happened to him. We must obey."

"We should at least inform Harafin."

"Harafin is busy," Gabral said.

Indeed, Harafin's voice rose above the clamor, calling for Nerys to explain his recent actions. Gabral was right. They couldn't interrupt without drawing everyone's attention. They would be forced to reveal their purposes before the entire council.

Would that be so wrong? Kevlin didn't know much about high nobility, but this summons ran counter to all his instincts.

Leander's explosive encounter with the emperor was still too fresh in his memory. He couldn't risk angering the keisara the way Leander had just enraged the emperor.

"All right," he said finally. "What exactly do we need to do?"

"Simple," Gabral said. "On the keisara's authority, we'll remove Remiel and escort him to the Keisara's Tower."

"She requires Kevlin to bring him alone," Ceren reminded them.

"Only because she didn't realize I was available. I'll accompany Kevlin and ensure the keisara's safety.

Kevlin chose not to argue. As much as he disliked Gabral, in this case he welcomed the help. Remiel may not be Actinopathic, but he'd proven himself an extremely dangerous man.

They descended to the Underground Palace. As they walked toward the long stair that led down to the dungeon level, Kevlin caught sight of a familiar slender form with bouncy brown hair.

"Marjani, wait."

"Hello, Sir Kevlin. What can I do for you?"

Kevlin drew Marjani aside. Gabral frowned at the delay so he gestured them on. "I'll catch up in a minute."

After they passed out of ear shot, Kevlin said, "Marjani, I need you to hunt down my brothers."

Marjani smiled and blushed. "I'd be happy to."

"Tell them to meet me at the Keisara's Tower. I may need their help.

Marjani raised an eyebrow. "A little cryptic, don't you think?"

"By necessity. Tell them it involves Remiel."

"I will."

"Hurry."

Knowing his brothers would come helped ease some of his worry. Marjani moved off with a purposeful stride and Kevlin jogged after Gabral and Ceren. He kept his hands clenched tight to quell a growing tremor in his fingers. He had plenty of time to deal with this and find some time with Harafin before the Trembling Madness became a real concern.

By the Lady, I hope we're not making a mistake.

78

TWISTED PRIORITIES

Harafin stood in the center of the council chamber and raised his hands for attention, reiterating the emperor's calls for order. He forced calm on his expression and his mind. He could not allow his personal emotions to interfere with these procedures. He wasn't sure he could salvage the mess Leander had made of things, but with a little time he was sure he could help.

"May I draw our attention back to the main reason we convened this meeting?" Harafin motioned for Nerys to approach. "There are serious accusations of lying and aiding the perpetrators of heinous crimes that must be answered."

Emperor Tegnazian gestured for him to proceed.

"Sentinel Nerys, are you prepared to answer truthfully?"

Nerys nodded, looking nervous, but determined as he faced the emperor. "May I point out, Your Excellency that recent events are being painted in the most negative light."

He held up his hands in a gesture of peace. "Let me be among the first to add my condolences to the families and friends of the slain. Terrible deeds were done yesterday and, as we all just witnessed, they have driven some to commit vicious crimes of hate."

"However, I feel obliged to point out that we must not apply the same condemnation so rightfully deserved against the perpetrators of those acts also to the tools they used. Tools are by their very nature neutral. Although certain artifacts were utilized to commit crime, might we still recognize and applaud the spectacular effectiveness of those artifacts?"

"You wish to applaud the murder of three men?" Ah'Shan asked.

"Of course not," Nerys said quickly. He glanced around the room at the angry stares on all sides and sighed. "Murder is a terrible thing. All I wish to point out is that the artifacts should not be condemned in the same breath as the murderer."

His eyes lit up with excitement. "Can't you see, they worked! Everything worked better than we could have imagined."

Harafin felt a powerful urge to beat the idiot into the ground. Did he really dare attempt to turn these proceedings into a marketing pitch?

Emperor Tegnazian scowled at Nerys. "This is not the time nor the place to trump the excellence of your wares, Sentinel. You shame yourself."

Nerys bowed low. "I am deeply sorry, Your Excellency. Please forgive me."

He made a great show of humility, but the damage was already done. Harafin noted several nobles and military officials regarding Nerys differently. For them, the discussion of truth just became secondary to the desire to acquire the very tools of destruction that had caused so much damage.

"Perhaps," Emperor Tegnazian said gravely, "That depends entirely on your explanation of lies spoken in connection with this investigation, and your flight from Justice that sparked the regrettable confrontation outside the Sentinel Tower."

"I confess I fled from Stalwart Leander," Nerys said. "The man attacked me in my shop and I feared for my life. He was completely unreasonable."

The emperor waved a dismissive hand. "We know all too well Leander's actions. What have you to say about the artifact used in the attack and murder of two Pallian Stalwarts and one Sentinel?"

Harafin reminded himself to stay calm. Leander's outburst offered Nerys the perfect opportunity to shift blame entirely to the Stalwarts. This entire interview was becoming a farce. He doubted Nerys actively supported the attackers. The man would see no profit in it.

"I admit I initially mis-represented the import of the multi-projectile distribution artifact."

"The what?"

"The box that fires half a hundred crossbow bolts in a matter of seconds."

A wave of whispered exclamations rippled around the room. Those nobles and soldiers already interested in Nerys's artifacts grew visibly excited. They would see only the tremendous potential of the device, and care far less that the perpetrator used it to release Tanathos from prison.

"Why did you do this?"

Nerys wrung his hands together. "I admit I feared that the box itself would be condemned."

"So you lied to protect your investment?"

"No," Nerys protested. "I lied to guarantee focus remained fixed on whoever committed that atrocity, not on the tools he used to achieve victory."

"Who committed the crime?"

"I cannot say for sure. I only know who purchased the item."

"Give me the name."

Nerys glanced around the room nervously. "May I interject, Your Excellency, that we generally hold in great confidence the identities of any who purchase our artifacts."

"Just give me the name."

"I will. It's just, I want it clear that I only reveal this name due to the exceptional circumstances, and under any other conditions . . ."

"Enough!" Emperor Tegnazian slammed an open palm on the top of the table. The report echoed like thunder through the room. "I understand completely that your greatest concern is to protect your profits. You try my patience. Give me the name."

"I sold the box to a man named Remiel."

"The same man currently imprisoned as a conspirator?"

"The very man." A fresh wave of whispered conversation rippled through the room.

Harafin frowned. "Nerys, you have a standing policy to sell only to nobility. This man posed as a servant. Why would you sell him this device?"

"He represented a benefactor who wished to remain anonymous. I chose to respect that wish."

"Why?"

Nerys hesitated. "Because he agreed to pay a hefty premium, and agreed to purchase a number of other artifacts."

"Such as?"

"Several shield cloaks and distribution rods."

Emperor Tegnazian stared down at the fidgeting Sentinel as silence settled back over the room. "Sentinel Nerys, your actions are disgraceful. Your lust for profit cost the lives of many, and contributed directly to instability in the realm and the escape of a most dangerous criminal. You will surrender all the revenue collected over the last week to be divided evenly among the families of the fallen."

Nerys paled, but the emperor waved away his protests. "As to your standing among the Sentinels, I leave that decision with Master Harafin."

He banged the broken head of the gavel on the table. "This council stands adjourned. The Ruling Council will meet in private."

People filed from the room, talking excitedly among themselves. They had much to discuss. Harafin joined the Ruling Council. He would deal with Nerys later, and was honestly not sure what he would decide. The man disgusted him, but did that merit demotion, or blocking him from his Actinopathic gift?

Nerys left the room, surrounded by a large knot of nobility and soldiers jostling for attention and calling out orders. The sight left a bitter taste in Harafin's mouth. No doubt Nerys would profit greatly from today's events, while one of the best men Harafin knew would pay a dear price.

While he waited for the room to clear, Harafin closed his eyes and extended his senses toward the Sentinel Tower. He needed something productive to do. He would restore the barrier shield around the Tower and add a few additional enhancements he'd been pondering in recent days.

79

GABRAL PROVES HIS WORTH

Kevlin stopped before the entrance to the Keisara's Tower. He held one of Remiel's chained arms, and Gabral held the other on the far side. The prisoner had not spoken, although he seemed more and more surprised as they passed through the various palaces to reach this location.

A pair of imperial guards, dressed in plate armor and full helms, flanked the entrance. That was unusual. Perhaps the keisara really did have viable intelligence. It appeared she was taking no chances with Remiel. That eased some of his lingering worry.

The guards snapped salutes, which Gabral returned. "Inform the keisara that Colonel Gabral is here with the prisoner Remiel."

"Where is Sir Kevlin?" asked one of the guards.

Gabral scowled at the man and Kevlin suppressed a grin. "I'm here."

The guards opened the door and one said, "Sir Kevlin, leave your sword here. I will escort you and your charge to the queen."

As Kevlin unbuckled his sword belt and laid it in the corner, Gabral said, "I will accompany him."

"We have orders only to allow Sir Kevlin to pass."

Gabral marched up to the much taller man. "I am Bearer of the Mace, and the Emperor's Champion. You will let me pass."

"Very well, but leave your weapon here."

Gabral barked a laugh and pushed past the man. For a second, it looked like the guard considered trying to stop him, but he wisely chose not to.

Kevlin pushed Remiel after Gabral. The three of them followed the other guard down an airy corridor draped in bright cloth, with a thick carpet running down the center. Kevlin marveled that they'd actually made it there. He had fully expected the heavy guard surrounding Remiel to deny access to the prisoner, let alone allow him to be removed.

Gabral's authority, coupled with a decree from the keisara proved sufficient. The Sentinels and Stalwarts assigned as guards may have been surprised, but they couldn't prevent the unusual interrogation.

At the end of the hall the guard pushed open a dark-stained wooden door carved with vines and fantastic creatures. They stepped into a surprisingly large, rectangular room, thirty paces long and half that distance wide. The walls rose a full twelve feet to a ceiling covered with a gigantic mosaic depicting a flower garden filled with a riot of colors. More fantastic creatures danced among the flowers. Nymphs and sprites and fawns and faeries and dozens more that Kevlin had never seen before.

Gigantic floor-to-ceiling windows filled the entire wall to their left, offering a spectacular view of the Tamerlane Sea. It felt like they perched directly over the waves. Kevlin realized the tower must be placed on the westernmost edge of the palace complex.

If he stood close to the windows, he'd probably glimpse the edge of the plateau directly below, where it fell away hundreds of feet to the pounding waves. That reminded him of the terrifying plunge down the face of that cliff with Tanathos and the heart-stopping moment when Harafin's magic arrested his fall just short of the jagged rocks.

He pulled his gaze from the incredible view and focused on the figure seated two-thirds of the way across the room on a low couch. Keisara Fideima Tamar Tegnazian.

She sat tall, her chin slightly raised, her golden hair falling in an intricate braid over one shoulder and down the front of an elegant cranberry colored taffeta gown. She also wore a green linen hat with a very wide brim that cast a gentle shadow across her face.

The rest of the room was surprisingly empty of furniture. Half a dozen straight-backed wooden chairs were scattered haphazardly around the room, as if someone had hastily removed the other furnishings but didn't quite finish the task. A pair of armed guards flanked a door set in the center of the right-hand wall. Another door was set in the wall behind the keisara.

The pretty maid Sitara stood flanking the keisara. Kevlin smiled in greeting. It was good to see a familiar face. Sitara didn't smile, but looked very solemn.

Keisara Fideima said in her rich, warm voice, "Greetings, Sir Kevlin. Thank you for coming so quickly."

Kevlin bowed.

Gabral also bowed. "I took the liberty of accompanying the prisoner, Your Majesty."

"Why would you do that when not commanded to do so?"

Gabral looked unsure for the first time. "I felt it appropriate, given the dangerous nature of this prisoner."

Kevlin glanced at Remiel and was surprised to see Remiel staring across the room, a look of astonishment on his face. He whispered, "Angel?"

Kevlin looked from Remiel to the keisara. No, not the keisara. Remiel was looking at Sitara.

She cast him a hint of a smile.

She hadn't smiled at Kevlin.

Kevlin grabbed Remiel's arm. "What's going on here? Sitara, how do you know this man?"

"I'll ask the questions here, Sir Kevlin," the keisara said.

"Of course. It's just, I'm surprised the prisoner seems to know Sitara. It could be important."

"I said I'll ask the questions. Be silent until commanded to speak, or I'll have you muzzled."

Why would she insist he deliver Remiel only to start threatening him? It usually took a few minutes for him to upset women enough for them to start throwing around threats of muzzles.

Gabral said, "He's an unlearned country fool, Your Majesty. Poor manners are to be expected."

"I will forgive the lack of manners once you answer my questions."

"Me?" This conversation was twisting completely out of line. "I thought you were questioning Remiel."

"In due time. First, I demand to know who is bearer of Oris and where is the stone?"

The last person who asked him that turned out to be mind-controlled. Not a good sign.

"Your Majesty, I don't see how that has any relevance . . ."

"I will determine what has relevance," the keisara snarled.

"One more time, mercenary," Gabral hissed. "Upset her one more time, and I'll beat you from this room."

"Answer my question," the keisara commanded in a ringing tone.

"I'm afraid I cannot."

"You dare defy my direct order." Her voice carried abundant threat.

"Not willingly. Master Harafin and your husband agreed this secret must be kept." Well, hopefully the emperor had agreed. If not, hopefully Leander had an extra seat on the banished wagon.

"Leave my husband out of this. In this tower, I rule, and you will obey my command!"

She rose to her feet and tilted her chin up to look down at him in that imperious gesture so many women adopted. When she did, despite the shadows of the wide, plumed hat, Kevlin got a clear look at her eyes.

They looked black.

He hated being right all the time.

"Answer her," Gabral demanded.

"You know I can't." He added in a whisper, "Look at her eyes."

"I'll do no such thing," Gabral huffed. "I know how to respect the keisara. Her command must be obeyed."

"She's not herself."

"You dare impugn the keisara's honor?"

"No, listen to me. Ceren was attacked just today. She . . . well, never mind. But look at her eyes."

"You're babbling. I knew it was a mistake to let you draw so close to nobility."

"Listen to me!"

"No, you listen to me. Answer the keisara, or I swear I will strike you down right here."

It was frustrating to realize Gabral's biggest character flaw was a not pride, not platform boots he sometimes wore to pretend he wasn't so short. It was lack of imagination.

He just couldn't think of anything new, but had to keep coming back to the tired idea of killing Kevlin. It was kind of tiring.

Kevlin wanted to shake Gabral and beat some sense into him, but getting into a fist-fight in the keisara's apartment would be a bad idea. How could Gabral not see the truth?

The keisara sat gracefully back onto the low couch and waved to one of the guards, "Bring my dear cousin Miren to me."

One of the guards saluted and exited the room. The keisara seemed content to wait, so Kevlin used the delay to try to think of a course of action. How could the enemy have struck here in the very heart of the palace?

He needed his brothers.

Kevlin tried the ethereal link he sometimes felt with his brothers, but felt nothing. Why now? He'd connected with them last time.

The connection was sporadic, but there had to be a way. He doubted the keisara would allow him to withdraw and summon Harafin and a legion of Stalwarts to help. He cast his thoughts back over every time he'd connected with his brothers.

Every time, he'd had magic. That was depressing. The connection must be limited just like his connection with Oris.

He needed magic.

The thought set his hands shaking. Of course he needed magic. He needed all the magic he could get. He deserved it.

No. He fought to control the sudden craving that undermined his will and distracted his thoughts. He did need magic, but just a little.

How could he get some? Harafin was far away, in counsel with the emperor on the far side of the Great Dome. It would take them half an hour to get here if they ran. He had no idea where Leander might be.

"Consider your actions carefully, mercenary," warned Gabral. "Choose your loyalties."

Gabral had the Mace. He had magic. "I need magic," Kevlin hissed. "Give me some, quick."

"You can use magic?" Remiel asked.

"Shut up or I'll break your jaw."

"As if I'd give you magic," Gabral sniffed dismissively. "You think I'd knowingly endanger the keisara?"

"I need it to help her. Can't you see, she's under duress?"

"You're insane. I will not bow and scrape to you like everyone else. I know how unstable you are."

"Just do it," Kevlin hissed. "This is important."

The door in the right-hand wall opened and the guard returned, leading Lady Miren. Her hair looked disheveled, as if she'd been sleeping, and her clothes looked skewed, as if she'd been forced to don them quickly. She looked confused, and more than a little irritated.

She took the scene in at a glance. She paused to straighten her clothes and made a little curtsy to Kevlin and Gabral. They bowed in turn.

"Cousin, you summoned me?"

Behind Lady Miren, the guards again took up position flanking the door. For the first time, Kevlin noticed that the guards' eyes also looked black. His frustration turned to anger. Things were about to get very ugly.

"Gabral, we're in danger."

"Don't try to threaten me. If you lose control here, I'll put you down like a rabid animal." He grasped the handle of the Mace. The special leather sheath that held it in place on his back *melted* away in its unusual way, and he drew the powerful weapon. He gave Kevlin a tight smile. "Just give me an excuse to use it."

Keisara Fideima said, "Miren, I'm happy you came. I think you can help me with a little problem."

Lady Miren curtsied and her smile seemed to brighten the room. "Anything. What can I do?"

"Wait there. All will become clear."

Keisara Fideima commanded, "Colonel Gabral, release the man Remiel and let him advance."

Kevlin ground his teeth together in impotent rage. The situation clearly had nothing to do with questioning Remiel, and everything to do with the enemy's next strike. They'd been fools thrice over to think they had the upper hand. The enemy had remained one step ahead at every turn. They had reacted with cunning and flexibility. Now he could do nothing as Remiel was about to walk free.

He had thought pitched battle was bad, but at least there one knew who to fight. Here in the palace, enemies skulked around every corner, with poisoned daggers concealed in their bodices.

Leander had sacrificed his station to try to bring the conspirators to justice. Even now, Harafin met in counsel with the emperor, questioning Nerys and discussing the next steps in routing the enemy. And yet the enemy was already striking again.

What could Kevlin do? He didn't know who to fight. If he moved against the keisara, whoever was controlling her might kill her outright. Would he then be blamed for her death just as Leander was being blamed for taking a stand against the Sentinels who blocked him from taking Nerys?

Gabral scowled at Kevlin again, then unlocked Remiel's chains. Kevlin should have insisted on keeping the key. He might have been able to pretend he lost it, or even swallow it to delay the inevitable.

Gabral pulled Remiel close and growled, "One wrong move and you die."

Remiel nodded, looking honestly terrified of the diminutive Colonel. Well, terrified of the Mace anyway. Remiel cautiously advanced and knelt before the keisara.

"I am yours to command, Your Majesty."

"Rise."

When he stood, Kevlin itched to clutch his belt dagger. This situation was preposterous. Remiel shouldn't be allowed to stand so close to the keisara. If he hurt her, they'd get the blame. No one would believe she was possessed. They'd have no proof.

Keisara Fideima drew a long dagger from behind her back. Remiel retreated a step, hands raised as he began begging for mercy.

"Shush." She reversed the dagger and handed it hilt-first to him.

"Your Majesty," Gabral said. "I protest. This man is a known criminal."

Even Gabral wasn't so dense he failed to see how bad things were getting. Kevlin needed to act, but what could he do? His sword lay against the wall outside the keisara's apartments and he had no magic.

The keisara said, "Silence, Colonel." She gestured with the dagger, and Remiel took it hesitantly.

"There," she said with a satisfied smile. "Now, Sir Kevlin, answer my question or this man will murder my dear cousin."

"You can't be serious," Lady Miren gasped.

"I protest," Gabral cried.

"She's possessed," Kevlin repeated. "Do you believe me now? We have to break the spell. Give me magic."

"Stop trying to twist the situation to your benefit. You will never command me."

Lady Miren spun to the guards flanking the door. "The keisara's ill. You have to help."

The soldiers made no response.

Remiel glanced at the queen and then at Sitara. He shrugged and advanced toward Lady Miren.

Gabral lifted the Mace and it burst into blue fire. "I cannot allow this, Your Majesty. Remiel, you take one more step toward that woman and I'll kill you."

Remiel froze.

"To interfere with me is treason," Keisara Fideima hissed.

"As bearer of the Mace and the emperor's champion, I have the right. Lady Miren is not to be harmed. I will extract the information you seek, or I'll kill this man myself."

He gestured toward Kevlin with the still-burning Mace.

Kevlin grabbed it.

Bad idea.

80

YOU NEVER REALLY KNOW SOME FRIENDS

It felt like twin bolts of lightning struck Kevlin simultaneously. One roared into him from the Mace, while the other burned up through his leg from where Oris lay hidden in his boot.

He jerked, his entire body convulsing under the magical onslaught. The magnitude of it rivaled the power that overran his mind and nearly killed him at Il'Aicharen.

The amulet flared to red-hot brilliance where it rested against his chest. It singed his skin, and blue light blazed from every opening in his clothing. The light mingled with the blue fire from the Mace that rolled up his arm and spread around his torso.

His thoughts scattered, and it took him a moment to realize he was only screaming on the inside. His mouth remained locked closed. Imagining screaming wasn't nearly as soothing.

He'd only wanted a little magic. Stealing it from one of the most powerful weapons ever known might not have been the best place to try. The magnitude of the power raging into him from the Mace was bad enough, but he wasn't prepared for Oris's reaction. The rock had never initiated contact with him before.

Intense white light blazed around him, and through him. It was very distracting, but it didn't appear that anyone else in the room could see it. They were gaping at the flames enveloping him, and Remiel seemed convinced he'd gone made and committed suicide.

The light changed his eyes. He now looked through physical forms to the magnificent spirits burning within each person's soul. Lady Miren's and Gabral's spirits burned pure white, while Remiel's looked dingy, like a long-used dish-rag. The keisara's pure spirit was ringed by clinging darkness, as were those of the guards stationed by the door.

Sitara's spirit surprised him. It was a flowing mixture of inky black and snowy white, whirling together but not mixing. The evil power possessing the others was affecting her worse.

The torrent of magic burst through his partially formed mental shields like the tidal wave Tanathos had unleashed against the fort at Il'Aicharen. It flooded his mind and his thoughts began to drown. Before he could really embrace the ensuing panic, he realized this was not the agonizing experience that Il'Aicharen had been.

This was glorious.

The magic freed his mind from the constraints of his physical form and left him floating on a river of power, able to go wherever he wished, to do anything he wanted.

Kevlin threw back his head and laughed. This was exactly what he deserved! This power was what he'd longed for ever since Il'Aicharen.

As if from a great distance, Gabral shouted, "What are you doing? Let go! The Mace is mine!"

The enraged Mace bearer threw a punch. To Kevlin's hyper-alert senses, the movement appeared sluggish. Reacting to it was as simple as forming a thought.

Blinding white light exploded from him and knocked Gabral from his feet. The short colonel lost his grip on the Mace and tumbled to the floor while everyone else in the room covered their eyes from the blinding flash.

Gabral stared from his empty hand to the Mace burning in Kevlin's grip. He looked like he was going to cry.

The moment was ruined when the deep magic filling Kevlin revolted. He tried to form shields, but the magic already filled him head to toe. It had slipped inside his defenses and he'd allowed it in.

Raging magic battered against his constraints like an enraged bull and shattered them. He would have staggered under the onslaught had he been able to move. His body remained immobile, burning with blue fire.

He didn't understand. He'd connected with Oris so the magic should be contained. Yet this magic, magnified to terrifying proportions, smashed against his defenses and threatened to drown him conscious will.

Kevlin groaned as he fought to raise new mental walls and summon forth his army of determination and resolve. Magic inundated his thoughts, submerging his defensive walls time and again, like an angry sea. Each time he struggled to cast it off, to retain his thoughts and sanity, but his resistance began to weaken.

He wondered why he should bother?

This magic freed him. It lifted him to greatness he could find in no other way. He should embrace it, ride the wave wherever it led, no matter the consequences.

He could achieve victory right now. No more hunting for elusive shadows. The enemy was close. He had the power to destroy them now.

He could do it. He could embrace the magic instead of fighting it, release it in one gigantic blow that would shatter this tower and the entire palace beyond. Many would die, but so would the enemy. So many innocents had already died in vain. There could be no more glorious end for anyone than to be sacrificed to this end.

Kevlin fought the insidious ideas, battling his own frustrated anger that weakened his resolve. The many sacrifices and setbacks they'd suffered fueled his urge to give in, just do it. Justice had been denied too long. He resisted, even as the fringes of his will began to fray.

Fire could be used.

Tiny wisps of flame flickered around him and throughout the room. They hung for a split second in the air before he extinguished them.

Or a whirlwind.

A breeze picked up, fluttering hair and bringing with it the threat of impending destruction. He gritted his teeth and pulled the magic back, denying it the life it needed to swell further to life.

Kevlin weaved where he stood, torn by conflicting desires, barely holding the magic in check. It pounded through him, a torrent pushing the limits of his control. In desperation, he reached for the connection to Oris and felt the stone's presence in his mind.

Take it back. I cannot handle it right now.

He felt no response from the stone, but drove the still-resisting magic back into the rock. At first it fought like a cornered lion and nearly burst from his control, but then its resistance snapped and it drained away.

As the last vestiges of magic faded, Kevlin's mind cleared and he remembered his brothers. He clutched after the magic but it slipped through his mental fingers like a sieve.

Before it faded completely, he reached for his brothers, and this time felt their minds.

Brothers. The enemy attacks the keisara. Come now!

The contact broke before he felt any reply.

Kevlin dropped the now-extinguished Mace to the floor with a metallic clang. Gabral snatched it up. He clutched it to him and glared at Kevlin, his grey eyes burning with hatred. Then he lifted it high and it burst into blue fire. He exhaled a great breath, as if he'd feared Kevlin had damaged it, or that the magic was gone.

Gabral snarled, "The Mace is *mine*, do you hear?"

"I'm sorry." Kevlin didn't want to fight Gabral. He ached from the mental and emotional drain of battling for control of the magic. "You should have listened to me and that wouldn't have happened."

"If you ever touch it again, I'll kill you."

He looked ready to carry out the threat right then and there, but instead stepped away, as if fearing Kevlin would once more steal the weapon.

"What does this mean?" Sitara asked. She stared at him, her expression surprised.

Keisara Fideima convulsed over her stomach and moaned. She clutched at her head, and dislodged the plumed hat. Her voice hissed between clenched teeth. "Will . . . not."

Sitara leaned over the keisara, her face worried.

Kevlin advanced. "Your Majesty, who is doing this to you?"

The keisara staggered to her feet and took two faltering steps toward him. She looked up, and the blackness drained from her eyes. For a second they shone bright, clear blue and she reached for Kevlin, her face desperately pleading

"Help me."

Then her eyes again faded to black.

Kevlin's heart sank and he shouted, "No! Fight it."

She retreated from him and bared her teeth like an animal.

"Kill them both! Traitors!"

The two guards stationed beside the door drew their swords and rushed toward Kevlin.

"I am no traitor," Gabral declared, outraged.

Kevlin shouted to Lady Miren, "Run! Get help!"

She ran for the door, but it was flung open from the other side and more guards charged into the room. Lady Miren yelped and tried to dodge, but the first guard slashed her across the ribs.

She screamed and tumbled away, a dark bloodstain already spreading across her waist. When she tried to rise, the guard punched her in the face and she crumpled, unmoving to the floor.

The two guards who had been stationed at the door closed on Kevlin. He drew his heavy belt dagger and flicked a stiletto into his left hand. He threw the stiletto from ten feet and took the first guard in the right eye. The man screamed and collapsed.

The second guard swung, and Kevlin ducked the whistling blade before it took his head off. He lunged under the man's sword arm, but the guard dropped his sword and caught Kevlin's wrist before he could drive the dagger home. The two grappled for control of the blade.

While the keisara silently watched the fight and more soldiers charged across the room toward Kevlin and Gabral, Sitara beckoned to Remiel. "It is enough. Kill the keisara."

"Are you sure?" His face paled and his hand holding the dagger shook.

"It has to be done. Trust me."

"I do, Angel." He hefted the dagger and circled the motionless keisara, approaching from behind.

Keisara Fideima made no move to resist.

This could not be happening.

With a burst of strength, Kevlin broke the guard's hold and clobbered him in the side of the head with the hilt of the dagger. The man fell like a stone.

Kevlin spun toward the keisara, flipped the dagger in his hand, and cocked his arm back to throw. Remiel stood directly behind her, shielded from anything Kevlin do from that distance.

Gabral moved to meet the dozen onrushing guards. He hefted the Mace and said, "Halt or I will strike you down."

They continued their charge.

The keisara stood five long strides away, but the distance might as well have been half a league. Kevlin couldn't reach her before Remiel struck.

Remiel's dagger glinted, as if winking at Kevlin as it paused in that last second Remiel lifted it high before plunging it toward the keisara's unprotected back.

Kevlin did the only thing he could do.

He threw his dagger.

The heavy weapon flipped once and struck true with a meaty *thunk*. It sank to the hilt in Keisara Fideima's right shoulder. She screamed and twisted.

It was enough.

Remiel's dagger plunged into her back below her opposite shoulder instead of into her heart.

She screamed again, her body rigid with shock. Her mouth moved in silent denial, her expression terrified. Then she crumpled to the floor. She lay motionless and could almost be sleeping. The widening pool of blood could almost be missed against the cranberry color of her dress.

"Villain!" Gabral shouted at Kevlin, but the charging soldiers prevented him from carrying out his threat to execute Kevlin.

"I had to do it," Kevlin shouted back.

Most of the soldiers moved against Gabral, but three of them came around the short colonel and closed on Kevlin. He drew the silver dagger from the base of his neck, but it would prove little use against three swords.

This was going to hurt.

The door they had originally entered was flung open and Drystan and Jerrik burst into the room. Shouting his traditional battle cry, Jerrik plowed into the knot of guards closing on Gabral. The entire group went down in a tangle of limbs and naked blades.

Drystan danced around the group and shouted, "Kevlin, catch!"

He tossed Kevlin's sword. Then he started rapping the heads of soldiers fighting Jerrik. His long spear proved extremely effective, whipping out and dropping one soldier after another.

Jerrik surged up from the press, a maniacal grin on his face as he punched one soldier after another in the face.

Kevlin ripped his sword from its sheath, shouting, "They're possessed. Try not to kill them."

Gabral snarled, "You do not command me!"

He clubbed one soldier in the head. The heavy, spiked ball sheared through the helm and smashed his skull. Blood and gray matter sprayed out, and the man toppled from his feet.

Kevlin engaged two guards, their sword ringing loud through the room. The third charged Drystan.

Being possessed didn't make the man any smarter. Drystan dropped him with a lightning-fast series of jabs with the butt end of his spear, then moved to help Jerrik and Gabral fight off the bulk of the soldiers.

"Stand down!" Kevlin shouted at the soldiers, but they only tried to decapitate him.

He ducked and slashed one soldier's knee. The man screamed and fell, and Kevlin tackled his companion. They fell together, with Kevlin on top. The man tried to push him off, but Kevlin pounded on his head with the hilt of his sword until the man stopped moving.

Jerrik heaved a soldier across the room. As the man collided with the wall, he called out, "A little crude, Kevlin, but effective."

He was one to talk.

Jerrik knocked the sword out of another soldier's hands with a heavy blow from his huge broadsword. He clubbed the unfortunate fellow and threw him into a clump of three soldiers facing Gabral. They fell in a heap and Jerrik brained them as they rose.

Kevlin spun back toward the keisara just as Sitara said to Remiel, "Finish her. Time to go."

Remiel leaned over the unconscious monarch to slit her throat.

Kevlin snapped the concealed stiletto into his right hand and threw the narrow blade at Remiel. It caught him in the side of the throat.

Remiel stumbled away, clutching at his neck as blood ran through his fingers. It was a serious wound, but not fatal. Kevlin needed more daggers.

"Stop interfering," Sitara shrieked, throwing out her arms.

A wave of hardened air blasted through the room. It caught the standing soldiers and tossed them like so many rag dolls across the room. Jerrik and Drystan tumbled along with them, cursing and flailing their arms. The group piled up along the far wall, and for the moment, no one moved.

The amulet captured the magic that struck Kevlin, and he felt no more than a light breeze. As soon as the magic entered his body, he *changed* it to gain control, and focused all of it into a spear of magic, which he threw at Remiel.

A golden shaft of light shot across the room and drove into Remiel's torso, tearing a gaping, smoking hole in his side and throwing him from his feet. He screamed, blood spewing from his lips. The surprisingly appetizing smell of roasted meat wafted through the air.

Two problems solved together. He was getting better at managing his time. With the magic gone, he didn't have to worry about the *Tai Pari,* and Remiel was down and out. He'd expire within minutes.

Sitara dropped to the floor beside Remiel and cradled his head in her lap. She placed glowing hands on his chest while tears stood in her eyes.

"Don't leave me," she cried. "I can't do this alone."

That clarified a few things.

Sitara wasn't possessed. She was the enemy.

"Sitara? Why would you do this?"

81

HINTS OF TROUBLE

Indira paused in a doorway to a small room in the hospital wing. Her healer's robe was stained and her midnight hair hung in a simple twist down her back like always when she worked. She found the familiar sights, smells, and feel of the hospital comforting. It helped relieve some of her lingering anxiety from the confrontation with the possessed Ceren.

Adalia shadowed her, her soul a spark of determination and good humor despite ongoing dangers. Her simple presence cheered Indira.

"Keelin, is everything all right?"

Drystan's willowy wife sat on a padded chair, holding her baby while a Pemburu Stalwart examined the child.

"Oh, hello Indira," Keelin said with a friendly smile. "We'll be fine, thanks. Rhys developed a fever so I brought him down to make sure it's nothing serious."

The Stalwart removed his hands from Rhys' head. "Your baby will be fine."

"I'm surprised Drystan isn't here with you," Indira said.

"He was, but Kevlin only just summoned him and Jerrik. He had to rush off to the Keisara's Tower of all places."

"What for?" Indira asked, a fresh knot of worry forming in her stomach. Kevlin ended up at the heart of too many of the ongoing troubles. She worried constantly for his safety.

"I really don't know. Some kind of emergency. I expect they'll sort it out."

Adalia snorted. "Knowing that lot, I 'spect they'll break something important."

"I hope not," Keelin said. "Not in that tower anyway."

Indira bade Keelin farewell and continued her rounds. She walked slowly, her mind troubled.

"Ye're worryin' agin," Adalia said.

"I'm just wondering what kind of trouble the boys could get into in the Keisara's Tower?"

Adalia shrugged. "Lots, prob'ly."

"Oh no," Indira exclaimed. "Lady Ceren went to the tower to visit the keisara."

Adalia nodded. "Might be bad, that."

Indira ran from the hospital, with Adalia on her heels, but she couldn't outrun her growing fear.

82

ONE STEP BEHIND

*M*aster!

Linked to Masego by the spell that enslaved her, Sitara sent out the thought in the direction she felt him to be.

What are you doing? She could clearly sense his surprise. *You stupid girl. Don't you have any idea how dangerous it is to talk like this?*

But he's here! She interrupted. *Kevlin's here. I need your help to take him.*

Don't let him leave, Masego commanded. *I am coming.*

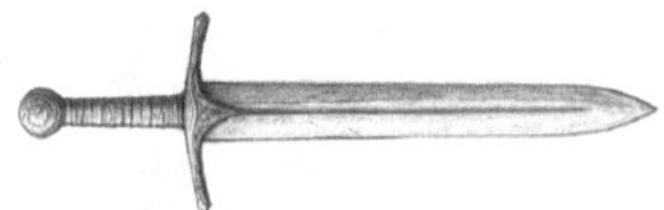

Harafin and the other members of the ruling council looked up as the doors to the large conference room where they still met banged open. Leander, dressed in full battle armor, strode into the room, flanked by a score of battle-ready Pallian Stalwarts. He looked angry, and Harafin recognized the danger signs.

His old friend was once again embracing the crazed fury of his youth. Harafin's heart fell, and he hoped his friend wasn't planning to do something stupid. When Leander had embraced the insanity of vengeance a century ago, he'd become one of the most dangerous men in the world.

Emperor Tegnazian scowled. "What are you doing here? I ordered you banished and I mean to see you cast out of the city immediately. Guards!"

Leander stopped in the center of the room and planted his feet. "Your guards are unable to attend at the moment."

"Murderer," Ambassador Janezeko breathed. The other ambassadors looked on fearfully.

"You've always been an idiot, Braden," Leander said. "I would never murder anyone."

"What do you call what you did earlier today?" the emperor shot back.

"Self-defense."

"I disagree."

"That is of no matter."

The emperor rose to his feet, sputtering with rage.

Leander said, "I'm not here to re-hash the past or challenge your ruling, no matter that you proved yourself a legendary fool."

"Get out," Emperor Tegnazian shouted. "Leave me, or by the gods I'll see you hanged."

"First, I demand to know why the prisoner Remiel was released."

"You have no right to demand anything here!" the emperor shouted. "Get out!"

"Wait," Harafin interjected. "Did you say Remiel was released?"

Leander nodded. "I received word only moments ago that he was released into the custody of Gabral and Kevlin on the keisara's order."

"Impossible." Emperor Tegnazian sank back to his chair. "If you're lying to me . . ."

"Tanathos escaped," Leander said. "I won't allow Remiel to do the same."

"You're in no position to allow or not allow anything," Emperor Tegnazian snapped.

"Enough," Harafin said. "This bickering isn't helping. This is the first we heard of Remiel's release. Why would the keisara issue such a command?"

"I don't know," the emperor said.

"Could they have been lying?" the hulking Ambassador Kescog asked.

"Unlikely," Harafin said, considering the strange situation. None of the explanations he came up with were encouraging. "Zuberi, is there any reason your wife would issue such an order?"

"No. None that I can imagine."

"What can it mean?" The lanky Ambassador Talamantez asked.

Harafin rose. "It means the enemy is again one step ahead of us."

Emperor Tegnazian gasped. "You can't mean . . ."

At that moment Harafin felt a tingle at the base of his neck. Someone had triggered the newly re-created and enhanced barrier shield around the Sentinel Tower. He raised a hand for silence and closed his eyes to concentrate.

He caught a faint echo of conversation.

But he's here! Kevlin's here. I need your help to take him.

Don't let him leave. I am coming.

The connection faded and Harafin cursed.

They were in the wrong place. Again.

He ran around the table, tossing chairs aside, and shouted, "To the Keisara's Tower! The enemy moves to strike there."

Emperor Tegnazian cried out, "Is my wife all right?"

Harafin dared not voice what he feared. That was enough of an answer. The emperor sprang to his feet and gave chase.

"To battle!" Ambassador Kescog shouted.

He led the other ambassadors to join the chase.

Leander beat them all to the door. He called out to the assembled Stalwarts, "Double-time. Clear a path!"

The Stalwarts pelted down the corridor, shouting for people to make way, and forcibly moving anyone too slow to comply.

As Harafin ran behind Leander, he wondered what they would find when they arrived. If the enemy arrived first, he doubted the keisara would survive.

He ran faster.

83

GAMES IN THE DARK

Sitara faced Kevlin. "It wasn't supposed to happen like this. You're supposed to help me."

"Of course I would have helped you. All you had to do was ask. None of this was necessary."

"It was," she cried. "My master commanded it."

Finally things were starting to make sense. "You're enthralled to Masego, aren't you?"

She dropped Remiel's head and retreated, her expression terrified. "I cannot speak of it."

"Not good enough," Drystan said, rising from the tangled mass of fallen soldiers. He kicked Jerrik in the ribs, producing a groan.

Gabral stepped past Kevlin. "Sitara, you are a servant of Darkness. You will answer our questions and you will face punishment for your crimes." The blue fire encasing the Mace ball flowed up his arm and surrounded him with its protective embrace.

"No," she begged. "Please, not like this."

"Hold on," Kevlin said. "Gabral, wait a minute."

Gabral spun back to Kevlin, the Mace raised to strike. "Don't interfere with me, mercenary. I'm in command and this creature will be brought to justice."

"It's Sitara," Kevlin protested. "We can work this out."

"Oh, I plan to," Gabral said, turning back to Sitara.

"Back off," Sitara cried, raising her hands.

Crimson fire roared around Gabral, charring the floor and chewing at the air. With it came a heavy scent of ash, mingled with the stench of something long dead.

The Mace's blue protective flames flared against Sitara's conjured fire and Gabral continued his advance with barely a pause.

"No," Sitara repeated. "This isn't how it's supposed to happen."

"Your plots are at an end," Gabral declared. "Surrender."

She cast a glance at Remiel's unmoving form and whispered, "There is no surrender, no escape."

She darted away from Gabral and circled the keisara's couch.

"You're just making it harder on yourself," he said, stalking after her.

"Harder for one of us," she said.

Sitara looked toward Kevlin again, and she looked like she wanted to speak. He longed to hear her story, understand what had happened to her. She had been such a sweet girl. Surely there had to be a way to salvage this mess.

She sighed, glanced at the approaching Gabral, and clapped her hands together above her head. A cloud of thick, rolling darkness enveloped her and expanded into the room.

Undaunted, Gabral strode into the darkness, the Mace burning with brilliant blue fire. For a second he was outlined through the dark haze.

Then he was gone.

"Drystan," Kevlin called. "I need a javelin."

Drystan instantly tossed one over and he caught the weapon, then ran around the spreading darkness toward the far door, which was already almost hidden from view.

"Stay out of the darkness," he told his brothers. "Be ready. If she emerges, bind her. I think she wants to surrender."

"I'm not so sure about that," Drystan said, gesturing at the growing dark cloud.

"I plan to give her the chance," he said. Hopefully Sitara heard him.

He had seen the light and darkness mixed within her soul. Evil had not conquered her spirit. He had a lot of experience recently casting off overwhelming external force. He had to believe she could do the same.

"We'll be ready," Drystan assured him as he worked to extricate himself from the tangle of bodies. Jerrik rose to his feet, shedding unconscious soldiers like water. He drew his small throwing axe from his belt. Should Sitara confront them, she wouldn't find them easy targets.

Kevlin plunged into the darkness, the javelin extended.

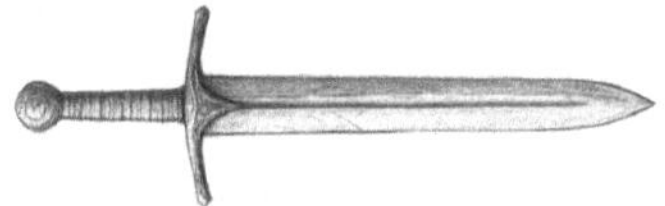

Crouching close to the floor, Sitara slipped to her left, away from where she could *feel* the Mace bearer advancing through her cloud of darkness. He was blundering forward in a straight line, seemingly determined to find her by sheer obstinacy.

He would be disappointed.

She didn't waste time considering ways to convince him to help. He was easily read. The man lacked imagination and vision. He'd try to destroy her.

Sitara just needed to keep them distracted until her hated master arrived. Let the angry colonel unleash his mighty weapon against Masego. Even her master couldn't stand against one of the Six.

It was Kevlin she must rely upon. If only Lady Ceren had completed the mission she'd embedded into her mind. With Kevlin already on her side, she could escape her enslavement. He wasn't actinopathic, but he wasn't a simple, non-gifted soul either. He was different. He was a hero. He was her one chance of salvation.

She extended her senses through the darkness as she slipped farther away from Gabral, closer to the rear door. Remiel lay just yards from her, his life ebbing away.

If they could defeat Masego quickly, she could rescue him. She needed to believe she could save him from the life he'd been trapped into. It offered a glimmer of hope that she could achieve her own dreams and return to freedom.

Feeling nothing else within the darkness, she took a few more cautious steps. It was time.

With a wicked grin, she cast her next spell.

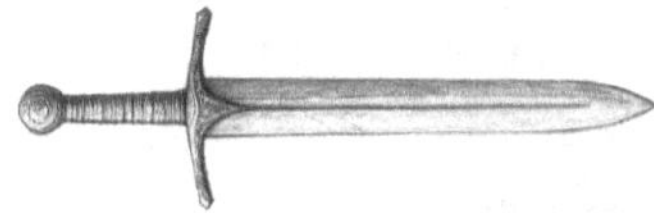

Gabral cursed as he pitched face-first onto the floor, tripped by an invisible obstacle. He landed in a puddle of some thick, viscous material.

Blood probably.

Just my luck. He struggled to push himself upright. *I'm going to be a gory mess when I present my victory to the emperor.*

He couldn't get up. He pushed again, but to no avail. Whatever he had fallen into held him down like glue.

"Where are you, you cowardly witch?" he roared, managing to stick his face into the sticky mess.

Forcing down his anger, he focused on the Mace and removed all restraints around the mighty weapon's power.

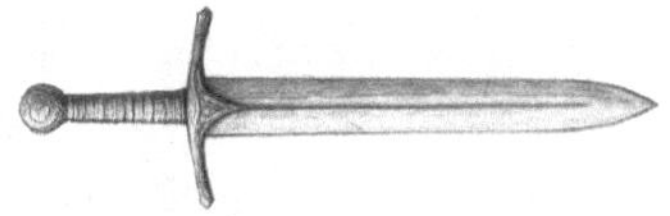

Kevlin cautiously crept through the darkness, blind as a ship running before a midnight gale. He had hoped the amulet would dissipate the mist, but it did nothing. The mist rolled around him but didn't quite touch him. He had no idea if that was the power of the amulet at work or not. It didn't help him find Sitara, and he felt no inrushing captured magic.

Then Gabral cursed, and it sounded like he fell. Kevlin almost called out to ask if he was all right. The Mace should have protected him.

Maybe he was just clumsy? Kevlin suppressed a chuckle. He would have loved to witness Gabral trip over his own feet.

Then tip of the javelin touched something.

Sitara?

She was the only other person in the darkness. Kevlin hated to hurt her, but they needed to end the games and force her to talk. So he lunged, and the javelin plunged into something solid. He twisted it.

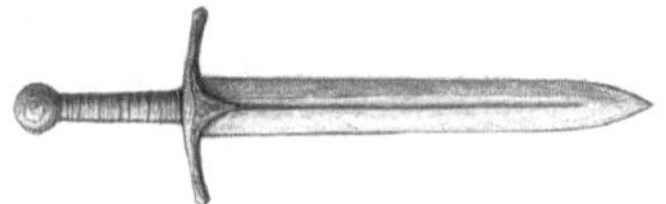

Sitara screamed.

Pain roared through her shoulder in a numbing wave. Only the discipline developed through Masego's training sessions allowed her to keep from fainting from shock.

She jerked backward, grabbed the shaft of the weapon piercing her, and pulled it free. She could feel someone on the other end of the shaft, trying to drive it into her again.

How had she not sensed them before?

The weapon jerked from her grasp and she dove sideways into a roll to avoid the next blow that was sure to come. She struck the floor hard and barely bit back a fresh cry as her wound flared with new pain.

Then a brilliant flash of blue light, brighter than the noonday sun, dawned in the center of her dark cloud. It burned away the concealing mist, revealing everything.

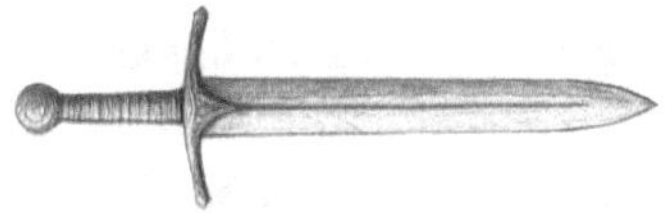

Gabral rose, his eyes glued to the figure of Sitara crawling away from Kevlin, not fifteen feet from where he stood.

She would not escape again. Kevlin, holding one of Drystan's javelins, also turned toward her.

"Hold!" Gabral snarled. "Let me handle this."

For once, the mercenary listened. Too bad, really. Gabral finally had ample excuse to execute the annoying man. He'd always known the day would come. It was just a matter of time.

He strode past Kevlin, focused on Sitara, who was climbing painfully to her feet, blood spreading on her right shoulder.

So Kevlin had scored a hit. So be it. The mercenary drew first blood, but he would win the victory. Sitara tried to escape, but she had nowhere left to run.

"You can't," she pleaded as her back struck the rear wall of the room. She conjured a wall of glowing darkness between them.

Gabral batted it aside. The wall shattered, blasting out one of the huge windows to his left. A chill wind rushed into the room, carrying the scent of the sea far below. He closed the distance to Sitara.

"Last chance."

"Leave me alone," she cried, raising a hand again.

He applauded her choice. It made his all the easier. With great satisfaction, Gabral plunged the long center spike at the top of the Mace between her breasts and into her heart.

She screamed as the force of the blow pinned her back against the wall. She stared down at the flaming weapon impaling her, her face shocked and terrified.

She tried to resist, but the power of the Mace filled her and denied her the ability to do so.

"No," she whispered before the blue flames enveloped her face and burned away the tears streaming from her light brown eyes.

Gabral stood before her, holding her upright by the power of the Mace, determined to extract truth from this evil creature. "You're now in my power. You will answer my questions."

The blue fire faded to bright blue light surrounding her. It pulsed with the regular, slow rhythm of her heartbeat as the final seconds of her life began ticking visibly away. The Mace would keep her alive until the force of her soul was spent. For those seconds, he could command her to obey.

"No."

"You cannot deny me. You will surrender to my will."

Sitara's lips quivered as she tried to resist.

Gabral increased the pressure on the Mace, the muscles on his arms standing out under the strain, and sweat beginning to trickle down his face.

"Her mind is amazingly well guarded," he muttered as the mercenary and his swordbrothers gathered around. "I've never seen anything like this."

"Sitara, why didn't you surrender?" Kevlin asked, leaning close. The fool looked sad.

"...*die first*.." she whispered, shaking her head weakly in protest. The regular pulsing of the Mace's light slowed in time with her heartbeat.

"No," Gabral commanded. "You will surrender and you will answer me."

Sitara screamed again, her body rigid as every muscle convulsed one final time. Then her will broke and she sagged against the Mace.

"There," Gabral said between teeth clenched. "Her defenses are broken. She will answer truthfully now."

"Tell us about your master," Kevlin demanded.

Gabral wanted to punch the insolent man. He'd wanted to ask that one.

She whispered, "He is Ma . . . se . . ."

Her body suddenly shook and she screamed again. She flailed at herself, scratching gouges in her own skin as she twisted and cried in agony. "No! No! I'm sorry, master!"

Blood began flowing freely from the continued scratching and she started weeping hysterically, muttering over and over, "Make it stop. Please make it stop."

"What's going on?" Drystan cried.

Kevlin grabbed her hands. "Stop it, Sitara. You're hurting yourself. Tell us how we can help."

"It's some other spell," Gabral said as he tried to maintain control. He'd held the Shadeleech Merab in similar Mace-bound confinement, but the Sigrun had intervened and possessed their servant. Merab had nearly killed Gabral, despite the Mace piercing his heart.

Gabral forced himself to stand his ground. He would not retreat from a tiny woman.

On my honor, I will win this fight, regardless of the cost.

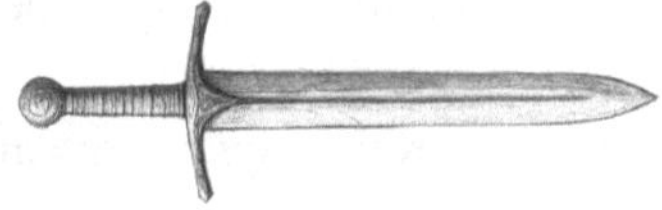

Without warning, an unseen power lifted Gabral from the floor and slammed him against the wall above Sitara's slumped form. He slid down the wall, unconscious.

The Mace's fires winked out and the heavy weapon dropped from Sitara's chest. It clanged to the floor as she slid down next to it.

Kevlin and his swordbrothers spun in surprise as cold laughter rang through the room. In the center of the room stood the Sentinel Felix.

84

TWISTED REALITY

"F elix?" Kevlin asked, confused.

The black-cloaked Sentinel said, "Am I late to the party, boys?"

Sitara jerked at the sound of his voice and whispered, "Masego. Help me."

"You!" Kevlin and his two brothers sprang into motion.

Too late.

Before Kevlin could bring the javelin to bear, iron shackles materialized out of the air and fastened themselves around his wrists and ankles. They yanked him into the air, arms and legs spread-eagled. He struggled in vain against them until they slammed him against the hard stone of the inner wall.

The shock of the impact rattled him and he groaned with pain. His head spun and lights danced before his eyes. He dimly registered Jerrik slamming into the wall beside him, three feet above the floor.

The distinctive clashing of steel on iron helped him focus. Again and again it echoed through the room. He blinked his vision into focus, and then stared.

Drystan. The lanky Einarri twisted and spun across the room in a blur of motion. He wielded his long knives in lightning strikes as he battled the iron shackles that darted around him, striking like snakes.

Kevlin watched in mute amazement as Drystan fought to remain free. He slashed and kicked and twisted and dodged, and somehow held the shackles at bay. All the while, he steadily worked his way closer to Felix.

The fat Sentinel's mouth twisted into a snarl and his brow furrowed in concentration as he directed his iron servants to finally take the final prisoner.

Drystan drew close enough to his target. He dropped one long-knife, yanked a javelin from its sheath on his back, and cast it in one smooth movement.

Kevlin silently willed it to strike true.

Felix was a Sentinel. Drystan never had a chance.

Scant inches from Felix's huge torso, the javelin halted in mid-air. Then it reversed direction and shot back at Drystan with incredible speed.

Drystan dove aside and the javelin whistled past his tumbling body, scraping his armored torso. He rolled, picked up his fallen knife, and landed on his feet.

The move cost him too much time. Even as he regained his feet, the iron shackles fastened themselves around his ankles and hoisted him off of the ground.

Drystan somehow maintained his balance even as the shackles pulled him into the air. He grabbed for another javelin, but Masego made a twisting motion with one finger. The shackles holding his feet spun him upside down. His head slammed against the floor and the blow stunned him.

Shackles fastened around Drystan's wrists. He was flipped upright again and his arms and legs extended wide. Felix laughed, a cold, mocking laugh, and sent Drystan hurtling into the wall beside Kevlin with a negligent flip of his hand.

How did everything get twisted around so badly? They had finally removed Remiel and captured Sitara. It wasn't fair. Why hadn't Felix attacked him with magic? All he needed was a little and he could unleash the power of Oris.

Still chuckling, Felix approached. The Sentinel's face twisted with hatred, and darkness burned in his eyes. His features looked different, as if the muscles under the skin had twisted impossibly far to distort his face into that of a stranger.

"Masego. . . help me."

The fat Sentinel turned toward the dying Sitara. He considered her, watching the blood trickle from the hole in the center of her chest.

"Very well." He pointed at Remiel, and the dying young man's body slid across the floor until it lay close beside Sitara.

Remiel groaned and his eyes fluttered open. He whispered, "Sitara, help me."

Masego said, "Last lesson, girl. Take the boy's life and save yourself, or die with him."

"Please . . ." she whispered faintly. She reached out a tentative hand and slipped it into Remiel's.

Felix turned his back on her.

"Oh, Bajaran," the whisper was barely audible. "I'm so sorry." A fresh tear dripped down her cheek, and her breath rattled in her chest.

Masego ignored the dying Sitara and approached Kevlin and his Swordbrothers.

"How is it possible?" Drystan asked groggily. "How could Harafin not have known it was you?"

Felix chuckled, making the soft laughter sound cruel. He closed his eyes and his body shuddered. It grew softer, fatter, and his features settled into those of Felix.

When he opened his eyes, he looked around with the clear blue eyes of Felix. He looked confused.

"Kevlin? What's going . . ."

His voice trailed off into a groan, and he doubled over in pain. His body hardened, his features twisted anew, and his eyes filled with darkness. Masego's mocking laugh rippled from Felix's lips.

"Oh, yes. Harafin and I are old friends. We've known each other for over a hundred years. He trusts me."

He patted his ample belly. "Well, he trusts the fool this body belongs to, anyway."

"Felix has proven very useful," he assured them. "No one can sense me while Felix is around." He laughed again as if the comment was unusually funny. "Felix will no longer be needed. Masego will claim the seat at the table of the Masters. All I need is the stone."

Kevlin's blood ran cold as he watched the man they had known as Felix. Ceren and the keisara had both been possessed, but they'd retained at least some of their own personalities. Masego controlled Felix completely. How had Felix fallen, and how long ago?

He shuddered to think of Felix standing in counsel with them over the past days. They had shared so much with him, all the while passing information on to the very enemy they hunted.

Realization struck and Kevlin said, "You cast the curse that almost killed the emperor."

"Of course. How better to lure you to me than threaten his life?"

"You attacked me in the catacombs," Kevlin said. "You started the cave-in."

Masego made a tiny bow. "Again, correct. I couldn't allow Tanathos to escape while I dragged you away."

"You failed."

Masego shrugged. "I always win in the end."

"You killed so many," Drystan said.

"A necessary price." He looked them over. "Just a few more to kill, and I'll be on my way."

"You're a coward," Kevlin said. "The only reason you're still alive is because you're so afraid of Harafin."

Masego gestured at an overturned chair lying nearby. It leaped into the air and struck Kevlin in the midsection with terrible force. Hanging suspended as he was, he could do nothing but watch it come, endure the explosion of pain that resulted, and try not to make any audible sound.

"Very brave," Masego applauded him mockingly. "But save your insults. I know your secret. You won't be able to goad me into touching you with magic."

Kevlin hated when his enemies held every advantage. Some of his most painful memories came from moments like that. He'd hoped to avoid making more of those.

Masego drew a little closer. "You cannot be touched by magic, but I can do anything I want with you when I use my magic on other things. Like those shackles, or that chair."

"What do you want?"

"Oris, of course."

"You know Harafin guards that secret."

"Don't play games with me," Masego snarled. He gestured and once more the chair beat Kevlin for him. It shattered on impact, but took one of his ribs with it.

Kevlin groaned from the searing pain. Every breath triggered fresh waves of agony. His head reeled, and for a moment he thought he was going to be sick. Vomiting with a broken rib was something he'd never done, and he really didn't want to try it now.

"I know somehow you're the key to the stone's location," Masego said. "Don't try to deny it and don't think I'm an idiot. We both know you know where it is. The only question is what it will take to get you to tell me."

Well that much honesty hurt as much as the next torture probably would. Kevlin had hoped Masego would rant and threaten for a while longer. Skipping that part was kind of insulting.

When he didn't speak, Masego only smiled. "I could torture you all for a while. As much as I would enjoy that, you'd probably think it noble to let me kill you."

"It would be more noble if I killed you."

Masego laughed. "How about I rip out your tongue after you've told me what I need?"

The possessed man smiled, a truly evil twisting of his face. It was absolutely unbelievable that the jovial Felix could share the same body as this madman.

"Don't worry," Masego said. "I have another idea that should help move things along a bit."

He turned and made a beckoning gesture. The same door Kevlin had used to enter the room moments ago opened and Marjani walked through. She ignored the jumbled pile of fallen soldiers, the shattered window, the dying keisara, and Kevlin and his brothers hanging on the wall.

"Marjani?" Kevlin called.

"Marjani, run!" Jerrik shouted.

She didn't respond, but walked calmly up to Masego, her face peaceful, her eyes half-closed as if on the verge of sleeping.

Masego stroked her hair and crooned, "Such a pretty thing, isn't she? I know you care about her. How far will you allow me to torment this lovely young lady?"

He grinned at the unbridled rage on Jerrik's face.

"Don't encourage him," Drystan whispered. "He'll only hurt her more if he sees it affecting you."

"Don't pretend you don't care about her," Masego said. "Remember, Felix was in your confidence, and Felix tells me everything."

He touched Marjani's forehead and she smiled up at him.

"Marjani, run!" Kevlin and Jerrik shouted uselessly.

She gave no indication of hearing them.

"Marjani," Kevlin cried. "Can't you hear me?"

Jerrik growled, "I swear by all that's holy I'll rip your heart out with my bare hands."

Masego stopped several feet away from them with Marjani standing close beside him. "This pretty little maid and I are now very good friends. She'll do anything I ask." He touched her cheek and asked softly, "Won't you, my dear?"

She nodded vigorously.

The sight of Marjani in thrall to Masego enraged Kevlin and he thrashed uselessly against his chains. She was a friend who was going to suffer for no other crime than knowing them.

"I'm gonna kill you," Jerrik declared.

"Please," Masego said. "Spare the bravado. You're completely in my power. The only thing you have any control over is how painful your deaths will be and how long it's going to take me to kill you. Have no doubt. You will die."

He turned to Marjani. "I would like you to please me."

She threw herself upon him, trying to embrace and kiss him, her face filled with mindless adoration. The sight nauseated Kevlin and he yanked against his chains again, but only barely managed to rattle them.

Masego pushed her back. "No. Not so fast. Let's take our time."

Marjani paused, waiting for his command, her eyes devoid of life. He smiled. "Dance for me."

She began to sway to music that rang only in her ears.

"Go ahead and take off that dress."

She began tearing at her clothing.

"No. Slowly, so our friends can enjoy the show." Once more she began swaying and moving to the inaudible music, and began to slowly unbutton her dress.

"You animal," Jerrik roared, his face red with rage as he thrashed against the chains holding him to the wall.

Masego smiled cruelly. "The dance will stop when I have Oris."

"I'm going to kill you," Jerrik shouted again.

The giant Donarri threw his head back and roared, straining with all of his mighty strength against the shackles. Blood began to trickle down his wrists where the iron cut into his skin.

"Pace yourself," Masego said. "You're going to wear yourself out too fast that way. We still have a lot of fun ahead of us."

Jerrik roared a long, desperate sound, his face red with the strain, and every muscle standing out as he redoubled his efforts. With a sudden *crack*, the small links of iron fastening the shackles to the chain holding his right wrist shattered.

Jerrik twisted and pulled with both hands, and the left one snapped too.

"You'll die first," Masego began.

With an ear-splitting roar, Jerrik ripped the shackles off his feet and dropped to the ground. Like an enraged bull, he charged the surprised Sentinel.

For a second Kevlin believed he was going to make it, that he would actually close the gap and crush Masego with one mighty fist.

Masego raised his hand and Jerrik ran into a shimmering amber wall scant inches from Masego's throat. He bounced back, his charge broken. He threw himself against it, battering the barrier with his fists.

Masego made a flicking gesture with one hand and an invisible force hurled Jerrik backward. He struck the stone wall so hard it shuttered. He slumped to the ground and lay in a crumpled mass, shaking with pain.

"I grow tired of this game," Masego said.

He gestured with his other hand and the still-dancing, Marjani was also thrown at the wall.

Jerrik lunged and caught her before she struck the wall, absorbing the impact with his own body. The two of them slumped to the floor and neither tried to rise again.

Masego said, "Perhaps something more direct. Kevlin, let's see how dear this secret is to you after you watch some of your friends burn."

He snapped his fingers and a ball of fire coalesced in the air before him. When Kevlin didn't respond, he threw out his hand and the ball of fire shot toward Jerrik and Marjani. There was nothing any of them could do but watch death roll toward them.

"Wait!" Kevlin shouted, thrashing helplessly against his bonds.

Masego grinned, his eyes blazing with eager anticipation as the fire hurtled toward the huddled forms of the two victims. In a last heroic effort, Jerrik pulled Marjani behind him, trying to protect her with his own body.

Kevlin screamed in impotent rage as the fire struck.

85

TOO MUCH OF A GOOD THING

With a great splash of flame, the fireball struck, and for a moment the roaring fire concealed Jerrik and Marjani. The heat blistered Kevlin's face and flames licked up the wall toward him and Drystan.

Then the flames dissipated. The two victims lay completely unharmed.

"What did you do?" Masego shouted. His sadistic glee changed in a heartbeat to unbridled rage.

"I will not allow you to harm anyone else."

That voice was like a song in Kevlin's heart.

Indira.

She stood just inside the door at the far end of the room. Still dressed in her stained Healer's robe, her midnight hair disheveled, she had never looked more beautiful. Adalia entered the room behind her and scanned the room, not looking shocked to see dead and dying scattered everywhere.

"About what we thought," she muttered.

Masego snarled and lashed out one hand. A crimson spear of magic arced through the air toward Indira. Just before reaching her, it shattered into thousands of glittering rainbow shards that floated around her like a halo.

Indira stepped farther into the room, her expression determined. "You will harm no one."

Twang!

With characteristic speed, Adalia loosed an arrow at the fat Sentinel. The shaft burst into flame, disintegrating before reaching him.

"Don't insult me," Masego said.

He looked at Adalia again and snapped his fingers. Fire erupted around her, enveloping her in a deadly storm.

The tiny archer stepped through the flame, scowling but unharmed. "This fellow be the one wot's been killin' folks, eh Indira?"

"Yes," Indira said, again advancing.

"You cannot interfere with me!" Masego shouted. He raised his arms and a fierce whirlwind sprang into life around the two women, shattering nearby furniture and flinging the pieces around the room in a deadly storm.

They walked through it unharmed, their hair not even blowing out of place. Kevlin grinned with renewed hope. Masego couldn't stop Indira. She'd slap him as soundly as she had Ceren.

Masego howled and pointed at the ceiling. With a terrifying *crack*, it gave way. Huge timbers and chunks of masonry cascaded over the two women with a thunderous roar. Stinging dust billowed into the room.

"Indira," Kevlin cried, worried despite his earlier optimism.

Masego bounced on his toes while he waited for the dust to clear. He probably hoped to catch a glimpse of their shattered corpses.

He was disappointed.

The debris had fall around the women, forming a natural doorway through which they could step. Dust coated their garments, and Adalia coughed a couple of times.

"Your evil magic has failed," Indira said. "You can do no more harm here."

"You can't stop me," Masego shouted, and raised his hands again. A thick wall of ice materialized in front of the women, stretching across the room and blocking them off.

"You should have kept Felix around," Kevlin mocked in an attempt to draw Masego's attention away from Indira. "He might have been able to learn the secret you want to know."

"Felix is a weakling." Masego spun to face Kevlin. He waved one hand, and another chair slammed into Kevlin. The pain rolled over him in a suffocating wave that pushed him into the welcome darkness of unconsciousness.

Kevlin came back to himself slowly, and wished he hadn't. He hurt. A lot. His torso throbbed like he'd been kicked by a horse for a month, and his wrists burned from the pressure of the shackles.

As soon as he moved, Masego shouted, "Tell me where the stone is." The fat Sentinel was now standing in front of him, his eyes blazing with barely controlled madness.

"Tell me!" Masego shouted again.

"I know where Oris is," Kevlin whispered through bloody lips.

"Tell me!"

"I'd have probably told Felix, but I'll never tell Masego."

Kevlin wanted to glance at the ice wall to see if Indira had found a way through yet, but didn't dare draw Masego's attention back to it.

"Tell me!" hollered Masego again.

He needed to try something new. Then again uselessly repeating the same demand over and over was a lot less painful than some of his other tactics.

Kevlin shook his head. "You're never going to find out."

"Tell me or I'll kill everyone you've ever loved."

As if he knew all of them.

"Felix, what did Kevlin do now?"

Gabral stood a little unsteady, clutching the Mace. At his feet, Sitara and Remiel lay close together, their hands clasped. Kevlin couldn't tell if they'd died yet or not.

He realized that Gabral didn't yet know about Masego. Before Kevlin could shout a warning, Masego pointed at Gabral. Flames erupted around his head and torso.

Gabral collapsed to the ground, falling beneath the fire. His hair was burning, his eyebrows had already singed off, and his face looked blistered. He screamed as Masego's fire dropped to cover him again.

Then the Mace burst into blue fire that scattered Masego's crimson flames. Gabral rolled to his hands and knees as the Mace's protective flames rolled up his arm and enveloped him.

"Felix is possessed by Masego," Kevlin shouted.

Gabral grunted and stood. "Then they'll die together."

"You first." Masego clapped his hands together, and a spear of crimson magic shot across the distance between them.

Gabral swatted the magic spear aside with the Mace. It exploded through the wall of ice blocking Indira and Adalia. Chunks of ice blasted past the two ladies and smashed into the wall. Several large chunks crashed right through the door, leaving its splintered remains swinging from the hinges.

Adalia was ready, arrow nocked, and she fired at Masego.

He snapped his fingers and the arrow changed course in mid-air and drove for Gabral's face.

Gabral ducked and shouted, "Leave off! I'll deal with this." He advanced on Masego, who circled him, moving into the center of the room.

Indira rushed past them both, heading for Kevlin. He grinned at her, yearning to take her into his arms.

"You really should help Gabral," he said.

"He doesn't need me," she said breathlessly. "You do."

She placed both hands on the center of his chest and looked into his eyes. "You must defeat Masego."

Her hands began to glow.

Magic poured into Kevlin from the amulet as it captured Indira's power. Kevlin shouted with triumph, *changed* it and reached for Oris. He connected with the stone, and magic flooded into him from it, filling him with welcome strength, heightened senses, and pure joy.

He looked past Indira, exulting in the clarity of magic-enhanced sight. Inside each person pulsed the light of life. Thankfully it still glowed inside the keisara, although it burned faint. She wouldn't live much longer without healing.

With a thought, Kevlin burst the shackles that held him pinned against the wall. He dropped to the floor close beside Indira. She tried to step back to give him room, but he wrapped her in his arms and kissed her full lips.

She leaned into him and kissed him passionately in return. That would motivate any man to become a hero.

"Thanks," he said when he released her.

"I trust you Kevlin. I know giving you magic is the right thing."

"Yeah, that helped too."

Then he headed for Masego, who still fought Gabral. The Mace bearer had closed to within a dozen feet of the Sentinel.

"If you kill me, Felix dies too," Masego said.

Gabral shrugged. "Sometimes victory comes with a price."

He'd said the same thing when he'd almost killed Kevlin in his attempt to take Tanathos. In extreme circumstances, Gabral was right, but Kevlin hated that the Mace bearer seemed so willing to accept those sacrifices.

Gabral lunged toward Masego. "You die now!"

Masego retreated and pointed at the floor.

A wide hole gaped open under Gabral's feet. The short colonel shouted in surprise as his victorious charge changed into an uncontrolled plunge to the lower level of the tower.

Masego grinned at the distant sound of Gabral's crashing impact echoing back up through the hole.

When he turned, Kevlin punched him in the jaw. Kevlin poured all of his anger and frustration that had been building for days. He plastered the Sentinel's nose against his face.

Let him try rearranging that feature. Masego fell, rolling just past the edge of the hole Gabral had just fallen through. He stumbled to his feet and shifted to the side, placing the hole between them.

As Kevlin moved to pursue him, Masego's form shuddered and softened into the features of Felix.

"I'm free," he shouted. No trace of Masego remained.

Kill him! Jerrik's thought echoed through Kevlin's mind.

Kevlin hesitated. Could Masego really be gone?

Felix's body shivered and settled once more into the hardened features of Masego. "That's the last time you ever see Felix," Masego said, spitting a mouthful of blood.

"Then I guess he's going to die with you."

Kevlin threw a dagger he'd picked up as he crossed the room. Just as he had in Tanathos's hidden fortress in Hallvarr, he focused on the blade and willed magic into it.

Brilliant white light blazed around the weapon as it flew for Masego's heart.

Masego batted it aside and made a clutching gesture with his hands. More magic poured into Kevlin as whatever spell Masego had attempted was nullified by the amulet.

Kevlin wished Harafin had trained him more in magical duels. The defensive measures they'd studied were crucial, but he lacked knowledge of how to attack.

Harafin had said to use one's imagination. Kevlin did. He willed the pulsing magic into a weapon capable of reaching Masego across the yawning, eight-foot gap. A long whip of fire materialized in his hand and he lashed out and wrapped the burning length around the man's legs.

Masego shattered the whip and replied with a ball of ice the size of a man's head.

Kevlin dodged, forming one of the shields Harafin had taught him. The missile careened off and shattered against the far wall.

Ice fragments pelted around Indira, but she remained untouched. Ice slashed into Drystan where he hung on the wall, and into Jerrik where he still lay against the wall on the floor.

"Sorry," he whispered. Hopefully Indira would extend her healing influence so he didn't hurt anyone else by accident. If only he could reach Masego with a sword.

Why not?

A long blade of pure-white light appeared in his hand. He swung it at Masego, who stood a dozen feet away. The blade stretched to cover the distance and Kevlin slashed at the fat man's head.

A blade of pure darkness materialized in Masego's hand, and he parried the strike just short of his face. Swift as thought, they sparred across the broken floor with blades of power. Sparks of magic erupted from the blades and cascaded high into the air, leaving tendrils of smoke hanging for several seconds.

Kevlin's world contracted as it always did when he fought with the sword, and his concentration became complete. Battle lust raged through him and drove back the pain from his recently broken rib and multiple bruises.

Masego might be skilled with magic, but he was no match for Kevlin with the sword. The distance between them proved meaningless as they fought with the weightless blades of magic.

Kevlin pressed the attack, adjusting quickly to the unique form of battle. He struck several times, off-balancing his opponent, beating down Masego's defenses and creating an opening for a finishing strike.

With a shout of triumph, he struck for Masego's heart. Masego released his own blade of darkness and caught the blade of light.

The magical blade connected them, sparking and crackling dangerously in Masego's grasp. The smell of charred flesh wafted to Kevlin. The fat man grimaced but held on tenaciously, trying to subdue the magic and bend it to his own will.

Kevlin called to Oris. The rock responded with a wave of magic that filled him to his uttermost capacity. He threw it all down the sword of light.

It rippled down the glowing blade with the brilliance of a miniature sun and struck Masego in a blinding explosion of light. He cried out and tumbled to the floor. His great black cloak billowed around him like a cloud and temporarily concealed him from view.

Kevlin stalked around the hole in the floor to deliver the fatal blow as Masego struggled within the folds of his cloak. Too much of a good thing could literally drive Kevlin insane.

The pulsing magic revolted against his control. Kevlin stumbled under the onslaught, clutching his head. He should have expected it, but he'd hoped it would obey for just another minute. Especially since Oris had given it to him.

The magic crashed against his defenses and a pounding headache formed between his temples. He had taken in so much magic, it assaulted his mind with stunning force.

Kevlin's hands shook as he fought to defend his mental shields and hold the magic at bay until it submitted again to his will. Only now he felt the growing, insidious lust for magic that came with the Trembling Madness.

All of a sudden he longed to embrace the insanity of the magic and release all restraint. Masego, the hidden enemy they'd hunted for so long, stood revealed. He had the power to destroy the hated man. All he had to do was strike now.

Kevlin glanced at Masego and snarled to see the fat man regaining his feet.

"You steal magic like a leech," Masego said, "but you lack the power to control it." He raised one hand, pointed at the low couch that Keisara Fideima had sat on earlier, and hurled it toward Kevlin.

When it struck, it would break him.

It never touched him.

Kevlin couldn't fight Masego and resist the Trembling Madness. Maybe Leander was right. Maybe sometimes it was right to embrace insanity for the greater good.

Time to test the theory.

Kevlin dropped all restraints.

Pain roared behind his eyes, blinding him for a split second and sending him staggering to the very brink of the hole in the floor. His mental defenses disintegrated, and magic surged through the breech, inundating him and drowning his mind in the *Tai Pari*.

Kevlin descended into madness.

After the first heartbeat of mind-numbing pain, he welcomed the magic that threatened to rip him to pieces. He embraced it as it tore through him and cast his mind over the precipice into chaos.

In that instant of surrender, a shockwave of blue-green light blasted out from him. It shattered the flying couch into a thousand wooden splinters that burst into flames and vaporized into drifting smoke. Undiminished, the wave struck Masego, rocking the surprised man back on his heels.

It shattered every window in the outer wall. Kevlin swayed drunkenly and he exulted with the joy of madness. He floated on a cloud of power. His vision tinged with rainbow light, and he laughed uncontrollably. The laughter sounded vaguely familiar, but he didn't care Fear and doubts evaporated, replaced by crazed confidence.

He was power. *He* was magic. No longer a simple, weak human.

No longer Kevlin.

He was . . . The Catalyst.

86

IDENTITY PROBLEMS

The name seemed fitting so the Catalyst assumed it. Magic pounded through him in a chaotic maelstrom that burned with an undeniable need to be released.

A man whose name no longer mattered, faced him, one hand raised and burning with power. The Catalyst snarled and his eyes blazed with fire as he roared a wordless howl of animal rage. There would be no challenge to his power.

He attacked with shapeless waves of pure energy. The challenger staggered under the onslaught, completely on the defensive as he battled to protect himself.

Magic deflected in every direction, ricocheting from the challenger as crimson bolts of power. Some ripped deep gouges in the stone floor. Others blasted through the gaping hole in the ceiling and exploded in the next room above. Many more burst out through the yawning opening where windows once stood and through which the wind now whistled. Others rebounded to the Catalyst, who absorbed them and cast them out again.

The onslaught soon overwhelmed the enemy and sent him tumbling across the room in a tangle of robes and black cloak. The Catalyst laughed again and dismissed the insignificant opponent. He turned slowly and searched for other outlets for the magic boiling through him. It must be released. The world must burn with it.

Remnants of a wall of ice across the room caught his attention. He shattered it, and burned away the chunks of ice before they could strike the floor.

The Catalyst smiled. This was good, but it wasn't enough.

He ignored the insignificant group of people crouched against the inner wall of the room who were shouting useless babble. Driven by the vortex of power in his mind, the Catalyst rose through the hole in the roof to the next level. Windows in every wall offered spectacular views of palaces, turrets, and long buildings.

The Catalyst frowned. He must stand atop the world. So many things to destroy. He ripped off the ceiling with a wave of his hand and rose through two more levels before smashing the roof. He rose to the highest level and surveyed the city from the uninterrupted view.

Embracing the pure joy of destruction, he pointed a finger that glowed like ten thousand stars at the peak of the nearest tower. It stood directly across from him and rivaled the Catalyst's height. From the depths of his mind, a name floated to the surface.

The Emperor's Tower.

He disintegrated it.

The Catalyst grinned as first the roof, and then the highest levels of the Emperor's Tower collapsed under the storm of magic. When it fell below the roof of the nearest palace, he shattered the entire top floor of that palace.

The lower levels of that palace began to glow with red-hot intensity, and the outer stones melted from the supernatural heat. Screams faintly reached his ears, encouraging him to do more to prove his dominance.

Pure blackness rose around him, an evil cloud attempting to suck out his life. He shattered it and new magic poured into him. He looked down through the tower's broken levels. The foolish challenger that he had forgotten about stood down there. The man now backed away, although he still looked prepared to fight.

The Catalyst snarled in rage and threw his hands wide. The room below filled with roaring fire.

No one died.

He could feel lives pulsing with steady life despite the fire that licked at the walls and consumed the furniture. He intensified the heat until the very stones began to melt.

Still no one died.

The Catalyst growled and prepared to redouble his efforts. He would to kill everyone in that room.

87

CHANGE OF PLAN

Harafin paused at an intersection of wide hallways on the back side of the Great Dome, not far from the border of the Emperor's Palace. Leander and a pair of Stalwarts slowed to a halt behind him, but said nothing. Farther back, Emperor Tegnazian and the ambassadors struggled to keep up.

Harafin ignored them all and placed a hand on a carved wooden post where the two hallways met. He bent over it, eyes closed in concentration, searching for the source of the surge of energy he'd felt through the floor even while running full speed.

"What is it?" Emperor Tegnazian asked through labored breaths as he drew close.

"Something . . ."

Harafin slipped his senses into the stone beyond the post and connected to the intricate web of magic embedded in every wall of the inner-city complex. There. It took only a few seconds to find. The magnitude of raw power in the keisara's apartments chilled him.

Despite a ripple of chilling fear, he cautiously reached farther with his thoughts.

Kevlin.

At the center of the storm, and only barely recognizable, stood Kevlin. That could only mean one thing. Not good.

He had to stop it. Reaching through the chaos, Harafin touched Kevlin's mind.

The reaction came instantly and burst against Harafin's carefully placed shields with awesome power. The blow rocked him to the core, and very nearly shattered his defenses. No one had come so close in almost two centuries.

Magic ripped through the distance between them a second time. It slammed into the old Sentinel, a physical blow that hurled him backward. He crashed to the floor and slid a dozen paces down the corridor. Leander reached his side an instant later and poured healing magic into him that removed the pain and restored his strength.

Harafin took a shuddering breath and looked up at his old friend, communicating everything in that one grave look.

"Are you all right," the emperor asked. When he nodded, the emperor asked, "Can you run? We need to get to my wife's chambers."

"I'm afraid not." Harafin allowed Leander to pull him to his feet as he mentally prepared for the coming trial.

"Then we'll send word to you," the emperor said and turned to leave.

Harafin grabbed the emperor's shoulder. "You misunderstand. I meant that we cannot go to her majesty's apartments. If we do, she will die."

"What's going on?" Emperor Tegnazian demanded.

Harafin didn't respond. He was already sprinting in a new direction. Toward the Great Dome.

"Basak," Leander called, and gestured after Harafin's retreating form.

Within seconds, Pallian Stalwarts pounded past Harafin despite his fast pace. They charged down the hall and again bodily removed everyone out of the way.

"What's going on?" the emperor called again as he gave chase.

"Your wife's life is now tied to a wider battle," Leander replied.

Harafin spoke softly to himself as he ran. "As are all of our lives."

88

DESTRUCTION VS PRESERVATION

The Catalyst laughed maniacally with the thrill of victory. The mind that had briefly touched his had been very strong, but no one could challenge him. He dismissed the vanquished enemy and turned his attention once more to the lower room and the frustrating tenacity of its inhabitants.

Time to kill them all. He formed his power into a long, spiraling column extending into the heavens. Through it he grasped the ponderous weight of the air and drew it downward. He'd seen this spell once, and he would make it even more destructive.

He twisted the air and drew it down faster, tighter. Out of the clear sky appeared a roaring tornado that descended past him into the tower below.

The wind screamed through the tower, and the gaping hole in the floor ripped wider. The wind tore at the structure and threatening to rip the entire top of the building apart and carry the fragments to the heavens. Floating in chaos, the Catalyst laughed, his arms wide, and magic pouring from him in staggering quantities to fuel the mighty whirlwind.

No one died.

The wind scoured the walls and shattered the floors between the various levels until the tower stood little more than an empty shell. It filled the room below with the overwhelming power of the elements unleashed, but it failed to move even a single person. Around each individual, a tiny eddy of calm held against the wind.

The Catalyst shook with rage and sparks of magic dripped from each strand of hair. He would not allow his power to be challenged. At his unspoken command, the whirlwind ceased.

The resulting calm lasted only a second before a blinding flash of lightning arced down from the clear sky to strike at one prone form. The accompanying crack of thunder shattered windows in nearby buildings, but the unconscious human form lay still, sleeping unconcerned and untouched by the deadly lightning.

Another bolt of lightning fell, followed a heartbeat later by a hundred more, all raining from the sky and striking at everyone in the room in a blinding tangle of searing power. Remnants of wood not carried off by the whirlwind caught fire, and every hair on the Catalyst's head stood on end as the air became dangerously charged.

No one died.

The Catalyst shrieked in fury, and flames billowed from his open mouth. Then he paused and stepped to the edge of the precipice and looked down on the form of one of the women who stood unharmed in the midst of the lightning storm.

She stood apart from the others, as if trying to position herself between them and danger. She looked up at him with tears streaming down her face. Somehow it was her power protecting these people.

She dared to defy him, shouting ridiculous, meaningless words of restraint and control.

She must die.

The Catalyst hurled his magic at her in a devastating wave of death that ripped the fabric of the air between them. It darkened the entire tower for a double heartbeat and sucked every bit of breathable air away. The resulting vacuum should destroy all life.

It did not.

His power dissipated and the cursed woman stood against him still. She looked surprised, but stood unharmed, as if he'd merely shouted curses at her. She called a name that no longer applied to him and beckoned him down.

He focused on the floor beneath her feet and released another wave of power. Cracks appeared and zig-zagged across the floor. Large sections fell with resounding booms to the level below. In seconds, holes gaped everywhere, but the floor remained solidly intact beneath everyone, connecting them in a twisted jigsaw of stone and wood.

The Catalyst howled with fury.

This hated witch-woman must die.

89

OLD MEN CAN JUMP

High up the inner side of the dome, two Stalwarts ran out onto a balcony set apart from other walkways on the seventh level. They paused, unsure where to go next.

Harafin sprinted out of the hallway onto the balcony and, without slowing, *leaped* over the railing into the vast empty space beyond.

Propelled by a burst of energy, Harafin sailed in a high arc far out into the center of the space beneath the Great Dome. People passing on the levels below pointed in wondering awe at the spectacle and shouted in concern at the expected long fall to the hard floor below.

One Sentinel, who stood on the main floor, gaped for a second in astonishment before the import of what he witnessed drove home. The truth chilled him to the bone with a sudden icy dread. He shouted, his voice magnified by actinic power.

"Everyone, run!"

As Harafin reached the pinnacle of his arc, directly under the center of the dome, he threw his hands out wide. Blue lightning exploded from his fingertips in crackling bolts that struck all around the inside of the dome.

The lightning didn't punch through the walls, but deflected perpendicular. Some raced up the heavy ribs that supported the dome while others ran horizontal, parallel to the distant floor. Where the bolts intersected, they split, and then split again. Within a double heartbeat, a grid-like pattern of incandescent power crisscrossed the entire upper side of the dome.

Ear-splitting thunderclaps shook the entire structure and sent people fleeing for exits with hands clutching their ears. Screams of fear were swallowed up by the rolling peals of thunder that reverberated for half a minute through the dome.

The sound buffeted Harafin like dozens of fists as he hung at the very apex of his flight for a long heartbeat. Just before beginning the terrifying plunge toward the hard floor of the mosaic map, he shouted a word of power.

It shook the entire massive structure. From every intersecting junction of lightning-like magic, new bolts of power arced back out to the center of the dome. Nine hundred and ninety-three bolts of power all met simultaneously to form a sphere of magic surrounding and supporting Harafin.

A final thunderclap, magnified a hundred times, reverberated through the dome. It rent the air and knocked from their feet people who had not yet fled. Those unfortunates ran in headlong panic from the sudden, terrifying spectacle.

Standing within the brilliantly glowing sphere of energy suspended beneath the center of the dome, Harafin intoned the next sequence of the spell. It would call upon the ancient magic embedded in the very fabric of the palace and activate the defensive spells that had long remained dormant.

The entire dome rang as if struck by an impossibly huge silver hammer. The air shimmered with rainbow light, as if the entire inner space under the dome bent and twisted inside a gigantic prism.

Vast amounts of magic stirred and came to life.

90

THE ULTIMATE TRUMP CARD

T he Catalyst paused. Ignoring the witch-woman who somehow defied him still, he focused on the structure beneath his feet. Powerful magic stirred deep in the bowels of the palace. Magic intended to thwart him.

His authority could not be challenged. He would rule all the dominion visible from this great height. He focused the power that so desperately sought for release and drove it against the new threat. All challengers would be ground to dust.

Somehow a foreign power absorbed his attack and bled the power away before it could fulfill its mission of destruction. He redoubled his efforts, and in a moment of insane clarity, it dawned upon him what he must do.

He must destroy everything. Only then would his power remain unchallenged.

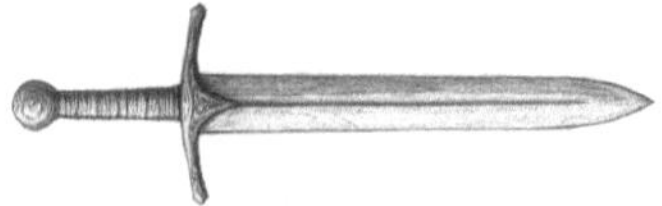

Beads of sweat dripped down Harafin's forehead as he worked, only to burn away from the heat of the pulsing energy that surrounded him. He focused completely on the task of fully activating the palace's defenses, but couldn't shake a growing shadow of fear.

He only needed another minute. If he could complete the sequence and fully activate the old magic, he could call upon the powers of the Sentinel High Council, and the enclaves scattered across the empire. The magic was awesomely powerful, strong enough even to bottle up the chaos of Kevlin out of control. They had always assumed there would be adequate time to activate the defenses.

He only needed a few more minutes. Even as the thought formed, the power under his hands swelled in a staggering wave and a torrent of magic drove against the partially activated defenses. Harafin grunted with the effort, pushed to the extreme edge of his capacity by the wild, untamed magic.

With the sphere of lightning protecting and enhancing his abilities, he wrested control over this first assault. Even with his enhanced abilities he could not contain it, so he re-directed it and released it back through the palace to dissipate outside.

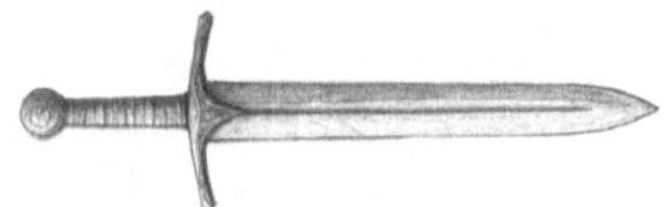

On the palace grounds, amazement spread as people paused to take note of a strange glow beginning to emanate from many of the palace buildings. In the sunken gardens and lawns across the palace complex, people started in surprise at the unexpected shocks they received walking on the grass.

People retreated in fear from the statues of the gods ringing the central courtyard. Their eyes glowed with blue fire.

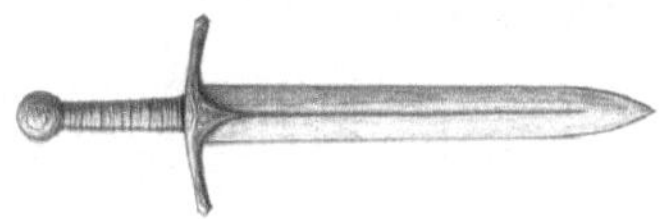

Harafin blew out a labored breath and faced the hard truth. He lacked the time necessary to complete the entire sequence. He couldn't finish the intricate process while simultaneously withstanding these attacks from Kevlin.

The boy should not be capable of such concentrated assaults, now while suffering a *Tai Pari*. Yet somehow he did. What he lacked in sophistication he more than made up for in simple magnitude. His attacks already threatened to overwhelm the defenses.

Harafin could not hesitate. With a focused effort of concentration, Harafin threw a mental command out to the air and drove it throughout the entire inner city.

The day of peril is come. Your strength is needed. This is a Critical-Urgent event.

So powerful echoed the command that many of those possessing no actinic gift paused to listen, sure they had heard something, but unable to say exactly what it was. All they knew was that the ghostly whisper filled them with a nameless fear.

Throughout every palace, those with actinic gifts, along with every Stalwart, cried out in alarm. Some stumbled under the force of the command. Universal fear reflected in every face, but their training took over and they sprang into action.

All through the inner city, they raced to nodes of power embedded in every structure and linked their minds to the palace defensive grid matrix. Their strength flowed up through the matrix to the lightning sphere cradling Harafin high in the air under the Great Dome.

The sphere blazed with light, and sparks of pure magic cascaded down toward the empty expanse below. The new influx of power stretched Harafin's abilities far beyond the limits of his natural frame.

The lines of magic forming the sphere began to shift, flowing from the simple grid pattern into symbols of power that further magnified the strength of the Sentinel within.

The receptacle of that vast power, Harafin became the key. Despite his age, in the invisible world of light and magic, he was an undisputed master. Wielding the power with the skill of a maestro, he wove his spells and worked his way through the increasingly complex patterns.

The emperor and the rest of the small group stared in stunned amazement across the wide empty space at Harafin hanging suspended in the magical sphere. They stood on the short balcony high up on the side of the Great Dome, the only witnesses to the awesome spectacle.

Leander stepped to the edge of the balcony and plunged his hand into one of the junctions of power situated just above his head. The lightning-like globe of pure magic sparked and crackled at the contact, but didn't harm the old Stalwart.

Leander bowed his head in concentration and poured his indomitable strength into the effort to support Harafin. The conduit of power connecting the node to Harafin's sphere flared to pure white brilliance.

Silently each of the Stalwarts followed their leader's example. They linked together into a long chain, with each man grasping the shoulder of the man in front of him. The last man was Basak, who connected the chain to Leander. The entire group began to glow softly, and the conduit to Harafin's sphere thickened and burned brighter still.

The chain of Stalwarts chanted, a soft litany filled with purpose, with faith, and with resolve. Within seconds, every gifted soul in the inner city united, the full force of their wills focused on one man.

Inside of the sphere of power, Harafin struggled to remain in control. The magnitude of power flowing through his fingers threatened to shatter his will even enhanced by the strength of so many others and from the magic of the palace itself.

He held on with iron determination, his control balanced on a knife's edge, with destruction looming at either side should his concentration slip for even a second. Were he to waver even a little, he would suffer his own *Tai Pari*, and all would be lost.

He did not waver. A new wave of power assaulted the matrix from the out-of-control Kevlin. Stronger than the last, it pushed Harafin to the very brink before he managed to deflect the power out through every available outlet.

If Kevlin kept this up, he'd drain all the latent magic from the area, leaving the actinopathic who supported Harafin powerless. Harafin could do nothing about it. So he clutched the living magic of the sphere and shouted the next word of power in the sequence.

Silence descended over the entire dome like a heavy blanket, so deep it silenced the ambassadors' muttered cries. For three long heartbeats, absolute quiet reigned.

Then every mural in the upper half of the dome shattered together with the sound of fifty thousand windows breaking. Every color imaginable exploded across the vast space under the dome in thousands of streaming rainbows made up of plaster shards.

As the shattered remnants of two centuries of effort fluttered down through the dome, the boundless expanse of golden metal that made up the lower layer of the dome glowed with pure amber light. Symbols of power, previously concealed beneath the murals, flared like miniature suns and set the millions of plaster shards glittering like tiny mirrors that filled the dome with reflected light.

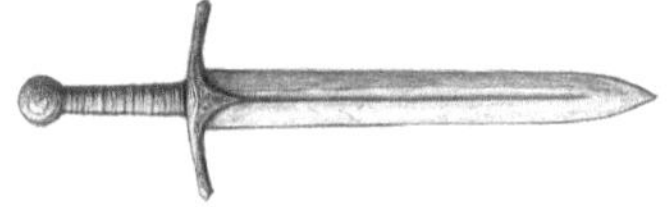

Emperor Tegnazian stared in awed disbelief at the spectacle of the fluttering remnants of the priceless murals drifting toward the distant floor. He then turned to the unbelievable sight of Harafin hanging suspended in the air far out in the nothingness beneath the Great Dome.

This couldn't be happening. As emperor, he knew of the magical defenses embedded within the very fabric of the palace. The spells had been woven two centuries ago during the initial building of the city, and had been reinforced and strengthened during every war with the Grakonians.

No one was ever supposed to use it. Intended as part of a last, desperate defensive measure should the empire be overrun by her enemies, the spells were not to be triggered except under imminent threat of destruction.

Where were the attacking armies? He hadn't even declared war on anyone. He should at least get to do that. He didn't understand what was going on, but as emperor he was supposed to know. Not knowing terrified him.

He was never supposed to be terrified. That made him angry.

"What can I do?" he shouted, hoping for someone to give him concrete direction, but dreading what they might say.

The burly Stalwart Basak whispered, "Stay back. Pray Harafin has the strength to defeat this threat."

"What threat?" demanded Duke Kescog from where he stood nearby, his hand clenching, as if searching for a weapon.

The Stalwart did not speak again, his entire effort focused on the invisible struggle they were engaged in.

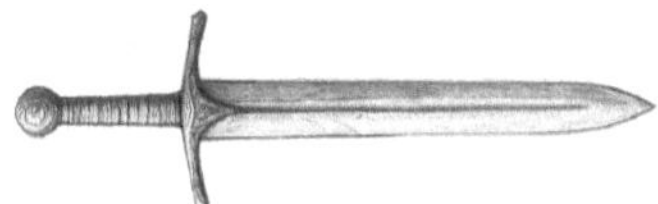

The Catalyst raged.

How could these puny mortals challenge his power? He drew even greater quantities of magic from the stone that served him, and thrust fingers of power down the length of the building. He drove his senses to the very foundation, intent on ripping the palace up by the roots and sending the entire structure crashing to the ground.

He could not. The foundation of the building was connected to the broader structure of the nearby palaces by the same magic that defied him. In fact, the entire inner city stood locked together, welded into an unbreakable whole.

Reaching farther, he called upon even more magic until his body began to swell, with blinding blue light blazing from every pore. He swayed, on the verge of complete disintegration.

The Catalyst was pleased. He struck at the nexus of the magic, at the heart of the matrix where the magic converged.

At Harafin and the sphere that contained him.

91

COMING UP SHORT

Indira paused for breath. Her throat burned from shouting at Kevlin, vainly trying to get his attention and reason with him. She tried to extend her shield of Faith over him like everyone else in the room, but couldn't reach him.

Adalia clung to her like a child, the normally fearless little archer terrified into speechless immobility. Even had Indira been able to tear herself from Adalia's grip, she couldn't climb the empty shell of the tower to reach Kevlin.

He might as well be in a different world. She stared up at him, her eyes filled with tears of disbelief, her soul aching with confusion and guilt. She had done this.

Ceren had warned her to stay away and she'd spurned that advice out of anger. She'd thought trusting Kevlin and following her heart could prevail.

She was so wrong. He had tried to kill her. The thought tore at her like a living dagger in her heart. She didn't know what to do. Everything had seemed so simple. She had been so filled with purpose, with conviction.

Now he had tried to kill her and threatened the entire city. She had triggered the *Tai Pari*. She, who worked so hard all her life to heal, would bear responsibility for every death that resulted.

Kevlin would probably die, and it was her fault. She might as well have slit his throat herself. The thought burned through her and gorge rose in her throat while tears stung her eyes.

She stared up at Kevlin, or what had been Kevlin, and couldn't recognize him. His body now burned with incandescent fire, and he seemed more a primal force of nature, than a man. This was not the man she knew, the man she loved.

It was Kevlin who had sparked a fire in her soul, who had opened the door to learning new aspects to her gift. Without her Faith, everyone in the tower would now be dead. Even his own swordbrothers who huddled with Marjani at the base of the wall, would have been killed by now had she not protected them.

They might not last long. The strain on her Faith was growing, a tangible weight that dragged her down with its unfamiliar burden. Always before, her Faith had been weightless, protecting her and granting the glorious gift of healing to ease the suffering of so many. Now her Faith was strained to the limits.

The ability to extend that Faith to others proactively was so new she had never tested the limits of her strength. Until now she hadn't even been sure it would work. With the shockingly destructive magic being unleashed against them all, those limits were being taxed.

For the first time in her life, her Faith was beginning to waver. A new feeling began to grow, chill and unfamiliar in the pit of her stomach.

Indira was afraid. How long until she began to doubt?

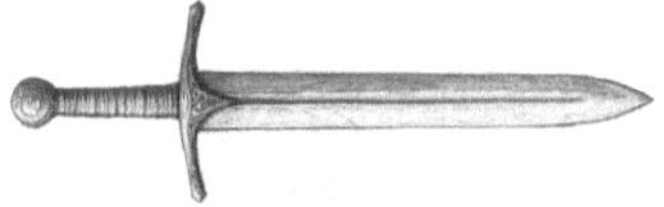

Harafin, Master of Light, wielded the power crackling in the air around him, and through him, with absolute precision. His hands and feet moved along the lines of magic forming the sphere, from one symbol of power to another, reinforcing and strengthening the spells strained to the uttermost limits by the new onslaught.

Constantly moving, he stepped to a dance that he alone could tread. One misstep, one incorrect movement, one split second loss of concentration, and the spell would shatter. With it, the entire palace would be destroyed.

Harafin locked his will into complete concentration, refusing to acknowledge the cold dread that threatened to drain his resolve and sap his strength.

That fear made the task of holding the shields against the staggering waves of magic hammering at them almost impossible. He could not recognize it, couldn't admit the unfathomable truth.

Despite his efforts, the fear continued to grow, a dread that whispered of the fast-approaching doom that he refused to acknowledge. He could not hold out for long.

He only needed a few more minutes.

He would not get them.

Despite the growing certainty of defeat, he fought on, mastering and controlling the wild magic that shredded the palace's defenses. He siphoned the power away from his enemy, and discharged it back through the defensive grid, and into the ground beneath.

He chose not to consider what would happen when the plateau could hold no more.

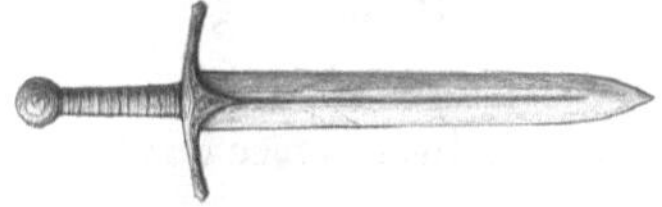

Indira dropped to her knees, unable to remain standing beneath the strain of holding her Faith in place.

Kevlin's focus had turned elsewhere, but the tower room was still filled with deadly magic that tore at her shield like a living thing. Adalia crouched next to her and buried her head in the folds of Indira's dress.

Tears of frustration and fear streamed down Indira's face. Doubt clouded her mind with its unfamiliar confusion. How could she have done this? Could she really say with complete honesty that she hadn't secretly feared this would happen? Yet she chose to ignore those fears, chose the selfish path.

An ominous groaning from far below rumbled up through the stones upon which she knelt. For the first time in her life, she realized that she was not strong enough.

They were all going to die.

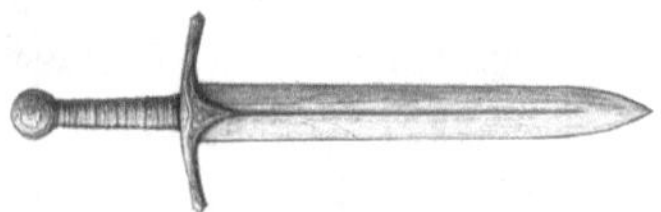

Inside the Great Dome, flashes of lightning began arcing between the lines of power connecting Harafin's sphere to the walls, crackling in the air and hinting at the growing danger.

Duke Kescog stepped between the emperor and the edge of the balcony in an attempt to shield him from whatever magic might be discharged in their direction. He faced likely destruction with bleak determination. If only he could strike back.

Ambassador Janezeko, his face white with fear, turned to the emperor. "Your Excellency, should we evacuate the palace?"

"There is nowhere to go," whispered Leander from his position at the edge of the balcony, still holding to the node of power. "You couldn't run far enough."

The indomitable old Stalwart's face was lined with strain, and his shoulders were beginning to shake, but he held fast to the node of power, his strength flowing still to support Harafin.

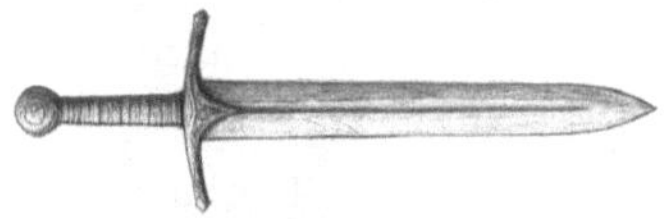

The Catalyst laughed in triumph. The enemy had repulsed his latest attack, but now he knew the enemy's secret. He had followed the tendrils of magic discharged from the enemy's stronghold down deep into the earth beneath the palace.

The earth was nearly saturated. Cracks were beginning to form far underground, undermining the integrity of the bedrock upon which the mountain rose. The entire mountain groaned, on the verge of cataclysmic destruction.

Deeper still, at the very root of the mountain, where a well of molten lava had lain dormant for centuries, the magic had pooled. The energy had seeped into the living rock, heating and stirring it until it began to boil.

The Catalyst was pleased. All events now moved for his good. He would not only destroy the palace, but would bring down the entire plateau in a moment of destruction like the world had never known.

The enemy was helping him do it.

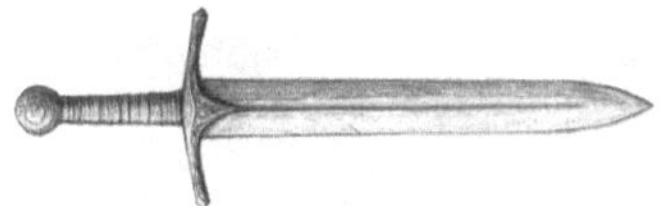

On the grounds throughout the inner city, the initial startled amazement felt by the populace was turning to fear. The air now felt charged, ominously heavy, like just before a terrible storm. Only moments ago an actual tornado had touched down atop the Keisara's Tower out of the clear sky. Now lightning and blazing fire burned high atop the shattered tower.

Something terribly wrong was happening. Then every beautiful fountain in all of the renowned sunken gardens exploded simultaneously. The *BOOM* shattered every window in the inner city, rocked ships in both harbors, and shredded the tops of waves far out to sea.

The water in the fountains evaporated in clouds of steam that floated across the palace, scalding clouds that sent people scurrying away. The steam dissipated and geysers of fire sprayed high into the air, visible to those in the city below as it shot higher than the inner city wall.

Lightning began arcing between the tops of towers and palaces all though the inner city. Thunderclaps merged together into one rolling peal that deafened those trapped in the inner city. Roof timbers burned and buildings began to crumble.

Even as people fled for the dubious safety inside of the palaces, trees lining the broad boulevards and parks exploded into deadly showers of splinters as the water within them vaporized into steam. A terrifying groaning began deep in the ground, and many walkways slowly began buckling upward. The ground started to steam, and in some places to actively bubble from the heat rising from the depths. Some statues began slowly sinking into the ground.

Screams echoed through the doomed inner city, and panic swept the populace. Some people raced down the Spokes for the gates under the thick inner-city wall in an attempt to flee the growing catastrophe. Others rushed into palaces or foolishly fled down to the lower levels in hopes that the bedrock of the plateau would provide safety.

Deep beneath the mountain the magma, now boiling, began forcing its way up through the newly formed cracks in the rocks, driven forward by an unstoppable force. That force would only be sated when the entire plateau exploded in a cataclysmic disaster of unprecedented proportions and destroyed the entire city that sprawled out across the nearby plain.

92

OVERLOAD

Locked in the desperate struggle to maintain control of the magic, Harafin sensed the danger. Unrestrained power swelled to a magnitude almost beyond comprehension. Tremors from deep within the heart of the mountain shivered up through the palace roots. They triggered alarms that radiated up through his fingers from the protective sphere.

He could not stop it. He barely held on against Kevlin's increasingly powerful attacks, and even that effort was on the brink of failure.

Harafin abandoned himself to the task and surrendered all hope of his own survival. He threw every ounce of his strength into maintaining the defensive grid a little while longer. Perhaps he could save some of the people. He drew even more heavily upon the strength of those supporting him.

It proved too much. Gifted men and women began dropping to the ground where they stood, drained of all strength. First one. Then a second.

Then ten.

Then fifty.

Exhausted both in mind and spirit, they fell. Their minds tumbled from the grid into welcome unconsciousness. The last thought they universally shared was of desperate terror.

They had failed.

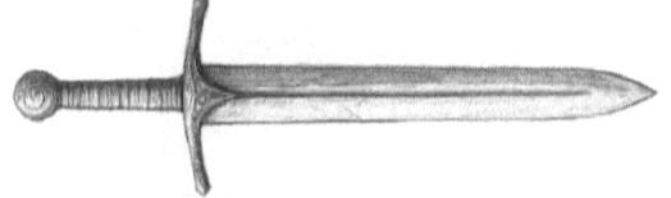

The Catalyst shouted in victory with a voice that rocked the tower. His body burned with power that was slowly tearing him apart at the most fundamental level. He exulted in the pure joy of becoming one with the wild, uncontrolled magic. This would prove the ultimate triumph.

Then he found the point where the grid was releasing magic into the earth, the safety valve keeping it from being overwhelmed.

He blocked it.

And poured magic into the palace foundation.

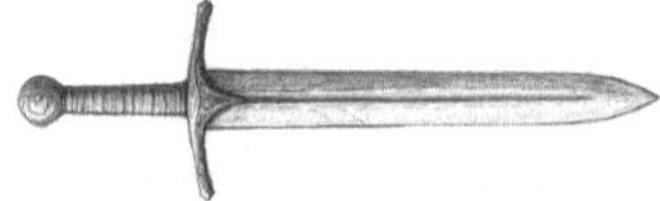

Instantly, Harafin felt the change. The magic no longer discharged out of the grid. Something blocked its release and the entire grid was now quickly becoming overloaded. With the loss of so many gifted from the grid, he lacked the capacity to handle it.

In a desperate attempt to buy some more time, he threw open new channels to release the magic.

Columns of fire erupted out of the ground in every sunken garden and soared hundreds of feet into the air. The towering flames consumed all breathable air and generated a deadly wind that raged through the gaps between buildings. Anyone exposed outside had only seconds to find shelter before the wind rose to hurricane strength and sucked the unwary or unlucky into the nearest column to be immolated in the inferno.

They did not all make it.

At the same time, a section of the cliff above the sea, wide enough for fifty men to have ridden through together simply disintegrated. A river of fire erupted through the gap.

Flames hurtled far out over the waters of the formal port and crashed down into the sea. Water boiled as the ancient elemental rivals clashed and consumed each other. A wave of steam churned hundreds of feet into the air and rolled over the ships sitting helplessly at anchor nearby.

It was not enough.

Despite everything he tried, Harafin could not vent enough magic safely from the grid. Already the wild magic was rising to a crescendo of destruction. If he threw aside any more restraints, the entire palace would be engulfed. None would survive.

Still moving through the steps required to maintain the grid, still fighting to delay the inevitable, Harafin could no longer refuse to accept the hard truth. He lacked the strength to win this battle. Everything he had fought for was about to be destroyed, and it was partially his fault.

As the grid matrix swelled to the bursting point, when he could no longer contain its explosive collapse, Harafin severed the connection to those Sentinels still part of the grid. It was the only way to protect their minds. It was the last gift he could grant them. Perhaps some few of them might survive the imminent destruction of the palace.

Only Leander remained.

93

LAST-DITCH EFFORT

The indomitable old Stalwart spoke to Harafin's mind. Despite the chaos about to engulf them, his Mindvoice spoke calmly, devoid of the crazed fury that had consumed him earlier today.

My strength is yours, brother, until the Light claims us.

Harafin smiled.

And severed the connection.

Leander stumbled back into the waiting arms of his brethren when the link broke. He turned toward the sphere of magic, and his old friend still caged within.

Inside the protective sphere, Harafin changed his movements, no longer working to preserve the grid matrix. All hope was lost, and he could no longer delay the inevitable. Instead, he focused all his fast-waning strength on preservation.

Harafin gripped two symbols of power so hard the lightning-like magic tore into the flesh of his hands. He braced his legs and shoulders against the strain as he assumed part of the load with his physical strength.

He shouted one final word of power.

The dome rang again as if struck by a giant silver hammer, and the entire structure blazed with blinding golden light. The light flowed like living water toward the four primary compass points, then rivers of pure light exploded out through the windows situated just above the seventh level walkways.

The light split and flashed away, pouring through the inner city, then farther, boiling down along all four major spoke thoroughfares.

People crowding the spokes all through the city cried out in fear as the light enveloped them with its glowing warmth. The air began to hum, and the sweet scent of honey and roses filled the air. People looked around with wondering expressions, some smiled hesitantly with a spark of renewed hope.

Then a single strand of light burned down the center of every Spoke and knocked aside anyone standing in its path. The strand of light hung suspended for a second, then blazed with pure white brilliance. It grew, forming solid walls of light that split every Spoke.

The walls of light began to expand, to push everyone off the Spokes. People cried out as they tumbled off the streets. Within three heartbeats, every Spoke lay completely empty, encased in brilliant white domes of light that reared higher than most of the flanking buildings.

Harafin blew out an exhausted breath and managed a weary smile despite the ponderous weight driving against his mind and heart. He'd done all he could to protect his people. His hands shook with absolute weariness as he tried to shift to the next symbol of power to maintain the grid matrix a little longer.

He slipped and fell to one knee.

The grid matrix collapsed.

The magic still caught within the inner-city defensive grid rebounded back against the sphere that stood at the nexus of the spell. The sphere glowed with a blinding brilliance for a single heartbeat as Harafin held at bay the overwhelming influx of the imploding matrix through sheer iron determination.

He held it for a single, painful heartbeat.

Then another.

Then Harafin's strength failed.

The sphere shrunk in on itself for half a heartbeat and an ominous silence enveloped the Great Dome.

Leander whispered, "Goodbye, my friend."

The sphere exploded in a dazzling sunburst that blinded those few looking directly at it and triggered a shockwave that hurled everyone on the short balcony backward like rag dolls.

Magic radiated back down through the supporting columns and through every node attached to the walls of the Great Dome. The entire top half of the enormous structure shattered into ten thousand white-hot pieces that tumbled miles out into the Tamerlane Sea or crashed down into forest or farmland beyond the plain of Tamera.

The explosion of the sphere catapulted Harafin high up toward where the apex of the dome had been. The thunderclap shook his body with bone-breaking force. He hung suspended for a second, arms and legs spread out limply like an offering on a broken altar.

Then he began the awful plunge to the stones far below. A thunderous booming *craaack* shook the plateau, and a mighty cloud of dust shuddered off the ground into the air. Every palace shook, and several smaller structures imploded, adding to the noise and the clouds of dust blowing across the city.

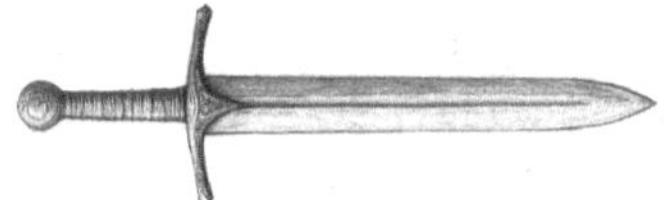

Leander, his head pounding, and every muscle shaking from exhaustion, pulled himself over the groaning forms of his companions. He clutched a piece of still-intact rail, and scanned the devastation beyond the edge.

There! A limp body plummeted toward the scarred and broken floor. With a cry of despair, Leander extended a hand, his lips calling a word of power that invoked a gift he no longer trusted, and once again he bent all his will to try to save a life.

Just before striking the floor, Harafin's body slid sideways, skidding off an invisible shield that attempted to soften the angle of impact.

It was almost enough.

The Sentinel, tiny in the distance, struck the floor hard and slid through the debris, leaving a bloody scar through the dirt-covered floor. He came to a stop and lay unmoving, his face grey, his eyes unseeing, and his ears unable to hear the terrifying rumble beginning deep under the floor upon which he lay.

The Catalyst shouted with victory.

Thus was the fate of all who opposed his supremacy. As the tower upon which he stood swayed dangerously, he called upon more power for the final, fatal blow that would shatter the very roots of the mountain and destroy everything within his domain.

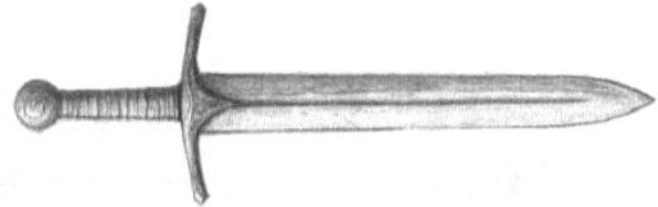

People were dying.

Indira could feel the despair, the terror, the overwhelming pain assaulting her senses from every direction. She could not save them.

She had failed.

As the tower swayed dangerously, and the insane monster that had once been Kevlin shouted with maniacal glee, she wept.

Even as she sorrowed with those she could not save, she threw the last of her strength, the last of her determination, off the brink into the realm of blind faith.

Following a prompting that she could not understand and lacked the will to question, she directed her healing powers across the room at two figures huddling helpless against the wall.

94

SPIN THE WHEEL

The Catalyst paused.

He sensed a new being nearby, a being of vast power, a being he should recognize. He turned slowly and quested out with fingers of power to locate and identify the newcomer. Somewhere above him, not far, and yet somehow not close either.

Akillik.

The air outside of the tower shimmered like the convergence of fifty rainbows and the young god stepped through. His Wheel blurred with speed as it raced in his hands. His eyes, serious as death, drew the Catalyst's gaze, and he laughed with the carefree abandon of a child.

The Catalyst laughed with Akillik, their voices merging and becoming indistinguishable as they exulted in the pure chaos of magic unleashed. The Catalyst threw his arms wide and welcomed Akillik like a brother.

Here faced him a being he had once feared, a being who understood. Here was a worthy adversary. Together they could battle for glory and, regardless of who won, destroy everything and leave behind this mortal shell forever.

"Well met, Kevlin," Akillik said as he drifted nearby.

"That name no longer applies to me."

The Catalyst threw out one hand and a torrential flood of raw magic roared out of him to consume the fickle god.

The Wheel in Akillik's hand flared with blinding light and eye-numbing darkness, and the Catalyst's magic dissipated. Akillik laughed again but no mirth reached his dead-serious eyes.

"You cannot hurt me. The time has not yet arrived when you can breach the realms."

The Catalyst shouted, "I will destroy you!" He unleashed another wave of raw power to rip the insolent godling to shreds.

Again his power melted away and Akillik hefted his fast-spinning Wheel. "Want to make a bet?"

The Catalyst grinned. Of course. That was the key to defeating this challenger. He must break the power of the Wheel.

"I do!"

Akillik raised one eyebrow and hefted the Wheel, which began to slow. "Say the words."

"If it spins true, we fight."

Akillik grinned in turn, and madness danced in his eyes. "Very well, but I choose the consequences if the Wheel spins against you."

Behind Akillik, the air shimmered again with rainbow light. The Catalyst sensed other beings. They hovered close and he caught glimpses of them, beings he knew so well and yet never expected to meet.

Salawin stood with arms folded, a stern frown on his face, his Sword of Truth strapped to his back. Serigala, in her form as the Lady Jagen, the Huntress, hovered closest, with an arrow already half-drawn on her legendary bow.

The youthful En'Lil floated on air beside her, his eyes wide, his face remarkably innocent. Beside him, Kamen stood as solid as the mountains among which he dwelled. His clean-shaven face looked peaceful and his eyes, although blazing with power, looked calm.

Asherah, goddess of the sea, the lovely Lady who claimed the hearts' devotion of every dedicated Meinarr sailor, stood in a flowing blue-green gown that fluttered as if from invisible currents. Her hair glittered like reflected sunlight through distant waves, and her eyes looked like the sea at the leading edge of a storm. She held one hand half-raised toward the Catalyst, as if preparing to grant a blessing, or perhaps level a curse.

Farther back, barely sensed in the distance, hovered two other figures. One carried a naked sword and, when the Catalyst caught a glimpse of him, a single drum beat in his soul. The chilling sound shook his confidence just a little with remembered fear.

Even farther back, a dark-cloaked figure clutched long lengths of burning chains that slowly writhed like serpents. The Catalyst caught the tiniest glimpse, but it was enough to shake him to the core. Then the hooded figure, dread EnKur himself, faded away.

"Do it," Lady Jagen said in an urgent whisper. "Let us end the threat here and now." She drew Her famous bow and fixed the deadly hooked tip of the arrow on the Catalyst.

Akillik leaned forward, his eyes wide with anticipation, and licked His lips. "Say it."

"Spin the Wheel!"

Living fire burned out through every pore and encased the Catalyst as he cast his fate into the hands of Akillik's infamous Luck.

The young god howled with laughter and threw the Wheel high into the air where it alternately burned like a miniature sun, or sucked all light from the sky.

It descended toward them, slowing, and then slowing farther. The Catalyst exulted. It was going to spin in his favor.

With a final half-turn, the Wheel stopped.

Black.

The Lady Jagen shrieked a triumphant cry and loosed her terrible arrow.

Akillik caught it.

Lady Jagen knocked a second arrow so fast it seemed to appear in Her hand. She drew, aimed the shaft at Akillik's forehead, and released all in the same fluid motion. The arrow leaped across the short distance, but vaporized just before touching Akillik.

He waved a dismissive hand. "Enough. I said I choose the consequence."

The other gods drew nearer, their excitement nearly palpable. Lady Jagen said, "Kill him."

The Catalyst drew back a pace. She spoke so quietly, and yet her voice bored into him with such power it shook him to the center of his soul. Even riding the uncontrolled wave of wild magic, he felt fear.

Akillik waved the other gods back and turned to face the Catalyst. He no longer laughed.

"First he suffers. Then he dies."

The words tore into the Catalyst's mind. They echoed the words of the prophecy spoken by Ah'Shan, and filled him with chill dread.

The boundless depths of magic surging through the Catalyst evaporated like the mist before a blazing sun. Bereft of magic, the Catalyst stumbled, slipped over the edge of the yawning gap in the floor, and fell.

Akillik grinned, and his eyes flashed with the same eye-numbing blackness as his Wheel. Every nerve in the Catalyst's body screamed in unison, as if every ounce of his soul was dipped in living fire.

Darkness rolled out from Akillik and consumed him.

95

BROTHERHOOD

Kevlin screamed so hard his voice cracked. Every breath burned, as if fire had singed his throat and lungs. His fingers and toes throbbed with sharp stabs of pain. It felt like they were encased in ice and freezing with agonizing swiftness.

He tasted blood, and his skin screamed like every piece of flesh had been rubbed raw with stones, but he heard nothing. His own screams echoed in his skull from a distance, but his ears felt like his head had been packed in wool.

Rough hands grabbed his shoulders, and Kevlin blinked open his eyes. Drystan and Jerrik stood over him, their faces frightened. They shouted at him, their mouths moving, but no sound reaching his ears.

Kevlin frowned. Why were they looking at him like that? What happened? He remembered nothing. His mind registered only the unending pain that threatened to cast him back into welcome blackness.

His brothers hoisted him to his feet. He looked around and gaped. Soldiers lay unconscious in a jumbled pile across the room. The keisara lay unmoving not far away. Blood smeared the floor around her and merged with her cranberry dress, making it look like her entire body was bleeding out.

How did they all come to be here? Complete devastation met his gaze wherever he turned. Cracks webbed the floor, and sections had fallen away in large blocks. The outer wall gaped open over a stomach-turning drop down to the plateau and then on to the Tamerlane Sea below. The waves crashing against the cliffs looked blackened, almost charred.

Then he saw Indira.

He remembered.

It all came crashing back in like a sledgehammer blow to the forehead. Kevlin rocked backward and would have fallen had his brothers not caught him. Memories pounded his awakening mind with truth he could not accept.

He tried to force the memories aside, deny them, but the truth blazed through his mind like living fire. With the truth came sounds, as if whatever had been blocking his ears melted away. Distant screams echoed throughout the city. The entire empty shell of the tower groaned as if it were dying.

Kevlin witnessed his actions, like a living nightmare. He cried out in horror as he remembered shattering the tower, raining destruction up on the city, and overwhelming the palace's defenses. How many people had he hurt or killed? How could he have embraced such insanity?

Outside the tower, smoke covered the inner city in a pall, while gigantic pillars of living fire towered over the city, still trying to vent the deadly concentration of magic he'd leveled against Harafin.

Then he remembered the worst part.

Kevlin groaned with horror as he slowly lifted his eyes to Indira. She stood not far away, with Adalia hovering in her shadow. Tears streaked her alabaster skin, and fear haunted the depths of her beautiful, dark eyes.

Kevlin sagged against his brothers' support. He had really done it. He had tried to kill Indira.

He wanted to leap out through the broken wall to the welcome bliss of death and end the horror of the memory, but even as he crouched to stand, the air in front of him shimmered with rainbow light. Akillik stepped through, his Wheel held motionless, with the light-consuming blackness still at the apex.

Jerrik cursed, and Drystan reached for a long-knife. Akillik ignored them both. He laughed with pure joy.

"Kevlin, I told you I'd own your soul."

"Wait," Kevlin said. "I wasn't myself. Please stop this." He gestured at the devastation he'd caused. "Please, let me try to fix this."

Akillik's laugh faded and he hefted the Wheel, drawing every eye. "You spun the Wheel, Kevlin, not me. No one escapes the consequences."

Even as Kevlin opened his mouth to protest, the magic that had drained away so abruptly when the Wheel spun against him, returned like a tidal wave and tore through the already breached defenses of his mind.

Indira watched in horror as Kevlin's eyes, clear and sane for that one brief instant, rolled back into his head. A scream of despair turned into a maniacal laugh.

Akillik joined the laughter before fading from view. She barely believed her eyes. Could she really have seen Him? More important, what had He meant?

Kevlin threw back his head and howled with insanity. Fire burned in his eyes and danced around his hands. Indira's heart sank.

She had lost him again.

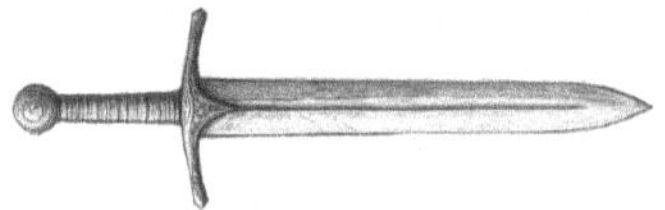

Kevlin's mind flooded as the magic roared through the breach and, unstoppable, assaulted his mind. The remembered horror of what he'd done when in thrall to the *Tai Pari* gave him the strength to withstand it for a single heartbeat before it hurled his mind out over the brink into insanity again.

Oris! Help me!

He connected with the stone and desperately grasped for its protective assistance.

Thou hast been given the tools thou dost require to succeed.

The thought gently swept through his soul, bringing with it a hint of calm reassurance. Then his mind was torn away by the torrent, his hold loosened by despair.

That was useless!

It hadn't helped. In his most desperate hour, all it could give him was empty reassurance? He very nearly cast aside the final tether to sanity and surrendered to the inevitable.

As his grip on sanity slipped like a sailor sucked under by a rip tide, another mind touched his own.

Control, Kevlin! Ukko's beard, man, remember your training.

Like a rock upon which he could stand and rise above the torrent, the thought came from Jerrik. With it came the huge warrior's strength, reinforcing the link to sanity and pulling his mind back from the brink.

Discipline your mind.

Drystan's voice rang with authority as it joined them. Calm assurance radiated through the link to Kevlin as Drystan adding his absolute self-control to the battle for Kevlin's sanity

You control your destiny. No force, no matter how powerful, can compel the resolved mind against its will.

With the added strength and discipline of his adopted brothers, Kevlin erected new mental barriers. The reinforced battlements of his mental fortress rose over the savaged ground of his mind.

The magic fought his efforts, like a rogue wave and attempted to swamp his will again. For a moment, he hung by a tenuous thread of pure stubbornness.

What if I can't control it? Kevlin cried as he desperately fought to remain in control.

Better we die than surrender, Drystan said calmly.

Die if you want, Jerrik's voice radiated through the conduit. *I need to finish my date.*

Kevlin gripped his head between his hands and swayed like a drunken sailor as he fought to withstand the onslaught. He populated his mental ramparts with an army of Donarri berserkers and swift-striking Einarri spearmen. He leaped off the turrets and led the counterstrike, tearing at the magic and commanding it to obey.

It struck again, a mighty blow that pounded his head like a hit from Leander's hammer. He dropped to his knees under the onslaught, but focused his thoughts on Indira.

I will not surrender. He repeated the phrase over and over, using it like a shield against the pain and despair.

Then the tide turned and Kevlin, standing on the rock of his brothers' strength and discipline, weathered the storm. The magic receded and submitted to his control.

He had won, but what price would he pay for the previous defeat?

Kevlin blew out a breath and staggered to his feet. He hurt everywhere, but once more he stood in control. Magic filled him, but now flowed placidly like a gentle, healing river of strength.

What a mess.

The air shimmered with rainbow light, and Akillik appeared again. The Wheel now spun fast in his hand, and he glared angrily at Kevlin.

"You can't beat me," Kevlin said and stood to face the youthful god.

"Ah, Kevlin, maybe taunting him isn't such a good idea," Drystan whispered.

Akillik floated close to Kevlin and raw power radiated from him like a wave of heat. Kevlin held his ground.

"No one escapes the consequences," Akillik, repeated. He grinned and leaned closer. "It will all be blamed on you."

Then he snapped his fingers and disappeared. The tower swayed and the floor tilted. Stones groaned, and everyone started sliding toward the broken outer wall.

Kevlin's swordbrothers both clutched at gaps in the floor to arrest their movement. Adalia screamed and grabbed onto Indira's robes. Indira stood on the tilting floor, unmoving, her eyes locked Kevlin.

He wanted to run to her, to think of some way to apologize, but there was no time. He understood Akillik's words all too well. The god intended to give calamity one final, tiny push and complete the devastation Kevlin started.

Kevlin hardened the air under his feet to keep from sliding farther and wrapped tethers of air around everyone else in the room. Then he closed his eyes and concentrated. His memories were cloudy, ethereal, like nightmares, but he remembered enough.

He threw his mind back down the length of the tower and through the lower levels of the Underground Palace, to the bedrock of the mountain below. There he found the surging, molten lava driving toward the surface and about to breach the lowest levels.

He could not stop it.

The titanic struggle against Harafin in the battle for the palace had resulted in cracks fissuring the entire bedrock of the mountain. The lava poured up through those cracks, driven by the strength of the earth, a power no man, no matter how he may be endowed with actinic energy, could hope to arrest. The cracks burst open wider, and the lava drove upward in an unstoppable tide that would inundate the entire city and kill every living being in a flood of fiery death.

Kevlin refused to give in to the terror that threatened to scatter his thoughts and leave him a screaming wreck. He could not face the responsibility for so much death. He would not allow it to happen.

The ground was saturated with wild magic. Kevlin wrested control of it and, following a prompting that came with an unexpected wave of peace, he focused that tremendous power against the rocks of the palace foundations.

Magic roared through Kevlin like a river of living strength. It strained his weakened control and he shook with the effort. He wasn't sure he could to this.

He had to.

Kevlin let go the fear that urged him to hold back, and committed to the effort. He gave himself to this one desperate attempt to save these people, committing to it as completely as he had to the insanity of chaos. If he failed, he deserved to die ten thousand times over for mass murder. Better to die in the effort and perhaps save a few.

Such magnitude of living power proved unwieldy, and Kevlin applied it clumsily. He directed it against the stones of the mountain and fused the smaller cracks in an attempt to shepherd the lava into controlled channels.

It was almost enough. As the lava surged upward toward the surface, Kevlin's senses touched on Harafin's last legacy, and he seized the tiny chance it provided.

Molten stone exploded up out of the earth.

96

APOCALYPSE REMODELING

M olten rock consumed the central plaza situated before the now-shattered Great Dome. The earth shook so hard buildings swayed and collapsed throughout the city. Lava exploded up through the breach and soared three hundred feet into the air before raining down upon the Inner City.

The concentric circles of power that made up the shield matrix around the palaces bent at Kevlin's command and funneled that falling lava down between the various palaces and onto the Spokes. The air became blisteringly hot and poisonous fumes hung over the deepening lava collecting on the wide avenues.

Then the lava began to flow. Slowly at first, and then faster as it was driven forward by the weight of lava still pushing up from below, it began to run down the Spokes. The depth increased as the free-standing shields Harafin had placed all down the Spokes like invisible tubes prevented the lava from spreading out into the rest of the city.

Rivers of molten rock poured through the gates of the Inner City. The gates burned like living torches proclaiming the entrance to EnKur's domain. The lava flowed through the wall and the depth rose to fill the high passageway. It crept inexorably down through the upper city, with the thickest concentrations on the Silver and Iron Spokes.

Molten lava rolled down them, through the center of the city, and eventually reached the arced stone bridges over the River Tam. There the shield tubes ended and the lava spilled over the edges of the bridges and into the wide river. Water boiled and clouds of steam rose a thousand feet into the sky and drifted over the city, driving inhabitants into any shelter they could find.

Lava consumed the famous Golden Road before torching the gate in the outer wall and flowing out to consume the docks. It continued past that inferno and plunged into the Formal Port. The violent contact of the elements rocked the harbor and covered the ships still at anchor with a sheen of superheated steam and ash.

A similar scene of devastation flowed down the long Port Spoke as lava ran the length of the boulevard above the sea until its path ended violently in the Common Port and the mouth of the Tam River.

Universal panic enveloped the city as superheated rock divided the empire's greatest metropolis and hemmed those sections on either side. The deadly steam clouds forced everyone indoors. Many people gathered their families around them and clung together in what they assumed would prove to be their last living moments.

Kevlin felt the fear radiate up through his magnified senses as a quarter of a million people trembled and faced the very real possibility of death. The weight of it reinforced his determination to save them.

The earth continued to shake and lightning arced overhead. The sun darkened behind the vapors and steam, and the city shook from the roaring of battling elements. Soon newly formed islands rose in the River Tam and in both ports. In the river, the islands of steaming black rock grew and fused with the stone bridges and blocked the river entirely. In the ports, they flowed far out into the water.

A sudden rain squall poured torrents of water out of the sky, as if the air were rejecting the vast quantities of magic recently released into it. The rain pounded down so heavy it filled the air to saturation, making it difficult to breathe.

The squall lasted several minutes and blew itself out as the flow of new lava slowed to a trickle. The air began to clear from the clouds of steam as a strong wind picked up off of the sea. The ground settled and the buildings of the city ceased their terrible shaking.

Calm settled over the city, so complete it was as shocking by its contrast as were the terrifying elements unleashed upon the city. People dared to hope that they might live out the day.

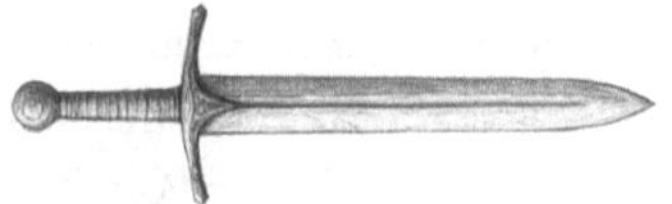

Kevlin fell to his knees. He felt empty, so far beyond exhaustion he could not describe it. Only a little magic remained creeping through him. Despite its healing effect, his body burned with a thousand pin-pricks of pain.

Between the *Tai Pari* and that final effort to preserve the city from total destruction, he'd been burned raw. He had ventured into realms from which he should not have returned, and his body paid the price.

Now that he knew the city would survive, he could hold on no longer. He fell to the warm stones of the floor and wished Leander were here to heal him.

Indira was here.

That thought brought his head up with a painful creak, and he sought the gentle healer. Their eyes locked across the room, and he wished he hadn't looked. The expression of haunted fear on her tear-streaked face would haunt him all his life.

He had tried to kill her.

He might have saved most of the city, but he would find no comfort. Even as he tried to grasp the magnitude of his crimes, a rustling of cloth caught his attention.

Masego.

97

DEATH IN A TINY PACKAGE

The fat man stood and faced Kevlin. The hard lines of his face looked confused, but not afraid. If anything, he looked hungry.

"The power you stole from me could not have fueled all this. What did you do?"

Gabral stepped through the charred remnants of the door on the far side of the room behind Masego. He was caked with dust and debris, and blood ran down his face from a cut to his scalp.

He glared at Masego. "Wrong question. You should be worried about what I am about to do."

He pointed the Mace at the possessed Sentinel. The long, top spike fired off the ball and shot across the room, directly at Masego's heart.

Masego extended a hand and the spike wavered in its flight and deflected past his shoulder, so close it rippled the fabric. Masego lifted both hands to unleash his powers back at Gabral, who was not yet protected by the fiery shield from the Mace.

Nothing happened.

Masego rounded on Kevlin and scowled. "You've exhausted nearly every scrap of latent power from the area, boy."

When Masego turned his back, Gabral sprinted into the room and, with surprising agility, traversed the cracked, broken floor toward Masego. He lifted the Mace high, and blue fire burst to life around the mighty weapon's head.

Then the fire flickered, and slowly faded out.

Gabral stopped and stared in disbelief at the Mace. He shook it a couple of times, but no fire reappeared. His face fell and his shoulders sagged.

Then rage replaced despair and he shouted angrily at Kevlin, "What did you do to the Mace?"

"Just about all the magic in this area's been used up, including yours." Sounded reasonable. Maybe Gabral would believe it.

Adalia stepped away from Indira and knocked an arrow. "Thank Jagen. Now I kin shoot this rabid dog."

She loosed the arrow at Masego.

He made a flicking gesture with one hand like he had the first time she tried to shoot him, which now seemed so long ago. It twitched, deflecting just wide enough to scrape his shoulder instead of impaling his chest.

"You're a dead man, Kevlin," Gabral promised before leaping a hole in the floor and resuming his charge across the cracked expanse toward Masego.

He hefted the Mace high. "You die first, villain."

Masego retreated, and for the first time looked worried. He threw out one hand at the charging Gabral, and the Mace bearer slipped and fell sprawling.

Masego dodged away, but Adalia fired another arrow at him. It slowed just enough for him to dive aside. He regained his feet near the shattered outer wall of the tower.

Gabral advanced again.

Masego held up both hands and shouted, "Stand back, or the keisara dies." He pointed at the injured monarch, and a light green mist began to form around her head.

Gabral skidded to a halt, and Adalia paused, bow drawn and aimed.

Kevlin forced himself to his knees and rallied the shreds of his strength. All he wanted to do was collapse to the comforting stones and sleep for a year. He hated Masego now more than ever. Couldn't he see they needed a break?

With thoughts rattling like a spar with a loose line, he tried to focus the little bit of magic he still possessed. He grabbed up a chair with trembling fingers of power and threw it at Masego.

It struck the fat man in the back, knocking him stumbling. The green mist dissipated from around the keisara.

Gabral lunged, but Masego's features shuddered and softened, and his eyes cleared. Felix held up his hands in surrender and shouted, "Gabral, thank the gods for you, man."

Gabral slowed to a stop two strides away. He frowned at Felix and held the Mace half-raised. "Where's Masego?"

"Gone. Help me, and we can make sure he never returns."

"Kill him," Jerrik said in a hard tone. "He can't be trusted."

"No, wait," said Kevlin.

Felix had always been a powerful ally. If they really could free him from Masego, they could accomplish a double blow against the forces of evil. Besides, after the devastation he'd unleashed upon the city, Kevlin hated to think anyone else needed to die.

"What do you propose?" Gabral asked Felix.

"Lend me the Mace. With its power, I can . . ."

Gabral's face turned red with rage and he lifted the weapon high. "The Mace is mine!"

The enraged Mace bearer swung a mighty blow that would have ripped apart Felix's head and shoulders.

Felix's face hardened into the features of Masego, and he rolled back from the blow. Light flashed between them, and Gabral shouted a loud curse and stumbled back several paces.

Masego snarled, "Your lack of vision seals your fate." He started to raise a hand to cast whatever final remnants of magic he'd scrounged together.

An arrow punched through his hand and pinned it to the wide expanse of his belly.

Masego howled as the unexpected blow turned him half around. Adalia knocked a second arrow in record time and drew again. Even as Masego tried to lift his other hand to use his powers, the fiery little archer released. The arrow drilled through his other hand and drove deep between his ribs.

Masego stumbled and fell to one knee. He groaned with pain, and his eyes glinted with panic.

"Enough," Gabral commanded. The short colonel advanced on Masego and said, "For your crimes, you are sentenced to death."

He struck.

Masego howled, and with a convulsive move, ripped his hands outward. Flesh tore and blood sprayed as the wounds gaped open and he yanked his hands free.

He lunged under Gabral's swing and caught the Mace bearer by the throat. The two of them swayed together and staggered to the very edge of the outer wall. Thick darkness gathered around them until only vague outlines of their forms were visible through the deepening shadow.

Kevlin tried to draw more power from Oris, but he lacked the strength, and the magic slipped through his mental fingers like water. Before he could try again, Adalia drew a third arrow.

"Indira, protect Gabral," she said.

Not waiting for a reply, she loosed the shaft.

The arrow leaped into the darkness, and someone screamed.

The shadow dissipated. Gabral fell to his hands and knees, coughing. The Mace dropped with a dull thud to the floor beside him, and his entire body shook.

Masego, his empty eyes staring up at the open sky, with the third arrow sticking out from his neck, stumbled back one fatal step . . .

. . . and fell out through the open outer wall.

Kevlin's brothers rushed to the edge in time to witness the fat man strike the ground far below. Kevlin managed to stumble over a moment later and peeked over the edge. Masego's body had ruptured on impact, and even from such a great height, Kevlin grimaced at the grisly scene.

He turned back to Gabral. The Mace bearer still knelt on the floor with a wild, haunted look in his eyes. He hugged himself with his arms, and his body shook with another tremor.

Indira dropped to her knees beside Gabral. "Are you all right?"

He opened his mouth twice before words came. "I . . . I am fine. He . . ." he glanced out the broken wall where Masego fell and shuddered again.

He coughed again, then straightened, his eyes clearing. He waved Indira's proffered healing hand away. "I'm fine now. See to those who can best use what limited resources you may be able to draw upon."

Gabral stood and lifted the Mace from the floor. He rounded on Kevlin and pointed the heavy weapon at Kevlin's heart. "Fix this, mercenary, or I swear to the gods I'll kill you."

"I'll take care of it," Kevlin promised.

He had no idea what to do. Harafin had talked about needing latent magic to draw upon when one's inner powers were exhausted, but they'd never discussed what power Oris or the Six used. Was it the same? Could he have broken it?

Drystan dropped to one knee beside Adalia to bring his head down level with hers. He took her hands in his. "That was a great shot."

"Aye. I'll drink to that," Jerrik said from where he was helping Marjani to her feet. She was awake, but looked around in open amazement. She'd slept through the whole thing. Lucky.

She gasped and leaped past Jerrik. Kevlin and the others turned to follow her as she sped across the room.

The keisara. Marjani slid to a halt beside the fallen monarch, kneeling in the blood-streaked floor. While she checked the unconscious woman's pulse, Indira joined her.

Kevlin wanted to stare at Indira, but the sight of her brought his horrific memories back to life and he couldn't bear to think of that.

Could he ever hope to look her in the eye again?

"She lives," Marjani cried.

"Let's keep it that way," Indira said. Her hands began to glow and her soft chant filled the devastated room. The sound was sweet torture to Kevlin.

He turned away and the enormous weight of everything that had happened, everything he'd done came crashing home. He'd pushed his battered body too far, and collapsed into welcome blackness.

98

CHAINS OF THE HEART

Indira exited the northeast entrance to the Northern Kingdoms Admin Palace and paused in the bright morning sunlight. The devastation of the inner city still shocked her. Only two days had passed. It would take weeks for any semblance of order to be restored.

Murky haze obscured distant objects, and the air smelled strongly of sulfur. Thankfully the ground had stopped shaking during the night. The first few aftershocks had triggered panic across the city and more had been injured. There were already too many injured, with too few Healers to tend them. Resources were stretched so thin, only the most critical cases were treated with the Healers' gifts.

Indira glanced at the jagged mountain of black volcanic rock that now occupied most of the central courtyard. Ridges of stone extended from that mountain like rough snakes along the tracks where the grand streets of the Spokes had once offered such easy access to the city. Now the volcanic stone filled the gates and stretched the length of the city.

All through the inner city, towers that ended in broken tops huddled beside palaces with burned roofs, broken windows, and cracked exteriors. The once-glorious expanse looked beaten and crippled. Rubble mixed with gray ash lay thick everywhere except for in the most heavily traveled areas where it had been shoveled back far enough to allow passage.

The shattered shell of the Great Dome crouched amidst the palaces. Where before it had shone as a beacon of hope and a symbol of the empire's pride, now its maimed silhouette seemed to represent all the suffering that had befallen the city.

Indira moved toward a small group standing in the charred remnants of the northern garden that ran all the way to the cliff face overlooking the devastated Formal Port. A squad of soldiers dressed in climbing gear flanked Ceren. She wore a black leather skirt split for riding and a russet leather jacket over a white silk blouse. Her auburn hair was pulled into a simple braid, and she wore long leather gloves.

Ceren offered a hesitant smile as Indira approached. Her eyes looked sad and her face drawn and tired.

Indira gave her a warm smile. "I heard you were leaving this morning."

"I didn't expect anyone to bother coming to see me off, not with so much still to be done."

"The others are all down in the city," Indira admitted.

Every able hand had been pressed into service since the cataclysmic events rocked the city. Injuries were widespread, although fatalities were amazingly low. The volcanic ridges that now split the city into isolated sections blocked easy travel and were proving a difficult problem to overcome.

"Are they working on the cuts?"

"Trying to."

Although the outer crust of lava had cooled the first night into a hard shell strong enough to bear a man's weight in many places, the deeper layers still burned hot enough to melt steel. Efforts to open cuts through the ridges to enable transfer of medical supplies, foodstuffs, and other critical supplies had so far been frustrated by the superheated lava.

"The Sentinels still haven't found a way through?" Ceren asked with a frown.

Indira shook her head. She'd been one of many dispatched to cross the ridges and offer aid to the trapped populace. The scenes of chaos and suffering she'd witnessed still chilled her. Many people had dared the dangers of crossing the ridges already and fled the city. Some had tried too soon and were seriously injured when a foot or a hand broke through the crust.

The situation was fast becoming a humanitarian disaster. Refugees crowded the countryside around the city, but could not utilize the wide, fertile plain that lay beyond the Imperial Highway. With new volcanic islands blocking its path, the River Tam had burst its banks and flooded the plain, compounding the already severe problems.

The cuts were desperately needed, but resources were spread too thin, and the Sentinels were all but helpless. The latent magic had been drained from the entire area. Their personal stores of power had all been sacrificed in the effort to defend the palace from Kevlin's insane assault. No one had ever seen such a dearth of actinic energy, so they could only guess at how long it would take to replenish.

Indira nodded toward the climbing harnesses and ropes. "You mean to descend the cliff?"

"No. We'll walk the outer wall as far as we can. We'll need the climbing gear to get over the new mountain blocking half the port."

"I'm surprised you found a seaworthy ship."

"Well, she's a ship. Hopefully seaworthy enough to see me home."

"Safe journey."

Ceren drew Indira away from the waiting soldiers and asked hesitantly, "How . . . how is Kevlin?"

Indira fought down a flash of anger that Ceren would dare ask about him. She reminded herself that Ceren had been driven to her actions by a rogue Sentinel. "He hasn't woken up yet. I'll check on him later."

Ceren sighed and looked down at her gloved hands. "It's better this way."

Indira resisted the urge to hug Ceren to help ease the hurt she so obviously still suffered. She reminded herself again that Ceren's actions had been forced upon her by another. The towering fury that had consumed her in the sunken garden still burned hot in her breast. She couldn't yet pretend all was well between them.

She felt ashamed and guilty for feeling that way, but she hadn't yet reconciled her heart and her mind. She said, "Ceren, don't blame yourself for what happened."

Ceren sighed, trying to maintain her image of strength. "I should have resisted more." She took Indira's hands and added in a whisper, "What I almost did . . . part of me didn't want to resist."

Indira retreated a step. Ceren really had wanted to steal Kevlin away. Her fury returned with undiminished strength and she curled her fingers into claws. She barely restrained the urge to lash out.

Ceren added quickly, "I never would have tried to seduce him or hurt him, but I do care for him." She sighed again. "Everything's still so muddled in my head."

Indira forced calm over her features and slowly relaxed her hands. "Evil is always seductive, and it twists any weakness into monstrosities."

"Oh, Indira," Ceren cried. "I'm so very sorry. What I did to him, what I did to you."

Seeing her in anguish helped a little. She couldn't let her leave like this. "You have to stop thinking about it that way. If you had been in control, you never would have."

Ceren smiled again, and tears glistened in her eyes. "Is it evil to care for Kevlin?"

Part of Indira wanted to snarl, *Yes!* But she managed to say instead, "It's evil to try to force his feelings, or control his will."

"Thank you for understanding." Ceren threw her arms around Indira.

Indira accepted the embrace and even managed to hug Ceren lightly in return. She tried to focus on the positive memories they'd shared. She had genuinely liked Ceren, and the noblewoman had proven a friend in many ways. Could she hate her now?

She wasn't sure what she felt. At the least, a new tension now existed between them. Ceren might have been compelled to do what she did, but she still did it. Kevlin had proven in the tower at the last that it was possible to resist those types of compulsions, even if driven to the very brink of death.

If Ceren ever tried to act on any feelings for Kevlin she still harbored, if she tried to be more than a very distant acquaintance . . . well, Indira would have a problem with that.

Her hands tingled again with the memory of slapping Ceren's face so hard it hurt. She'd bruised her hands in the fight in the sunken garden, but she'd refused to heal them. Now she squeezed Ceren just a bit tighter and promised herself she'd try to maintain a cordial friendship.

Until Ceren forced her to change her mind.

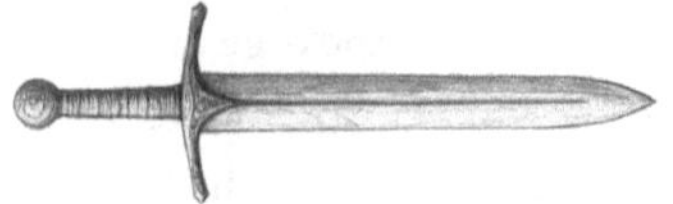

Kevlin blinked his eyes and opened them slowly. They felt plastered with sand and ached from the small movement. Feeling returned slowly to the rest of his body, and he wished it hadn't. Every muscle complained, and he felt weak.

Movement drew his eyes and he managed to focus. Indira stood over him, dressed in her green Healer's robe, with her long, midnight hair in a loose twist. Her robe looked dirty and her face marked with grime, but the sight of her took his breath away.

The lingering grogginess evaporated, and all the memories returned like an avalanche. Indira held his gaze for a moment before withdrawing.

Kevlin tried to leap out of bed to go to her, to beg forgiveness, to make things right. He couldn't move.

Thick iron bands encircled his hands, feet, and even his throat. Heavy chains secured them to the bed. Kevlin struggled, but could do little more than rock side to side.

Indira, now standing several strides away said, "Relax, Kevlin. You're going to hurt yourself."

"What's going on?"

"You are restrained on Harafin's orders."

Kevlin settled back and forgot about the rising panic at being so tightly restricted. Everything faded under the exultant thrill to hear Harafin's name. His murky memories were not clear, but he'd feared the worst.

"Harafin's all right?"

"He lives. He is very weak, though. He nearly died when . . . " Indira's voice trailed off.

When I lost control.

Bitter self-loathing consumed him. "It's probably better this way." He closed his eyes and mustered his courage to ask the next question. "When are they going to execute me?"

Indira gasped. "Don't say that."

Kevlin could see little of the room other than the low wooden ceiling and one plain wooden wall beside the bed upon which he lay shackled. It felt small, though, like a prison cell.

He gave Indira a wry smile. "Indira, you know what I did. You think they're just going to forget that?"

Indira drew a little closer. "Are you . . . under control?"

"Yes."

He nearly added, "Of course," but realized he couldn't say that. Not now, perhaps not ever again.

"No one is talking execution, Kevlin. In fact, I'm not sure anyone really knows what happened."

"How can they not know?"

She drew closer. "Think about it. Very few of us were there when . . . "

"When I lost control and almost destroyed everything," Kevlin said harshly.

She motioned him to be quiet and drew closer still until she stood right beside the bed. He could almost touch the hem of her robe, but couldn't quite twist his fingers far enough. Being so close and still prevented from any contact was maddening.

"Please stop talking about that," she said softly. Her dark eyes looked so earnest, he forgot to speak for a moment and just looked at her, savoring the fact that she was safe and still speaking with him.

"I won't hide from the consequences of what I did."

Akillik's final words rang in his mind, and he wondered if this was what He meant all along. *First I suffer, then I die.*

"Don't talk about it, Kevlin," Indira said more strongly. "In a few days, you'll be gone. For now, everyone has more than enough to do."

"What's happening?"

Indira related to him how everyone had been mobilized with rescue and relief efforts. She told him about the difficulties with the cuts through the volcanic ridges. In several places, earth had been brought in to form long ramps on either side, so some goods were being moved and were beginning to alleviate some of the suffering.

The more she spoke, the more Kevlin hated himself. He'd done all that. He dared not ask how many people had died as a result of his actions. She painted a clear enough picture of the suffering and overwhelming problems that still plagued the city. Things wouldn't return to normal for months. It would take years to rebuild everything.

"Why don't the Sentinels help?" With their actinopathic powers, they should be able to make short work of cutting the volcanic ridges, even with the still-hot cores.

Indira shook her head. "There's no latent magic to draw upon." The Sentinel's personal stores had returned to a small degree, but they'd been needed to assist with more pressing demands.

Kevlin was surprised to learn that the dearth of actinic power was affecting the Stalwarts and Healers too.

"How is that possible? I thought Stalwarts received their gifts from their gods?"

Indira shrugged. "So did we all, but there's more of a link to latent magic than we knew. We can do some healing, but our powers are weak and we have to rest often. We can barely treat the most critical cases.""I wonder what the connection is."

Indira shrugged again. "No one really knows. Leander has several ideas, but I haven't had much time to speak with him."

"How is he?"

Indira looked down at her hands, twisting the fabric of her robe. "He is well, and he throws himself into the effort to help."

"What are you not telling me?"

Tears blossomed in her lovely eyes and she savagely wiped them away. "The emperor still means to banish him, still means to strip his title."

He cursed the chains that prevented him from comforting her.

She managed a weak smile. "Despite how much needs to be done here, part of me can't wait to be gone. I want to be away from all this, and I want to feel my gift at full strength again."

"You keep talking about leaving."

"We all are. We're going to the far western border as soon as they secure a ship."

"Who?"

"I thought you'd remember. The Ruling Council discussed the need to send a mission to inspect the western fortifications before winter snows."

"I do, sort of, but I hadn't expected it to affect us."

"I think Harafin had a hand in it."

"Who's going?"

Indira explained that the council decided that every kingdom should be represented. It was to be heralded as a vital mission, used to distract the population from their troubles and demonstrate national unity.

Leave it to the ambassadors to turn a simple mission into something far more complicated than it had to be. He was surprised to learn that he had been appointed to represent Hallvarr on account of his recent appointment to the noble class there. Drystan and Jerrik would represent their kingdoms, and Gabral would represent the emperor and Tamarr.

Freyarr and Meinarr would appoint representatives prior to departure. Everything was thrown together hastily amidst the chaos of the past couple of days. Due to the lateness of the season, they needed to embark soon, and even then they might not beat the snows.

Kevlin focused on the mission. It gave him something to do, a goal to embrace. Perhaps it could help drive back dark feelings of lingering despair from the suffering he'd caused. If he could do some good, maybe he could atone for some of the destruction he'd caused.

He'd faced failure before, although not of this scale. From his experience and from what he'd learned from Leander, he knew wallowing in self-loathing wouldn't help. He needed to serve, to work harder than ever to try to restore some of what he'd done.

"Very well. A mission to the west. Will you let me up now so I can try to help before we leave?"

"I will." She retreated a step and said a little nervously, "But first I have to show you something." She drew from a pocket the amulet on its silver chain.

Kevlin cried out in alarm and thrashed against the restraining iron bands. He needed the amulet's protection. Didn't she know that?

Fear flooded through him. He needed it or he'd never get to touch magic again. Panic colored his vision and he snarled and fought harder against the chains. He'd throttle her! He'd . . .

Aghast at what he'd felt, at how quickly he'd fallen under the insidious power of the Trembling Madness, Kevlin fell back against the bed. Maybe she should just leave him like this. Better yet, maybe she should have someone throw him into the sea. It would prove safer for everyone.

Indira stood watching him, one hand raised to her mouth, a look of anguish on her face. The sight of her watching him like that helped him regain control.

"I'm sorry," he said, "You surprised me."

"I do this on Harafin's orders. I will watch over this for you until . . . well, until later."

Kevlin forced calm on himself. "Indira, Harafin's right. It's too dangerous for me right now. I trust you more than anyone. No matter what I might say later, don't give it back to me."

"I won't."

"I'm in control. Please let me up."

Indira unchained him and helped him sit up. He rose to his feet, but a wave of dizziness nearly toppled him. Indira caught him.

They stood together, arms wrapped around each other, and he never wanted to let go. She overwhelmed every sense. The warm touch of her skin seemed to burn into his hands and roll up his arms. His eyes drank in the perfect contours of her lovely face, her alabaster skin, the silky sheen of her ebony hair. Her gentle scent caressed his nose, and he breathed deep to inhale as much as possible. He never wanted to exhale again and lose it.

"Kevlin." The rich sound of her voice speaking his name thrilled him, warming him to the center. He tightened his grip on her waist.

She tried to draw away, but he held her firm in his arms. He looked deep into her dark eyes and yearned to stay there forever. "Indira, I'm . . ."

He couldn't finish. What could he say? He couldn't promise never to hurt her again, never to lose control. Look at how quickly he succumbed just moments ago. No, he could *never* fall under the Trembling Madness again.

That truth filled him with iron resolve. He could never relent. By all the gods, by all that had ever been considered holy, he would accept whatever death before surrendering his will again. He would never break this oath.

He wanted to share the oath with her, but hesitated. He'd tried to kill her. He couldn't bring himself to speak of it aloud, but the truth hung between them. Could she ever see past that? Could he ever ask her to?

Indira surprised him by grabbing the back of his neck and pulling his head down into a passionate kiss.

His mother had always taught him to follow a woman's lead. Kevlin's lips tingled at the touch of her full, soft lips pressed hard against his. She clutched him tight and kissed him with a hunger he'd never felt from her before.

They held each other tight in the small cell, and the passion of that kiss held all the hope, all the fear, all the longing that boiled through him. Hope illuminated his soul and passion ignited in his heart.

He kissed her hungrily, savoring every second. He ran one hand through her long, silky hair and she grinned and grabbed his head with both hands. Her dark eyes glowed with emotion, and if he hadn't been so busy kissing her he would have shouted at the top of his lungs with exultant joy.

Despite everything that had happened, she still cared for him. He no longer doubted, no longer cared about the consequences. This woman belonged with him.

Indira finally broke away and retreated. She brushed her robe and with a visible effort composed herself. Kevlin took a step after her, but she held up a restraining hand.

"I can't." Tears glistened in her eyes. "It's too dangerous. I can't hurt you like that again."

What?

How could she say that? That made no sense at all.

A look of agony flitted across her face and he realized she'd been harboring some twisted sense of responsibility for what happened.

"You didn't hurt me," he assured her. "I hurt you. I hurt everyone."

"No," she said with conviction. "It was my fault. I gave you magic." She looked down and added in a whisper, "I trusted . . ."

Kevlin moved toward her, but she scurried back to the door of the small room. "Indira, of everyone we could blame for events that happened, you are not one of them."

She blinked away tears and shook her head slowly. She gave him a weak smile. "I cannot trust . . . us . . . again."

Then she yanked open the door and bolted. Of all the ridiculous ways to view recent events, that one was the worst.

Kevlin's strength failed him and he dropped heavily onto the bed. He stared after her, barely believing what he'd heard. How could she do this? He'd felt her passion. It was real. How could she turn away now? The soaring joy he'd felt just a moment ago crashed in his chest and withered to ash.

He couldn't go after her. After what he'd done, he couldn't force her to care. He had no right to expect anything. She'd kissed him, by Jagen's unholy temper. That had to mean something, didn't it?

Kevlin sat there for a long time, suffering just as Akillik promised he would. That made him angry.

Kevlin rose and shook a hand at the blank ceiling. "I won't let you do this to me. I'll show you!"

He'd keep the oath, he'd prove to Indira she could still trust him. Despite fear that threatened to rob his resolve of its power, he repeated over and over in his mind that he would do it.

Then he headed for the door. He needed to find Leander.

99

A Promising Journey

Kevlin stood at the rail of the *Ceara* near the boarding ladder, watching the bustling activity as sailors prepared the ship to depart. He tried to focus on the upcoming journey. He clung to the mission and made every effort to consume his mind and energy with it.

It was the only way to fight the growing fear that kept his stomach in a perpetual knot. He clenched his hands to hide the steadily intensifying shakiness. Thinking about it only it stoked the hunger for magic to a fever pitch.

I will not relent. It was becoming increasingly difficult to repeat the oath and really mean it.

Today was the tenth day since he nearly destroyed the city. He'd held to the oath and avoided all magic, but already he felt drained from the constant effort. The insidious pull of the Trembling Madness tugged at his mind, like whispers at the edge of his consciousness. If he allowed his thoughts to drift, it drew them like steel to a lodestone.

He dreaded the day he'd have to touch magic again. Could he control it? There was no way to know, so he determined to postpone the attempt until he could find a way to be sure. At the least, he wanted to be far from any population centers.

One more reason to focus on this trip. Although part of him yearned to stay and spend himself working to repair some of the damage he'd caused, the rational part of his mind welcomed the chance to leave. He had to get away to distance himself from so many potential victims. He'd hurt them enough.

Besides, lingering questions still circulated about what had really happened here in Tamera. He could make no restitution from the gallows. At first, that's what he had expected to do, but Leander had helped him see a better way.

The old Stalwart had laid a hand on his shoulder. "Remember Kevlin, I know how you feel. I too committed terrible atrocities when lost to insanity. The burden is a heavy one, and it will always be with you. However, you must not let it eat you alive and destroy you. Instead, you must use it as motivation to work even harder to accomplish enough good to partially atone for the debt you owe."

"I don't know how you do it," Kevlin had said, voice thick with emotion.

"I managed by focusing on one day at a time, and by leaning on friends who could help me bear the burden."

"Thank you." It wasn't much, but it had been enough.

He'd take the advice to heart. He'd find a way to make things right. That hope helped him begin the process of regaining his composure and resuming his duties.

Now as he waited for the last of the party to row out to the ship where it swung gently at anchor in the Formal Port, he stared at the aftermath of destruction and wondered again how any of them had survived it.

Jagged volcanic rock had consumed most of the usable docks, and still blocked the few that remained. Latent magic was still woefully low, but some of the Sentinels had regained enough inner strength to become more useful by degrees. In the past three days, over a dozen cuts had been completed through the ridges of volcanic stone. Goods and people were flowing again. The city was easing back from the brink of constant chaos.

Kevlin watched as sailors and dock workers swarmed around the distant gate. A cut had been completed there, allowing access to the badly damaged port. Half a dozen shore boats, heavily loaded with cargo and passengers were being rowed slowly out to the *Ceara*. They were the last, and then the ship would be ready to sail with the tide.

So much destruction. Kevlin shuddered again. He didn't know how many people had died in those horrifying minutes. In a way it didn't matter. All that mattered was that people had died, and he was responsible.

The knowledge that he'd avoided facing the emperor's justice, at least in the short term, didn't help. He was still amazed that he hadn't been summarily executed.

Worse, the emperor had actually thanked him for helping save the keisara from Sitara and Remiel. She'd survived, thanks to heroic efforts from Indira and Basak, who had arrived shortly after Kevlin passed out. Kevlin had feared the emperor would punish him for throwing that dagger and wounding Keisara Fideima, but Emperor Tegnazian had understood it was all that had saved her life.

Kevlin had still felt distinctly uncomfortable in the man's presence. Surely Harafin had shared at least some of what had happened with him. Could he really not know anything of Kevlin's involvement? If he did know, what arguments could Harafin have possibly made that might have convinced him to keep the truth silent?

What price would the emperor eventually require? Akillik's jubilant laugher rang through Kevlin's mind and again he heard the fickle god's last words. Maybe that was it. Maybe Emperor Tegnazian expected him to suffer more living than he could through execution.

Kevlin looked down at his clenched hands and swore he would weather whatever storm Akillik might launch against him. He would survive it, he would make restitution, he would win Indira back.

He forced himself to focus on the activity on the ship. It was still early morning, just after dawn. Despite the cold, the *Ceara* and several other vessels that had best weathered the storm of destruction made ready to sail.

Drystan and Jerrik appeared from belowdecks and joined Kevlin at the rails as the group of shore boats approached the ship. They held two dozen imperial guards, along with the last of the luggage and cargo.

"Are things settling down yet?" Kevlin asked.

Jerrik grunted. "They're arguing like a pack of rabid monkeys."

"You should really be down there, Kevlin," said Drystan. "Harafin's still arguing that you're the appointed leader."

"I don't want it."

"Do you really want to serve under Gabral again?" Jerrik asked.

That gave Kevlin pause. With the Trembling Madness growing in his soul along with the fear of losing control and hurting the people he loved most in the world, leading this expedition held no appeal. Unfortunately, in their haste to send the group on its way, the Ruling Council had left the question of leadership unusually vague. Everyone seemed to think they'd been appointed leader.

Gabral, who led the fifty imperial guards who were their escort, insisted he was the military commander and the rightful leader. Harafin insisted the emperor had appointed Kevlin leader. Leander, who had been stripped of his title as Styrskena and banished from Tamera, still led a full score of battle-ready Pallian Stalwarts. He stated simply that he led the Pallians, and if anyone wanted anything from them, they'd have to ask nicely.

The Freyarr appointee on the mission was a lovely young noblewoman named Lawren Farthegn, who was a personal assistant to Ambassador Janezeko. She insisted she was the senior diplomat and therefore entitled to lead. The Meinarr appointee, a friendly, middle-aged woman named Nainsi, said she didn't care who led during the journey, but she insisted on taking the lead in the actual inspection of the border fortifications.

Kevlin had slipped away from the increasingly heated argument moments ago with Captain Sankar, who busied himself with preparing the vessel to depart. Now that the last contingent of soldiers was climbing aboard and hoisting the last of the goods, they would soon be setting sail.

Kevlin glanced back at the ravaged city and wondered if everything would be back to normal by the time the group returned from the long mission. There was still so much to do, so much to understand.

Masego's body had been burned and his ashes spread far out at sea. Remiel's body had been found buried under a pile of rubble and there was almost not enough left to bother burying.

Sitara's body was never found.

"Whoever ends up leading, this is going to be an interesting trip," Drystan said with a wry grin.

"I'm just glad we're up here and not down there," Kevlin added.

"Let them fight it out for a while, then you should join them and stand for yourself," Jerrik said.

At that moment, Captain Sankar shouted, "Hop to it lads! Raise anchor, set your course west by north-west."

Sailors scrambled into the rigging. The sheets snapped in the morning breeze and the ship heeled slightly as it came about.

"Well, brothers," Drystan said, placing a hand on each of their shoulders and staring out at the harbor as it began to recede slowly, "I think we're in for quite a journey."

"Aye," Jerrik said. "Let's hope there's at least a couple of good fights ahead of us."

Not a war, Kevlin thought. *Not yet.*

The sound of Akillik's wild laughter rang in his mind, followed by a single, deep drum beat.

100

A Trailing Shadow

*Y*ou are sure?

There is no doubt. You have your orders. Succeed this time or die in the attempt. You will not receive another opportunity.

The connection broke. Tanathos sat for a moment, enjoying the exultant feeling of expected revenge. Fate, it seemed, intended to give him another opportunity. He would not fail a third time

"Slave," he called.

Immediately the tent flap parted and a Makrasha stuck its deformed head inside.

"Get Syntyk in here."

His second in command appeared a moment later.

"It is time," he said with a cold smile. "Tell the captains we sail on the next tide."

OTHER WORKS BY FRANK MORIN

Find all books on www.frankmorin.org
and at: bio.to/authorfrankmorin

The Catalyst

Oath & Shadow, Book One

The Petralist Series
(Epic YA fantasy)

Set in Stone, Book One
A Stone's Throw, Book Two
No Stone Unturned, Book Three
Affinity for War, Book Four
The Queen's Quarry, Book Five
The King's Craft, Book Six
Blood of the Tallan, Book Seven
When Torcs Fly, A Petralist Origins novella: Tomas and Cameron
Game of Garlands, A Petralist Origins novella: Anika
Builder of Intrigue, A Petralist Origins novella: Ailsa
Sweetbreads, A petralist short story collection.

Bacon Master of the Apocalypse Series

(Humorous fantasy)
Bacon Master of the Apocalypse, Book one
Pawn of the Pantryon, Book two.

The Facetakers Series
(Urban Fantasy Time-Travel Thrillers)

Saving Face, Book One
Memory Hunter, Book Two
Rune Warrior, Book Three
Aeon Champion, Book Four (release in September 2020)

Books to Read Online One Chapter at a Time

Nexus Runner – litRPG fantasy on Royal Road

Short Stories

"Odin's Eye," included in A Game of Horns: A Red Unicorn Anthology
"The Essence," included in the Dragon Writers: An Anthology
"The Seventh Strike," included in Cursed Collectibles: An Anthology

ABOUT THE AUTHOR

Frank Morin loves great stories, great food, and great humor. He is an outdoor enthusiast, and loves to travel for inspiration.

Frank is the author of fast-paced adventures with quirky humor including:

- The Petralist – epic YA fantasy series

- The Facetakers – Urban fantasy thriller series

- *Bacon Master of the Apocalypse* – humorous epic fantasy

- The Catalys – Classic epic fantasy

- Nexus Runner – litRPG fantasy adventure

He and his wife are often found hiking, camping, Scuba diving, or traveling to research new books. Find out more about his novels and his shorter fiction, or join his readers group at: https://bio.to/authorfrankmorin.